AT THE EDGE OF THE SOLID WORLD

AT THE EDGE OF THE SOLID WORLD

DANIEL DAVIS WOOD

BRIO

That illusion of a world so shaped that it echoes every groan, of human beings so tied together by common needs and fears that a twitch at one wrist jerks another, where however strange your experience other people have had it too, where however far you travel in your own mind someone has been there before you—is all an illusion. We do not know our own souls, let alone the souls of others.

—Virginia Woolf

If every event which occurred could be given a name, there would be no need for stories. As things are here, life outstrips our vocabulary. A word is missing and so the story has to be told.

—John Berger

I've long considered myself a heathen in every sense of the word. Not just an unbeliever, impatient with supernatural fancies, nor just an iconoclast bent on provocation. Not just someone spiteful of piety and notions of worlds beyond this one. I'm also a creature of the heath and heather. If there's a god to speak to me, it dwells out there in the uplands, in the austerity and muck. That's where a person can feel the elements converse. That's where we're most abandoned, cast back onto ourselves; where one is compelled to shrink before the naked Earth, the only truly absolute power, to appreciate its impossible magnitude, its indifference to one's presence. That's where you can know for sure that the only holy thing in this life is the body, because the soul doesn't live a moment longer than its shell.

I

These are the things I remember:

I stirred when a warmth and wetness touched my back. Snowflakes lashed the window only inches from my eyes. A flurry whipped through the dark in swirls of flickering white, then rushed at the glass with a gust and exploded and scattered over the ground. Behind me shallow breaths were teasing the hair on the nape of my neck. I propped myself up on an elbow and angled around to carefully, carefully draw back the covers. The glow of light on the snowdrifts outside cast a haze across the bed. My wife, I saw, slept deeply despite the damp that spread out around her. Her waters had broken and soaked through her nightclothes and now they'd flooded the sheets and the mattress.

I let out a sigh and let myself drop onto my pillow again. I lay there with the gale thrashing at my back as I watched the rise and fall, the gentle rise and fall, of my wife beside me breathing. The light traced an arc along the broad curve of her belly. It swelled with each breath she drew, relaxed with each exhalation. I lay there and I felt between us a momentary decoupling, the opening of a disjuncture in the life we shared. I wonder now how far I could've prolonged the feeling if I'd remained as I was, so still, and made no move to rouse her. Awake and alert in the present, I watched her sleep on and moment by moment withdraw from the flow of time. She couldn't see, as I could see, that the world she'd known when she'd closed her eyes was already gone, lost to us, and a new world had taken its place.

The wheels of the cases I'd filled with clothes stuck fast in the snow in the car park. Sliding doors swished open and released a burst of heat. We faced the ghostly fluorescence of an emergency access corridor. A nurse hurried out towards us, bracing herself against the cold, and in words at the very limits of what I knew of her language she urged us to tell her quickly what had happened, what was wrong. My wife straggled forward through piles of powder. Her figure and gait announced much of what the nurse sought to know. The nurse reached out to take her hand, to guide her through the open doors. I battled luggage against stubborn mounds of snow and struggled not to slip on the underlying ice. I heard my wife adopt the nurse's native tongue to ask her if she might switch to the only language I speak. Then without waiting for an answer either way, my wife made the switch herself and spoke rapidly of what had happened. The broken waters, the snowstorm, the two hours' drive on slippery roads. The absence of any aches or pains and the unnerving lack of contractions.

The nurse led my wife down the corridor, one hand at her back, and together they turned a corner and abruptly vanished from view. I left the luggage by the doors and dashed back into the snow, to the car. From the boot I retrieved the capsule seat we thought we'd need for the journey home. Then I dragged our stuff inside and placed the capsule on top of the pile and set off to see where my wife had been taken. I gave her name to another nurse and was led to a spartan room. A small round table and two plastic chairs, a bed beside a tiny window. She sat calmly on a folded blanket, clad in a sky-blue hospital gown, while a new nurse knelt beside her and drew blood from the crook of her arm. Bag by bag, item by item, I hurried up and down a stairwell off the corridor and transferred our belongings to the corner of the room. I returned to my wife as the nurse extracted the needle with care and pressed a shred of cotton against the puncture. Urine samples were taken next and after that a midwife arrived to conduct the more urgent assessments. My wife lay on her back. I watched the calm disappear from her eyes. I watched her clench herself against the things she knew were coming. Feet into stirrups, thighs apart, a gloved hand probing in ways that triggered at first a wince and then a hardening of the gaze.

The due date we'd been given was still two weeks away. Nearly four hours had elapsed since the waters had broken. So far, labour hadn't involved so much as a cramp or a twinge. Should any of this give us reason to worry? We asked the nurses, we asked the midwife, but just as a doctor entered the room to discuss our plans for the birth my wife buckled over, crashed to her knees, struck by the violence of a contraction as if belted with a weapon. Something fierce inside her seized her, wrenched her innards and bent her double, dragging a groan through her throat. She was panting for breath, almost gasping, by the time I'd managed to hoist her up again. The doctor vied for her attention and put his face in front of hers, nearly nose to nose, and when he was certain she'd focused on him he gave her a knowing smile. He muttered something I took to be a dismissal of our concerns. My wife understood what he meant but clearly didn't like his tone. She swung around to find me beside her, agony radiant in her eyes, and just as she seemed about to speak she lurched away and shot out an arm to hold herself against whatever she could reach. A hand hooked onto the edge of the table, fingers scrambled for purchase on one of the plastic chairs, and in this awkward position, clutching at the furniture around her, my wife kept herself upright but hunched as she quivered with spasms of pain.

Offer comfort to the wounded. Alleviate their suffering. Do whatever it takes to bring them the peace they crave. That's the inherent tendency, that's the animal instinct. I felt it flare in the core of myself and burn through the whole of my body. I felt it sear my bloodstream with its command to help, to *act*. The doctor dematerialised. The nurses dissolved into air. I stepped towards my wife and took her in my arms. She made no shift in her posture to register my touch. Softly I cupped my hands over hers. I leant in to place a kiss on her forehead. I could taste the sweat that slicked her brow and I felt with my lips the heat of her skin and the strands of hair that stuck to it. I broke away slowly, kept my eyes on hers, but then from over my shoulder I heard the calm voice of the doctor. He stood behind me and snatched my wife's attention with commentary too articulate for me to comprehend. As she mulled over his words I stole a moment to step aside, towards the window, and tap out a message on my phone. We'd agreed that I should alert our families as soon as the contractions hit. An absence of thirty seconds. Three short words, an exclamation point. I pressed a button to send the update and just like that, even before I'd slipped the phone back into my pocket, my brief account of events unfolding right then inside a hospital room in the snowbound heart of the Alps had blitzed across the planet to land in the hands of my parents and hers, with dings and chimes and flashes of light, at dusk on a bright summer's day in Australia. A wounded glare assailed me when I turned back to my wife. Betrayal, resentment, disdain. A squint through slit eyes, a motion of the jaw as of grinding teeth. Her expression froze me where I stood.

I opened my mouth to speak but before I could make a sound another contraction brought her low. She staggered forward, reached for me, interlocked her fingers with mine and with her other hand she grappled for my shoulder. She crunched my knuckles and clawed at my back. Her entire body convulsed, snapped like a lash, then she went limp and faltered at the waist. She fell forward, onto me, before she dropped and slumped into a cower. With her fingers splayed on the floor she rocked on the balls of her feet. I knelt down beside her and tried to command her attention. She looked at me but didn't see me. Tears welled in her eyes, a flush blazed up from her cheeks to her temples. She held me with an empty stare and suddenly I understood her anger of a moment ago. She'd been taken hostage by reflexes at odds with her thoughts. All her wants and inclinations, all the birthing arrangements we'd made, all of those had been suppressed by the screech of synaptic mayhem. When she watched me step aside, she saw me flaunting the freedom she'd lost. I wasn't just sending a message home in accordance with our plans. I was breaking out of the fog that had encompassed her, the fog that shrank her world around her immediate bodily needs.

So of course she glared at me. A curl of the lip, mottled cheeks. Betrayal, resentment, disdain. Then her body claimed control once again and a cloud occluded her eyes. She fell away from me, fell back into herself, and I found then, as I find now, that I know no words to convey the sense of impotence that overcame me. I'm not sure that this or any other language can capture it. To see that pain latch onto her. To watch it immobilise and debilitate her. To feel capable of nothing more than standing as a spectator to her trauma. To hold back, unmoving, as the nurses and the doctor intervened where I couldn't. I stood there at the darkened window, I looked out at the world beneath a mantle of snow, I tried to keep my distance while the experts gave my wife more help than I was able to offer. What was the worth of my being there at all? Why not flay the skin from my body, let my veins run dry and wither, strip away all the sinews and flense the flesh from my bones? All I was was a pair of eyes staring out at my wife from the aether. Never before had I felt so totally distinct from her, situated at such a remove, even as every atom in me thrummed with empathy tuned to a pitch that made me want to scream. But the other bodies in that room rushed to do their work, bringing themselves between us to give her the relief she craved, and with their purpose and expertise they left me to my inertia. Absolutely still, but absolutely attentive, I watched them and I resolved that if all I could do was stand and stare then I would at least bear witness to every detail of every event opening up before me. Be wholly attuned to the moment. Let nothing occur without notice. Observe, catalogue, and testify. Iterate.

Hours passed in chaos. Half the day was chaos. One nurse flicked on a computer screen and bathed the room in sickly light. Another connected my wife to a snarl of cords and wires, plastering her with electrode pads and abdominal transducers. Digital graphs leapt to life, testing the baseline heart rate of our unborn child and tracking the oxygen levels in utero. Other nurses came and went, brought things for comfort and took things away. Cold compresses, warm compresses. Balms and ointments, sedatives, salves. Minimal food, regular drinks. Boiled sweets and herbal teas. I tried to ignore the periodical rattling of my phone, the buzzing of my parents and in-laws begging for an update. I wouldn't vacate the scene again, not even momentarily. I would stay present; I would remember. I stood back and watched. Staff rotated as some took respite and others ended their shifts. They rearranged the furniture so my wife could pace the room. They made and remade the bed and kept the lights on low. When daybreak came the darkness beyond the window disappeared. The sun rose over the peaks of the mountains. It lit up the snow on the streets outside, dazzled the soft new surface of the world. Someone drew the curtains to take the edge off the brightness. The curtains trapped the heat that crept in through vents in the floor. Stickiness pooled in my armpits and groin and I felt the first dull thud of a migraine pounding into my skull.

Whenever my wife lay down she'd seize my hands with terrifying strength, crisscrossing my skin with bright red marks where she dug in her nails. When she tottered to her feet she'd hobble halfway to the window and stand and sway from side to side, eyes turned up to the ceiling, murmuring like a shaman in communion with another realm. Then she'd contort and arch her spine, she'd stoop and haul herself back to the bed, and with strands of soggy hair spread across the pillow she'd cast about for me again and reach out once more to grip my hands and the whole routine would repeat. Despite this the doctor insisted that there was as yet no medical need for interventions. Our child's arrival was imminent, he said, so we could and should persist with our plans for a natural delivery. But really these moments of incident, of motion and discussion, rocked us in surges, in waves, intermittently. Most of our time in that room was thickened by indistinct swathes of silence, of regulated breathing and controlled recuperation, punctuated by the sporadic violence of a body against itself.

Eventually the contractions became more than could be withstood. Their duration didn't decrease, their frequency didn't rise. Their intensity did not wane in the least. If anything, they gathered strength. My wife stopped moaning and started howling and then she turned to pleading for mercy. She begged for someone to simply lay hands on the life inside her and wrest it out. She wept and choked on her tears, and cursed into the surrounding air, until her eyes dilated and her eyelids fluttered and she gave herself up to fatigue. Exhaustion swept over her body like a sudden onrush of wind. It washed the colour from her face and dragged her into a sleep so intense that even successive contractions couldn't wake her. I sat beside her, stunned, and watched her torso shudder each time her muscles cramped and relaxed. The skin on her swollen stomach drew taut and slackened, drew taut and slackened, with the rhythm of waves smashing over the sand before being sucked back to sea. I felt the ache in my head build into an attack on my vision, and so, to regain my own composure, I sat and watched over my wife in her state of uncanny calm. She slept through the mayhem around her and she slept through the tumult inside.

A second doctor entered the room to confer briefly with his colleague. Together they announced their intention to induce the birth. I missed their meaning the first time they spoke but the new doctor translated for me. The other doctor woke my wife, a series of forceful taps on the wrist, and when she came around he began to explain the situation. Eighteen hours had passed since the waters had broken; further delay increased the risk of bacterial infection and recent changes inside the womb had given the specialists cause for concern. The new doctor reached for the bedside screen and angled it so my wife and I could see. He pointed to a horizontal line. It oscillated with peaks and troughs at regular, reliable intervals. That, he said, was our child's baseline heart rate. Next he pointed to a darker line that ran parallel to the first until its tail end ticked up and swerved suddenly down. That was the current heart rate, he said, and, as we could see, it had become volatile, slowing and speeding and slowing again. Its pattern gave shape to a cycle of protracted, heightened stress followed by drastic enervation. That cycle had to be broken, right now, to avoid the very worst, to not jeopardise the birth.

Induction required an epidural that had been arranged before anyone told us. The doctors hadn't even finished speaking when two technicians wheeled into the room a monster of a machine, a slap-dash hulk of tubes and coils, valves and bellows, electronic keypads and needles as long as fingers. One technician helped my wife roll onto her side. The other worked with the first doctor to ready the anaesthetics. The new doctor hurried me towards the bed to make way for the equipment. The sudden movement stoked the pain in my head and I felt as if my brain might blow apart. I winced, I'm sure, as I knelt beside my wife and laid a hand on her cheek. She locked her eyes onto mine and did not let them break away.

Now I could see the first technician standing directly behind her. I watched him hold her steady with one hand on her shoulder. With his other hand he prodded different places along her spine. When he found the optimal spot his colleague approached my wife with a needle. I watched the needle vanish behind her and I watched for her reaction. I watched a grimace twist her face into a knot of creases and furrows, I watched her draw in her elbows and knees, I watched her hold on to the torsion while she waited for the sting in her back to fade away. Nobody could later explain to us why it didn't, why nothing changed. The contractions wouldn't ease. They came and went, and came and went, each one striking with all the force of the one before it. Nobody could tell us, either, why the induction hadn't worked. The child still wouldn't arrive. The interventions appeared to bring the birth no closer. We'd hoped they might hasten the moment in which we'd at last become the parents we longed to be. Instead we returned to the process. Recumbent on the bed. Regulated breathing and controlled recuperation. Standing up when contractions hit and bearing down on command. We returned to the haze of having no idea of what was coming next, or when.

Just after midday the child's heart went haywire. Erratic scrawls devoured the screen of the electrocardiograph. The triple digits above the graph plunged and seemed bound for zero. The shrieking of the machines sent shards of pain through my head. One of the doctors ordered an emergency caesarean and left the room to prepare for surgery. His colleague remained behind to oversee one last attempt at a natural delivery. Nurses wheedled my wife into returning to the bed. I stood above and behind her while she reached up and held my hands. The doctor knelt at her feet. I could see his face, masked, between my wife's raised knees. As he started to speak to her, with unimpeachable seriousness but in words that meant nothing to me, I looked away from him and looked down at my wife and tried to lock eyes again. This time, though, she did not reciprocate. She looked up into the air, at nothing, but less with a glaze or an emptiness than with the appearance of someone transfixed before a mirror. She seemed as if she was somehow contemplating her own reflection, meeting herself in vacant space and scrutinising her own mien to sound out the depths of her resilience. Then I watched her haul her resilience to the surface. Her entire being swelled with new breath, the rush of blood, the force of energy summoned up and focused on a single act. I could see her marshalling all the dynamism she had left to work with, gathering every last trace of her strength and channelling it into one final push at giving life to the child inside her. The doctor stammered out words that seemed no longer to issue instructions on what my wife should do, that seemed instead to offer spontaneous, almost panicked responses to what she was already doing. She arched her back, she pushed, she screamed. The doctor's voice grew urgent, excited. My wife tore into the veins in my wrists, kicked free of the doctor's hold on her ankles, and then she released the first real words she'd managed to utter in hours as she wailed that she could feel it, she could *feel* it coming out.

This is how it came at last. The second doctor returned to the room in the company of a third. The new arrival swanned around with an air of seniority, a multinational CEO summoned from his private yacht, and instantly both of his colleagues were deferential towards him. He consulted with them, then gave them instructions, then spoke calmly to my wife as she writhed on the bed beneath him. When he stopped speaking he shot me a glance that asked without words if I concurred with what he'd said. He'd spoken to my wife as a formality, knowing she couldn't really follow what he put to her, and he'd assumed I'd heard and understood so that I could speak on her behalf to give consent to his plans. I wavered. I probably nodded. My vision swam and thunder resounded through my head. I didn't speak out, I'm sure of that, and the doctor saw my silence as tacit accord. He turned to one side and pulled towards himself a tray of specialist instruments that someone had stationed nearby. Probes and clamps and scalpels. Nurses had gathered around my wife. One of them held a damp cloth to her forehead. Another tried to soothe her as she sobbed and groaned. Then the other two doctors returned to their superior and the three of them huddled together at the foot of the bed. The lead doctor snapped on a latex glove and plucked something sharp off the tray. I saw a flash of silver and in one swift movement the doctor touched the blade to my wife and cut. She convulsed with a flex and a flump, as if she'd just sustained a bolt of electricity, and as soon as a scream poured out of her I saw blood spill between her legs and trickle over the doctor's gloves. The other two doctors bent in to staunch the flow. One of them held two haemostats, the other a needle and thread. When the lead doctor rose to his feet and took a step back from the bed, I saw that in his arms he was cradling an infant. The child lay unmoving with its head reclined in the palm of his hand. It seemed shrunken, even shrivelled, with a mop of black hair and skin of spectral blue beneath smears of blood and mucus. In my mind I heard a false echo of the bawling I'd expected. I searched its face for signs of life but it kept its eyes closed tight and made no sound at all.

I realised then that my wife had fallen silent as well. She'd stopped screaming and now she seemed to be holding her breath as she focused intensely on the child. With no apparent thought of what she was actually doing, she began to unbutton the hospital gown she'd been wearing throughout the delivery. The doctor approached us and quickly showed me the child's sex, and then he laid her, skin to skin, tummy down, upon my wife's chest. The girl was still blue, still bloodied, still motionless and silent, but none of that seemed to trouble the doctor and none of it troubled my wife. Words elude me when I think of how best to name the look that washed over my wife's face as she tilted her head to one side and peered down at the child. Ecstasy comes to mind, but it also cheapens what took hold of her. She appeared to possess no awareness of the world outside her field of vision, no concern for any of its trivial phenomena. She struck me as having been overcome by something primal, something animal, something that lacks a term of its own because it is prior to all language. She was burning, resplendent with adoration, and the instant love she felt for our daughter seemed to throb out from her beating heart and through her skin and upwards into the girl.

The pallor of the child warmed into a ruddy red and I noticed, then, that she too lay there drawing shallow but steady breaths. Muscle by muscle, limb by limb, motion worked its way into her body. One tiny foot curled its toes. An open hand scrunched into a fist. Eyelids strained and then shot open, and as the blinding light of the room inundated her vision my daughter forced her lips to part and let out a feeble cry. It's easy to look back on that moment and say, very simply, that what I felt then was something I'd never felt before. It's more truthful, though, to look back and say that what I felt wasn't a feeling at all in the usual sense of the word. It wasn't like bliss or despair, it wasn't like fear or contentment. It didn't pierce my heart, it didn't quicken my pulse. I didn't feel it *inside*. I felt it on the outside, I felt it on my skin. It came over me like a fire, a crackling blaze rushing fast across the surface of my body. It came as a scorching awareness of the outer limits of my being, of all the places where I as a living creature met the enveloping space of the world. It was a shock of radical selfhood, as if all the emotions I'd expended over so many hours in that stifling, sweat-soaked room had receded from its furthest reaches to lodge again in the flesh and blood that were mine alone. It brought with it an air of calm, a calm that broke distinctly with the chaos of the preceding hours, a calm that began to wear away the worst of the pain in my head, and the force of that pain diminished further still when my wife turned to me, turned her eyes upwards to find mine again, and spoke to me, in a shattered voice, of the life we had created.

She's so beautiful, she said.

Yes, I agreed. She is.

Beautiful, in that moment, changed its definition. It had something to do with her helplessness, her vulnerability, her sudden exposure to forces she had no concept of. Drying bodily fluids matted her hair to her scalp. White, chalky vernix speckled her skin, clumps of it in her armpits and in the folds of her neck. The fat wet tube of the umbilical cord hung limp and translucent from her stomach. A nurse in scrubs came up to me and handed me a pair of scissors. She took the cord in her fist and with a nod invited me to cut. Black sludge oozed over the blades. The nurse clamped off the stub of the cord, tied a knot and tossed the remnants into a bin for biomedical waste. Minutes later the placenta slopped onto the floor. My wife felt nothing when it came. I managed to catch a glimpse of it, a glistening mound of clotted blood with veins all through it like the roots of a tree in soil. Quickly, though, the nurse heaved it into the bin and wheeled the bin out of the room while another nurse entered with a mop and dolloped soapsuds on the floor.

Eventually a new nurse arrived to help my wife start breastfeeding. With nimble fingers she stroked a nipple to coax out the colostrum, but at first nothing would flow. Then she began to massage the breast, putting pressure on the milk glands. Our daughter moaned, kept her eyes closed, and guided by scent alone she switched her nose back and forth and cast about for nourishment. When she couldn't latch on she thrashed in frustration, swinging her heavy head this way and that, until at last a slick of something emerged and she leapt at it, licked it, gained traction on the nipple, and finally nuzzled her face against the breast and drank. She worked hard to gulp down the milk, biting my wife with her empty gums, but there wasn't enough milk and soon it ran dry. Then she threw back her head and yowled, refused to be calmed, wouldn't suffer being rocked or swaddled. When I picked her up and paced the room, she kicked and cried in protest. When I passed her back to my wife, she raised her pitch and squalled. Finally she ran out of breath and just collapsed, defeated. Her head dropped onto my wife's shoulder and instantly the girl fell asleep. My wife and I exchanged panicked glances, startled by the sudden silence.

The nurse told us both not to worry. In her halting pidgin she added that this sort of thing happened often. Now was a good time for a health check, she said, and a chance to get our daughter dressed before we tried to feed her again. She took the girl in her hands and asked me to follow her out of the room. The two of us left my wife behind in bed. We moved down the corridor and entered a dark annex where the nurse laid the girl on a changing mat. She measured her and weighed her and took her picture for the hospital records. With a brush she dabbed ink from a pot onto the pristine sole of my daughter's foot, then she pressed the foot to a piece of card to leave a print. She wrapped a nappy around the girl, fastened it in place, and pulled open the doors of a cabinet to pass me a handful of tiny clothes. She said she wanted to tend to my wife a little more, to take a look at her stitches and make sure the pain was abating, and with that she abruptly excused herself and left the room.

I wrangled my daughter's arms and legs into a jumpsuit far too big, stunned by the lack of resistance from a child so exhausted she didn't wake when I rolled her side to side. I savoured the swish of my fingers against her dusky skin, and the sweetness of her smell as the vernix dried and flaked. Finally, alone for the first time since the onset of labour, I took my phone from my pocket and snapped a photograph of her face. Eyes closed, entirely at peace, her manifest perfection bore no trace of the torment of her arrival. With the press of a button I cast her picture into the wake of my initial message. Hours beforehand her grandparents had been alerted to her impending arrival. Now in only a second, halfway around the world and more than a full day's travel from our door, they'd be able to see the face of the granddaughter whose presence they had yet to know.

Then the nurse returned to me. My wife, she said, was being transferred to a recovery room. She retrieved for me a bassinet with transparent plastic sides and fixed it to the frame of a trolley that came almost to waist height. I laid my daughter inside and wheeled her down the corridor, then with the help of the nurse I found my wife in a new bed and parked the trolley beside her pillow. The frame held the bassinet at the level of her eyes. My wife was able to lay on her side with our daughter stationed next to her. She could watch the girl through the plastic without having to shift position. While I waited for the nurse to leave, I sent another message to our families in Australia. For them a new day would have dawned and I knew they'd now be expecting a call, but I told them we had no headspace for coherent conversation and I promised we'd speak with them after we'd had a chance to get some rest. When the nurse left the room at last, when she left the two of us, weary, alone with our newborn daughter, I felt free to lay down as well. I found a little clearing on the mattress and wrapped my arms around my wife. She seemed to have been mostly relieved of her pain and I'd been relieved, too, of the pressure in my skull. From behind her I held her close to me. I felt her move against me with each breath she drew and released.

She coasted into sleep almost as soon as our bodies touched. I could feel my own eyelids aching to close, to push away the world outside myself, and so with the day's last flickers of lucid thought I reached out once more, over my wife, to touch our sleeping child. I swept my palm softly over her scalp and laid a gentle hand upon her cheek. Before sleep overtook me, I remember, I stole one final look at her, at her entire person. She slept in a thicket of winter clothes. She was a picture of absolute calm. Despite her stillness and the faded bedsheets and the dim light of the hospital room, when I looked at her then I saw a figure like the star at the heart of a spiralling galaxy, a gathering point of pure potential encircled by a halo of countless possible futures. I looked at her and saw horizons without limit. I felt as if, in time, nothing would be beyond her. I felt hope for her, for the person she was destined to become, for every person she might yet be capable of becoming.

Acting on some instinct I could only guess at, the girl reached up with her tiny hand and took the tip of my index finger. She curled her own fingers around my knuckle and nail, and I let her hold me like that as I drifted into darkness. I surrendered to my fatigue at last, overwhelmed by a deep and powerful gratitude. Gratitude. It came, I knew, from the simple fact that the girl had fought her way into existence. I was grateful for her having made it just to this point in her life, and for my having been there to witness her first precious hours. I was grateful for the relief of the doubts I'd harboured for months, a relief she afforded me solely by being there and lying there with me. I was grateful for the knowledge, or really the reassurance, that on this occasion my wife and I had succeeded where only recently we'd failed.

A little less than a year beforehand, my wife had come to me with daubs of blood on her skirt and down her calves. We'd just finished up a late breakfast on a day we'd both arranged to work from home. I'd returned to the laptop, to prepare the year's final classes, when I heard her cry out and rush down the hallway to where I sat surrounded by papers. She opened her mouth to say something but found she couldn't speak. She choked on the knowledge of all we'd been through over the past three months. She'd missed a period at the end of autumn. It turned out to have hinted at what we proved with a take-home test. An obstetrician smeared jelly on skin and waved a wand over it. A little white dot on a monochrome screen. A printout of the sonogram, a due date after midsummer. Discussions of names, bedroom furnishings, negotiations for maternity leave. Long debates about parenting styles and the ethics of all the decisions we'd have to make on our child's behalf. We were impassioned, we were fanciful, we indulged in hours of wild, blissful speculation. We were giving voice to the different people we were bound to become, giving shape to the new identities we would fashion for ourselves. We pieced together a birthing plan and itemised the conditions for a calm and comfortable delivery. Then that morning, just after breakfast, my wife went to the toilet and when she stood to flush she noticed spots of red on the seat. She came to me speechless and took my hand to lead me to the bathroom. I followed her not knowing what disturbance she wanted to show me, shaken by the sight of the blood, thrown off-balance by the surprise, and when I saw what had robbed her of speech I lost my bearings, I sensed a lustrous haze gnawing at the edges of vision, and I felt in my chest a suffocating pressure as the space we'd entered collapsed on itself and started to crush me where I stood.

I had my phone in my hand. I pressed it hard to my ear. I listened to the dial tone as I raced around the house and raged for someone to pick up. I tore open a backpack and threw in clothes and hospital papers. When I finally heard a voice on the line I unleashed a cascade of words. I didn't even think to ask if my language would be understood. I tried to describe what I'd seen. I started and stopped, started again. Then I realised the voice was asking me, instructing me, to take a breath to gather my thoughts and then be methodical, be precise with all the details. I returned to the bathroom and started over. My wife leant against the sink and wept with one hand shielding her eyes. I was asked if I was able to actually see the foetus. First I looked to my wife and felt an urge to console her, and then, impelled to answer the questions, I searched about for any hint of something certain, something I could say for sure. The next voice I heard was my own. Yes, I said. I could see it. I could see it on the floor.

I knelt beside the toilet. I switched on speaker mode and set down the phone on the tiles. With one hand cupped I reached out for the tiny thing in front of me, and slowly, exercising consummate care, I brushed it into my palm and raised it to examine it. I was fascinated. I was appalled. Is there a word for the state of being both at the same time? Is there a word for being spellbound by something that otherwise makes you recoil? Smaller than the tip of a finger, clotted in sticky crimson, it weighed nothing at all and showed no real signs of a human existence, and yet I knew it possessed, inside, the myriad chambers and valves of a heart, a nervous system, a functioning brain, bones and joints, wrists, ankles, fingernails and taste buds and so much more. The voice on the phone crackled into the air and asked me what exactly I could see. A frail red thing with delicate arms and curled legs, all conjoined to a slender torso. An overlarge ovoid head that awoke in my deepest self, almost absurdly, an instinct to protect and defend, to act on innate bonds of kinship, which until then I hadn't even imagined lay buried, dormant, within me.

From the phone came the words I dreaded to hear even though I could sense their approach. The voice informed me gently, but in unambiguous terms, that if a foetus was no longer inside the womb only ten weeks after conception, then regrettably my wife had suffered a miscarriage and the child could not be saved. At that announcement I was ambushed by questions impossible to answer. Was the foetus in my hand enduring any pain? Did it have the receptors and pathways that would allow it to feel suffering? Had the right cells connected themselves so as to transmit the signals? Did the brain have the structure needed to receive and interpret them? These weren't philosophical questions. These were biological questions that stoked in me an insatiable need to know the extent of a life whose development had come to a halt. What had afflicted that child, I wondered, when blood-flow had displaced it from the warmth it nestled in?

The voice offered us an apology in a largely formal way, articulating various expressions of sorrow and reassuring platitudes. Of course I knew, intellectually, that we'd been told the truth. Even so, I couldn't accept it, I couldn't integrate the knowledge into my experience. I knew when I saw the carnage in front of me that it could not have come from anything other than a miscarriage. But when I turned the word over in my mind, testing its sound and probing its meaning, I knew, I *knew*, that there was no way for a miscarriage ever to be ours to suffer. My wife had been scrupulous in her preparations for pregnancy. She'd primed herself with exercise and vitamins and other mineral supplements. She'd diligently avoided anything that would increase the odds of malformation, eggs and soft cheeses and all the rest. She'd calculated her prime nutritional intake, balanced it against the energy expended on an average day. With a raw and rasping throat I reeled off a long list of all the precautions we'd taken to fortify ourselves against assaults like the one we faced in the bathroom, desperate and frenzied and irate at the keen injustice of what I saw.

My wife had felt no twinges or cramps, no warning signs in her abdomen, no indication that anything inside her was amiss. She hadn't even felt anything during the miscarriage itself. She'd noticed what had happened only after it had happened. She'd risen from the toilet seat and seen the blood and viscous fluids. She'd edged away from the mess, noticed the blood still streaming from her, and then she'd found the foetus lying on the floor. She hadn't felt it leave her. She hadn't felt it fall. The miscarriage set upon her from nowhere and in a sense she never sustained it. I didn't know how to come to terms with an event that we experienced only as an impact, not as an occurrence. I wanted simply to delegate my life to someone else for a time, to offload its demands onto someone stronger, and so I slipped through the following hours almost catatonically. Things that astonish me now, in hindsight, were met at the time with dull acquiescence. The voice on the phone instructed me to take certain measures, to follow protocols. I did as advised without any conviction that I was doing anything at all. Don't rush to hospital now, I was told. Call your obstetrician. Request an emergency visit. Take your time and talk it over with your consultant. Don't be afraid to ask for help from a mental health practitioner. I know it can be difficult if—

Time refused to alter itself. That was the greatest difficulty. The call was ended, not by me, at 10.17 in the morning. I still cupped the foetus in my hand. My wife still supported herself at the sink, still heaved with sobs and still had tears down her face. At 10.17 the day ahead stretched out wide before us. We were entombed in a moment that felt somehow eternal, interminable, as long as we two were static, unable to move forward, physically incapable of performing the first actions that would break with what had happened in that space. I wanted to just leap ahead to another, later moment in which that one, that moment, was already far behind in our past and I was involved in a new course of events. I wanted to not have to commit myself to pushing on through a thicket of time whose far side I couldn't see, wading through a bog of turmoil whose depths I couldn't know. I wanted to not be stalled there, treading water, mired in the immeasurable muck between the aftermath of the miscarriage and whatever was due to come next.

In a hallway cupboard I found a tiny ornamental box. Marble art, vivid swirls, splatters of primary colours. I lifted the lid with my free hand and found inside the sort of padding that had once been a bed for jewellery. I laid the foetus on the padding and I passed the box to my wife. I told her to take her time with it and I left her to replace the lid whenever she felt ready. I knelt in the frost at the edge of the forest outside our bedroom window. Amid the pines and silver birches stood a yew tree I was fond of. I liked the way its bole seemed to have been twined together from countless strands of bark. Taking a trowel to where its roots twisted into the earth, I made an attempt at digging a grave. I scooped up clods of slush to expose wet soil, not yet frozen, then I dug down further and flecked my hands with mud.

My wife approached me from behind. I only became aware of her presence when I heard her clothes swish as she moved. I turned around to face her and saw that she'd stopped crying. She held the box in one hand and the lid in the other. She passed them both to me and said she couldn't do it. I took them from her and turned back to the hole and lowered the box into it. I remember looking down at the tiny scarlet thing inside, and I remember not so much feeling but consciously thinking that I'd never before seen anything as plainly sad as that. Still and glistening but also somehow washed out, dun, like a piece of rubber. An identity stolen away from us before it had even come into being.

I fixed the lid atop the box and with the trowel I scraped the soil over it. Then I took a step away from the yew. When faced with something like that, I realised, there's no such thing as laying it to rest. There's not even such a thing as rest. I had scraped the soil. I had buried the box. Worse than having lost something precious was the feeling that I had destroyed it. Because I'd been the one to put it out of sight, I felt as if I'd also been the one to end the life, and all the conceivable lives, that might have lain ahead of it.

We'd secured a late appointment with the obstetrician. I'd called him from the depths of that intermediate state, after the voice had instructed me on what to do with myself. He'd been the one to suggest the burial. I'd asked him if he needed to see the evidence for himself, if my wife and I should bring the foetus with us to his clinic. How haggard I might have looked if I'd done that didn't even cross my mind. But he told me no, he told us both to take our time, he said we should say our farewells in whatever manner we thought appropriate and then we should come to see him when we felt prepared to do so. We did the best we could. All notions of work disappeared in the meantime. Marking end-of-term assessments, compiling and finalising grades, writing formative reports and letters of recommendation, all of it was sacrificed to the new and urgent unknown we'd fallen into.

The two hours' drive came as a relief, an endeavour with a blessed objective we could work towards. Finally we arrived and embarked on a terrible reprise of the past. My wife lay down once again on the examination bed. I sat beside her in a hard black chair. Jelly slathered over her stomach. The wand pressed firm against her skin. What appeared on the monochrome screen was much more black than white. What we understood from the visuals was made explicit in the doctor's words. Cold and irrevocable facts, a new and bitter status quo. When the doctor left the room to sign a discharge notice, my wife rolled onto her side and turned towards the wall. She couldn't tolerate having me within her field of vision. She lay there and stared at the pure white plaster. She used that spell of privacy to say nothing to me whatsoever, and to do it in a way that made it tantamount to something said. A silence unfolded around us where we sat close together but worlds apart. It bled out into the air of the room and congealed in the empty space between my body and hers.

On the drive home I tried to assuage my wife with words that were hardly worth saying. I set a hand on her knee in a futile gesture of comfort. She jolted it off and flicked on the AC and cranked up the heat to a level I couldn't stand. Dry mouth, rough throat. The drumbeat of an oncoming headache. My wife tilted her head to one side, pressed her temple against the cool glass of the window. Fine white mist, white noise, thickened around us in the valleys we sped through. In the rear-view mirror I saw the billowing spray of melting snow kicked up by the tyres. We raced along the motorway and I realised then that it was exactly where we needed to be. Near to a hundred miles an hour, every passing nanosecond meant a swift and total change in location but no change in the backdrop. Bitumen, roadside barriers, overhanging streetlights. Onward momentum, a breakneck rush, no time to take stock, no time to catch breath, and yet the things in front of our eyes and the things we saw flashing by outside were more or less the same as what we'd seen a mile back and what we'd see a mile ahead and all we could really do as we moved so fast through space was connect each mile to the next and the one after that. We'd been whiplashed into a life we hadn't foreseen. Now we braced for a return to the remains of the life we'd been building together. We knew what awaited us at home. We knew that as soon as we entered the house we'd be back in the midst of the mayhem we'd left behind.

There are few things more awful than ending a moment of respite to return to a life in pieces, staggering through the minutes and hours of simply moving here and there as if traversing a vast and blinding field of static. The most awful part of it all is having returned and having to live on. Your biology doesn't care that the life you'd been building has crumbled. You stand there withdrawn, surveying the wreckage, and you feel the air seep into your lungs and you feel the blood burst through your heart and you despise the body you're in because it dishonours your despair and forces you to survive. It pushes you past the point at which your life has ended and, just to spite you, it persists.

My key scratched into and out of the lock. Bitterness shot through me, hot and fierce, as the handle and the hinges creaked.

My wife couldn't face the scene in the bathroom. She took herself to bed and closed the bedroom door. First I stood awhile at the kitchen window. Twilight reduced the trees outside to jagged thorns of black. Then from the cupboard beneath the sink I retrieved a bucket, a rag, a bottle of disinfectant. I set to work on the bathroom. I must have scrubbed down the surfaces hard, with vigour, and scraped away dried fluids, but my memory has rinsed itself of the details. All I remember now is looking up from my labours, a little short of breath, to find the bathroom restored to its usual condition as if a janitor had sorted it out and stolen away unseen. I'd fallen under an anaesthesia that kept my own behaviour from me, that cleaved me from my alertness to the passing of my time.

After that I cobbled together something to settle our stomachs. A pot of boiling water and a few different greens from the freezer. I knocked on the bedroom door, told my wife I'd soon have dinner ready. As I served it at our kitchen table, I heard her leave the bedroom and then I heard the bathroom latch. I sat at the table and awaited her return. I heard the flush of the toilet, the click of the opening door. My wife lowered herself into the seat opposite mine. Dinnertime was the distant crunching of beans and sprouts. Nothing was said of the state of the house or of what its cleanliness concealed. After a few mouthfuls of food, enough to ease her hunger pangs, my wife stopped eating and stared down at her plate. When I saw her sitting there, arms crossed over her chest and eyes roaming over the table, I stopped as well and watched her and waited for some cue to act. Only the quiet prevailed. I heard no other sound besides our breathing. She seemed to be making an effort to avoid eye contact. Finally she broke the silence with a whisper that sounded like something engineered to mortify me.

We shouldn't have waited so long, she said. Should we?

It was the question that left me speechless. It was the way it begged me, almost innocuously, to agree with what was really an accusation against me. My wife was thirty-four years old. We both knew the statistics on fertility complications in women of her age. We both knew that I was the one who'd insisted we wait until we had stable jobs and a stable home before we considered conceiving a child. We both knew that in the years before we were married, we'd talked it over on many occasions and for a long time I'd made it plain that I didn't want any children. In her quiet lament I heard my wife hint that perhaps I wasn't upset by what we'd just gone through. I heard her hint that perhaps I even felt relieved.

I shrank into myself and said nothing. I didn't agree with what she'd said but I didn't speak against it. I saw it as a symptom of her shock, her distress, and for that reason I let it slide. What that meant, I see in hindsight, was that I let her notions simmer and stew.

She went to bed before I did and left me to clean the kitchen. When I slid under the bedsheets I felt her awake beside me. I turned to her and placed my hands on her back, beneath the fabric of her nightclothes, and asked her what I could do for her. Nothing, she said, and she added that she only wished she wasn't now, in this moment, so far from her parents. We both knew that I was the one who'd agitated to live the expatriate lifestyle. We both knew that my relationship with Australia had always been belligerent, at best, and that from as far back as before we met I'd wanted to settle elsewhere. I mumbled an apology and took my hands away and turned aside from her. I woke in the morning after a night of fractious sleep to find her leaning against the jamb at the entrance to the bathroom. We both knew that I'd been the one to pursue the opportunities that drew us to the Alps, to lead us into a life far away from the senseless rush of the city, to suggest that this would be the best place for us to raise any children we might have. She let her gaze wander over the tiles as she spoke. If only we didn't live so far from everything we need, she said.

There are things about this phase in our lives that it wouldn't be right to say. It wouldn't be right to say that our hardship brought us closer. My wife took to looking back on all the decisions we'd arrived at as a couple, then unpicking the logic behind them and isolating its faults. She saw our situation as the result of all the choices we'd made and for that reason she questioned the sense of each one. She found an outlet for her sorrow in sentiments like these, I know, but in voicing them she chipped away at the integrity of the people we'd striven to become. In the questions she posed I saw a rot eating into the fibres of our selves. In the flaws she pinpointed I saw a campaign to unwind the history that made us who we were. Even so, it wouldn't be right to say that whenever we were together we bristled with unspoken anger. The anger was intermittent, igniting between us like glints from the friction of striking stones, and what enveloped us outside our outbursts was a sort of anomie.

Midsummer came and went. Daylight dwindled and brittle brown leaves rustled over the floor of the forest. Most of the time we ate our meals in separate places, we went to bed at different times, we woke and embarked on our days independent of one another. Sprinkles of snow brought a hush to the mountains. Dawn began to break long after the world had already woken and darkness fell a few hours before the working day had ended. Christmas entailed only cursory commemorations, simple gifts and phone calls to family overseas. Then we entered a new year and we returned to our routines and adhered to them like automata. Yet, too, it wouldn't be right to say we started to break apart, held back from human touch, never gave ourselves up to the murmuring wants that had a will of their own. At night the cold that crept into our bedroom pressed us closer together. Both of our bodies built up warmth beneath the sheets. We'd wake in darkness with limbs entangled. We'd hold tight for a time and then release, and through the languid hours of early morning we'd find each other again. It wouldn't be right to say that we felt moved by passion. The blood finds a way to meet its ends. Desperation, irritation, and a need for crude distraction will serve its purposes equally well when affection fades.

The thaw had just arrived, icicles dripping from eaves, when my wife came to me with a blue line on another take-home test. I'd returned from work and dropped onto the sofa. She'd met me at the door but didn't burst out with the news. She waited until I'd settled before she showed me the proof. It wouldn't be right to say that I was instantly overjoyed. We'd been through all this once before. Caution tamped down whatever flutters of joy I felt on reflex. The only feeling I allowed myself, the only one I couldn't halt, was the sudden relief that descended on me with the force of a smashing wave. Relief at receiving news I didn't know I was waiting for, even though I needed urgently to hear it. Relief at seeing clearly now that this, this new conception, was the farther shore, exactly the destination the two of us needed to reach because any other outcome would have driven us further apart. So we swung into three months of a recursive loop. An appointment with the obstetrician and a stomach exposed to his touch. Jelly on skin, the wand, and then, once more, the magic. A monochrome screen. A white speck surrounded by darkness. A vision of the same thing we'd seen the last time we saw our last child. This time, though, the fact of its existence was by far a greater source of wonder than simply laying eyes on it. The doctor offered curt congratulations and gave us a due date not long before Christmas.

The last of winter melted away over the following weeks, and throughout the spring something in our marriage slowly rekindled. One step at a time, we met all the milestones we hadn't reached the year before. On the day the new pregnancy entered its eleventh week, we celebrated with dinner at a favourite restaurant in Brienz. Ultrasounds at twelve, twenty, and twenty-six weeks let us marvel at the growth of the life inside the womb. We saw the valves of the heart jerk open and close in alternation. We watched the notches and discs of the spine assemble into a flexible column. We tracked the progress of musculature sheathing bones and organs. As the body steadily built itself, we gave our entire summer to preparing for its arrival. We painted barnyard animals over the bedroom walls. We stitched up curtains covered in stars and whorls of cosmic dust. We bought and received oodles of toys. Goofy smiles and googly eyes colonised an entire corner of what would become a bedroom. We collected a little library, dreaming ahead to the day we'd be able to sit and read aloud to our child. We became the living clichés of expectant parents. I hammered together a changing table and a wooden cot. My wife dropped a lambskin rug on the floor and dangled mobiles from the ceiling. We hoarded rattles, stockpiled nappies, indulged in rambling deliberations about the relative merits of monsters and dinosaurs on pyjamas. We became tender again.

All the while I knew that our preparations were really so much more than paltry, practical steps towards taking care of a child. They were spurious activities, ways of relieving ourselves of the spells of anticipation that shot up within us at some point every day. They were attempts to calm the fervent impatience we felt to skip ahead to the end, to transport ourselves to the day of delivery, and meet the person, whole and healthy, who'd be with us for the rest of our years. From time to time, at night, before bed, I'd try to put this feeling into words. Let everything that follows from here stand as a testament to my aspirations. I know it also stands as a record of my naïveté. I'd sit at the table with pen and paper and I'd address a letter to my child. I wrote pages and pages of letters, entire books of letters. I wrote in the knowledge that this time I was more at ease with the future I faced. I was ready to raise a child. In fact, I was longing to do it. With no idea of even which gender to expect, I'd try and try again to express what I felt about the kind of person my child might become. I wrote in the hope that I could articulate the disposition I wanted to shape. The qualities I wanted to cultivate. The knowledge I wanted to bestow, the interests I wanted to share, the guidance I wanted to give. The sensibilities I'd usher into someone else's being. Many of these came to me with the sobriety of someone afforded a second chance, a way of thinking past the point at which my earlier, amorphous thoughts about parenthood had been thwarted by the miscarriage. Many of them returned to me, too, as I sat in the hospital, after the birth, and doted on my daughter for the very first time.

I was a teacher back then and I launched myself at the task with a teacher's lofty ideals. Above all, I suppose, I wanted to nurture in my daughter an openness to whatever the world might put before her eyes. I wanted her to be alert to its infinite forms, to appreciate its endless possibilities. I'd long ago resolved to be this way myself, and I realise now that as I wrote about and towards and for my daughter, I was also, at the same time, delineating both the person I'd consciously become and the father I now sought to be. Attentive to all things unfolding around me. Calm and patient and generous with my sympathies. Magnanimous in the classical sense, endlessly forgiving and expansive of soul. I hoped to be, in a word, capacious. I wanted to bring about for my child a world defined by largeness of space and a worldview defined by largeness of heart. Planetary, epochal largeness. I wanted to point to those parts of the world that tremble with difference and discord, and I wanted to help my child learn to strike fine and subtle harmonies between them.

I cringe at myself when I look back now at those moments of anticipation. I'm awestruck by my simplicity, by the scale of my obliviousness, by my failure to consider that I'd be defrauded of my dreams. I woke in the recovery room with daylight brimming the curtains. I woke with my arm around my wife, the two of us cramped in a single bed, and the first thing I felt was the pull of a weight on my hand. I rose from the mattress, a couple of inches, and saw a tiny fist still holding fast to my finger. Let's say I smiled at the thought that I'd been in touch with my daughter like this while we slept. I eased myself up a little further, careful not to wake my wife, and peered in at the girl through the clear sides of the bassinet. She pressed her face against the plastic. She kept her lips pursed, I saw, and the ruffle of hair on her head gave her a fringe that reached her eyebrows. She'd lost none of the serenity of the instant she fell asleep. But then as I relaxed, reclining again on the bed, I noticed that her hold on my finger didn't shift or slacken. I angled over my wife to move closer to the sleeping child. Now I saw that her exhalations left no smudge, no steam, on the plastic that touched the tip of her nose. I moved in closer still and saw that her face had once more taken on an unusual pallor, an ashen shade. Carefully, for what felt like an aeon, I watched for signs of breath and pulse, palpitations, tremors, the rise and fall of her chest, I watched for any movement of any kind at all. I watched her intently and I wanted not to believe that I was seeing, really seeing, a stillness I never imagined I'd see.

I sat upright and fumbled for the emergency button. On my feet I rounded the bed, socks swishing over linoleum. Snatching at the bassinet, I wheeled it to the window. I waited there for a nurse to arrive. I didn't take my eyes from my daughter. Still her chest, her entire body, made no movement whatsoever. I bent over where she lay to place my ear to her mouth, to listen for a sigh or feel some trace of breath. I placed the underside of my wrist beneath her nostrils, to detect a burst of warmth or even just a wisp. With the tips of my fingers I touched her cheek. Her face was stunningly, shockingly cold. I stood upright again and looked down at the body beneath me and recognised, then, how awfully empty it seemed, how vacant of involuntary motion, of anything restive or fleeting beneath skin with the texture of wax. I hovered over it, I remember, unsure of what to do with my hands. I clenched and unclenched them, flexed them, flailed them. I watched them begin to twitch and I waved them without thought, as if I'd sensed that my daughter's life had somehow dispersed into air and I was answering an urge to catch it before it could dissipate, to gather it all together again and drive it back inside her body to bring her back to me.

Finally the door swung open. A nurse bustled into the room. My panic rendered her face indistinct, reduced her to her presence and her functions. She dashed towards my daughter and reached in to touch the child as if to take a pulse. In a breathless voice she said something I couldn't understand. She took the bassinet in both hands and dragged it to the door. The squeak of the wheels across the linoleum was loud enough to wake my wife. What's that? she said, she groaned, as she strained her eyes to focus. She sat up in bed and found the bassinet no longer beside her. She saw the nurse at the door and turned to find me still by the window. What's wrong? she said. What's happening? I rushed to explain what I'd seen, what I'd done, but all my words came out as babble. I didn't just babble, I leapt outside my own body and watched myself babble and even with an awareness of it I couldn't control what I said. The nurse said something else, this time addressed to my wife, and hustled the bassinet into the hallway and out of sight. She must have known the truth at a glance, or at least within seconds of taking our daughter away. As she left the room my wife's face drained of colour. She thumped onto her feet and darted after the nurse. I tried again to tell her what had happened but still I could only jabber, only sputter drivel. She burst through the door, into the hallway, hobbling towards the bassinet. I stood back and saw her stop the nurse, seize at our child, grab an infant hand that moved only when she made it. The nurse manoeuvred into my wife's line of sight. She issued orders in a tone of rising alarm and pried my wife's fingers from our child's wrist. She spun on her heels and pushed the girl away from us, through two large swinging doors, and then she was out of sight. The doors creaked closed in unison. A puff of air rushed down the empty corridor.

My wife stood alone and stationary not far from where I lingered, but the distance felt so insurmountable that I lost all will to make myself move to her side. With another puff of air the doors broke open again and the nurse returned. Our daughter wasn't with her. She went to my wife, laid a hand on her shoulder, ushered her back to our room. I trailed them at a remove. My wife, I could hear, was sobbing. I pulled the door closed behind me while the nurse led my wife to the bed and gestured for her to sit. My wife sat as instructed. I steadied myself against a wall. Then the nurse spoke, still in her own language, and I was left to infer the meaning of her words from the changes they wrought on my wife's composure. I watched my wife with care as she listened, scrying her demeanour for some sense of the message the nurse conveyed. I watched her with no feeling for how to comprehend what I saw. A hollowness came to her eyes. She blinked quickly in confusion. The news drained the life from her face the way a midwinter dusk drags light from the sky.

What I learnt later was that the nurse had said she was sorry to have to tell us our daughter had passed away. I'd known enough German to have gathered her meaning if she'd bluntly told us our daughter had died, but her euphemism, *Ich glaube, dass—vielleicht, dass sie ist entschlafen*, gave me to understand that, at worst, the girl had fallen unconscious. Then she said something more, something to the effect of having suspicions of the cause, and at that instant an intercom hissed on the wall by the head of the bed. The nurse pressed a button to speak with a man of higher rank. When the intercom clicked off she turned to us to deliver a preliminary diagnosis. She told us our daughter had suffered from a condition that I'd eventually learn is known as a total anomalous pulmonary venous connection. She might have added that this condition was worsened, and perhaps intensified, by an undetected venous obstruction. What she meant was that our daughter exhibited several malformations of the heart. These malformations were barely perceptible even though they severely impeded the functioning of her circulatory system. They weakened the flow of blood through her veins and, worse, they weakened her heart's capacity to retain it. Her heart, we learnt, had effectively pumped itself dry. She had holes in the veins that should have supplied the rest of her organs with blood rich in oxygen. She had a blockage in the veins that should have returned deoxygenated blood to the lungs. All through the night, one hundred and fifty beats per minute, each contraction of her heart expressed a trickle of blood through the holes, and compounded whatever the blockage was, so that her body had no way of circulating fresh air. All through the dark hours, in fifty thousand impossibly tiny increments, our daughter leaked blood into the tissue that padded her oesophagus, her trachea, her diaphragm, her vital organs. Her own heart sapped her of life. When she died, we were later informed, she would have felt no pain. She would have slipped away, exhausted, too weak even to whimper.

I stood there mutely and listened to the nurse but I felt myself lagging behind. I had no way to be certain that what I thought she was saying was in fact what she'd just said. I couldn't be sure that the sounds I heard her making were actually the words I matched to them, or that those words had meanings to match the meanings of their cognates in English. I wasn't able to know how strong a grip I had on the situation, and for the second time in as many days I felt, between my wife and myself, the opening of a disjuncture in the life we shared. She understood perfectly what the nurse was saying. She was already there, a step ahead of me, closer to the reality I couldn't discern just yet. As long as I didn't properly understand the truth, it wouldn't really be true for me at all, and I wondered briefly if I could somehow play dumb and postpone my comprehension of the events unfurling around me. I wanted to delay my departure to the world my wife had already arrived in. I wanted only to sit there and listen to the sounds of her exchange with the nurse while shrugging off the sense. But just as I began to drift and toy with fancies like these, my wife began mumbling questions to the nurse and in the tenor of the nurse's responses I saw the truth grow clear. I'd been the one my daughter held on to as she died, passed away, by degrees. I'd been the one sleeping soundly beside her while she bled to death without a sound. I turned to my wife and watched her silence herself with a choke. She bit her bottom lip. My eyes burned, my vision blurred, my nerves set on edge so sharply that I didn't just witness my wife's distress but felt it vibrating across the open space between us. I hung my head and knew I had no notion of how I might ease her anguish.

Without explanation the nurse excused herself and strode to the door. With a click of the handle behind her she left me alone with my wife. Why had we been deserted like this? To discuss the facts or to process our grief or to ponder how we ought to respond? To comfort one another? I had no sensitivity to ways of offering comfort. In the absence of the medical staff I had a feeling of being abandoned, of having been cut adrift, by people I now needed more than I needed my wife. Right then I wanted anything but to be left alone with her. I wanted someone to stay with me, to buffer me from her incandescent distress. I wanted relief from the onus of having to help her through her trauma while my own was still so raw. We faced one another without quite facing anything. Spontaneous tears stung my eyes but I cried without a sound, I think, and I stepped towards my wife with one hand out to touch her, if not to put her at ease then at least to break our stagnation. She rose to her feet and escaped to a nearby wall before I could reach her. She pressed her face to the surface of the wall without saying a word, only sighing. I stayed by the foot of the bed and watched her standing away from me, nose and forehead against the pastel yellow paint. Then I lowered myself onto the bed and sat with my feet where the bassinet had been stationed. I remember, very distinctly, looking down at my socks on the shiny floor and realising just how powerfully, how completely, my life, our lives, would be marked by the emptiness of the space they occupied. Every event henceforth, every experience, would be shadowed by the indelible absence of a child who had departed before she could know she was beloved. The vacancy she left behind would follow me forever. Wherever I went and whatever I did, I knew, I knew with all the certainty of receiving a criminal sentence, I knew I'd always be dragging behind me a cavity in the world where she should have been. All my future actions would be dogged not by the girl herself, not by a trace of her presence, but by her withdrawal, by the rescission of the arrival I'd believed would bring a very different change to my life.

A knock at the door announced the return of a professional. I rose from the bed and my wife turned away from the wall as the door inched open. A doctor stepped inside. We hadn't seen him before. He had a chubby round face and black hair in a quiff. He had eyes I struggled to see as the light from the window turned his glasses into discs of shining white. He told us in eloquent English that he'd come to confirm the diagnosis. His words were perfect and precise. He spoke of the superior vena cava and the hepatic vein. He spoke of ventricular hypertrophy and the left innominate vein. Informed suspicions only, he said, pending evidential support. He cast a glance at my wife, saw her pallid look, came to me with a sheaf of papers covered in foreign print. The papers, he said, required signed permission. Without parental consent, he said, the autopsy couldn't proceed.

My head began to spin. The world began to spin. Then came another knock and the door inched open again. An enormous spray of flowers obscured the face of a young woman. A vase of violets and daisies, poppies and peony roses, struck an absurd contrast with the white of the walls. The woman set down the vase on a table, right beside a pile of folded clothes for a newborn. She smiled as she released the vase but stopped smiling when she saw our expressions. The flowers had come from my parents. They'd ordered them after receiving the picture I'd sent the day before. I had to sign something for the woman as well. I took the receipt and pen she gave me and put a mark on a dotted line. At that she left the room sheepishly, head down past the explosion of petals, but just as the doctor drew breath to resume his discussion with me the phone in my pocket rang. I pulled it out and checked the screen. My parents wanted to speak. I couldn't stomach talking to them. I couldn't stomach having to unweave the story I knew they'd already written around themselves, the story that crescendoed with the birth of their first grandchild and reached its climax with their imminent chance to cradle the infant. I rejected the call and stuffed the phone back into my pocket. Without facing the doctor again I reached for the papers he held out to me. I took them from him, along with the pen he offered, and, obediently, I signed. I signed away my right to see my daughter in her state of rest. From the wall my wife watched me in silence. With her silence she forfeited her only real chance to protest. I passed the papers back to the doctor and when he took them I went numb. My wife, I knew, was numb already.

The doctor whispered his thanks with a sombre nod. Then he cleared his throat to change the subject and he didn't wait for a response before he started on it.

Given what has happened, he said, we must now begin to consider how to pay your daughter the respect she is due.

I should have despised him for forcing me to direct my attention to what he deemed important here, for guiding me towards a subject of more profound desolation. I should have despised him but I didn't. In that state of mind, I see now, the most gracious thing that any other person could have done for me would have been to free me from the burden of independent thought, to somehow absolve me of the weight of being who I was.

The doctor passed me a selection of pamphlets about various possibilities. Most of them were nonsense to me. I could only infer the flimsiest meanings from the pictures that accompanied the text. Burial options. Plots to purchase. Coffins, cremations, ceremonial affairs. One sheet listed a dozen funeral directors and their contact details.

Naturally, the doctor said, I can't even imagine how difficult it must be for you and your wife to think of these issues right now, at this time. Nevertheless, it's all for the best if, over the next few days, you give some thought to your daughter's resting arrangements. He gestured at the list of names. Any one of these men will see to it, he said, that your daughter is appropriately presented after we confirm the diagnosis.

I understood him to mean that each of them would take pains to conceal the autopsy scars. I couldn't avoid anticipating the wounds, crescents of livid red with bruises of grey at the edges. I shook my head in an effort to dismiss the grotesque sight.

I can't do it, I told the doctor, I can't, I can't do it, and I couldn't say anything else.

The doctor nodded and looked to my wife to see if she might have calmed, if she might be ready to respond. She hadn't calmed, she wasn't ready, she'd grown more pallid than before. She'd disappeared deep into herself. The doctor nodded once more before conceding that he could ask around, could maybe find an assistant to make some calls on our behalf. Then he tapped my shoulder with a reassuring paw and stepped again towards the door. I thought he intended to leave. I thought he would leave us to ourselves. Instead he opened the door and turned back to me.

If you have a moment, he said, there's something further we must discuss.

I'd only just brushed past the doctor, he'd only just closed the door behind me, when the phone in my pocket rang again. My parents hadn't accepted my silence. The growl and jingle, rattle and ringtone, echoed down the empty hallway. I couldn't see what more the doctor would want from me, but I knew he wouldn't have called me away if it wasn't bound to be egregious. My parents, now, were my escape. I said I had to speak to them and at a trot I fled. The phone cried out anew in my hand. I hurried to the men's room at the far end of the corridor and I pressed the button to take the call as I shouldered in.

Blistering light, bright tiles, the sting of citrus disinfectant. A cubicle. I lowered the lid on a toilet seat, sat down and locked the door. I pressed the phone to my forehead and held it there without a sound. A squawk came from the speaker. My mother sounded buoyant. On reflex I put the phone to my ear and offered an apology for not having answered earlier, for not having called before going to bed, for not having kept everyone updated now that it was almost eleven in the morning and she and my father in Brisbane and my in-laws in Sydney were no doubt sitting around in the dark awaiting contact from me. She told me not to be silly, not to worry about apologies. She just wanted to know how mother and child were faring and she wanted to hear the details of the troubled labour. Instead of sharing the details I told her the story of what had happened when I woke.

I'd rejected the earlier call for fear of knowing I'd have to speak of these things and knowing I wouldn't be able. I dreaded having to focus all my faltering energies, to concentrate my failing powers, on the task of tensing every muscle in my body, my diaphragm, my throat, my jaw, just to release the words. Now I made no effort to withhold anything. I gave no thought to what I said and I have no memory of it. All I remember is the wailing at the other end of the line, the tinny howl, the fading lament as I held the phone away from my ear. Then I heard a bump, a shuffle, my father seizing the handset, followed by a string of commands barked out in a panic. He told me to tell him what had happened, from the very beginning, to tell again what I'd just told my mother. I ended the call. I left her to tell him what he wanted to hear. I left it to the two of them to call my in-laws and tell them as well. I breathed in deeply, breathed in the burn of Clorox, and breathed out and in and out again, committing myself to a rhythm as steady as any I could maintain.

I don't know how long I sat in the cubicle. I only know I determined to sit there long enough for the news to reach everyone who needed to hear it. Only then did I feel it was time to rise and return to my wife. I found her in a chair in the corner of the recovery room. A nurse knelt by her side to help her affix a pump to her breasts. She'd produced enough milk for a child to drink its fill, but now without a child her breasts had begun to leak. The nurse pressed a button to activate the pump while my wife looked away from her and away from me. I moved to the table near the window, caught the sweet scent of the flowers, and quietly I retreated to the wall and tried to disappear. A message buzzed and dinged in my pocket. I took out my phone to learn that my parents had already brought forward their flight. Now they were due to board their plane in a matter of hours. My in-laws had done likewise, although they'd depart from further south, and both sets of parents would unite in Singapore before boarding the same flight to Zürich. All four would be with us in a day and a half. I laid the phone on the table, beside a sheaf of yet more medical papers, and there I noticed, on top of the documents, a commemorative card produced by the hospital. The cover showed the first photograph anyone had ever taken of my daughter. The text above her face offered congratulations on the birth. Her footprint marked the interior in mauve. I sat down, dumb, and stared at the text for a time I cannot reckon.

Just after midday the doctor returned. He rapped on the door and poked his head into the room. The nurse had begun to disassemble the pump. My wife shifted anxiously when she saw who'd arrived and took care to avoid the doctor's eyes. He asked me to follow him into the hallway. This time I had no means of escape. He closed the door behind me once more and then handed me a pamphlet for a funeral parlour by Lake Brienz. A member of staff had arranged a simple service, he told me. The day after tomorrow. Twelve o'clock.

I thanked him and made to return to the room.

Unfortunately, he added, detaining me with a hand at my elbow, there is, as I mentioned before, one more matter to discuss. I must confess it's not easy to say this. He bowed his head, almost in shame, and allowed himself a moment of thought before he looked at me again. Unfortunately, he said, the law and the policies of this hospital provide beds for patients and their immediate relatives only. Your daughter will be released to you tomorrow, after we conclude the examination this afternoon, so, of course, for tonight you and your wife are entitled to remain in the room you have been allocated. In the morning, however, there will be nothing here, in a technical sense, to allow your stay.

I stared at him in disbelief. I felt my mouth go dry. I had to swallow before I could speak. I had to force the saliva.

We are grieving parents, I said. My wife is still in recovery. Our daughter's body will remain here in your morgue. Why should we leave? Where would we go?

He couldn't actually answer my questions. I do apologise, he said, I truly do. He shook his head in what looked to me like frustration. I apologise and I sympathise with your dilemma, but we have no legal basis on which to allow you to stay here after tomorrow.

We live two hours away, I said. Longer than that if more snow sets in.

I know that. I do. I'm aware of your situation. I've argued for accommodations. I have taken your case to my superiors and they have appealed to the board, twice in fact, and the governors understand the nuances of your situation, but there is nothing we can do to alter the law. It is inflexible, despite our best hopes to find a way around it. Please accept our apologies. But please also understand that we are unable to change this.

I leant back against the door and closed my eyes. I felt a stabbing in my temples. I didn't want to go home. So soon after all this, this madness, I couldn't bring myself to do it. A new peal of thunder sent a new pulse through my head. I opened my eyes again.

Okay, I said. Okay, okay. If we have to leave, we will. I didn't say it because I meant it. I said it for an expedient end. I said it because I needed to get the doctor out of my face.

I turned and barged through the door and blasted back into the room. My wife hadn't moved from her chair. The nurse stood at the table where she was packing the pump into its case. Both of them were silent and both, I saw, had been crying. No doubt they'd heard everything. The corridor couldn't contain my exchange with the doctor.

At my return the nurse made haste to leave with her equipment and a couple of bottles of milk. When she was gone my wife stared straight ahead as if peering down a tunnel.

I don't want to go home, she said. I can't go home right now.

I couldn't argue with her refusals. I agreed to find a hotel for the next few days and I spent that afternoon making calls, hunting for vacancies at affordable rates, booking a place near the hospital and then contacting the funeral home to discuss our options. By dusk our departure was assured. We spent that night in the hospital bed without a minute of sleep. We lay together, awake but silent, haunted by what had happened there only the night before. I could feel the fury of my wife's thoughts. I could feel the raging heat of her inchoate anger. But I couldn't begin to guess what else troubled her, what worse, what more she felt as she endured the paroxysms of her mind. I suppose I was a victim of my own confusion and fury, and of the same sense of injustice that stung me the first time we lost a child. I couldn't credit my own suspicions of what my wife was going through. I couldn't credit my own efforts to suppose, to imagine, what she was feeling. I held her as tight as I could even as I knew she'd drifted away from me, beyond my reach, in every sense but the literal one.

First light urged me to my feet. My wife remained beneath the blanket. I knew she hadn't fallen asleep even though she didn't move. I dragged the curtains from the window. Outside, I saw, the snowfall had stopped. The sun rose up behind the Jungfrau. It burned off the night sky in a bloom of white while the peaks remained in shadow. Still we had a few hours to wait before our discharge would be finalised. I spent the time reopening the suitcase I'd already packed and refolding all the clothes. Among the clothes were a shirt not much bigger than my hand and leggings with ankles wide enough for only two of my fingers. I found a pair of socks as well, impossibly small in my palm, and a bonnet with a smiling polar bear sewn onto the front. A tension in my forehead bleached the colour from my vision, pumped heat into my eyes. For a long time I sat on the edge of the bed and blindly fingered the ribbons on the bonnet in a stupor of speechless rage.

At ten the doctor returned. The autopsy had been conducted, he said, and the results had confirmed his suspicions. He stood before us awaiting a response. What response could he have expected? My wife and I exchanged glances, each of us as mute as the other, then we nodded blankly like a pair of simpletons. We just wanted to see our daughter one last time. So the doctor led us down a sonorous stairwell, through a labyrinth of corridors, into a subterranean morgue of buffed steel and exposed concrete. He had spared us the sight of the girl retrieved from cold storage, the body bag unzipped to reveal the face. Our daughter lay there already, naked and small and stiff.

Few people ever have to see the things we saw in that room. Fewer can prepare themselves for having to see them.

I thought I'd break down, collapse to the floor, bellow until my throat began to bleed. Instead I took a step towards my daughter and studied her without a flinch, without so much as a sound. She did not look human. She didn't resemble the child I'd seen before. She had a human form but her skin, the colour of smoke, looked now as if it had been moulded from clay and left to dry in the air. Her chest had been cut open and sewn together again. The scars were as red as I'd imagined and matched by rims of red around her eyes. My wife, behind me, leant her shoulder against a wall and waited for me to finish looking. She looked at me, at my back, as I looked down at our child. I felt an overwhelming urge to address the body somehow, to linger over it and mutter some final words of love or consolation, but at the same time I felt as if the body dampened all sound in the room, took the words from me before I could speak them aloud. I couldn't dredge up any words that felt in any way adequate to address the thing in front of me.

Far more difficult than seeing my daughter was leaving the hospital without her. I loaded our luggage into the car and placed the empty capsule in the back. My wife climbed into the passenger seat. She sat wrapped in a fleece and a jacket padded with down, while I rounded the bumper, scraper in hand, and began chipping ice off the windscreen. I hacked at it, sawed at it, stripped away my gloves to strengthen my grip on the handle, scattered shards and splinters over my knuckles. I was out of breath when I took my seat at the steering wheel. I yanked at the door, slammed it shut, put my hands on the wheel and my feet on the pedals, and began to hyperventilate. I couldn't slow down my breathing and I couldn't stop myself from releasing every breath I took. Before I realised I'd started to cry, I was already crying beyond control. The tears welled up so fast and clouded my vision so quickly that at first I thought I'd gone blind. I felt the flow of time distending and deflating, contracting and elongating in otherworldly ways, so that I would now need hours if not days to accomplish trivial things like sitting at the wheel of a car and starting the engine while events of immense importance arose and then ebbed away before I'd had time to attend to them. Our daughter, I realised, had been dead for only a day. Even so, I realised as well, by the time I sat at that wheel she'd been dead for longer than she'd ever been alive.

The hotel clerk hummed with unnatural happiness. She assumed my wife and I were tourists and she tried to sell us tickets for the train to the Jungfraujoch. The room we received demoralised me as soon as I opened the door. The problem was nothing particular. The problem was that the room had nothing particular to it. It could've been any room anywhere. It felt like every room everywhere. In the wake of our loss I couldn't stand walking into a space in which, by design, our departure would be followed by an erasure of all traces of our having been there. I couldn't even stand knowing that we'd entered the room following on from everyone else who'd stayed before us and been erased. I couldn't get my head around the logic of a building intended to turn its occupants into ghosts. I felt suddenly faint, as if my substance was thinning out into nothingness, and I had to hold myself against a wall to bind myself together. I bought a bottle of red wine that evening and spilled a glass on the carpet. I sat on the bed and relished watching the red stain the beige.

My wife and I stood at the window and looked out over Unterseen. Lumps of dirty snow bedecked the cobbled streets. We opened the latch to let the cold inside. A freezing wind lifted off the turquoise churn of the Aare. We lay on the bed and stared at the ceiling. We had twelve hours to wait before our parents touched down and twenty before the service. Events that were moving at speed when we surveyed them from afar were excruciating to experience from one minute to the next. We switched on the television and then we switched it off, we debated what to eat for dinner and then decided we weren't hungry, we fumbled through every conceivable way of distracting ourselves from the torture of sheltering in that room and awaiting the next event. Finally, as a last resort, as a retreat towards the one thing we'd supposed would be worse than endless waiting, we broached the brutal subject we'd been trying to evade.

We need to locate a plot, I said.

No, said my wife. Cremation. *Please.* She should rest wherever we want her to.

I shrugged when I shouldn't have done. With that shrug I resigned myself to a decision I'd later realise was intolerable, insufferable. I signed off with all the numbness I'd seen in my wife, the shell-shocked nonchalance, when I scratched my consent on the papers to permit the autopsy. I magnified the scale of my daughter's desecration while being too narrowly focused on the search for appropriate words in the blistering heat of the now. I moved the discussion forward when I should've lingered, should've thought about what the outright loss of the body, its atomisation and disposal, might someday mean to me.

Well, then, I said, we need to think of what to say.

We'd opted for a ceremony, rather than simply consigning the body without a service, but neither of us knew how we wanted it to run. How can anyone know how to honour a child less than one day old? We didn't know what to say at the service or if we should let our parents say something or even if we should allow anything at all to be said. We floated ideas, a Shakespearean sonnet, a verse from the Psalms or Proverbs, but we settled on nothing specific because I struggled to overcome my feeling that a child whose life had ended before she ever cultivated tastes of her own couldn't possibly care what was said about her one way or another. We fell asleep with the issue unresolved.

Our parents disembarked the train in mismatched pairs. They didn't disguise anything. On their faces they wore the trials of breakneck travel, two transcontinental flights followed by hours on the train from the airport, and these strains overlaid the naked distress of the situation that had summoned them. My father, unshaven, grimaced as he took a case from my mother-in-law and hauled it onto the platform. She followed on his heels, accepting the hand he extended to her, and stumbled into the winter sunlight wearing enormous shades and a parka lined with fake fur. Behind her stood her husband, a foot taller than my father, and he clambered through the door with a frown as a duffel bag swung from his elbow. My mother showed herself last, joining the group with a valise clutched in one hand and a pair of earmuffs in the other. The morning was still young. All of them looked bedraggled. Sleeplessness had scorched their eyes and put a slouch into their postures. My wife and I moved towards them, greeted them all, voiced our gratitude for their presence, and yet, we found, none of these people were in any state to talk to us. We became, perversely, their sources of moral support. Our mothers embraced us and bleated into our shoulders. Our fathers pitched themselves at practical concerns. Mine wanted nothing but medical facts, hounding us for any details that might offer grounds on which to sue for negligence or outright malpractice. My wife's father wanted to know how he could help with the funeral, checking that we were of clear enough minds to ensure that we'd do justice to the memory of our child.

I can't be the one to say whether or not justice was done. I don't know what justice could possibly look like in that scenario. I'm not even sure that our memory of our child gave us anything of substance to do justice to. With our parents we went to a department store where we bought new clothes, a black suit and a black dress, because all we had in our luggage at this point were dirty sweaters and shirts and trousers. Our parents paid for everything. We all went back to the hotel. Still too early for the new arrivals to check in. We ate croissants from a convenience store as one by one our parents used our shower to freshen up. Then my wife and I put on our new clothes without having had time to wash them first, and finally, around midday, the six of us made our way to the lakeside funeral parlour. In a small, stuffy room with peach-coloured walls and faded salmon carpet, we met the old man who'd been recommended to us. He wore thin-rimmed spectacles and a short-cropped moustache and a slight but compassionate smile. He seemed undaunted by having only six attendees in a cavernous hall with seats for a hundred. He mumbled a prayer of his choice in Swiss German and consolations in broken English. I'm sure the prayer was word perfect, but his condolences for our loss came out in variations on the future tense.

Behind the man, a small, simple coffin sat on a conveyor belt. The lid had been sealed shut. I assumed I'd consented to that being done when I'd called the parlour from the hospital. I assumed we'd stuck with the plan even when I'd called from the hotel to confirm that we wanted a cremation. I wish now I'd intervened when I saw the result. I wish I'd asked the man to suspend the service, to open the lid, to give me one last look at my daughter. Actually, I wish I'd stepped in right then to stop the ceremony. What happened next, I realise now, was the fountainhead of all the difficulties to follow. I was an accessory to it. By my inaction, I gave it an authorisation I didn't intend; I gave it my passive, perverse sanction. I didn't have the presence of mind to say so at the time, but still, I know, that's what I did.

It happened like this. The old man finished speaking and pressed a button beside the conveyor belt. The belt jolted to life with a hum. The coffin slipped out of view, through an archway built into a wall. It took my daughter into the flames, behind the scenes, where I could no longer see her. As it trundled along, irrevocably, I felt overcome by the slow understanding that I didn't want my daughter to be reduced to dust. But she was, irrevocably, and then the ceremony came to an end and we were served refreshments. We found ourselves in a room with a window looking onto the pebbled shore of the lake. At our disposal we had a trestle table displaying an urn of steaming water, tea and coffee, also a platter of unseasonal fruit and tiny sandwiches sliced into triangles. Nobody felt much like eating.

Nobody was swooned by the view. Nobody had anything more to say. Our time in that room was spent listening to the ticking of the radiator and watching condensation gather between the panes of the double-glazing.

After a wait of perhaps an hour the old man creaked open the door. Moving at a stride I didn't expect from one so meek, he made a beeline for me with both hands outstretched. All other heads swivelled to track him. Humbly but unceremoniously, he presented me with an urn containing my daughter's ashes. I took it from him in much the way I imagine I'd receive a cudgel. It had a dull, gunmetal surface with a matte finish and handles of stainless steel. With the remains returned to us, entered into my care, I felt a revitalised unwillingness to part with them, to let go of my daughter again. I was, I am, a heathen, in every sense of the word, but I'd thrown aside the one thing I should've preserved in order to keep the memory of my daughter from the torment of eternal life.

Our parents stayed with us another three weeks. They found rooms in our hotel and maxed out their credit cards in covering their own expenses and splitting the cost of ours. We spent Christmas Day in the dining salon of a guesthouse near the river. We drank warm beer and ate cured meats and tried as hard as we could not to think about the state of our lives and not to reawaken any memories of the previous Christmas.

In the week leading up to Christmas itself, and throughout the week that followed, we faced a swarm of other irritants and confrontations. Every day we had to swat them away and soldier on without complaint. Every day, while they harassed us, we had to bite our tongues and wait for them to retreat. At one point my mother suggested that we might find it easier to return to our home in the mountains if we had our parents to help us settle in again. My in-laws made a few attempts at dragging us back to Australia. Several times they wondered aloud if we might scatter the ashes there. My father-in-law even floated the idea that my wife and I could simply renounce our expatriate lives and return to more familiar surroundings without so much as a backward glance. It wasn't the last time he'd detonate bombs like those, and it wasn't the worst of the things he'd lob at me before we parted ways. My mother shared his views, I knew, though she didn't dare admit it. My father, meanwhile, advised us to look at the new year as a watershed, a moment that would mark the boundary of our misfortune, as if it would miraculously gift us a chance to cast off our grief for good.

I rarely responded to anything so asinine. I rarely had the grace or the patience. Most of the time I'd swallow my words and shake my head without a sound. I'd wait for the silence to grow large enough to push the conversation in a different direction. That was my way of running down the clock. Although our parents had brought forward their arrival, they hadn't yet delayed their departure. All four were still scheduled to fly out, as planned, the day before New Year's Eve. The only thing I had to do was bide my time until they were gone. I couldn't say exactly what I wanted from them while they were with us, but I knew for sure that I didn't want any of what they foisted on me. I didn't want them to keep on asking what they could do for me and my wife. I didn't want them to go further than that and guess at our needs when we could only shrug off their questions. I didn't want to be confronted, over and over again, with a vision of myself as someone marred by the simple lack of some basic material comfort, some *thing* that someone might supply, to restore me to who I should've been, if only I could name it. I couldn't and I didn't. Perhaps it's better to say I wouldn't. I wasn't me anymore, I felt, and I didn't want to be. I didn't want restoration. If I wanted anything, I wanted the very opposite. I wanted to stand as an agent of ruin, a glorious wretch in endless pursuit of impossible reparations for his injuries. I saw myself as a man hollowed out, literally scraped clean on the inside, vital organs ripped from my sternum and replaced with something dense and heavy, some fluid dragging me into myself, as if the cavity inside me sloshed about with tar. I wanted recompense for this feeling of deformity. I wanted redress for a grievance beyond compensation, retribution for the irreversible wrong I'd been compelled to incur. I knew I couldn't reclaim what I'd lost, but the loss itself I refused to sustain. I'd been hurt and I wanted others to hurt in turn. I wanted the world to know my pain and I was electric with the impulse to inflict it wherever I could.

The night before our parents left we all dined out in a Chinese restaurant close to the hotel and that was where I relinquished control of my energies at last. We were sitting through an awkward pause while waiting for our drinks to arrive when my mother spoke up in a tentative tone. She wondered if it might be good for my wife, and for me, if the four of them stayed a little longer. Another week, she said, maybe two. To see in the new year together, to drive us back to our home and ease the shock of returning to regular life. Immediately my father said he thought it sounded sensible. Both my in-laws nodded and murmured their agreement. The speed of the consensus told me they'd already talked this over. I pictured the four of them holed up in one of the rooms they'd rented, jet-lagged and wide awake in the dark of early morning, deliberating over strategies for not taking their leave of us until they could assure themselves they'd provided as much support as possible. But a longer stay and further support meant, to me, more time spent on sharing sorrows and still more unsolicited suggestions on how best to arrange our affairs. I couldn't bear to digest more of that than the feast I'd already been force-fed.

I thumped the table and began to scream. At first I didn't scream any words. I screamed out a gravelly cry. I did it just as reflexively as if, instead of speaking to me, the people around me had reached for me and sliced me open and stuck their soiled fingers into the bloody trench of the wound. Then I harangued them, I berated them, I begged them to pack up and leave. I told them I didn't want their help anymore, I told them I didn't want *them* anymore, I told them I wanted all of us to return to the places we belonged, to the homes that were ours and ours alone, and there to come to terms with our troubles in our own ways and on our own time. I told them I resented their meddling in my life. I told them I despised their presence, just the fact that they were *there*, the way it burdened me with obligations I could not take up. To nod along agreeably as they aired their concerns over and over. To become their grateful dependent again, giving thanks for every meal, every train ticket, every pot of tea and cup of coffee they insisted on buying us, and to be haggled into submission whenever I opened my wallet to pay for anything myself. To be polite and humbly accept their charity, their solicitude, the outpourings of their bleeding hearts. I despised the way they clutched at me, latched onto me like shackles, threatened to drag themselves behind me as I retreated home or else to drag me back across the planet to a place I'd escaped long ago. Of course I understand that this outburst seems, in retrospect, cruel and callous. I agree that my wife and I were privileged to receive the support of our parents, that we benefitted from generosity we didn't have to ask for. I agree that I was cold to reject what they offered. I can only say that there's no way to control a mind and a heart so far gone, so profoundly in extremis, nor to control the words that fly from their depths.

How better can I account for my actions? At some point I know I stopped screaming and I let my anger drop. I don't remember how long it took. I only remember feeling so hot in the head I thought I'd burn up from within. For a time I lost my sight. Brilliant white flames devoured everything around me. I had visions of fire behind my eyes and I felt a sensation of scalding on the underside of all my skin. When the flames dissolved and my sight returned I found myself encircled by a dozen strangers, onlookers, staring back at me, at all of us, in rising panic, in bewilderment, in unveiled concern for the safety of everyone at the table but me. My father held firm to my shoulder, dug his thumb into my collarbone. My father-in-law had risen to intercede, to stand between me and my wife, one hand out behind him to keep her at a distance. Tears had ruined the faces of my mother and mother-in-law, jittering mascara down their cheeks, and my wife looked at me as if stunned by the sight of a creature she'd only ever heard about in legend. I mumbled an apology, not rehearsed but certainly rote, to puncture the tension that grew in our midst. Everyone could tell it wasn't heartfelt. But, I suppose, back then I still had enough standing with those people that for my sake they behaved as if my expressions of sorrow were sincere.

We returned to the hotel in silence. We gave the rest of the evening to small talk. The next day my wife and I woke early to help our parents pack their luggage so they could leave for home as planned. We waited beside their carriage until the train pulled away from the platform. I watched her watch them depart. She watched the departure through tears. She looked as if she'd just straggled to the end of a second funeral.

We swerved back home through the mountains without speaking to one another. Our house, when we entered, was unbearable to be in. A mound of envelopes had built up behind the front door, each letter tumbling from the postage slot onto the same patch of hallway. I tried to sweep the mail aside with my foot while my wife groped about for the light switch. Illumination jolted the darkness back to the state we'd left the house in. On the carpet beside the sofa we'd made a bed from a bundle of colourful blankets. On top we'd left a dummy and a chewable rubber giraffe. Nearby stood a wooden arch decorated with dangling shapes. At the far end of the dining table, ready for use in a couple of months, we'd cleared space for a pre-assembled highchair and on the seat we'd piled up a placemat, a handful of bibs, a plastic bowl, a spoon. In the corner of the living room a Christmas tree, unwatered, stretched its spindly branches over a hoard of presents blanketed in fallen needles. Not a single one of those presents was intended for either of us.

For months on end, for the duration of the autumn, we'd subtracted ourselves from the time we were actually living through.

Obsessively, devotedly, we'd reoriented towards a future removed from the passing days and we'd set about accumulating new belongings to prepare for it. Deep in my innards I felt the churn of something coming up. I wanted it to come. I wanted to throw up on everything that fell before my eyes. I wanted to smear the vomit over anything I didn't hit directly. We'd acquired a huge amount of stuff to fill the empty spaces of our home, all the paraphernalia we thought we'd need to furnish the life we'd hoped to give our child. There was nothing frivolous about what we did, nothing done without forethought. It was, it had been, a deeply imaginative exercise, a detailed envisioning of the substance of our lives as parents, a construction of the tactile space in which our new selves would flourish. When we looked at the objects that clogged up our home, we didn't see them simply as totems of our loss, as headstones in a makeshift children's cemetery. Each one was a receptacle, a shelter for a fragment of soul, in which we'd invested a tiny shard of the person we thought she might be. But each one needed a living, breathing, growing child to touch it, to throw it, to drop it on the ground, to smudge it with sticky fingerprints, to break it or to cherish it, to lose it or hide it or wake up one day and abandon it for something new. Without touch there was no way for any object to release the shard inside it, no way for the soul to reconvene and return to its rightful body. Looking over them now I felt as if our child was somehow still within them, in pieces, aching to be freed and yet forever locked away. The sight of them streaked anger through me and at the same time robbed me of breath. I hacked. I dry-heaved. All those possessions, unmoving but humming with life, crowded around us so tightly that they sucked the air out of our house.

Our bed was a mound of crinkled covers. We'd left the house in too much panic to straighten it out. The fabric was crisp and dark where the waters had broken. I tugged at the fitted sheet and found it taut with dried fluids, then I thrashed out the top sheet and the blankets and let them drop back down. I smoothed them and plumped the pillows. I looked down at the bed and knew at a glance I couldn't bring myself to sleep in it.

Beside me loomed the angular frame of something else we'd bought. A bassinet on wheels, with three protective sides and a pair of latches on the fourth. The latches could be affixed to the frame of our own bed so that, with one side open, we'd be able to let our child share a sleeping space with us.

My wife stepped into the room behind me. I heard the squeak of the door on its hinges, the hush of her bare feet on the carpet. She brushed past me and lowered herself onto the bed, pulled the sheet and blanket aside and slipped under them fully clothed. I turned to leave her alone but I hadn't reached the door when I heard a violent snap of metal. I spun around to find her levering the second latch of the bassinet. She thumbed it open and then gave the entire structure a shove to get it away from her.

She rolled over and faced the window, the snow and the darkness outside. I took the frame by one end and dragged it, backwards, out of the room. I jostled it through the door, angled it round a corner, pushed it against the hallway wall. I edged back into the bedroom to reach for the door, to pull it closed. I saw my wife sigh and shift beneath the sheets. Quietly I sealed off the room; I didn't say goodnight.

My life at this time, my entire state of being, obtained its hue from minor movements as unglamorous, as unassuming, as these. There's nothing bold about what follows, and very little that could be called decisive. The roar that ripped into the white noise of my days was conducted through the static hiss of my habits. Taking a seat at a table. Tapping at the computer. Closing blinds against the sun. Cleaning dishes or making tea or coffee. Stepping outside for air, or into a warming shower. These things were the background hum of my daily affairs. Back then, they also opened thresholds between one version of myself and the next.

From where I stood in the hallway, I could see the front door and the pile of letters I'd scattered with my feet. I drifted down towards the envelopes and dropped to the floor, exhausted, to begin trawling through them. Cross-legged, my back to the wall, I pinched at the first envelope and turned it over in my hands. As I shuffled through the mail I felt the flow of time reverse. I shredded, tore, cast aside. Condolence cards from family and friends in Australia. Most of them also contained letters of greater length, and every one of the letters began with the admission that the person who'd written it didn't know what to say. Beneath these were twenty or thirty other, more colourful cards. They were the joyous responses to the first message I'd sent my parents and in-laws, posted from that limbo between the announcement of labour and the confirmation of death. They'd found their way to our home from a dozen distant places to congratulate us on the birth of a child who was already dead by the time they fell through the slot in the door. Each one captured, preserved forever, something ephemeral, something already gone. But by far the worst of the mail sat at the bottom of the pile. Inside an envelope from the hospital I found the congratulatory card: the picture taken by a nurse, my daughter overcome by sleep, opening onto the footprint stamped in pale purple ink. We'd left it behind by mistake and then forgotten about it. I wished someone would've thrown it away. I didn't want it in front of me, I didn't want to look at it, I didn't want such a tangible trace of a person I wouldn't see again. But now that I'd received it, now that I could hold it, I knew I couldn't be rid of it; I couldn't let myself let it go.

Nor could I trash the final letter, the first one to be sent. It came from the cantonal government. Generated by a machine, as soon as a record of our daughter's arrival went into the hospital computers, it summoned me to an appointment one week hence in Interlaken. I had to bring my child with me. The authorities needed to take her picture before they could certify her birth. I assumed that the correspondence relating to her death would arrive in the new year, when postal services returned to normal. Only the next day, when I called to cancel the appointment, would I see how plainly stupid that assumption was.

Leaning against the hallway wall, I closed my eyes. I tilted back my head and pushed my fingers through my hair. I pressed my spine hard against the frontier of the world I'd built for myself. Still I felt cramped and crowded in, pinched at by the wreckage that surrounded me, and so, to return to the here and now, I forced open my eyes and I slowly, deliberately began to enumerate the unspoken things that I knew were true. The truth was that my wife and I had done worse than fail to speak to one another. The truth was that we'd avoided speaking about true things we knew full well. The statistics held no mystery for us. In the aftermath of the miscarriage we'd both looked into them. By and large, marriages don't withstand the difficulties we faced in ours. They tend to crumble when they make a bid for permanence on the basis of things that don't survive. Why should our marriage defy the odds? How were we any stronger or more special than the average? The loss of the life we'd conceived was, we knew, a tinder to the life we'd made together and now we were waiting, just waiting, to wake up strapped to the pyre. The truth was that our loss gave us grounds to anticipate worse, and by not speaking of it we were bringing the worst upon ourselves. We knew this and still we didn't speak, didn't work to bridge the growing divide, didn't do anything but wait for what we felt would happen to happen at last.

We are now no longer married. That's the place we've ended up. But in surveying the distance between here and there, in looking back at what we once had and charting the trajectory of our descent, I'm anxious to avoid simplicity. There was nothing simple about it. It was not an experience of liberation or closure or rebuilding. It didn't involve wilful rancour or wrongdoing. It was a period of fluctuations, false starts, backtracking, disorientation. The descent was not a direct one, a continuous downward drift. We went through weeks of malaise spiked by brief, occasional gushes of confused intensity. We vacillated. We prevaricated. We duped ourselves, bought into false hopes and illusions, and we tried, meekly, to salvage things. There is no point A and point B to the events that have brought us to where we are now. There's the nerve centre of our loss and an explosion of ganglia. There are a billion lines of thought that have all at once branched out from a seed of grief to compete for our commitment. There's nothing straightforward about it. Right from the start, there never was.

Leaning against the wall, I closed my eyes again. In a very literal sense I felt myself spinning out of control. The emptiness of our house opened up around me like a boundless vacuum, a vacuum that devoured me and my wife and severed us from one another. It wrenched us apart in the same way that the farthest reaches of outer space would rend the bond between a pair of wayward astronauts, casting us both into solitude and leaving each of us hurtling head over heels, far from solid ground and forever towards the distant stars. I spun in terror of this isolation, this prison without bars, having been flung into the blackness inside my own head and abandoned to a bombardment of thoughts I couldn't control. I wanted to scream, I couldn't scream, I felt extending around me a void that would swallow my screams into silence. I wanted to open my eyes, I couldn't, I wanted to see that all things within my grasp were in fact steady and stable, weren't really spinning away, but I felt, too, as if a glaucoma had gathered beneath my eyelids. All I could see were flickers of white. All I could see was a throbbing haze of faraway lights, a long and pale glow overlaying an awful expanse of oblivion. Hundreds of lights in congregation, so many and so blurred together that I couldn't take their number or even guess at it.

At first the lights pulsed in tandem with the beating of my heart. Then they started to beat distinctly, in a syncopated frenzy, as each one took on a frequency and rhythm of its own. As I spun they swung above and around me in broad, swooping arcs, a starscape revolving at sensational speed, and I watched them dilute the purity of the black with so much scattered lustre, so much indecipherable noise. Smears of luminescence. Spurts of silver streaking through ink. I spun so fast I couldn't tell whether there was, at the core of each shining light, something solid, a source to be tuned in to, or only noise, an inane clangour. I flattened my back against the wall, I forced my eyes shut even tighter. I pressed myself deeper into the black, deeper into my shimmering cell. Surrounded by coils of dust in boundless space. Surrounded by spiralling nebulae braided in a sash. Exactly what had I fallen into? What place? What solipsism? Was I encompassed not by static but by satellites, third parties, whose flickers and pulses were signals, transmissions of meaning in want of capture and release? Or had I plunged into an inner space beyond whose hum was only my own mind: only, terribly, more of me?

PART I

PERIHELION

DEMIROVIĆ

From Interlaken the eastbound train skirts the shoreline of Lake Brienz. Outside, in winter, there's nothing to see. White mist loiters over the dull silver slate of the water. Sky and mountains are hidden from view, shrouded in colourless murk or iced over or smothered in snow. That's why the story from Sydney stole my attention. Every carriage is fitted with a screen that scrolls through the day's most urgent headlines. No soundbites or commentary, no filmed footage. Just a summary of an important event brought to life by a single photograph.

Diplomats in suits engaged in negotiations at the European Central Bank.

Guerrilla fighters, begrimed in dust, trudged through the rubble of Aleppo.

Times Square glowed in the winter dark but was entirely empty, abandoned, as temperatures in America plunged to record lows.

Then came a scene from suburban Australia. On a blazing summer's day, so visibly hot that the image itself seemed to ripple, a policeman embraced a woman who roared, bereft, with her eyes scrunched closed and face upturned to the perfect blue of the sky. The photographer had frozen the very moment of her fracturing, the instant her life had shattered. The summary mentioned something about a child, perhaps a group of children, but before I could decipher the words the screen refreshed and cycled back to the economists in Frankfurt. I couldn't read the news at a glance. I needed time to unpick the strings of alien phrases, to reverse the declension of articles and unwind the conjugation of verbs. I kept my eyes fixed to the screen and waited, on edge, for the story to reappear. I had no idea at the time that it would keep me awake for days to come.

I'd ventured out to Interlaken to escape the smog polluting our house. Languor, lethargy, stifled intentions and sloth. All this was the stuff of the days before the appointment. I'd take my time rising from bed each morning before moving myself to the sofa and then, a while later, I'd stand and walk to some other room, and once I'd traversed sufficient space I'd cast about for something new to hold or rest against. Those days felt the way dreams feel when they fade back into life, when the vividness of their events blurs into a miasma of moods. I lost myself to listlessness. I washed dishes that were already clean and swept away snow while it went on falling. I slouched at my computer and waded from website to website without really reading a word of anything I clicked on. At that time, I remember thinking, the strength of the torpor that took hold of my body was proof of the depth of the grief in my soul. Giving myself up to my worst impulses was a way of honouring the magnitude of what I'd lost. By the day of the appointment, though, I was glad to have reason to go elsewhere, to have something new to concentrate on.

I'd opted for the train to the city because I knew that if I drove I would've kept on driving without looking back. The train gave me a direction I couldn't deviate from, committed me to returning home at the end of the day. The appointment gave me focus, a clear objective, and the issues that needed resolving gave me something definite to think on. Intransigent authorities and bureaucratic functionaries emerged as targets for the fury that bubbled inside me like lava building towards an eruption. The beautiful systems they assembled made no leeway for the sloppiness of lives lived close to the ground. The Swiss were unable to issue a death certificate for my daughter without issuing a birth certificate first. But they couldn't issue a birth certificate without confirmation from Canberra that she was, by descent, Australian. The Australians denied all our requests for the relevant documentation, arguing that applications for citizenship could not be processed posthumously, and so, inside the computers that govern the world, their denials left my daughter both alive and officially stateless.

The Swiss asked me to meet with a man who needed my input to resolve the problem. I found him in a muggy office that still smelled faintly of Christmas. Cinnamon cookies, coffee with cloves, a lump of leftover stollen.

All he had to do, I said, was uncheck the box that designated my daughter as a living resident of his country and instead check the box directly underneath it.

By law, he told me, he couldn't do that, and so the problem was bound to persist.

What more did he hope to draw from me then? Why did he sit there and say nothing else as if he expected me to find a solution? I despised him, despised his country, despised his supposedly irresolvable problems, and finally I let slip my good manners and did not hold back my mounting fire. I couldn't see how to bargain with an office that behaved as if a clear and immediate condition of reality was somehow not valid until the office itself said so, as if through its words alone it could admit or revoke the existence of a human being with no respect at all for facts of flesh and blood. I couldn't see how to engage a system that lagged so far behind experience, or how to disabuse it of the assumption that its pronouncements were commensurate to the fabric of the world. I especially couldn't see how to keep calm in the face of a state apparatus whose refusals to document the death of my daughter left me and my wife living in its fiction.

I exploded at the man and suddenly I felt a thrill. I began to relish the problems I faced and the problems I caused him. A problem was something I felt I could seize, hold fast, invest myself in. I raised my voice, belittled the man, mocked the petty concerns of his labours. I'd been craving something like that outburst, I saw. I'd been hunting for something to hook onto, to grapple with, to stabilise myself. I'd been casting about for something substantial outside the confines of my skull. I set off for home with an appetite for more and I didn't have to wait long before circumstances served it up.

The train rocked from side to side through banks of rising snow. My carriage was empty except for an old man at the far end. Ahead of me the news on the screen cycled back to the picture of the woman in anguish. This time the story stayed up long enough for me to make sense of the words. With sense came a lurch in the belly. Something awful had happened in Sydney. A group of children had been attacked by a man possessing a deadly weapon. Injuries weren't described. Casualties weren't numbered. The weapon wasn't named and motives weren't divulged. The shock and the terror of the atrocity were left to the picture alone to convey.

The only other piece of the story mentioned on the screen was something that made it local to my part of the world, something about a victim's parents and their connection to Switzerland. For a time I could only guess how any of this might involve someone so far from the scene. When the train pulled into Brienz, however, the old man in my carriage shuffled off and left on his seat a copy of the evening tabloid from Lucerne. I stumbled forward to reach for the paper as the train bumped into motion again, and with a powerful hunger for details I sat and started swishing through the pages.

The middle of the paper featured a double-page spread on the attack. I unfolded a proper report with a slew of pictures embedded in the text. I saw a red-brick building cordoned off on a street corner somewhere in Sydney's eastern suburbs. Crime-scene tape blocked access to the premises and a police car outside the entrance flashed its lights. The building, I learnt, was a day-care centre. It had been broken into by a man with a heavyweight hunting knife. Four pre-school children were dead. Seven others had been injured. Three of the injured were on life support. Two adults had also been killed. Witnesses had spotted a man fleeing the scene. Dark skin, dark hair, slim build, a workman's clothes. Police had issued a statement to say they'd apprehended someone fitting the description. The photographs printed alongside the announcement made a mosaic of distress. Parents clambered anxiously out of cars that had mounted the kerb. Day-care staff in bloodstained clothes shielded screaming children from the cameras. A father embraced his daughter, almost crushing her against his chest, while a man and a woman in a neighbouring picture gripped one another in the throes of bereavement.

The woman in the policeman's arms did not appear in the tabloid, but the largest photograph there showed a couple in an identical pose. I saw a middle-aged woman with half-moon glasses and eyes wide with panic. Her mouth had dropped open in disbelief, sheer incomprehension, as she tilted her head to rest a cheek on the shoulder of her husband. With worry lines pinching his brow, scoring the bridge of his nose, he clenched his jaw and raised his eyes to squint into the distance. He looked to me like a man attempting to scrutinise an inscrutable future. Facing him, but out of focus, were two policemen in Swiss uniforms. So this man, too, had come up against the membrane between what he knew from experience and the office with jurisdiction over life and death.

The caption beneath the picture explained the situation. The man and his wife had just lost their daughter in Sydney. The picture seemed to have been taken at the moment they received the news. They'd spent a week outside Australia, leaving their daughter under the care of her aunt. They'd been on a flight into Zürich, to catch a connecting flight back home, at the time of the attack. Police had waited for them to land before they could inform them of their loss. Journalists and photographers had waited, too, to witness their belated arrival in a world very different from the one in which they'd taken flight. The newspaper identified them only as Herr and Frau Demirović from Randwick, New South Wales.

Look at me there by myself in that train. Faded jeans, a crumpled hoodie, a limp scarf over my shoulders. An accordion folder, desperately clutched, containing the heft of all the papers the authorities wanted to see. Heavy boots and a winter coat splotched with melting snow. An empty seat to either side and a row of three more opposite. Perching my feet on the seat facing mine, I laid the newspaper on my knees and examined the photograph. Aloof, hunched over, with shoulders swaying as the carriage rode the rails, I must have looked like a man hermetically sealed inside a world of his own making. Even though I sat forward to inspect two people I'd never seen before, I scoured their faces for features now familiar to me. To outside observers I knew they'd look like the model of a strong, supportive couple. In the media, I was sure, they'd play the roles of a husband and wife whose impossible situation was survivable because each of them would help the other muddle through the grief. Theirs would be a tale of courageous overcoming. For the credulous, or the romantic, they would withstand the trauma of their loss owing to the adamantine strength of their bond. But I knew from experience how their relationship might have already fractured. Where others would see fortitude, all I could see were splinters.

In the tilt of the woman's head, in the slackening of her jaw, I recognised what I'd noticed in my wife when the nurse took our daughter away. I recognised her shock at receiving a report from so far beyond the horizon of what she'd assumed was possible, and at having realised that the hours she'd spent on the plane to Zürich had cocooned her in a past that everyone outside already knew was irrecoverable. In her husband's distant gaze and in his stance, in the awkward arms with which he didn't quite enfold his wife, in the hands with which he didn't quite comfort her, I saw the resonance of the uncertainty that I knew would cripple him. Between this husband and wife there yawned a distance that echoed what was opening up elsewhere in my life. In his posture I saw a mimicry of my own paralysis upon receiving news of the death of my child, my loss of faith in my own reflexive movements. I saw, too, the expatriate in him, the rootless man whose loss untethers him from his own being. I saw it in his self-consciousness, his immediate assertion of self-control, the way it distorted the sincerity of his shock. I saw a man who was, like me, so completely at a loss for what to do next that he didn't even know whether or not to just let himself feel what he must have felt. I saw him second-guessing his own instinctual expressions of grief, halting in a bid to arrest his turmoil, to subdue it. I saw him seeing himself through the lenses of the cameras around him and not so much embodying his grief as staging it for spectators.

Is it arrogant of me to make confessions like these? Isn't it arrogant to have teased out insights so specious from a single candid photograph? To have felt I possessed some privileged access to that man's state of mind? To have seen myself as uniquely capable of interpreting his performance? To have done these things when there was no way that my sorrows could equal the scale of his? But arrogant is what I was, believing that I alone could receive the messages broadcast in the demeanour of a person whose grief was as acute as mine. I sat back in my seat, dropped my feet to the floor, and with a whip of the hand I tossed the paper away. I found I couldn't look at his picture any longer. The paper hit the opposite seat and flopped onto the floor. Actually, I realised, the truth was more complex than just wanting him out of my sight. As I bent to pick up the paper I felt I was being watched from behind. I cast a glance over my shoulder but found the carriage as empty as before. I blushed, I remember, as if, against all logic, someone had in fact been there, watching me invisibly, to see me act like a fool when I turned to find myself alone. Settling back into the seat while darkness amassed outside the train, I caught my reflection in the window beside me and that's when I understood. The eyes I'd felt observing me didn't belong to anyone else. They were my own eyes, seeing myself, when I fixed them on the stranger's face.

I set my eyes forward again and looked ahead at the news as the stories cycled back through the day's developments. Diplomats. Soldiers. Times Square. Sydney. Unbelievable sunshine and the woman in the policeman's arms. Something recoiled in my stomach. Something churned inside and pushed me to the verge of vomiting.

The sight of the woman didn't cause it. What caused it was exactly that, the realisation that I was looking at her and feeling for her not a thing. I wasn't cold. I was drained. My sympathies had dried up. That man in the picture, Demirović, had been a vortex for all my reserves. Everything had flowed towards him and now there was nothing left. I wished I could unsee his face and worried I'd made myself vulnerable to depletion by someone like him. I'd supposed that my grief had hurled me into a solitude I'd never break. It was, I'd thought, a solitude so profound, so intense, that my experience of it seemed to cast me beyond the bounds of sympathy. But then I'd seen Demirović and felt convinced I knew exactly what beset him.

What I couldn't see at first was that my new conviction stole something precious from me. My grief was the measure of the love I'd felt for my daughter. It stood as proof of how much heart I'd invested in something I could never retrieve. If it wasn't unique to me, then what was the value of my love? It's true that I'd wanted to find a way of dissolving my solitude, to find another soul who could know my sorrows from the inside. No surprise that when I found him I gave him all the common feeling I could muster. But it was also true that finding him meant losing a part of my person, seeing that I shared with him something I'd thought belonged exclusively to me. His body spoke the same language as mine and gave voice to an experience that echoed what I'd been through. You could distort the surface of things but inside, at the core, there was only correspondence. Change a few details of appearance and situation. The turmoil and the murk remain the same. Here, then, is my question. When I attempt to account for myself, how can I own what I say?

I bashed the slush off my boots, beating my heels against brick. Days of constant snowfall had made it long past time to clear a proper path from the road to the house. Condolence cards and unpaid bills mounted up inside the front door again. Onto the pile fell the accordion folder. At the far end of the hallway I could see my wife. She didn't turn to greet me. She sat at the kitchen table, facing the window by the forest, with the glow of the laptop outlining her head and shoulders in unearthly white. That's how I'd seen her sitting most days since we'd returned. More and more she'd withdrawn from me by retreating from the spaces we shared. She moved into the margins of rooms, kept away from open centres where contact might be made. She skewed the gravity of our house. She wouldn't answer the door, not even when acquaintances and colleagues came to commiserate with us, and she wouldn't offer any hint of what might draw her back from the edges. I couldn't intuit the simplest things about what she wanted now. Where she wanted to be if not here. What she wanted me to do from day to day. Whether she wanted me near her at all. Whether she wanted anything other than what she already had. Whether she was capable of wanting anymore.

I approached her from behind. I began to talk. I told her about the day's events. I confessed to my loss of temper and bemoaned the bureaucratic standstill. Beside the laptop I saw the crumbs and crust of a couple of slices of toast. She shifted in her seat while I spoke and once or twice she nodded to acknowledge the things I said, but otherwise she kept her eyes on the screen and her fingers on the keyboard and none of the news I brought her piqued her interest enough to make her turn.

Would it be right to say we'd begun avoiding each other? Our bodies passed at oblique angles in the hallway or the entrance to the bathroom. Even her most benign behaviour seemed to disclose a despair I couldn't appreciate or a malice directed at me alone. When she washed the dishes, I heard her washing too loudly. I was sure she clinked plates and glasses together to signal her anger at something I'd done. When she rummaged about in the bedroom wardrobe, she drew out the squeak of the doors on their hinges and clapped them suddenly shut. The shock of the latch in the lock seemed addressed to me, I thought, but I couldn't say what it meant. She'd begun to speak to me through a twisted sort of semaphore, gesturing messages for me to decrypt as best I could without a cipher. But an action whose meaning isn't clear, isn't fixed, is an action of infinite import, a boundless burst of significance in its purely potential form. The noises that I was convinced held more for me than hubbub became, instead, only noisier still, a cacophony of clattering.

Anyway, eventually, she stood up and shut the laptop, took her plate to the kitchen sink and dropped it in and went to bed. When she was gone I opened the laptop and pulled an old tub of ice cream from the freezer. I ate what scrapings were left while I trawled through the news online. On the websites of the Australian broadsheets I found a trove of horror stories, scores of accounts of unbearable suffering. I found each report waiting for me on the other side of a link that I could see had been accessed already. The front page of the *Herald* was a tableau of bright eyes and wide grins, the faces of the slaughtered children, above a profusion of scenes like the ones I had seen on the train. Tearstruck infants in terror. A man and a woman tightly bound as if holding one another intact. Police officers at a podium from which they spoke to the press. Off to one side, jarringly, Demirović was overjoyed. Next to the familiar shot in which he held his wife at the airport, the *Herald* showcased another, clearer picture of his face. In its own way, in its context, it was more shocking, more uncanny, than the first one. It looked like a portrait of the employee of the week at some small firm servicing a suburban clientele. He faced the camera front-on and beamed. He wore a yellow polo shirt and an unguarded smile that really reached his eyes. He had close-cropped black hair and the olive complexion of a man who enjoyed a life in the sun. He was surrounded by the glow of white pixels in the negative space of the website, and beneath him a banner flashed back and forth between promotions for a touchscreen tablet and cut-price airfares to Bali. He seemed too staid, too steady, for the gallery of distress his face appeared in. He seemed like a blue-collar worker with a white-collar sense of self. He seemed like the sort of man who'd know how to supervise staff in a retail park or industrial estate, maybe appraising the efforts of contract labourers or managing the performance of a new apprentice.

In fact, I discovered as I sank into the news, that was almost exactly the sort of person the man turned out to be. I clicked on his portrait to read a rundown on the two parents who were coming to be seen as the most tragic survivors of the attack. Hassan Demirović owned and managed a whitegoods store in Maroubra and oversaw satellite outlets in a few surrounding areas. At the time of the attack he and his wife, Jessica, had been abroad in Europe. They'd only intended to be gone for a week and they'd entrusted their daughter, aged three, to his sister-in-law, who lived within walking distance of the day-care centre. Their trip turned out to have been jointly sponsored by the Bosnian Community Council of Sydney and the Eastern Suburbs Chamber of Commerce. Both organisations claimed Demirović as a distinguished member. They'd agreed to fund his plans for some sort of public speaking engagement in the town where he'd grown up.

Višegrad lies on the Drina, I learnt, in the middle of the territory that was once Yugoslavia. What wasn't reported directly, but what I deduced from the age of the man, was that he must have been a refugee from the carnage under Milošević. How much worse did that make his turmoil now? Demirović hadn't just lost his daughter in appalling circumstances. He'd fled unspeakable violence and sought asylum far from home, and by some miracle he'd been granted safe haven, and he'd settled and started a family, but now fresh violence had claimed his child while he was far away and enjoying the new-found peace of the homeland he'd left in chaos. How could you fully acknowledge the unreality of his situation? How could you say how much worse his personal history made it? Impossible to set one trauma beside another and calculate an addition or an exponential sum. Impossible to measure their aggregate intensity in the units of an unknowable scale or else in relation to others of their kind. You could really only look on and gape.

Where was he suffering right then, at that moment, while I sat at my kitchen table and read about his ordeal? Thirty-thousand feet above the Gulf of Oman on a plane departing Dubai? Looking out a window at the wastelands of Mongolia, turning slowly towards a connecting flight in Beijing or Bangkok? No doubt sweating through the makeshift darkness of hundreds of plastic blinds drawn down, their edges fizzing with sunshine, to fabricate a European night in an aircraft heading into midday on the equator. Knees against the back of the seat in front. An ache in his haunches from being seated so long. Was he a drinker? What, then? Whiskey? Gin? Would he swig it or sip it or just sit there and swish it around?

I rose from the chair and arched my back, extended my arms to the ceiling. Beside me I saw myself standing, stretching, in the kitchen window that night had made a mirror. I sat again and scratched at the stubble on my chin. I remember the movements of my fingers, the shadows in my eye sockets, the gauntness the overhead light gave my face. I remember Demirović imprisoned in the cabin of that plane. I remember seeing him ease an itch where he, too, had neglected to shave, and I remember him peering into his own eyes dimly reflected in the tiny screen he was forced to sit and stare at. I remember the two of us, at the same time, each confined to a separate enclosure.

Cut off from the course of events, that's where we shared common ground. Dusk was settling over Australia. In a cold storage cell in a morgue in Sydney, his daughter lay dead on a slab. On similar slabs in similar cells lay the bodies of three more children and two of the adults who'd cared for them. Across the city more than half-a-dozen others nursed wounds of varying severity. Police officers consulted legal experts to lay out a strategy for interrogating the suspect they'd apprehended. Barristers and senior counsel busied themselves with the finer points of defence and prosecution. Forensics experts combed through the crime scene to gather evidence for use in court. The drivetime airwaves detonated national indignation. Outraged calls for legal reform exploded across the internet in social forums and comments under news reports. Meeting rooms in Canberra thrived with parliamentary aides preparing statements for politicians. All of this was clearly, powerfully, a world away from both of us. In the early hours of a winter morning, I sat at a computer placed atop a wooden table in the kitchen of a house in the Alps. In spectacular heat in the middle of the day, Hassan Demirović sat in his cramped little place in economy class on a flight not even halfway through. My wife lay buried under a stack of blankets in the bed on the other side of the kitchen wall. Jessica Demirović, I supposed, sat beside her husband with her head once again tilted onto his shoulder, perhaps unmoving and tensed, perhaps lolling gently as she tumbled into sleep. We were each of us discrete, sheathed in our own little pocket of silence. We were all at a distance from the conflagration consuming Australia, and further still from where we had been when the first sparks were struck.

Višegrad appears to the eye as a tranquil refuge from the conurbations of continental Europe. It crouches down in a gash through the landscape, a scar of green torn into the earth by glacial movements millennia ago. The pressure of the retreating ice moulded the limestone hills that now carve into the sky, topped with beech and silver fir. The runoff from the ice-melt gnawed into the lowlands between the hills, eventually spilling out across the valley to form the River Drina. At a break in the ravine through which it flows, the Drina intersects with the smaller, slighter waters of the Rzav and wends away, eastward, to the foothills of the Carpathians. People of one tribe or another, one nation or another, had been making that place their home for thousands of years by the time the Ottomans arrived in the sixteenth century. The Grand Vizier of the Ottoman Empire saw the strategic importance of the site. He decided to overrule the natural shaping of the land and bind together the banks of the river. A bridge was built, a masterpiece of engineering. Eleven gigantic masonry arches, each one almost fifty feet thick, plunged into the aquamarine of the Drina. They spanned the river and severed it laterally, slicing through the water to separate its placid southern end from the rapids to the north.

But as the river ran under the bridge and past the town and into the hills, and churned on through the Drina Valley up to the Pannonian Plain, it would, in time, exert a divisive force once again. Twenty miles from Višegrad, centuries after the expulsion of the Ottomans, the Drina would come to form Bosnia's border with Serbia. In the meantime, Višegrad became the stuff of postcards of Eastern Europe. Tiny white houses with pointed red roofs clustered along the water's edge. The onion dome of an Orthodox church nestled among the minarets of mosques. It was quaint and peaceful and picturesque, absolutely emblematic of a UNESCO World Heritage Site. Seeing the beauty of the place took me by surprise. Sarajevo and Srebrenica marked the extent of what I knew of Bosnia. Paramilitary forces and bloodshed, concentration camps and the violence of the mob. I'd never pictured the country as containing a sliver of paradise. Yet when I looked at Višegrad and imagined it as the theatre of Demirović's youth, I wished I could also say that I grew up in such a sanctum. Then, of course, I came across details of the disasters that had blighted it. I pursued links to websites that spawned archives of documentary footage, I binged on a jumble of Bosnian blog posts and news reports translated with algorithmic awkwardness, and as I read I saw visions of the horrors that all those beautiful pictures had hidden.

One summer's night in 1992, the Višegrad police received a call about the bodies. West of the town of Bajina Bašta, downstream from Višegrad on the Serbian side of the Drina, a hydroelectric power plant had been experiencing problems for some time and the manager decided he couldn't take it anymore. The problems began when the culverts started clogging up with corpses. At first the manager ordered his men to retrieve them without complaint. He thought it best to fish the victims from the river and put them to rest in a consecrated space on the periphery of the dam. In the beginning the bodies arrived one at a time or, at worst, in pairs. A supervisor on the dawn shift had been running a site inspection when he found an old woman, facedown, bobbing beneath a balustrade. A couple of cleaners with high-pressure hoses had manoeuvred around the side of a pylon to discover a young girl and, nearby, her mother or perhaps an aunt. Soon, though, the river swept in so many people, and so many all at once, that machinery began to malfunction. Clusters of corpses, five or six together, eddied towards the dam and lodged in the inner workings. Roped at the ankles, cuffed at the wrists, their numbers rose as the days went by and the holding pen outside the dam grew into a mound of waterlogged flesh. Not all the bodies could be caught or recovered. More and more became submerged and lost in the works of the plant. Filters broke down and turbines jammed. Power outages followed, right across the region, and then came complaints from the military authorities. Finally the manager had to call for professional divers, had to send them into the depths of the penstock to recover the corpses that hadn't surfaced. That's when he picked up the phone. He didn't want to tread on any toes, least of all those of the new man in Višegrad, but the situation he faced had become intolerable. He asked the police to ask the General if he'd please instruct his men to leave the bridge alone.

What word would you use to name what happened there each night that summer? This is not a rhetorical question. It was, I learnt, the very question that lured Demirović back to the war zone, the question that pulled him half a world away from his new and stable home and his beloved daughter. What happened was that the people of Višegrad became the playthings of a man they called the Butcher. What happened was that his arrival caused the population to collapse. Even today the town's citizenry is barely half the size it was when the violence broke out. What happened has since been eclipsed by the greater brutality at nearby places like Goražde, and by the atrocities of Ratko Mladić, but that's exactly why what happened deserves to be named and retrieved from the shadows of history.

The Butcher set out for the town on his own initiative and seized it for his amusement. Upon arrival in Višegrad, his first move was to take command of all the hotels. He expelled the guests and the staff and he gave the empty rooms to the men who fought in his private battalion. They were known as the White Eagles. Like the Butcher himself, like Mladić, like Milošević, they were Bosnian Serbs willing to lay down their lives for the survival of their cherished Republika Srpska. They'd stationed themselves on the vanguard of the newborn Serbian nation, and they worked to wipe out those who had voted against its existence. They'd boycotted the referendum at which a majority of Croats and Bosniak Muslims declared support instead for the independence of Bosnia and Herzegovina, and with the military on their side they'd begun to purify their republic of its ethnic contaminants. Višegrad was a Bosniak stronghold. Its twenty thousand inhabitants included more than fourteen thousand Muslims. The town was a bullseye on the map of Republika Srpska, and the Butcher, Milan Lukić, was the arrow poised to strike it.

But simply explaining what happened doesn't begin to do it justice. Knowing the facts isn't nearly the same as understanding how they came to be. Constitutions and referenda and nation states in decay and transition. What did any of that have to do with the bridge across the Drina? How did the politics of Lukić and his followers motivate their behaviour? Where did you have to look to see the politics in their carnival of horrors? Thinking of them in political terms credits them with a more refined disposition than their actions warrant. The animus of what they did was sadism, that's all: a brute thirst for blood.

First the hotels became rape camps. In the dining rooms and lobbies the White Eagles would take turns abusing girls as young as twelve. Often the girls saw suicide as their only hope for escape. Then, throughout the town, houses were requisitioned and transformed into furnaces. Women and girls were herded inside and the structures were set alight. When the White Eagles wearied of the labour involved in organising these firestorms, they blackened the pavements with ash from human pyres. Men and women, mostly Muslims, were forced at gunpoint to huddle together to be doused with petrol and set ablaze. Later on, perhaps in search of novel ways to slaughter their victims, the soldiers decided to take the bridge as their favoured weapon of terror. Every night, truckloads of civilians would be driven onto the road that spanned the Ottoman arches. They'd be forced outside and lined up along the low wall that guards against a fall. The lucky ones would be shot, or they'd have their throats slit, and then they'd be hauled over the edge to drop, dead, into the Drina. But luck, by definition, evades all except a very few.

Eyewitness reports and survivors' stories made me ill when I came across them. A soldier approached a mother pleading for the life of her six-month-old child. He tore the infant from its mother's arms and hurled it into the air to impale it on a knife. He forced the mother to lick its blood before he sliced open her stomach and threw the both of them into the water. Other victims were shepherded onto the banks, to wade into the river with soldiers at their backs. As they struggled against the flow, the soldiers, armed with knives, would reach down to cut the Achilles tendons. In agony the wounded would thrash, would fight to stay afloat, but they didn't have the strength anymore to stand or swim. The river would pull them under and leave only a plume of blood in their wake.

One man was crucified on the door of his house. The door was wrenched off its hinges and thrown into the Drina with the man still nailed to it. Another man was shackled with chains that were then bolted onto a rock in the river. He drowned and was left to bob in the waves like a buoy at sea. A woman who managed to flee the city later recalled the time she'd found, at the water's edge, a garbage bag filled with severed heads. All the eyes had been removed for reasons she couldn't imagine. A girl who survived told of how one day, as a matter of new routine, the soldiers began shooting at the bodies they hurled off the bridge. She said they'd realised that several people had escaped by plunging into the water and only pretending to drown, lying as still as possible while the current carried them off.

A number of young boys survived their wounds after being left to die. They heaved themselves out of the water, clutching at the stumps of trees and crawling onto the banks, then spent weeks in hiding in a downstream forest. They set about recovering corpses from the river, dragging the bloated bodies out of the torrent to bury them with a measure of respect. They worked in the dark of night, they said, to avoid the snipers who prowled the woods. They guessed they buried close to three hundred people. Later investigations found that, at best, those boys recovered one in twenty of the bodies that floated by. It's hard to say whether this happened before or after the carnage drew complaints from the power plant over the border. All that's clear is that those complaints did nothing to stop the bloodshed. They never really stood a chance. Electricity is a hallmark of a functioning civilisation. Its benefits are entirely social and utilitarian. It affords none of the gratuitous pleasures of hearing desperate pleas and protests, none of the thrills of distress or guttural groans or the cries of the condemned. Milan Lukić and his men couldn't possibly have seen the point of it.

Somewhere in all this butchery, too, was the man with the

distant gaze. Look at the eyes that looked at the cameras that closed in around him as he took his wife in his arms. What cruelties had exploded in front of him all those years ago? I could see those eyes, in a younger face, in a crowd of terrified children fleeing the bonfire of flesh at one end of the bridge. I could see them peering out of the window of a house beside a colonised hotel, watching the comings and goings of girls rounded up by sneering men in fatigues. I could see them emerging slowly from the river, rising above the surface to scan for soldiers on the banks. I could see them in the background of all the violence I imagined because I could find no clear account of what they had actually witnessed, of what Demirović had been forced to behold, of what terrors that boy had braved to remove himself, alone, to Australia.

In the capsule biography I found online, the Eastern Suburbs Chamber of Commerce came across as disgustingly coy. It made an escape from ethnic cleansing look like nothing more than a rejection of old-fashioned class warfare. I shouldn't have expected otherwise. The organisation's patron of honour turned out to be a conservative senator and former member of the state cabinet. Even so, the omission of the most distressing details took me by surprise. As a young man, the website said, Hassan Demirović had fled the military encroachments of communist forces in Bosnia and established his own small business in Sydney in 1998. He'd met his wife two years later, and off to the side of the text was an old picture of them both. A decade younger than they were now, outside one of his whitegoods outlets, they stood hand-in-hand and smiled broadly at the camera. The caption made a point of the fact that he'd married a local. Jessica Demirović, it said, had grown up in Tamarama. Pointedly, too, considering the conservative audience, she wasn't wearing a headscarf and her picture was now so outdated that it suggested she'd never worn one. How much else wasn't there to be seen, then? What more was not a part of the picture made available to the public? No mention of the journey that had brought the man to Australia. Only a note to say he'd settled there. No mention of his loss of his parents, if in fact he lost them at all; no mention of his departure from them, if instead he left them behind. No remarks on the felt effects of his distance from his homeland, no hint of his faith and piety, and nothing whatsoever of his trauma as a refugee. Yet his recent return to Višegrad, sponsored by the Chamber of Commerce, surely had been motivated by every last one of those aspects of his identity.

In 1995, Bosnia-Herzegovina received international recognition of its independence and sovereignty. In 2004, the International Criminal Tribunal for the former Yugoslavia issued its final indictments against the Milošević regime for crimes against humanity. In the wake of these indictments, the communal caretakers of the Bosniak Muslim cemetery in Višegrad erected a memorial to all the innocents who had been slaughtered at the behest of Milan Lukić. Inscribed in the stone was a brief acknowledgement of the irrecoverable loss of too many children, women, and men, too many killed and missing Bosniaks. The dead were referred to as victims of genocide. Who could honestly impugn the wording? Višegrad was a site for the unfolding of a genocide. What other word could describe what happened there? No alternative took its place for the better part of a decade. Three weeks before Christmas, however, while my wife and I were preparing for the birth of our daughter, the mayor of Višegrad decided that silence, or evasion, would be preferable. Backed by members of the Republika Srpska special forces, he ordered the removal of the word from the site. Of course his plan sparked dissent and protests. A courageous woman who survived the rape camps led the charge. But what person in a position of power was ever going to listen to her? The removal went ahead as ordered.

Imagine being the man who took the angle grinder to the stone. Someone's hand, the hand of a dedicated craftsman, had chiselled the word into granite, etching it out with precision in an act of extraordinary respect and restitution. Now another hand would ruin it, deface it with screeching machinery, a hand that belonged to a person who could have refused to remove the word, could have chosen not to do it, but who decided to do as told, who complied with the orders he'd been given. He felt in his palm the weight of the grinder, flexed his fingers around the handle, pressed the trigger and held the spinning disc to those few contentious letters and wiped them out of existence. That's power, isn't it? In an instant the dead became only victims. Victims of what? Of nothing specific, nothing worthy of mention. Victims of a stunted sentence, of something known but purposefully unnamed. The woman who led the initial protests had courage enough to continue. She and a growing army of allies, all of them Bosniak widows, marched on the memorial and rewrote the missing word in furious streaks of scarlet lipstick. But by dusk of the day after that, by the time Demirović arrived in the cemetery, the stone had been wiped clean again and the victims of Milan Lukić were once more victims of nothing.

The Murdoch papers, especially, told the story in greater detail. Demirović had been raising awareness locally, in Sydney, ever since the Bosnian press began reporting on the protests. He'd made his own plans to travel to Višegrad to speak out publicly on behalf of Australia's Bosniak community. Once there, he'd been more or less anonymous. He was no fêted dignitary. Survivors of the Bosniak diaspora had travelled from all over the world to protest. Demirović was one of a couple dozen. Only those who'd supported his journey from Sydney recognised his distinction. The Chamber of Commerce had sponsored him as a voice of capital, an anti-communist success story, and so already, before he'd even returned home, the Chamber website carried a report of his remarks alongside a picture of him speaking at the memorial. He wore a dark teal greatcoat, its broad lapels spreading over his chest, and he stood open-mouthed, mid-utterance, looking out at the surrounding crowd and gripping tight, with both hands, to the papers that held the words of his address.

He'd been outraged by the attempt to erase the past of his people, he said, and indeed the past of his family. His mother had been among the dozens of women raped and then blown apart by a grenade at the outbreak of the conflicts in 1992. He still didn't know what had happened to his sister. He guessed that hers was one of the two thousand bodies found in Lake Perućac, not far from Bajina Bašta, when engineers drained the reservoir to perform repairs on the dam. Only a few hundred were finally exhumed and identified. Before they could all be tended to, the authorities, mostly Serbs, demanded that the water be refilled. As for his father, Demirović said, a soldier had shot him clean through the head in full view of any number of onlookers and with no repercussions. He'd been out on the street to collect his son from the house of a family friend. He was perhaps a minute's walk away. The boy at the door had seen him coming, seen the soldier walking towards him, seen the pistol raised to the temple as the two men passed one another. He saw the flash of the bullet's blast, saw his father's body fall, saw the murderer walk on by as if he'd done nothing more than slap a bothersome mosquito. That's what spurred the boy to run. He ran as soon as he could.

Demirović sought sanctuary in the wild, in the peaks of the Dinarides, and travelled on foot through fields and forests and over the border into Croatia. He stowed away on freight trains bound for the Adriatic. From the eastern shore he escaped across the waves to Italy. He remembered he'd heard he had distant relations somewhere in the Veneto. He tracked them down over many months and with their help he applied for asylum. He spent more than a year in the bureaucratic limbo of the global pool of people seeking refuge from the Balkans. Just after his eighteenth birthday he was called up at last and given a seat on a plane bound for the far side of the world.

That's what it took for him to escape the inferno of Višegrad, he said. Gunshots alone wouldn't have sent him into flight. Indiscriminate slaughter wouldn't have done it either. Invasion, occupation, and even outright warfare were all things he felt he would have been able to withstand. What terrified him, what he ran from, was what could only be called genocide. It wasn't simply the fear that someday his blood might be spilled. It was the knowledge that spilling his blood wouldn't slake the thirst of whoever managed to do it. It was the constant awareness that his fear would dissipate only when every last trace of him and of everyone who belonged to his bloodline had been wiped off the Earth and lost from living memory. His speech, as I read it, was aggrieved, sorrowful, righteous, impassioned. He didn't dread the thought of endless conflict, he said. He dreaded the thought of an endless *chase*, a future devoured by hunters who he knew would never tire, and he couldn't stand by and look on in silence as the only word sufficient to describe the sinister intent of his pursuers was eliminated from a structure designed to hold it.

Who would be surprised that the removal of that word would provoke that response from that man? I was: not taken by the fact of it, but blindsided by the news. I rose from my chair at the kitchen table and stood to brace myself at the sink. I bent over the mouth of the drain and stared down into the pipes. I felt inside myself a sort of blossoming sentiment, a warm quease filling me up with the shame of watching a man act like a fool but feeling too embarrassed to rebuke his idiocy. I felt that Demirović had done something stupid and I blushed with humiliation on his behalf. It wasn't the same as feeling he'd said something he should have kept to himself. The substance of his address did justice to the situation that called for it. What I mean is that something seemed amiss in the balance of his transactions.

I didn't know quite how to unpick the knot of thoughts I felt forming in my head. Terrible things had happened to him and worse had happened to many of the people he'd grown up with. Over time, bound together as a concept, those things came to be distilled into a single word. Maybe, too, the word itself had become their equivalent, holding a value equal to the things it represented. But what value did that word really have? Its existence would never alter what had happened. Its destruction couldn't revoke or invalidate the settled facts of history. It was just a word. It had no bearing on the mechanics of what was *lived*, the tactility of daily life in Višegrad or anywhere else. Everything that was true of the past would still be true without it. And yet, and yet. The furious refugee who stepped up to share his anger with a sympathetic crowd, the exuberant employee who shone a smile at the camera taking his portrait, the husband in shock who held his wife in the corridor of an airport in Switzerland, that man felt as if that one word bore such exceptional significance, was so densely and uniquely freighted with meaning, that its erasure was worth resisting absolutely, with intricate arrangements to protest the injustice, with a stretch of time spent inconveniently far from home, with uncountable hours given to the pangs of global travel, and with energies beyond reckoning discharged on many more words delivered in public in order to inflame the emotions of his listeners and seize the attention of a polity that had so far dismissed their concerns. The crusade to preserve that word, to prevent the desecration of everything it stood for, was worth the investment of every resource at his disposal. Time and money, stamina, patience, the stable structures of the life he'd made for himself in Australia. All of it was part of the price he decided he was prepared to pay. It was the cost of resolving to demonstrate how zealously he'd stand behind the value he saw in a scant eight letters, an insubstantial sound on the tongue. It was also, worst of all, a price that did not include being at such a remove from his daughter in her last few precious moments of life, and this, I realised, was why I felt embarrassed for him. I could see what he couldn't have seen when he left for Višegrad. I felt certain that if he could have anticipated the future, if he'd had any inkling of what might happen in his absence, he would not have gone. He would never have agreed to the transaction imposed on him, would not have behaved as if protecting the memory of thousands of victims of genocide was truly worth his distance from his one and only daughter when she took her dying breath. But he had no way to suspect he'd rouse the fate that was taken as almost predetermined in every account of his loss. In each report he was, and was forever doomed to be, a man who fuelled his protest with a sacrifice he couldn't have dreamt he'd end up making.

Now seems like the time to stop and look at what was really happening there. At least that point was the one at which I stopped and saw myself. Risen from my seat, bent at the waist, I crouched over the glowing laptop. Beside it I'd gathered the remnants of a sleepless night. Empty bottles of beer, the empty tub of ice cream, half a block of cheese with a knife jabbed into it. I met my own eyes reflected in the smudges on the glass. The white of the screen ate into the rest of my face. With fingers pressed to the trackpad I tapped and tapped, compulsively, flicking back and forth between breaking news and the history of Višegrad. In the end I set things up to let a stockpile of pictures download offscreen, overlaying them with a window that showed the headlines I refreshed with mounting impatience.

For what? For whatever came forth. Demirović and his wife remained in the margins of time. Subconsciously I must have taken a shot at the maths. Four in the morning in Switzerland, near midday in Sydney. The two of them wouldn't touch down for another six or seven hours. Even so, that didn't stop the story from unravelling in new ways. How many policy wonks and investigators and government spokespeople were gobbling sandwiches at their desks and teleconferencing to collaborate on releasing a deluge of new details? The media pack would be baying for more than the scraps thrown out so far. If you wanted to keep the public content, you had to feed the hungry mouths in time to make the evening news. Odds on an infodump after lunch seemed better than even to me. I hovered above the laptop as if suspended in its ambience and I waited, checked, went on waiting. I glanced outside at the falling snow, flakes slowly shredding apart the resolute darkness, and then I returned to the screen again and gave my waking hours to waiting for something new to happen. Even like that I still had a gall that takes me aback when I think on it now. Even with my own insipid reflection crooked over the keyboard, I still looked Demirović in the face and thought of *him* as a man in shame.

The truth is that what he'd been trying to do wasn't a mystery to me. I would've seen it if only I'd looked more closely at the experiences of my daily assault. At best my command of German put me on equal footing with a two-year-old. I was ashamed of it at the time, I'm ashamed of it to this day. I should've learnt more of the language than I did. Even minor dealings flustered me. They dropped me into the depths of a discourse I could understand only shallowly. Buying a beer at the pub on the corner, describing an ailment to my doctor, stopping a stranger on the street for directions in an unfamiliar city, all these encounters were belaboured and approximate. Every time I heard someone speak I froze and hoped I could gather a meaning close to the one they intended. Everything I heard had multiple senses, simultaneously, and every noun in a language with four cases became an erratic flicker. Every time I had to speak I faltered and stopped and started again, and I feared my words would come out in a sequence that made them make no sense. Everything I managed to say felt like a metaphor for what I really meant, or a restatement or refinement of something I'd spat out earlier. I'd hew out an ingress to my subject at a slantwise angle, or else I'd try to approach it by plotting a sidereal progression. I'd find one way of expressing myself, then I'd find some other way, then I'd think of a third approach, maybe even a fourth and fifth, and I'd just hope my listener would deduce my meaning by calculating the common denominator underlying each of my slipshod variants.

Forget about genuine communication. Forget about voicing the things I wanted to say. I spoke to the world using echolocation, words as good as dopplers. I strained against a muzzle even when aiming for something as simple as asking to receive my change in coins. What had Demirović actually tried to do? To point out the gross misconception caused by one word out of place. To speak against it at greater length, to clarify a muddied meaning. I should've seen it earlier. What more had my life become than the very same quest for clarity, day after day on a more domestic scale? The only times I hadn't needed to contrive my manoeuvres in advance were the times my wife and I spoke together. That was true at least until the thread between us frayed. Then the fraying loosed me into a world entirely my own. Up until we came apart she'd been my last link to my native tongue and my lifeline to everything I couldn't comprehend. Long before we met, she'd studied abroad in Berlin. She alternated ways of speaking, from English to German and back again, with all the ease of shifting weight from one foot to another. A chasm gaped at me when I thought on the distance between where we'd started out and where, by chance, we'd arrived.

I'd met my wife in her hometown, Sydney, at an awkward stage when the both of us were wondering what to do with ourselves. I'm not sure we ever actually figured it out. What happened happened almost as if we lived on autopilot. We intertwined our lives, spliced two singulars into the plural, and we'd spent a couple of years mapping out our shared existence before we agreed to pitch in a different direction. The opportunity came without warning, thanks to an old colleague of mine. I knew him from the time I'd spent toiling at the edge of Britain. Scotland had been our stomping ground. We'd started our training as teachers together. Not the intellectual stuff, only the classroom practices, although we had similar backgrounds and overlapping interests. He'd arrived from Chicago by way of London, I'd arrived from Brisbane by way of Boston, and the two of us set our sights on working around the world by leapfrogging from one international school to the next. Well, it played out as planned for him. He found himself an overseas placement shortly before I went back home. My luck was more sporadic, less sustained. Casual contracts, menial jobs, peppered with unemployment and ending in debility. Anyway, six years later, entirely out of the blue, he tracked me down online to offer an opportunity.

He'd been working for a while at a school in the Berner Oberland, he said. His students were the kids of diplomats and bankers. Many of them were American, most were Anglophone. A handful of eastern Asians weren't, but desperately wanted to be. Now he'd landed a gig in Seoul. He'd been itching for a change of scene. Result: the school he was leaving needed to find someone else to teach the subjects we both specialised in. History and politics, post-Enlightenment, and mostly American, too, concerned with civic processes, with civil rights and liberties. His new contract would kick in any day, so the school leaders hoped to replace him pronto. They'd probably take whoever was first to raise a hand. Plus, he assured me, since my wife had skills in the local language, they'd find a job for her as well. Polyglot Germans in her classes. Expatriate Americans in mine. It sounded like a dream. My colleague didn't have to say anything else to convince me to pack up and go. I had to say more to convince my wife, but soon enough she yielded. I had fresh bait to entice her along. A year earlier we'd taken some weeks to travel the length of eastern Australia. For a while after we'd returned to life in Sydney, the uplands of Tasmania had retained her affections. I relied on memories of the trip to win her to my cause, coupled with vivid promises of similar scenery in Switzerland and a married life of greater financial security. I suppose that means she left her home at my urging, moved by my entreaties and my energetic assurances. In some way, though, I've always supposed it means she agreed to leave for my sake.

Outside, I saw, the snow had stopped falling, and now the first glint of sunlight touched the teeth of the Alps. The day ahead promised to be clear and spectacular. In the distance, white serrations cut into the streak of blue that rose above their false horizon.

Between them, lodged in their corries and saddles, glaciers sprawled out above sweeping valleys. Beneath the snow and ice, I knew, an entirely different realm lay in slumber. In my mind's eye I could melt away the whiteness, circle through time to midsummer, and see it all exposed and flourishing. Lichens and mosses glistening on stone in wide expanses of scree. Dales of lavender and scarlet, hills of flowering heather and stands of redcurrants, raspberries, rosehip. Streams bubbling up from mountain springs, glacial runoff carving ribbons of water into gneiss. Tufts of bog cotton on the surface of stagnant fells. Doesn't it sound romantic? It was; it is. Sprouts of sphagnum, blackened pits of peat. Snarls of bramble, spears of miscanthus, the glimmering micas of schist and quartz. Rocky scarps and austere summits punished by relentless wind. I could look out at that landscape and rewind time, two hundred years, and know that Goethe had walked those hills, and Byron and Wordsworth, and Mark Twain and Fenimore Cooper. Alpenstocks in hand, donkeys shod and mounted, they'd taken to the trails that riddled the upland plateaux. The scenery over there, the cliffs and the rivers and bellowing falls, sparkled with the words those men left in their wake. Awestruck poetry, spellbound prose. Testimonies to the wonders they'd beheld and adored. Wastrels of human expression compared with the wonders themselves.

That was the landscape I knew before I saw it for myself: a landscape of things revered and written about. Not the actual terrain or topography, but the sights and sounds those men had harnessed to the page. Also my thoughts of the things they didn't include in the picture. The dank stench of donkey hide after a downpour. A fly taking off from a cowpat to choke up a traveller's throat. The smack of steaming urine on a clod of mud or a dusty rock. Every day each one of them would've heard the hiss it makes. Even Goethe had to dismount to relieve his bladder from time to time. Even Byron had to find bushes to unbutton behind. They made themselves into men of words but they were bodies, too, just like everyone else, and it was as bodies that they'd been there, trod the dirt, inhaled the air, occupied space. That fact, as much as their legacies, made me eager to live in a place that carried a tinge of their being. I mention this only to delimit the expanse of the chasm, to stand at the far side of the gorge and look back on what I plunged into. What a laugh. The tightrope walk from sweltering Sydney to the snowscapes of the Bernese Alps. It seemed like a lark at the time. To think I could make it across without falling. Now it only seems like a joke, with my life as the punchline.

What I couldn't admit aloud, though, was that, as a force, landscape was as repellent to me as much as it was attractive. I wasn't just drawn to the mountains. I felt driven out of Australia, driven from the land, driven away by the land itself. Whenever I tried to explain this to others, never in so many words, always in response to their musings on why I'd settled so far from home, I don't think I ever avoided sounding disgruntled. As if I didn't want to be there because I can't abide the sun and I don't like surf and sand. That was true in a simple sense, the place never spoke to my soul in ways other places can, but that wasn't why I needed distance. I still don't know how to explain myself. Part of what repelled me was the impenetrable island mentality. I know how I sound when I say things like that. Entitled, overprivileged, judgmental and condescending. But I don't just mean I recoiled at my exposure to the gimcrack culture, the shallow larrikinism, the self-absorbed, insular politics. I don't just mean the ethos of constant complaint, of narcissism and prudery, the stuff of any rote critique from any liberal you might approach on an inner-city street. I mean that the land does things to me, things I can no longer submit to. It whittles me down to a nub. The heat there is heat like no other. Solid ground and sultry air conspire into a furnace. The scorch of the sun bombards the earth, drives in deep and then seeps out from the soil. It irradiates the atmosphere, washes the blue from the sky, singes the surface of the sea with flickers of gold. It stifles from all angles. It clings and clasps and throttles. It's a heat that squeezes something out of people. Something sinister, often violent. Something subcutaneous, under the skin of the nation, something always ready to break free and bite.

I won't pretend there's anything profound about these complaints. I can't even really pretend that they amount to more than complaints against myself. My pedigree isn't a secret. It's easy enough to see the poison in my blood. A family rooted in settlement, in the dispossession of the peoples of the Australian deserts, in the dispossession of the peasants who sojourned from the far ends of the world to seize those wastelands with all the fervour of desperados come to the Gates of Paradise. Deep inside, when standing on that soil, I'd always had the sense that nothing of what I saw or felt around me was something I could think of as *mine*. This sense wasn't at all political. It wasn't a sense I could speak to in the language of Eddie Mabo or the Wik, with appeals to heritage going back millennia, nor in the crude insistence on superiority favoured by Pauline Hanson and those knuckleheads in Cronulla. It couldn't be reduced to a hunger for some abstract right, it didn't come from some inner struggle to feel as if I was entitled to occupy that land. It was bound, if I can put it this way, to the history of my body, and the disposition of my flesh in the air of that brutal continent. It was a very corporeal sense that the body I wore was no more suited to standing on that expanse of earth than to taking rest on the rim of a volcano. It did not belong there. On the most fundamental level of my being, I did not belong there. I should have been shrouded in mist, tramping through sleet, stalking fens and grassy fells, not flailing about for an affinity with a land swept flat to the horizon.

So all my complaints against Australia were really my ways of taking issue with what I felt it did to me. My heart was home to something ugly, something serpentine, coiled up in ducts and chambers and apt to circulate through arteries and veins. Being in Australia stirred it from sleep, prodded it, antagonised it. Three times in my life, I have been charged with physical assault. Against my name, in Queensland, I have a suspended sentence and two others discharged through community reparations. I've lost jobs after outbursts of anger, after threats of violence against people in authority and members of the public. I've had a meaningful relationship reach a premature end because I came to inspire fear in a woman I thought I loved. All of these things occurred in Australia. None of them occurred in the presence of my wife. She'd heard of them in summary: I never tried to hide who I was, or told lies to blunt her awareness of what I could be. She was, in a way, the beneficiary of the steps I'd taken to control myself when I could no longer stand my own spite. I left Queensland to tame it. I made resolutions and quickened new hopes to push it farther into my past. I embarked on an effort to live more consciously, to subject my conduct to a code I'd deeply considered; I sheathed myself in the armour of new, firm principles, principles to adhere to without deviation, though the armour served less to protect me from the world than to encase what I might release into it. Maybe my wife alleviated the burden of that armour during our early years together. Maybe her presence soothed me enough to soften my alienation. Or maybe we just left Australia before she'd had a chance to see what I could do when my will was weakened.

My parents and in-laws saw that weakening on their final night in Interlaken. My wife saw it as well, at last, or saw as much as she could glimpse from behind the defences of her father. Without doubt, that night, the reins on my rage fell slack only because I'd been entrapped by meddlers who prodded me until I lost my grip. Their suggestions that I should return to Australia were what provoked me, provoked that thing *in* me. I unleash nothing willingly. Every day I burnish my armour anew. I guess that's why I tend not to see myself as a terrible person. I see myself as a beast forced to spend too much of its life in confinement. Australia starved the beast, agitated it, cornered it and caged it, kicked it again and again until it lashed out. But a land of stark and vivid seasons, of generous warmth in summer, frost and snow in deepest winter, a land with rhythms to which my body was innately attuned, that land could muzzle the beast and calm it, soothe it back to sleep. At the stem of my distaste for Australia, and my longing for a more accommodating world, was just the old dilemma of wanting a place I could experience as *mine*. Not a place of my own choosing. A place, instead, that felt as if it had chosen me; one to which my body was indigenous. A place that answered my call by calling back, calling me out from my exile.

With a click I refreshed the news and a breaking story shot to the top of the screen. Most of what it said left me unsurprised. Australia was in mourning. Bereaved families were bracing themselves for the funerals of four children lost too soon. Outraged members of the public flagged the need for tighter security at day-care centres nationwide. Representatives of teachers' unions had struck a provisional agreement with the ministers for education and workplace relations. It was time, they announced, to raise the standards of the background checks required of employees who didn't work directly with children but still worked in proximity to them. What I did find surprising, though, was the announcement made by police. They didn't intend to charge their suspect with murder or assault or grievous bodily harm. They intended to charge him under anti-terrorism legislation. They didn't think he was crazy or out of control. They saw his actions as the result of premeditation and malice aforethought. They'd prosecute him for the massacre, they announced, on the grounds that he'd committed it as an act of political violence motivated by an extremist ideology.

Multiple eyewitnesses, unnamed throughout the report, had described the suspect as a man of Middle Eastern appearance. So things had grown more specific since he'd simply been dark-skinned. Before he entered the day-care centre, the witnesses agreed, he'd been seen on the grass outside, on his knees, bent over papers he'd placed on the ground. Apparently some people believed the pages contained Qur'anic verses, words to bow before in prayer. The report didn't say exactly who believed this. It emerged instead as a general belief, a belief that just happened to be in the air. I didn't doubt the truth of it but I could also smell the interests behind it, the fermenting stench of underhand transactions. Cash for comments, on the record, guaranteed to remain anonymous. An allowance for people to describe the suspect however they wanted, without fear of reprisal. An incentive for people to say whatever they thought would bring in money.

All the requisite caveats arrived only at the end of the report. They hid their substance behind a thicket of tortured euphemisms and bureaucratic circumlocutions. Police officials summarised the incident in the present perfect tense. No *was*, no *is*, no attempt to construe the massacre as an event experienced in real time by living, breathing human beings. It appears, they said, that the gentleman in question, by which they meant the suspect, has been sighted in possession of a weapon, and on and on in such hobbled formulations. The name of the suspect, according to the report, had been provided to the journalist on confidential terms and would be released upon approval from the investigating authorities.

Only towards the final lines did a glimmer of humanity return, although even then it was the humanity of the cliché, as if the people who came forth to have their voices heard were simply echoing what they'd heard in reports like this one many times before. A colleague of the suspect described him as a gentle person, soft-spoken, well dressed, respectful and reliable, quietly dedicated to the work he performed in maintaining the grounds of the day-care centre. One mother shared an anecdote about how he'd once come to her aid outside the building. An aggressive parking warden was threatening to fine her, she said, because she'd overstayed her time in a space with an ironclad limit, but the suspect had intervened on her behalf to persuade the warden to show lenience. Then, too, there was the woman who lived around the corner from the day-care centre and knew the suspect as an acquaintance. She expressed shock that he could ever have treated those children with such violence, such *venom*. He'd once repaired a leaky pipe in her kitchen pro bono, she said, and he seemed for all the world like a man who'd never hurt a soul. Neither would I, of course. That's what I thought as I read the woman's words. Who would want to hurt anyone? For what tangible gain? But I knew things, too, that that woman didn't appear to know. I couldn't deny that the body has its own ways of expressing what the tongue cannot. I couldn't deny that this was all the more true when the speaker feels his tongue babbling on without any real hope that he'll ever be understood.

On those rare winter days that end up blazing, dawn in the Alps can be heard long before it makes itself seen. Even as the sun lingers behind the mountains, it heralds its arrival with a wave of gentle warmth. The wave crests over the sharp, serrated spires and washes across the snowscapes beneath them, and if you wake up early enough, or if you've stayed awake long enough, you can listen to its passage through the darkness.

The icicles that dangle from gutters start to drip. In a matter of moments, all else being silent, the dripping will surround you, will encompass the house you shelter in, with the cantankerous *rat-a-tat* of a demented tattoo. Then comes the hiss of sintering snow. The warmth in the air shears away the crystals on the surface of the drifts, and as the uppermost flakes fizzle into a flow of tinkling water, daybreak arrives amid an entourage of rhythms. The hiss shrouds the world in a field of static. The percussion of the ice-melt rises to a clamour. Every so often you'll hear the slosh of snow slipping off a roof, the spatter of clods tumbling from the branches of overburdened pines. Then with a faint aureole of white, the sun, its body still hidden, erodes the farthest reaches of the dark. Over two or three hours it eases into the sky, backed up by the sounds it calls out with its warmth, the sounds of winter being worn away, until at last the growing brightness stirs the first birds and inspires songs and it's clear that dawn is done. The day has begun its business. The stillness of night is over. Things start happening all around, inundating the senses, as the conditions for solitude recede with the rotation of the planet.

I slumped at the laptop but turned to face the window. With exhaustion biting the backs of my eyes, I watched the day come into being. But by the time the creeping sun had risen, the havoc that disturbed me no longer came from outside. It didn't matter that I hadn't heard a sound from inside the bedroom. It didn't matter that the door remained closed, barricading me from all signs of life within. I could feel my wife's awakening like a blast sending shock waves through the air. I could feel the throb of her consciousness on the other side of the wall, the whirring of thoughts that spun out of control as if reeled off without pause on an over-cranked machine. Impossible to know what those thoughts might have been. Impossible without hearing them given voice. They accrued behind the door, accumulating an explosive pressure; they sucked the space to breathe from the bedroom and filled it with possibilities like smoke from a candle burning under a bell jar.

I ached to know when the door would creak open, when the pressure would be released. I hoped my wife would come home, so to speak, and say something to me, something calm and ordered and confessional, something pained and intimate and true, something to let me know where she was in her life and to bring me into that place with her, but even so I knew all this was far too much to hope for. At the very least, I hungered for her to leave the bedroom, to occupy some other part of the house, if for no better reason than to end her profusion of unimaginable things, the notions she wrought outside my presence. I didn't know then, and couldn't have known, that when she finally made her thoughts available to me, when at dusk she spoke them plainly, I'd suffer an even greater hunger to undo the damage, to grapple them out of the air and drive them into her mouth again, to stuff them down her throat and carry on with our tortured days as if she'd never uttered a word.

She didn't emerge until almost noon. By then, I'd learnt, Hassan and Jessica Demirović had landed in Australia. Eleven o'clock in Zürich was nine at night in Sydney and that's when their plane touched the tarmac. I'd wasted the preceding hours compulsively haranguing the laptop, refreshing the story, feeding my hunger for new information by picturing the aircraft and the mourning couple inside it. I saw the last rays of the sun bathe the runway red, and pierce the porthole window, now open, with a spear of amber. I saw the indigo swell of the Pacific at dusk, border control booths lit up as darkness took the windows, a gaggle of restless photographers in the arrivals hall. I saw the grieving husband and wife become overnight celebrities, the stuff of tabloid dreams. Eventually the screen updated and I saw reality dovetail with the images in my mind. Eleven o'clock in the morning, maybe half past the hour. Then I saw my wife. She slipped out of the bedroom and quietly closed the door behind her. She shot me a glance that told me she could see I hadn't slept. There was at least some sympathy in it. She looked like she'd spent most of the night awake as well.

She walked into the kitchen and made herself some toast. The crackle of crumbs scraped away with a knife, the scratch of butter grazed onto bread.

She came out of the kitchen and sat on the sofa behind me. She crunched the toast between her teeth. I eyed the laptop one more time, scanned the story for whatever new details it contained, then I reached for the screen and flipped it down.

While my wife ate, I wandered about the house. I gathered papers I'd left in various places, shuffled them into a bundle. I washed the dishes I'd dirtied overnight and I swept the kitchen floor. I showered and dressed, I did the laundry. I made a cup of tea while I waited for the happening of whatever my wife wanted to happen. I made her a cup of tea and took it to her on the sofa. I found her there already nursing a drink, a glass of white wine, probably old, no longer palatable, although she didn't seem to have taken a sip.

By now the afternoon had entered its early hours, but, at that time of year, that part of the day already felt late. In the Alps in the dead of winter, where the sun will have vanished by three o'clock, even the end of lunchtime carries a promise of imminent darkness.

Without a word I placed the steaming tea on the table beside the sofa. That's when I saw what my wife had been doing while I'd given myself to busywork. On the armrest nearest her was the commemorative card from the hospital. It lay there open, having been taken up and read, but my wife had set it down so that the interior, our daughter's footprint, couldn't now be seen. Only the cover was visible: my daughter, asleep, beneath a burst of congratulations in cartoon letters that flashed with golden glitter.

I didn't walk away when I felt I should've. I stood there and watched my wife, beside her and almost behind her, almost looming over her shoulder. I stood and watched her as she gazed at nothing in particular, watched her for a minute, two minutes, three. I watched without making a move to leave her to herself again, to leave her there in peace. At the time I thought I was showing kindness, offering genuine charity, using my presence to invite a meaningful exchange in which she could disburden herself of her thoughts. Looking back now I see I was baiting her, daring her to speak to me, even if only to tell me to go away, because I could no longer stand the silence that had taken hold of us.

But she just sat there and stared ahead. She was, in her own way, forcing me to speak. I resisted. I followed her gaze with my own. I realised then that she wasn't simply staring into space. She'd thrown her attention across the room, to the kitchen table, and she'd secured it to the spot from which she'd taken the card. Now, aside from the laptop, the only thing left in that spot was the gunmetal urn, the canister of ashes. My wife fixated on it as if approaching the pinnacle of a mountain, as if the rest of the world had grown dim, diminished, and a special light had fallen upon a site of holy meaning. Movement by imperceptible movement, moment by unendurable moment, I could sense the coming of a revolution in the state of affairs we'd sunk into. Something fresh and fervent, I felt, was being brought about. It had already crossed the threshold, bristling into the air around us, and there was no mistaking now that it would show itself by the time one of us was ready to walk away from this encounter. Through my actions, through her actions, the atmosphere of the room had grown dense with the weight of something inevitable, something foreordained, but something that also needed someone to puncture and drain it.

Why don't you tell me what you're thinking about? I said as calmly as I could.

My wife didn't turn to look at me. She kept her eyes on the ashes for a time, then broke off to look down at the card. For an instant she seemed to be ready to speak but she didn't make a sound. She looked up again, looked ahead, at the urn. Finally she found her words and addressed them to me without looking my way.

Are you asking me to actually tell you what I'm thinking about? she said. Or are you asking me why I haven't told you yet?

I couldn't look at the urn with her. I looked away and let my gaze meander. Only when it settled again on the card did it come to rest. I looked down at the bombastic cover, at my daughter's face, so placid, and I saw inside without really seeing. I saw the footprint. I saw the foot from which the print had been taken. I saw the sole covered in faded purple ink. I saw the tiny toes, the wrinkles, the skin flaked with dried fluids and taking on a blush.

Well, I said, what I mean is, all I want to know is what's on your mind right now.

She raised her shoulders in a shrug. Right now? she said. Right now, what's on my mind is really, I guess, just a whole long series of questions.

Questions. Okay. Like what?

Really, she said, just a whole long list of what-ifs.

With those words I felt, in my gut, the tip of the dagger. More what-ifs. Not the first round of hypotheticals she had wielded to wound me. How was I supposed to respond? I could warn her off her line of thought. I could remind her, as if she didn't know it already, that desperately chasing after what-ifs means diving into a rabbit hole. Or I could shoot for compassion. I could play the exorcist, entice the what-ifs to show themselves like demons pulled screaming from their host. In the end, though, I didn't need to prompt her. She'd already drawn blood and something in her wanted it to flow.

What if I'd made more of an effort to wake up throughout the night? she said. What if I'd made myself wake up more often to try breastfeeding until she latched on? I woke up three times, once every three hours, with a nurse to help me, just like I was supposed to. Mostly, though, it was a disaster. I'd sit in the chair and fumble around and she'd moan a lot and sort of desperately try to drink. But even when she managed to get a few drops, she'd collapse from exhaustion and then she was out. What if I'd kept on trying to wake her up? What if I'd decided not to go back to bed and lie there waiting for the nurse to return?

Come on, I said. Having her drink more milk wouldn't have done a thing to save her.

Drinking more milk isn't the point. The point is that I could've intervened if I hadn't been asleep. What if I'd made myself wake up at shorter intervals? I would've noticed earlier how lethargic she was becoming. I would've had a reason to ask the nurses to check her more carefully or hook her up to a monitor or something, I don't know what. Or what if I'd done something even simpler, like turning on the lights? I would've seen her colour change, wouldn't I? With my own eyes. I would've seen the blood draining from her skin.

But you didn't do it, I said. I wanted to halt her there. I didn't want her to pursue these thoughts. And anyway, I added, it's too late now for any of that. It's too late.

She chewed at her bottom lip, bit down to hold something in.

Then she said, Ask me why I didn't do it.

Why you didn't do what?

Why I didn't turn on the lights.

All right. Okay, then. Why?

Because I didn't want *you* to be woken.

With those words the dagger sliced me open. It was true that I'd slept through the night without waking. But until my wife told me all this about the several attempts at breastfeeding, I hadn't wanted to face the possibility that there had been activity around me. When I woke with my daughter's hand holding fast to my finger, exactly as it had been when I drifted off, I knew full well that it was unlikely she'd been holding on all night. I'd suspected, even then, that someone, if only a nurse, had prised us apart to monitor my daughter and then refastened her grip. In retrospect I'd considered, too, that my wife might have wrested her free to take her away, to try to feed her, then returned her to me, guiding her to hold me again, while I slept on without a clue. But I didn't want to give voice to any of these possibilities, nor hear them given voice by another, because I didn't want to admit the reality of what I knew now was my negligence, my selfish obliviousness.

What if you'd been more awake? my wife said. What if you'd been awake enough to feel something while she held on to you? Like a disturbance or, you know, some sort of irregularity. Or what if I'd gone for the other option? What if I just hadn't given her back to you when I laid her down again? What if I'd let her hold my hand instead?

Those weren't really questions. They were accusations. Up until now, I suddenly saw, my wife and I had tangled ourselves not in a single, wilful silence, but in a braid of many. Our silences came in different strains that intertwined like voices in some baroque composition. It wasn't just that we'd stopped speaking. We'd woven other things into the moments we'd spent together without saying a word, all the things we never would've said even if we'd been on speaking terms. We'd reinforced those things, in turn, with all the details we couldn't have brought ourselves to dwell on even if we'd spoken of them, and we'd threaded the details with all the feelings we couldn't have shared even if we'd devoted hours to discussing the particulars. Now she'd taken a blade to it all, sliced the braid of silences and shook out the tresses of the unsaid things we'd bound. What I heard my wife saying as I felt the silences unravel was that I'd been guilty of fatal neglect, that my greed for sleep left me culpable for what had happened in that room. This came atop the sinkhole of counterfactuals she'd already steeped herself in, the fact that we'd both be living better lives if we'd never moved so far from where we'd been raised, the fact that she'd withheld her reservations about my enthusiasm to settle abroad, the fact that we would've been able to contain the situation if we hadn't set up residence so remote from basic services, and so what I really heard my wife saying was that even if I couldn't be held directly responsible for our daughter's death, I was at least the force that propelled us through the choices that brought it about. Small difference between those two states of damnation. But even worse than the disclosures that broke our silence were all the implicit questions, entwined in the questions my wife actually asked, which I guessed she was still too timid to unleash. She left it to me to release them, to make plain what was covert in her hypotheticals.

Well, I said. What if you'd had the chance to marry someone else? What if you'd never met me at all and you'd gone off to build your life with a completely different person? Or, for that matter, what if you'd *been* a different person? Born to different parents? Brought up in a different place? What if you'd made choices earlier in your life, so much earlier that you couldn't possibly remember making them, which led you down an entirely separate path with greater likelihood of getting your hands on whatever it is you think I've stolen from you? But then, I said, if it comes to that, why not keep it as simple as can be? What if you and I had just made a different child? I mean, at the bottom of everything, isn't that really what you want to have done? What if the daughter we conceived had been a different daughter? Problem solved. You'd no longer be one of those parents who feels like they've failed an infant in need. Better than that, you'd no longer be one of those who feels like their own flesh and blood has torpedoed their quaint little dreams of domestic bliss.

If I'd been a man of sound enough mind to maintain rational thought while my temper flared, I suppose I would've expected my wife to stand up and walk away after the third or fourth question. I never expected her to stay seated as long as she did. Eventually, though, without a word of departure, without even acknowledging my presence in any way other than by removing herself from it, she rose from the sofa and retreated to the bedroom.

Before she left she set her glass of wine on the table. The tea beside it was no longer steaming. In her absence, in the sudden vacuum of energy, I stood still and looked down at the glass. Then I scooped it up and drained it. The wine tasted pickled and warm. I forced it down with a wince. I took some time to think of what I ought to do next. I took so long that by the time I'd decided, all I could see through the kitchen window was the dark.

I sauntered back to the laptop with the empty glass still in my hand. I let my attention swing this way and that as I crossed to the kitchen table. I felt like a man electrified, jolted by a live current, now casting about as if hunting high and low for mercy, dowsing the room in search of some reprieve. I lifted up the laptop screen and waited for the news to refresh. Nearby, I saw, the gunmetal surface of the urn captured my silhouette. Strange, I realised, so strange to be in such a malformation of the scenario I'd dreamt of. Weeks ago I'd pictured myself much like this, awake late at night, restless for hours long into the morning, but only because I'd be changing soiled nappies or pacing the hallway to calm a howling infant, not compulsively checking the foreign news for updates on the story of a man I knew only via a photograph I'd glimpsed by chance on a train. Suddenly, though, with a flicker on the screen, banner ads popped into position and the news I craved began to populate the empty spaces. I set the wineglass on the bench and lowered myself into my seat. At last the screen offered something to sustain me, something

I hadn't anticipated. It took me out of myself for a moment before I plunged in deeper.

In enormous letters across the top, a headline: REUNITED. Beneath it were two pictures. On the left was a photograph I'd seen before my wife stepped out of the bedroom. Husband and wife in mourning, debilitated by their ordeal, squeezed together with lowered heads as they braved the gauntlet of cameras. In the picture on the right, oversaturated and shamelessly culled from the social media feed of some friend or family member, a toddler, a girl, smiled deliriously at whoever had been taking her snapshot. Wearing a swimsuit patterned with flowers, standing on a suburban lawn with a sprinkler whirring beside her, she bent at the waist to look into the lens with a fantastic grin. She wore brown hair in a bob with a dangling fringe. She squinted her eyes in joy, bathed in a splash of sunlight. I knew I couldn't let my wife see the picture, I knew it'd only send her into a deeper rut, but I knew as well that I could not look away.

The caption gave the girl's name as Alanna. She looked like a three-year-old girl. She looked like exactly the child she'd been. That's what made it so painful to see her face.

Perhaps what happened next was sparked by my row with my wife. Perhaps the sculling of the wine had taken a toll on my perception. Perhaps it came from sleeplessness or perhaps it came from that picture, the girl with the brilliant smile. Perhaps it came from somewhere else altogether. I turned aside from the screen and I saw, on the white rug adjacent to the sofa, a girl of the same age sitting with her back to me and letting her head flop from side to side on her shoulders.

My eyeballs stung with lack of sleep. I closed them and held them shut, assuming the apparition would have vanished when I opened them again. Instead I heard a child's music. I heard the girl humming to herself, inventing a sweet atonal tune. When my vision returned and the room swam back into view, the girl still sat on the rug. She didn't move to look at me, didn't seem to know or care that

I sat there watching her. She went on humming a jumble of notes, none of which gave form to any melody, and let her head drop onto one shoulder before lifting it again and letting it drop onto the other.

Not for an instant did I believe I was seeing a ghost. I knew as soon as I saw her that I wasn't really seeing her. There was no three-year-old girl in my house. There wasn't a three-year-old girl in my *life*. What I could see had to be hallucinatory. I harboured no illusions about that. I knew that anyone watching me watching the girl would have seen me staring into abject emptiness. But knowing these things only took me so far. Being conscious that this couldn't be real did not make my experience of it any less immersive. I couldn't deny that I still saw the girl. I couldn't deny I still *wanted* to see her. Once I understood who I was seeing, who had come to me as a visitation, I stopped wanting for her to fade away or disappear in a blink. More than that, I didn't want to deny myself the chance to see her as closely, and as clearly, as I could.

Edging myself off my seat, I moved towards her cautiously, anxious not to disturb her. She wore her hair in pigtails that jiggled each time she swung her head. As I drew near I quailed at the palpable reality of her. She wore no spectral veil. No fog of abstraction enshrouded her or streamlined her into something too simple for real life. Her features were as finely marked and imprinted as any other textures of the material world. Light from a lamp in the corner of the room played over the skin on her arms, shimmering and then extending shadows with each swish and flail. Errant strands of hair lit up, shining distinctly around her ears, and she wore denim overalls that creased and rumpled where she bent her body to move in time with her music. Closer still, I could smell the fabric softener on her clothes and the sweetness of the shampoo in her braids. I crouched down, astonished, terrified, and inched towards her, around her, at the periphery of her vision, until my motions caught her attention and she turned to face me and smiled.

I sank to the floor, knelt on the rug. I must have been gaping like a fool. I reached out a hand to touch her face. Sudden confusion came over her. She didn't know what I wanted. I placed my palm against her cheek, her smooth skin, and felt her hair tickle the back of my wrist. I asked her what she was singing. She didn't give it a name, only went on humming. Miracles don't exist. I reminded myself of that. Even so, I couldn't escape the feeling that I'd been gifted something impossible. I'd been granted an opportunity to appreciate simply being there, to relish the physical sensation, the pure and immediate experience, of placing myself in the presence of someone I'd believed forever lost from my life. Not to make amends for my failure to protect her. Not even to weep in front of her with a belated goodbye. Not that the encounter was in any way diminished. To see her and touch her was enough, was as much as I dared consider, and it bewitched me with the magic of dissolving all my concerns about what had happened before she appeared. I touched her face, gently, and felt myself smile back at her. Behind her, beyond her, on the kitchen table, I could see the urn of ashes. What meagre traces she'd left in the world were hoarded now in that tiny tomb. Perhaps, I thought, what was happening had its source in those remains. Even if this apparition sprang from my own inner troubles, perhaps those ashes were the anchor that held it in place for me.

I woke when I heard a door pulled shut. A cramp ran right through my body. I'd fallen asleep on the rug. Staggering to my feet, one hand on the sofa for support, I glanced down the hallway and saw the bedroom door ajar. My wife must have gone to the bathroom. I moved back to the laptop. A notebook lay open on the keyboard, a pen on one of its pages. Beside the screen I found an orange peel on a plate and an almost empty glass of water. My wife must have been working there. I leant towards the screen. The clock in the corner told me I'd been out for nearly ten hours. The news stories with visited links told me that my wife was across the details of events underway overseas. The latest report struck an ominous note. At the beginning of the business day, hundreds of people from all over Sydney had travelled to Maroubra specifically to buy whitegoods from the workplace of Hassan Demirović. A picture showed them lined up at the doors and crowding the suburban footpaths, trailing a queue around the block and up Anzac Parade to the army barracks. One participant described the gathering as a spontaneous demonstration of solidarity. You could count on the Australian public to send a message, he said. They'd come to Maroubra to show their support for a man who only wanted a fair go to build a decent life for his family. They'd come as well to take a stand against the sort of malicious characters who deserved no place in their country. That's what Australian mateship is often really about. Aggro buddies flocking together to exert a rough-hewn penal authority over people they despise.

The toilet flushed, the bathroom door unlatched and opened. I stood up again, stepped away from the screen, and as I waited for my wife to return I saw some of what she'd scratched onto the pages of the notebook.

Dep. ZRH via DXB—BKK—SIN.

Dep. GVA via HKG—KUL—ICN.

Dates, durations, departure times. Tickets plus taxes in dollars and francs.

You must be sore, she said when she came back to the laptop. Couldn't have been comfortable sleeping so long on the ground.

I pointed to the notebook. What's this? I said.

She slid onto her seat at the table. I've been sketching out some options, she said. She clicked a tab on the screen, wiped away the news, called up a list of flights. Then she spun to face me and she spoke. I'm not asking for your permission on this, she began. I've decided. I want to spend some time in Sydney. I'd like it if you'd come with me. I think it'd be good for us both, a healthy break from everything putting pressure on us here. But there's more to it than that. It's not about respite. I think you have a right to be there, probably even an obligation. She tilted her head towards the urn, beside her notebook. The thing is, she said, I want to take our daughter to Australia. I want her to feel the warmth of the sun. I want her to feel the flow of the sea. I have this sense that she'll never find peace, and we'll never find it either, if she's not laid to rest on soil that's native to both of us. So I want to go home for a while, she insisted, and that's where I want us to scatter her ashes.

CHILD

Sometime in the thick of the years I spent in Scotland, I happened to hear a song that has haunted me ever since. Morbid winter, dense white mist. Raindrops froze as they fell from the sky. I sought refuge in a record shop, back when almost every corner had one, somewhere between Bank Street and the Lawnmarket in Edinburgh. At the window I stood and watched the hail attack the glass. I had a mind to wait out the weather, only as long as it took to break, but then I heard the voice. A young woman clearly in mourning. No instruments whatsoever, nothing at all like the chart hits usually blaring in those places. Only vocals, pristine, demure, and fretful, too, as if enfeebled by a sorrow that couldn't be borne any longer. Every syllable soared with the force of the singer's sadness, stretched out beyond its natural length, wavered and was held aloft by the sincere, unashamed melancholy of a plaint welling up directly from a wounded heart. *Though pleasant is—this winter night*, she sang,

I feel
some drops
of rain ...

Then she let her words fade out before she drew breath and resumed her lament. *I never had—but one—true love*, she sang,

in green woods
he lies
slain ...

And again, a fading away, a moment without sound, until there came a resurgence of song and a heartfelt promise: *I'll do so much—for you—my love*, she sang, *as any—maiden—may*, and then:

I'll sit and mourn
upon your grave
a twelvemonth
and a day …

I wondered, as I watched the falling of the rain outside, where in the world I'd been swept away to. The song, the singer, abducted me, snatched me out of my surroundings and plunged me into another place and time. The spitting hail dispersed. The street outside disappeared. The shop and its wares blinked out of existence and their absence exposed an entirely different locale. A hillside forest somewhere in Britain. All the squelching of a winter's mud and yet, at the same time, a verdant copse. The trunks of ancient trees had grown thick with pelts of moss. Twisted branches bobbed in a breeze, leaves twinkled with runnels of dew, and all around me water dribbled over emerald grass. Into this scene, the singer arrived. Long, flowing hair, pale white skin, and a thin, timorous frame. She was fifteen, sixteen years old. Clothed in black, a gown damp and dirty at the hem, she shuffled through a clearing where the greenery was broken by a patch of soil freshly turned. Beneath the soil lay the corpse of a man not more than a year or two older than she.

This young woman, here, has unwittingly stepped into what folklore calls a thin place. Much, much later, long after I first heard her song, I would learn of this. Between the human world and the otherworld, the shadow realm, the metaphysical dwelling of the folk known as *aes síth*, the fey, the whole discordant retinue of fairies and elves, of ghosts and sprites, of pixies and brownies and nymphs, there exists a sort of fabric, to be thought of as a membrane, which keeps the inhabitants of each plane of existence where they rightfully belong. Sometimes, however, this fabric wears thin, deteriorates, disintegrates, exposing a point of access to another realm. If you happen to enter a thin place, you might peer into the world beyond our world, as if gazing through the mesh of a bridal veil, and you might even step over the threshold to mingle with the spirits who live there. Equally, though, the spirits might peer back and flit forth to approach you, to trick you and torment you, or to take you as the object of their affections and steal you away for their sport.

Typically, thin places exist wherever water pools or flows. You can see them in surfaces that capture reflections with other faces underneath. The rush of water generates friction against the membrane between worlds. Its energy is abrasive, eroding the barrier, so that the phenomena of one dimension can seep into the other. This is why we listen to the flow of brooks and streams and say that they babble or murmur. Generations ago, they were seen literally as conduits for otherworldly voices, the lines along which the fey would transmit messages from puddle to plunge pool to tarn and back again. This is why we use the word *gossip* to describe the disembodied chatter that goes on behind our backs. Centuries ago, that word was coined to denote the plopping sound of water hitting water, the glottal blubbering of a rivulet as it runs across rocks to plash into a pond. But other, similar movements in nature can just as easily open a thin place for wayfarers to pass through or stumble upon. In forests dense and overgrown, the trees converse in fricatives as branches rub against boughs. When thickets of brambles are exposed to the wind, thorny leaves shave away the air itself. On hillocks covered in tufts of turf, each twitching blade of grass mauls the open space that marks the surface of the world we fail to see beyond.

How the young man came to lay in that forest, I can't say for sure. Pick any one of a number of possibilities. Ambushed by a highway gang. Mistaken for a marauder. Bested in a duel. We are, after all, three or four centuries in the past. I can't say who buried him, either, or from whom the young woman learnt of his death, or how she knew where to find his grave. The singer revealed none of these things. Instead, while I expected to hear more of her private sufferings, the loss of her beloved and the loneliness of her bereavement, the singer dropped the character's voice and leapt ahead to a scene of occult eeriness. *The twelvemonth—and—a day—being up*, she sang,

the ghost
began
to speak,

and instantly, in my mind's eye, I saw him, I *saw* him, and I could see as well the spellbound awe on his lover's face. In the darkness of another winter's night, beneath the fallen leaves of autumn, the soil stirred and the ghoulish boy appeared. He rose from his grave like a wisp of smoke from a candle sputtering out. The tinkle of his chainmail armour, the stench of sulphur and horsehide. Tinged with an unearthly cyan, his skin was glossed by moonbeams that broke through the canopy of the forest. He turned to his lover and addressed her. Jawline tense, cheeks hollowed, he strained the muscles in his neck and he spoke words that made the young woman shrink from him.

She expected, as I expected, to hear him express his gratitude for her fidelity to him, for having endured the hardships of her vigil, for proving her love and dedication through her suffering. But the ghost had no patience for sentimentality. He turned to her in anger, incensed, and rasped out his resentment. *Why come you here—and mourn—for me*, he cried, *and refuse—to let—me sleep?* I saw him rush at her, swoop towards her, bring his face close so as to lock his eyes on hers, and then, with an admixture of rage and impotence and desperate pleading, I heard him pose his question. *What do you want—of me—my love?* he asked:

O, what
is it
you crave?

And then I heard the girl, terrified, adoring of him, as she reduced her voice to a mumble, timid and submissive, and said,

One more kiss
of your lily-white lips,
then I
shall leave
your grave …

But he could only meet her gentleness with ire. He gathered up his strength and howled and rose from the soil, dragging behind him the flames of hell. *O, don't you see—the fire—sweetheart?* he moaned, *the blaze—of burning blue?* and he gestured at the collapsing ground, at the pit beneath his feet, the mouth of the inferno, as he afflicted his lover with accusations of betrayal and blame for his eternal anguish:

The flames torment
my tortured soul
for I've
the love
of you!

I blanched at the pity of his complaint when I heard it the first time. Her unabating love for him caused him pain she didn't want him to suffer. Her devotion to him, her unwillingness to let him go, protracted his punishment in the netherworld. Her grief, unrelinquished, wouldn't allay his agony. It was exactly what fuelled it. But how could it diminish? Her love wouldn't let it. Her heart damned him to everlasting woe. *And if you weren't—my darling dear,* he sang, *tho' I know you well—to be*, and he drew his sword from his sheath and swung it around to rest its blade at her throat while he sang,

I'd rend you into
pieces small
as leaves
upon
the trees ...

And yet, and yet, he couldn't follow through with the blow. He couldn't end her life just to end his own suffering. So he remained there, singing his lament, and she remained at his mercy, worsening his fate, and the song drew to a close with the dilemma unresolved. What was the young woman to do? Accept his absence and cast him from her life? Continue to love him and keep him shackled to his pain? But how could she actually choose to do what was best for him? How could she overcome her grief? It was the proof of her love.

To lose it somehow, or let it go, would be to show the world that she no longer felt anything for him. How could she give him the peace he longed for without denying her heart? But how could it be better to twist him into a fiend he never was?

When the music disappeared I moved from the window and approached the woman at the sales desk. I asked her if she could tell me the name of the song I'd just heard. She couldn't. She checked the stereo system. The song came from an unlabelled CD, she said, a mixtape left in the shop by someone who used to work there. All she could give me was a meaningless number. She checked the display on the stereo. It didn't credit an artist or offer a title, she said, but only showed what she guessed was the filename assigned to it before it was burned to the disc. Not much use, she said, but here it is anyway. Seventy-eight.

Only when I reached Switzerland did I learn what it meant and where it came from. I managed to track down the song again, and hundreds of others like it as well, and over the years it became an integral part of my life. It was the song I returned to after my wife announced her wish to scatter our daughter's ashes in Sydney. That I returned to it then, returned to it almost reflexively, told me more about myself than I had the energy to put into words. I called it up from the catalogue of music I kept on the laptop.

My wife was nowhere to be seen. She'd taken her winter boots from the pile beside the front door. She'd lifted her goose-down jacket from the coat rack in the hallway. When I glanced through the kitchen window I noticed a trail of prints in the snow on the forest floor. She'd left the house and left me with time to myself. I knew what she wanted me to use the solitude for. I knew I wouldn't use it for any purposes other than my own. I sat at the laptop and clicked the icon that would play the song, seventy-eight, on a continuous loop. I listened to it once, I listened to it again, I listened to it repeatedly and listened to what it had to say. I heard it express the thoughts I'd sensed intuitively before I'd had a chance to think them clearly on my own, the thoughts I hadn't expressed to my wife at the time she revealed her intentions. I would obstruct every effort she made to take my daughter from me. I realised that early the following day, as the music played on around me and the singer sang out in mourning. The ashes had to stay close to us, no matter the pain of not scattering them. We'd already done enough desecration in having burned the body. For that reason and for the potency of the remains, for their power to induce a vision of my child, a vision I could touch and even hold in my hands, I could never consent to letting them go.

So, in the sorrowful tones of the singer, I recognised a sentiment that swept over me as well, heaved and rolled through me and gave me the resistance of stone. My wife, I knew, would try at first to persuade me to follow her to Sydney, then she'd urge me to join her, she'd admonish me for hindering her, and eventually she'd bluntly demand compliance. She might as well have grown herself to gargantuan proportions and taken a stance astride the globe. One foot in the northern hemisphere, one foot in the southern, and soon enough she'd shift her weight to list towards Australia. With a harpoon shot through my spleen and her hand upon the winch, she'd try to crank in the chain and drag me wherever she wanted to go. I resented her wish that I'd meekly follow. She'd pit me against my own best self, the self I'd built myself into, and even built for *her*, on the foundations of the code that compelled me to maintain composure. She'd leave me with no way to be true to the love I felt for someone lost, someone who might yet return to me, taking on a vivid form, at moments I couldn't foresee. I'd have to become the steadfast obstacle, the boulder blocking her path. I'd have to make myself resolute, fasten myself to the ground I stood on. My sheer determination would become my monument to my child, commensurate to what I felt bereft of.

That's why I opened the laptop. I called up an empty document. I found a willing listener in the blinking cursor. The keyboard heeded without complaint whatever words I threw at it. Over the course of a day, wired on coffee and indignation, I set down much of what I've written here so far. Not as written, not exactly. Not with all the explanatory stuff, the things that led us to the point we'd reached. Just the experiences I'd not spoken about, now given expression in urgent form. Sometimes only in bullet points, sometimes in lists of dates with events condensed into keywords. Sometimes in garbled notes to elaborate on later. Even so, those rude outlines would be enough for catharsis. Out it all came in a gush. My impressions of the birth of our daughter. My memories of the miscarriage. My panic in the hospital, my fury at my parents and in-laws. The bureaucracy in Interlaken. Hassan Demirović and his loss. Milan Lukić and his crimes. The removal of the word *genocide* from the memorial in Višegrad, the solidarity gatherings in suburban Maroubra. My wife, her what-ifs, her plans. The apparition on the carpet. The sight of the girl, the smell, the sensation of an impossible touch. All of it. All of it. I purged myself of everything, all the bitter impurities I'd been building up since the birth, and I fixed it all to the physical world in undeniable black and white. See? You've got the result in your hands.

Imran bin Musa. That was the name of the man behind the slaughter in Sydney. Between bouts of splurging text into the document I'd created, I toggled browser tabs to stay on top of the news. I streamed it all, ministerial press conferences, blowhard opinionators, drivetime talkback radio. Fact-files popped up in the margins of news stories. Who is Imran bin Musa? The stuff of political nightmares and the dreams of paranoid tabloids. Countless hacks reporting for too many cheap rags had spent years sketching out the ghoul that haunted the imagination of Australia and now here he stood: a man who invested that monster with life. Every paper had published exactly the same picture. It had originally accompanied residency documents provided to police, under confidentiality, by officials at the Department of Immigration. Imran bin Musa appeared to be about the same age as Hassan Demirović, maybe a few years younger. He was indeed a dark-skinned man. He had short-cropped black hair and a thin, almost adolescent face, sunken cheeks and a slight, narrow jaw, with eyes enshadowed by heavy brows. He held dual citizenship from Jordan and Iraq and he'd arrived in Australian waters, crammed aboard a rickety boat alongside countless others, having fled the anarchy in Fallujah more than a decade ago. Bodies beaten to pulp, burned alive, dragged through the streets and strung up, immolated, charred beyond recognition, above the turgid grey of the Euphrates. Warm winds peeled carbonised flakes from limbs, flung the dust of disintegrated skin as far east as Baghdad. This was the start of the horrors he'd run from. I struggled to understand why he'd hung around waiting for more before he made his move. I couldn't see any advantage in not leaving immediately.

At this stage, though, the story of his flight, the finer points of his sufferings, the clinical condition of his mental health, the findings of the psychological assessments he'd been subjected to when he arrived in Australia, were all filtered through departmental spokespeople whose ethics I couldn't grasp. That's one way of saying they appalled me. Without hesitation, it seemed, one official after another appeased the public pressure for swift vengeance, no frivolity, and they openly gave airtime to thought experiments with horrifying legal implications. Or maybe I just didn't get it, didn't see where they were coming from. Maybe I didn't appreciate the subtlety of what they stepped up to say because I'd taken myself too far outside the public discussion. Maybe intensity of feeling depends on proximity to a grievance. I sat in a quiet room far away, clicking from story to story, eavesdropping on broadcasts, raking through whatever new facts I could find, while the people of Australia cowered under the cacophony, the frenzied pronouncements of commentators frothing at the mouth. Moralisers ruled the airwaves with appeals to everyday fascism dressed up as realpolitik. Legal pundits poked holes in a prosecutorial framework not punitive enough to slake the people's thirst for retribution. Opportunistic parliamentarians fed off the politics of fear, and trolls took over comment threads online where passions swarmed to stultify anyone so docile as to seek a moment's pause to think things through.

But the chaos of the conversation at least made one thing clear. Confusion was not springing up organically but being sown by those hordes of patriots who saw it as their duty to act aggrieved. Because, look. Here was a man of Muslim heritage. He was due to be charged under the anti-terrorism provisions of Australian law. He'd been motivated to murder those children thanks to a radical religious ideology. Let's take all that at face value. Why, then, did he do what he did instead of something else? How do you square his violence with an opaque political agenda? In what credible way could that massacre have been a means to an end? Why didn't he go further to achieve whatever it is that he wanted? Why not aim for celebrity or, better still, martyrdom? Why attack and then just submit to arrest? Why not take hostages? Why not send the place into lockdown? Why not stage executions, draw out the reign of terror, bait the police into putting the building under siege? People seemed to be genuinely baffled but they didn't want to probe the causes of their confusion. They behaved as if there simply had to be a perceptible, intelligible objective to the man's haphazard bloodshed and they all had to try harder to figure out what it might be.

Not just external observers, either. Sydney's Muslim authorities had condemned Imran bin Musa. The imam at Lakemba Mosque denounced him in a public address attended by thousands of the faithful in the western suburbs. The head clerics of the Supreme Shiite Council issued a statement expressing their horror at his actions. Leaders of Muslim communities from all across the city unanimously disowned him, insisted he'd never attended their services or ceremonies, and repudiated, in advance, whatever agenda he might have had. They jointly agreed to co-operate with police so that everyone, everywhere, could understand as soon as possible the motives and objectives of Imran bin Musa. In the meantime they expressed their wish to be present at the funerals of the fallen children. They hoped to attend as a gesture of communal healing. In the wake of the tragedy, they said, this healing was something that everyone had a duty to promote. Obviously they said this in the face of opposition, even drawing threats of armed resistance to their right to set foot on whatever soil the children would be laid to rest in. It was against the backdrop of this browbeating, this gnashing of teeth, that the Minister for Immigration began to play his games.

How will this incident shape the future direction of government policies regulating Australia's intake of asylum seekers and refugees? A faceless reporter at a press conference, a disembodied voice on my laptop screen, put the question bluntly to the stern man commanding the podium.

Successive federal governments, going back many decades, have tightened and strengthened the relevant policies, the minister said. But clearly now is the time to accept that we need our laws to be more stringent.

There was something disturbing about the expression that played across his craggy face. At first it looked like a sneer or some strange permanent frown. Actually, though, his lips drooped at the corners, almost as if his mouth had been stuck on upside-down, and what looked like a sneer was really the grin of a man aglow with glee.

We could knock ourselves out making carefully reasoned arguments against what I'm saying here, he said. It's important to concede that much, I think. We could produce all sorts of statistics and make any number of pleas for clemency. Fair enough. Ultimately, though, I think that in this case a bit of common sense goes a very long way. Really, I think, most fair-minded folk can agree that when a killer is motivated solely by a thirst for blood, by just a beastly determination to end innocent lives, that killer won't now, and never will, acknowledge the legitimacy of our respectful debate. When we try to argue against what a person like that is willing to do, the minister said, for all our earnestness, his actions are basically laughter in our faces. We end up looking like impotent fools.

The minister pursed his downturned lips. This was his way of miming thought.

Predictably, he went on, an organised political opposition has already begun to suggest that the actions of Imran bin Musa can be put down to mental illness. It's said that the suspect has been traumatised by the turmoil in Fallujah, by the hardships of his search for asylum, by his years in immigration detention on Christmas Island and Nauru. But do these claims of trauma have any basis in reality? The minister pondered the question aloud. He'd received advice confirming that Imran bin Musa had been out of detention, steadily employed, resident in a comfortable flat, for years by the time he committed his crime. And even if that hadn't been the case, he said, compare the circumstances of his detention with the circumstances he'd fled. You've got a city torn apart by Islamic insurgents, you've got the grinding poverty of life on the run, you've got the awful dread of drowning in a smuggler's leaky vessel, and then you've got taxpayer-funded medical care, food on schedule, and sea breezes cooling your bunkhouse on Phosphate Hill. Whatever cause for trauma Imran bin Musa might've had, the minister said, it was long gone by the time he picked up his knife. Actually, it was long gone by the time he arrived on our shores. Now, of course, we're left to deal with the trauma he has *caused*, trauma that will have a legacy here, among our fellow citizens, for many, many years to come.

The minister arched an eyebrow. Were we ready for what he was about to do?

At that, impromptu, he reeled off all the solutions tried and failed by his predecessors. You could excise islands from Australia's territorial waters, he said, but in the end that still wouldn't stop people like bin Musa from reaching the mainland. You could send a naval fleet to intercept dinghies overflowing with human traffic, you could physically drag those vessels to a foreign country, an outpost in the Pacific, and you could fully fund detention facilities all the way over there, but that wasn't enough to stop people like bin Musa either. You could offer refugees only temporary residency, thinking of it as a way of deterring future arrivals. You could abolish temporary residency, thinking of it as a way of encouraging assimilation. But then, you know, Imran bin Musa had the terms of his residency chopped and changed, this way and that, and none of what he was given was enough to prevent him from doing what he did. You could try other things. Send these people to the steam-house prisons of Malaysia. Send them to sweat it out on Manus Island. Or don't send them anywhere. Repeal the Pacific Solution. Process applications for asylum here at home. Or get the foreign infrastructure working again. Reinstate the Pacific Solution the next time the government changes hands. Turn the tap on, turn the tap off. Up and down, back and forth, try this, try the next thing, on and on, on and on. Everything I've just mentioned, said the Minister for Immigration, has been part of the asylum seeker and refugee policies of the Australian Government at one stage or another. None of it stopped Imran bin Musa. So it raises the question, doesn't it? he said. What is the right way for us to act now?

Not that he intended to propose any answers of his own. He was there, as I said, to play games with the public. The flat dismissal of previous attempts at managing the inflow of boats, the dismissal of the value of even making those attempts, plus the implication that there existed somewhere in the wide blue sky a definitive solution to this perennial problem, plus the total absence of any clue as to what that solution might look like or how it might be put into practice, all this, all this swagger, this was what the people who watched him saw as the strong, decisive leadership they almost fetishised. Not as the chaos of overdetermined masculinity. Not as the confusion of a man trying desperately to stage a theatrical performance. This was, for his onlookers, true and powerful authority, never to be questioned on its merits, or its ethics, and especially its optics.

So the minister fielded questions from his audience and intermingled his answers with questions of his own, questions that segued into nothing more incisive than the shrugging of shoulders. Would Imran bin Musa be returned to detention somewhere? Would he be transferred to the processing centre in Papua New Guinea? Would he be reprocessed from scratch? Wouldn't reprocessing inevitably result in a denial of his appeal for asylum? Would he then be repatriated or simply sent to prison? What would happen if, instead, he were to be returned to Nauru? Huge numbers of detainees there had recently embarked on a hunger strike. Dozens, including children, had sewn their lips shut in protest at the filth they were forced to live in. Others set themselves on fire. Self-harm was endemic and suicide rates were rising. Would the government expect a legal challenge on the grounds that a move to Nauru would jeopardise the suspect's human rights? Would the government have to revoke his residency entitlement in order to send him anywhere, to overcome allegations of perceived mistreatment? If his residency was revoked, what precedent would this set for other asylum seekers and refugees currently in Australia?

Let's not speculate on the outcome of other cases, said the minister.

What would happen, then, if Imran bin Musa lost his residency and no other nation would take him in? Would he be subject to indefinite detention? Shouldn't he be subject to it anyway? But wouldn't a deliberate return to indefinite detention contravene habeas corpus and the judicial entitlements that flow from it? Up until now, the minister was reminded, the government had approached the indefinite detention of asylum seekers as a necessary evil of bureaucracy, reserved only for those claimants who struggled to provide documentary evidence for the particulars of their application. Imran bin Musa was a man whose claim had been approved long ago. Could the government knowingly, purposefully return him to indefinite detention? Could it deliberately lock him away, without the possibility of release or even appeal? Could it force him to live through a succession of days that led onwards into a future in which no single day would be different from any other? Could it really do that, essentially annihilating his life to come, and dismissing, as if with a godlike foreknowledge, all possibility of regret or reformation, reparations or remorse? Why, then, wouldn't the government take measures simply to kill him outright? Wasn't that really what this entire discussion was about? Should capital punishment be reintroduced so that a man like this might receive the justice the people felt he deserved? Bundle together the lives he took and all the other lives he brought to ruin. How do you tally up the worth of everything he destroyed? Aren't those lost lives at least equal to the remainder of the years Imran bin

Musa will live to see? How can the loss be balanced except by taking those years from him?

All these questions were put to the minister in polite and reasonable tones, in the received pronunciation of the professional journalist. But then, while the reporters were taking care to maintain their manners, a racket of bells and chirrups broke out and unsettled them. Perhaps there had been some warning, a ping in the background or off to the side, while the minister finished garbling an answer to a question. In the lull before the next question, however, a sudden din of digital tones led the journalists to drop their eyes, almost as one, from the podium to the phones in their hands.

A second, quieter wave of alerts washed over the crowd while the first receded, and the journalists were on the move before the last sound had faded. Most of them already knew what the public would know soon enough. One hour hence, I learnt a few minutes later, the Eastern Suburbs Chamber of Commerce would hold a press conference in Bondi. The father from overseas had something he wanted to say. Advance notice made it sound as if he planned to deliver a victim impact statement. It was even possible that he'd make remarks directly addressed to the minister, his advisers, and his departmental staff. Actually, though, when Hassan Demirović went on to ascend a podium of his own, he'd end up straying far from anything so formal, so scripted. He'd offer the reporters what they sought, reserves of sympathy to exploit, and he'd also bend their stories towards a challenge they didn't foresee.

None of my doubts about the minister's honourable intentions would have come as a surprise to anyone familiar with where my wife and I had settled. I'd be underselling it, despite the lofty wording, if I said that our place of work had a long history of advancing an ethos of liberal humanitarianism. The school had sprung up from the cinders of the Holocaust. The spirit of the institution came into being in Germany, just after the First World War, when a philosopher from Thuringia scraped together enough money to establish a place of learning and communal boarding. He founded a campus in the Odenwald, dangerously close to Nuremberg and Münich, and there he began to attract infamy as an eccentric. He lectured exclusively in aphorisms and cultivated a wispy white beard that descended to his waist. He fasted, meditated, periodically kept *shtum*. He corresponded often with men like Einstein and Gandhi. He clothed himself in thick black robes that dragged through the dirt behind him, and, on warmer days, he found contentment in wearing nothing at all.

Here he is. Past middle age with sprouts of grey hair on his chest and down his back. Long skinny legs, a paunch, bare naked, head to toe, with arms raised to the heavens. Sunlight on his skin, a breeze caressing the surface of his ageing body. Eyes shut to relish the sweetest scents of summer, to revel in the tunes of twittering birds and the chirp of crickets in distant fields. Probably ticks latched onto him as well, sinking their teeth into sensitive places, or leeches drew blood from the soles of his feet, or horseflies raised welts across his shoulders, but it's hard to imagine he cared much about these punishments. He was a famous Romantic, a Goethe for the modern age, and he couldn't seriously entertain the idea that noble nature would be anything less than hospitable to man.

In time, of course, the currents of power surged towards the Nazis. A year after the Reichstag fire, Bernhard Rust, Hitler's Minister for Education, decided he didn't like what he'd heard about the Odenwaldschule. He didn't like the philosopher's permissiveness or the influence the man exerted over his students, his adoring protégés. More than anything else, Rust couldn't understand why the school accepted so many Jewish children and why they were permitted to mingle freely with the others. The whole thing would have to be shut down. The SS raided the dormitories in the dead of night. One alert boy, apparently an insomniac, saw the soldiers approaching and sounded the alarm. The philosopher and most of his wards escaped the gunfire that broke out behind them. Those who stood their ground did not survive. Those who ran retreated first to the thickets of the Schwarzwald. For ten days, maybe two weeks, they lived off roots and berries and slept under bracken and blankets of leaves. Then, southbound, they edged across the border into Switzerland. Neutral territory. Guaranteed refuge. Even so, there was no assurance of a warm welcome or a stable life.

Over the next fourteen years, the philosopher ran a peripatetic school. Its rootlessness lasted longer than the reign of the Nazi Party. It was long enough for the school to churn through several cohorts of students, and long enough for many of them to become orphans in absentia as their parents were fed to the furnaces of Topf and Sons. First the sojourners chanced the rugged uplands of the Canton of Neuchâtel. They tried to settle by Mont Racine, but they were swindled out of the land they'd claimed and found themselves again uprooted, forced to trudge on, compelled to relocate. They sought haven on the shores of Lake Biel, in the mountains of the Jura, along the length of the River Aare, each time granted leave to remain in one place for a while before local authorities displaced them again. At last they entered the Berner Oberland, more or less an enclave cut off from the rest of the country by a warren of difficult Alpine passes. At last they found a place to rest on the slopes of a graceful peak, slopes renowned for receiving more sunlight than the summit.

That's where my wife and I ended up. By the time we arrived, more than sixty years later, much had changed even as much remained fixed and a little dated. Now all the buildings were fitted with radiators and running water. The platz at the heart of the campus had become a basketball court. Buses ran between the residential chalets and the village in the valley below. Still, though, students who liked to have milk at breakfast had to take training in animal husbandry, and precious resources were shared by the entire school community. The simplest traditions of the original cohort had been passed down with care to later generations, and when my wife and I arrived we found ourselves swarmed by bewildering communal habits. Sometimes quaint, sometimes infuriating, these habits had survived the decades like parasites nestled in the tissues of the student body. Among them was an avowed appreciation of the old folk cultures of Europe, and especially an appreciation of their traditional songs.

Once a week, every week, teachers and students alike would assemble to sing a round of folk songs led by the choirmaster. I don't mean songs like the greatest hits of the sixties, I don't mean banjos and cymbals or pleas for an end to hunger and war. I mean the real things, the historical artefacts, the actual songs of the *volk*. I mean relics of the Romantic era, as poetic as any canonical ode, but not declaimed from a mountaintop, nor penned by a sanctified genius, and, for that reason, not commemorated or preserved so as to endure. These songs were written centuries ago by people long forgotten: composed, or more often improvised, by journeymen in stables and mews, by milkmaids gathered around village wells or market stalls, by the household servants of the landed gentry who sang to themselves, beneath their breath, quietly, while sweeping the larder floor or resting around the hearth, in those stolen moments between one task and the next. These songs, folk songs of an authentic kind, survived on the breath of the students as much as in the notations on the page, and one of them, I discovered in time, was the song of the woman confronted by the ghost of her lover.

Every morning during my first term at the school, I taught a junior class on the American Civil War. History and politics, mostly American, had always been my ground. Even though some colleagues found it surprising, faintly amusing, that a man with an Australian accent and a Scottish teacher's certification should end up resettling in Switzerland to lead classes on the United States, these facets of who I was always overlapped. Both of my parents have lived in Australia for most of their lives, but neither of them is native born. My father immigrated from London, my mother from New York. When I first tried escaping abroad, then, I had a couple of options open to me, but America was my destination of choice. I left as soon as I could, as soon as I was a legal adult, and set about reinventing myself in Boston, Massachusetts. I enrolled in college there and imbibed the history etched into the streets. I spent a few years using the place as a springboard for exploring other parts of the country, and even started the process of permanent settlement until I graduated, broke, with no meaningful prospects, with no future that I could discern ahead of me. That was when I learnt, by chance, that the birthright bequeathed to me through my father meant I could train as a teacher in Britain at no personal cost. I signed up without hesitation and bummed a ticket to Edinburgh, testing the limits of my parents' lines of credit, then I set off on a one-way journey and embarked on another round of reinvention. I carried with me no residue of my past, as far as I could tell, except a muscle memory of wanting to flee Australia and a couple of books full of notes on things I'd gleaned in the States.

In fact, far from being incongruous, these aspects of myself fused together one day in the Alps, in a way that left me startled. It happened one morning in early autumn, five or six weeks into the job. The timetable gave me twenty minutes to prep for the juniors I was guiding through the Anaconda Plan. With the campus in full splendour, with hornbeams taking on the pigments of desert sands, I went to the printing room to duplicate some handouts. As I came to the photocopier I saw a sheet of paper left behind, facedown, on the glass plate. I picked it up and turned it over, and I found myself holding the lyrics that had haunted me ever since that icy afternoon in Edinburgh. Surprising to hear those words again, even if only in my head, and to visualise the story of woe they told, from the first evocation of the winter night to the fury of the afflicted ghost. Surprising as well to feel the shock waves of a collapse in the distance between two points in time, and to think that such an antiquated element of the culture of this school could have taken up residence in my life, in my being, before I even became aware that such a place existed. But most surprising of all were the words someone had scrawled at the top of the page. The writer had given the song its rightful title, 'The Unquiet Grave', along with two other details. The first was the number seventy-eight, which, I now understood, must have signified more than just the name of a file burned onto a disc. The second looked like an actual name, which turned out to be the name of a man, placed beside the number and cordoned off in parentheses. The name was Child and the story of the man took me back to Boston.

Picture a frog with the proportions of a person. Picture amphibian features sheathed in ill-fitting human skin. Picture a drooping mouth, arching like a bow above a weak chin and folds of loose flesh, and picture squinting eyes made bulbous by circular spectacles. Picture a pasty white face, beaded with sweat, and white hair fuzzing on a smooth, shiny dome like a fringe of pond scum on a head just emerging from beneath the squalid froth. Picture all this and you'll see Francis James Child in the flesh: a scholar of great repute, though his friends called him Stubby Jim. Born in Boston in 1825, dead in his early seventies, he was lost to history long before there was even a dream of the school that would revere the songs that bear his name.

What none of my colleagues there were aware of, however, was that Child had spent his best years roaming the school's historical terrain. He embarked on his graduate studies in the old universities of Prussia, wandered the holloways of the Schwarzwald, even attended lectures by the Brothers Grimm. Compiling his groundbreaking scholarship on foot, vagabonding from place to place with research notes in hand, he steeped himself in the folklore of the hamlets along the Rhine, the Danube, the Elbe. Then, at age twenty-five, a professorial post at his alma mater, Harvard College, lured him away from the fascinations of the strange and back home to the known and familiar. Once in Massachusetts again, he married, became a father, and began to live a more domestic life. But that's not to say his life was sedentary. He dedicated the rest of his days to the tireless study of folk cultures, of regional lore, and most of all the old tales of the British Isles.

Rarely were those tales told. Almost always, they were sung as ballads. Few of them have become as precious to me as 'The Unquiet Grave', but not even the most precious of them can equal their collective power. Totalling more than three hundred, they are altogether a wonder to behold, a captivating parade of fantasy and fantasia, a carousel of the sublime tinged by the sinister and the carnivalesque, a glimmering, tinkling, whirling pageant of magic and malice, desire and death, laughter, despair, bravery, trickery, and, above all, love. Conniving, exploitative lords and ladies receive their comeuppance at the hands of imps and sprites. Courageous knights slay troublesome dragons in honour of some fair maiden whose heart they hope to win. Princesses, splendidly gowned and beribboned, offer their bodies to peasant boys whose romantic overtures are forbidden by custom. As these young women grow heavy with children, they shame their noble fathers and then, if they are not imprisoned in some dark corner of a family manor, they are disowned, disinherited, exiled to distant lands, never again to be spoken of by those with whom they share bonds of blood.

This is all, of course, highly wrought, emotionally charged, melodramatic stuff, and all the more glorious for the shamelessness of its pitch to wring the heart of every possible feeling. The fey folk dart back and forth between worlds, through thin places that open on the surfaces of lakes or in the narrow spaces between trees in sunlit glades. All it takes to lure them hither is a misplaced word on the lips. Names, in the ballads, are things of extraordinary potency, formidable weapons laden with magic. A single utterance is sufficient to summon some power from elsewhere, even if a name is only whispered aloud in error. Usually, once in our world, these creatures carry off human captives; they accost their prey, or inebriate them, or woo them with sweet nothings, mellifluous promises, and then they snatch and imprison them. Sometimes children are stolen from bed. Sometimes women meet suitors who are secretly more than human, sometimes men strike bargains with supernatural tricksters. Time and again, unwary people are taken from home and plunged into a realm not for mortals, a realm from which there is no clear escape.

As one tale flows into the next, too, characters return and recur. Song after song, ballad after ballad, Sweet William and Fair Margaret are doomed to love one another to death, and Janey and Mary are both too dumpy, too plain, to draw the eyes of the men who win their affections. Curses are cast and tragedy ensues when lines are unwittingly crossed. Suitors for virgins are sought and found, much to the happiness of the maidens' parents, only to be press-ganged into naval service, sent away to sail the seas, and lost with their ships to the pillaging of the waves. Elfin gentlemen linger in dells and hollows, and stand tall upon barren hilltops, the better to espy and seduce the women who pass by on their way to market. Young lovers drown in torrential rivers as they flee their overbearing elders. Ailing kings lament the destruction of their estates by enemies attacking with newfound vigour. Scoundrels and rogues rape the housebound wives of barons who aren't at home. Highwaymen hold up travellers only to be met by magicians who turn the tables.

Fortunes are made by roundabout means. Fates are sealed by social status. True love rarely prevails. Evil deeds aren't always avenged. The songs, the tales, open onto a world of misfortune and grand injustice, warning of the need for eternal vigilance, for persistent suspicion of charity and chance blessings. Yet, at the same time, they testify to the innermost hopes and ambitions of the common people, the harried peasants, who first sang them into being. What makes them magnificent, for me, is that even though none are credited to a particular person, you can sense in the situations they contrive, and you can hear in the words that weave their stories, the pangs of particular hearts, the particular longings that spring from deep emotional wounds. Those wounds are the wounds of people who clearly wished that their lives might be elsewise and that the world they'd been cast into might at some level pulse with a spiritual substance more enlivening, more vital, than the drudgery of their days.

Now picture a plank of wood. A fine herringbone pattern etched into a surface of taupe. Burnished by generations of feet, smooth but lacking a shine, it is pressed upon by a polished black shoe and it yields with a creak. It doesn't sit flush with the planks around it. Underfoot, it shifts a little and rises at one end. A whine, a squeak, slips out from where one edge rubs against another. This was the first thing I pictured when I tried to see Child as a man of flesh and blood, of indrawn breath and body mass. I pictured his house as a New England colonial mansion. Spacious rooms with ample light, a wraparound porch, a parlour with bay windows, a regal sofa setting and a pianola. Through the middle of the house, linking the front door with the kitchen at the rear, a hallway ran alongside a staircase to the second level. At the base of the stairs a floorboard had long ago come loose. The man set his foot on it as he came down from his study. The creak made him halt, gave him pause. Steadying himself with one pampered hand outstretched, he grasped the oaken knob at the end of the bannister. He glanced down at his feet and studied the boards beneath him. I saw him squint but then that's it. That's all I could see of him at first.

When I found the words to 'The Unquiet Grave' facedown in the photocopier, I had no trouble following the trail back to his biography. The title, the number, and the name, keywords in a search box, opened onto cybernetic pathways that led me to who he was, where he came from, where he went, and what he did. As I read wider and deeper, though, I realised I already knew his work, and not just from overhearing one song. Years before Switzerland, before I met my wife in Sydney, I'd been struck down by a spell of illness that demanded a deliberate, effortful recovery. I couldn't just kick back in bed and wait for my body to take care of itself. The short version of the story is that I ended up, basically convalescent, in a remote house on the rugged coast south of Aberdeen. It was the private beachside retreat of the parents of someone I'd been involved with for a while. She convinced them to let me stay there as long as I felt the need. They kept the place comfortably furnished, I saw when I arrived, and the bookshelves sagged under a couple-hundred titles. One of the books that caught my eye was an ex-library volume stamped with the label LOCAL HISTORY. *In Search of the Thin Places of Alba*, it was called, ostentatiously subtitled *A Journey Through Time, on Foot.*

I doubt I'd remember the title at all if I hadn't asked for the book to be sent to me in Switzerland. Long after the last time we'd spoken, the same day I discovered the lyrics to 'The Unquiet Grave', I retraced my steps through years of ancient emails and recovered the address of my onetime lover. I sent her an impromptu message, peppered with well wishes and apologies for my silence, in the blind hope that she hadn't trashed the old account and settled in to a new one. Then I laid out my reason for writing and asked if she'd please have her parents check their shelves for the book about the thin places. Could they post it to me in the Alps? I needed it pretty urgently, I said, or at least I felt an urgency to hold it again and leaf through it. I knew they'd have to go out of their way. I promised to pay whatever it might cost them to drive to their retreat from their home in Fife, and I even said I'd sweeten the deal with a case of wine as a token of appreciation. She wrote back with some notes on her life and delivery details for the alcohol. I had the book in hand within a week. I read it right through the day it arrived. I smuggled it into a staff meeting, scanned it while walking the corridors, neglected essays in need of grading until midnight had come and gone. The book turned out not to focus solely on Child, I found, but still I could see him wending through its chapters. He slipped in and out of view as the pages traced a path linking up all the known sites on which the familiar fabric of Scotland had worn thin.

Child, I learnt, spent decades amassing a formidable reservoir of folktales and songs under an unassuming title: *The English and Scottish Popular Ballads*. But there was nothing unassuming about the result. First, in 1860, he published his collection all at once. Eight volumes, more than three hundred pages each, altogether contained about two hundred songs. Then, twenty years later, he revised and began to republish it. Five enormous volumes, each one five hundred pages, were released to the world in increments, one at a time, over fifteen years. Of this second round of songs, however, only half had appeared in the eight-volume set. On the whole, then, thirteen volumes, five thousand pages in length, gave posterity to more than three hundred songs. In the National Library of Scotland in Edinburgh, the first editions, quarto size, take up a full three feet of shelf space. Just to see them there, crinkled brown leaves bound in vellum, is to look upon a manifestation of what strikes the eye, very truly, as a lifetime's work. What's most impressive, though, is not the size of the volumes, nor even the array of songs, but the number of variations on each song and the sheer degree of the labour involved in pinning them down.

Plainly the maths doesn't play out as expected. Take another look at the figures. The lyrics of three hundred songs shouldn't need five thousand pages. They only take up so many because each one exists in a number of variant forms, usually a dozen or so. To keep them in order, Child divided them up according to the stories they told and numbered them from one to three hundred and five. 'The Unquiet Grave' happened to be assigned the number seventy-eight. After that, with the stories so numbered, Child brought together the multiple versions of every story, versions that differed sometimes in significant ways, sometimes only subtly, and he gave each one its own letter. In fact, I learnt, there are ten distinct versions of 'The Unquiet Grave': 78A through 78G, followed by 78Ha, Hb, and Hc. Their idiosyncrasies are intriguing. In some versions, the young woman doesn't visit the grave of her lover at all. The ghost simply rises and speaks to itself, in solitude. In other versions, it's the woman who has been killed so that the man is the one in mourning. Sometimes there's no ghost to be seen. The woman simply recalls her lover's face and unleashes her lament at his untroubled graveside. Then, just once, the ghost is able to satisfy her pleas, leaning in close to embrace her and console her with a kiss. Now take this spectrum of variations and layer it over each of the songs, all three hundred, one at a time. That's how you fill out five thousand pages, providing you've got the stamina for it.

I admired Child's dedication to his cause. I also felt an affinity with his method. He didn't strike me as a man obsessed with variety for its own sake. Variation seemed instead to give him a way of approaching precision. Call it a switchback path, spiked with spurs and offshoots. If exactitude is beyond your expressive capabilities, all you can do is say something that approaches what you mean and then say it over and over again in a different formulation each time. You'll never pin down the meaning exactly, but pull together all your variants and you'll see them haunted by its ideal, each one containing a piece of the sense you want to convey. So I saw Child groping towards the perfection of the songs he recorded, and my own struggles with the unfamiliar language around me came to look like shadows thrown by the light of his efforts. But more than all that, what I really admired about him was his doggedness, his muscular determination to give the songs a written form that would outlast their singing. The breathlessness. The exhaustion of the quest. The tenderness of limb. Assembled in physical space, cover to cover in a row, his collected songs make for a solid body of work, and it's the bodily heft of it all, the bodily experience of bringing it into existence, that I still find most impressive about Child. Why? The question has been put to me by others, by teachers and students I used to work with. Of all things to appreciate, why appreciate that? Why couldn't I be like everyone else and just enjoy the songs?

I can only answer indirectly, by asking a question of a different sort. Have you ever seen anything so beautiful, and yet so lonesome, as a single shimmering firefly held in the palm of your hand? I've seen it just once, after dusk one spring evening, at the end of a day in the mountains. I set out for home across the moorland beneath the sickle curve of the Schwarzhorn. I had to keep my eyes on my feet to pick out a path alongside a bog. When I looked up I found, wavering across my field of vision, lilting above the water and the reeds, an awesome, surreal starscape of bioluminescence. Fireflies swayed like motes awash in eddying air. Thousands of pinpoints of sparkling green drifted aimlessly, weightlessly, side to side, glowing against the rising darkness and tracing curlicues into the distance. As I moved onwards I spooked them. In a panic they dispersed and scattered across the moor. They fled from me, my clutches, and their absence encased me in empty air from which I couldn't reach out to draw them back. I stopped and stood as still as I was able. By freezing myself I hoped I could lure them to me again. I wanted to see if I could hold one, if I could entice it to cast its light on my skin. Moments passed, minutes passed. By and by a firefly came dawdling along in front of my eyes. As slowly and soundlessly as I'd ever moved, I raised both hands behind it and brought them together to cup it inside. What can I say of what happened then? It hovered in the tiny cavern I'd created, a pale glow on my palms and my interlocked fingers, but there it seemed somehow diminished, as if it had lost its luminosity. Only when I flicked it back into the air did it flare up as bright as before, hurtling like a meteorite into the galaxy of the others, and as I watched it zoom away I realised that what I really wanted to hold was something beyond grasping, something my hands could never capture or contain. I didn't want to hold just one and I didn't want my touch to dim them. I wanted to corral them all into a space of my control and I wanted them to blaze, to burn. But there was no way to confine them all, I knew, and even if there had been, even if I could reap the gains of calling them my own, I could never offset the loss of the light that made them what they were. Captivity would extinguish exactly the brilliance that made me want them.

Child didn't share my misgivings, or if he did he went on collecting despite the lonesome beauty of the corpses he pinned to the page. Perhaps he saw that the songs were dying out anyway, already afflicted by the touch of death. Perhaps he felt duty bound to minister to the dying, to salvage a few last traces of life before they expired. What I mean is that, by the time he tramped through Scotland, the songs he recorded there were already the afterglow, the fading light, of a swarm long ago scattered to the periphery of its habitat. His arrival had been preceded by more than a century of clearances. First in the Borders and Lowlands, then in the Highlands and Islands, generations of crofters had been expelled from their ancestral homes as aristocratic landlords coerced them into leaving. They had to make room for the enclosure of the commons, the private acquisition of the open grounds on which they'd made their livelihoods and which, by custom, they shared. Sometimes enticed abroad by promises that usually proved false, more often forced to flee at the point of a gun or a bayonet, their mass emigrations emptied out entire valleys once glorious with life.

On foot they fled the corries of the Cairngorms, the straths of the Spey and Naver. Clutching fast to all their worldly belongings, bundles of clothes and parcels of precious things, they climbed and staggered and stumbled, bedraggled, fatigued, worn by the moans of their starving children, up to the high roads that ran along ridges or down to the passes through graceful glens that would lead them on, one and all, to uncertain new lives elsewhere. Sometimes east towards the coastal plains. Sometimes west towards the salt water lochs. Either way, their landlords didn't care where they ended up. Just as long as they begged someone else for mercy, scrounged someplace else for sustenance, and stopped being so bothersome as to insist on making a living from the land.

Within a couple of generations, the Highlands had been hollowed out. The heart of Scotland had pumped itself dry, flushing the lifeblood out of the culture, until the interior was barren of human warmth. The crofters' settlements were fenced in and given to sheep on the graze. Humble dwellings and houses of worship were left to the elements, relentless wind, vicious rain, and over time they crumbled into indistinct rubble, piles of shattered rock. All that remained of the crofters' traditional ways were the songs they carried with them, inside themselves, and spun into music as they turned their backs on the land and walked off.

When Child showed up in the mid-nineteenth century, foraging for songs passed down only from mouth to ear, the variations he found were often the scars of the clearances. People who'd once lived cheek by jowl split up, shambled along diverging paths. Before their expulsion, they'd sung the same words to the songs they knew in common. Afterwards, as the decades wore on, with countless miles between them, they forgot exactly how they once sang the songs, but they also fought against forgetting. Time and failing memories didn't change the tales, but the contours of the stories shifted, characters merged or swapped places, and some of the words rotted off, replaced with approximations. Child, decades later, tried to catch their fading light. What chance that posterity would side with those who'd suffered a terrible wrong? More likely than not, the few folk who still carried the songs, even in variant forms, would soon enough weary of them. The tunes would be forgotten under the pressures of new lives. The old ways would be stolen by time, and the words would slough off from memories of how the songs were meant to be sung. Eventually there'd be nobody who could remember the songs at all. That's why Child wrote them down. Even at the risk of diminishing their glow, he tried to halt their decline, arrest their extinction. Notebook open, pen to the page, a bulwark against fragility and forgetting.

But could there be an image of Child any more anaemic than that? There he is, in my mind's eye, collecting his precious ballads. He scratches their words onto paper with the nib of a pen dipped in ink. He pores over his disorderly jottings and collates them, gives them a sequence, catalogues them with codes that make them subject to his control. I've never been satisfied to see his life's work that way, summed up in the raw behaviour of its creation. It's a bloodless view of what he did because it robs him of real motivation. That's why I've always needed the plank of wood. The floorboard creaks beneath his feet, beneath the weight of his body. I need to picture Child as a creature capable of breath. Drawing it and expelling it. Holding it for a time, carefully releasing it, and investing it with a voice in control of pitch and tone. He can't have collected so many songs if driven solely by a scholar's belief in the disinterested pursuit of truth. He can't have been besotted with the mere act of collecting, effectively disregarding the preciousness of the jewels. The time he devoted to recording the words of the ballads, the dedication of his energies over half his life, these things speak to me of simple, unwavering adoration for the pleasures he found in the songs. He had to have collected them so that they might still be sung. I see him as a man who would carry them inside his body if he could be sure they'd survive there. I see him, in fact, as a man who really only acquiesced to having them written, knowing too well the necessity of it after learning too intimately, too painfully, how easily bodies can waste away.

So Child, descending the stairs, comes to stand atop the plank of wood. It creaks beneath his weight. He halts in the hallway, grasps for the handrail, and when he draws breath the floorboard creaks again. He peers down at the source of the complaint, the burnished spot beneath his feet, but, as ever, his thoughts sweep him off to someplace far away, sometime long ago. He takes a moment to sift through his options before he makes his selection. Then he raises his eyes again, eyes drawn into a squint behind the lenses of his spectacles, and he releases his breath with a song set lovingly upon it. This one is an old favourite of his, a ballad of joy and sorrow. He knows all the words by heart and with his tongue he conjures their tune.

Hassan Demirović braced himself before his audience. His appearance made me stop my bashing at the keyboard. On one side of him, a furled Australian flag. On the other side, a fern with enormous fronds. His wife, like mine, was nowhere to be seen. His fingers held fast to the lectern, and he loomed above his notes with his shoulders hunched. He wore a dull suit, a white shirt and grey blazer. The overhead lights beat down on him but his posture cast his face in shadow. For some moments I watched him hold his stance as if frozen. Did he know the cameras were already rolling, feeding the broadsheet websites? Did he think the footage wasn't streaming just because he hadn't yet signalled his readiness to speak?

He drew and released a deep breath, deep enough for me to notice through the blur of the footage the swell and collapse of his figure. He embodied fatigue with a physical weight, fatigue like a burden he couldn't carry anymore. In his motions, and in his lack of motion, he gave his grief a palpable presence. It radiated outwards from the figure on the laptop screen, smouldering off him and filling my house with its smothering might. Finally he corrected himself and stood a little straighter. He reached into the breast pocket of his blazer and removed a pair of glasses. When he'd settled the glasses onto his nose, he looked up and peered into the camera. Journalists, off-screen, readied themselves for his remarks. Photographers jumped into action with shutters clicking, casting flashes across his face.

Demirović didn't give them what they wanted straightaway. He took the time he needed to gather his resolve. A frown, a furrowed brow. Shoulders tensed and knuckles white as he strengthened his grip on the lectern. All the familiar motions of someone who didn't quite know what to do with his hands.

Only when he stood steady did he begin to speak. He began in a voice that made his greeting hoarse. Good afternoon, he said, and cleared his throat. Then he thanked the gathered reporters for coming all this way to hear him, and calmly announced his intention to speak as if addressing the Australian people as a whole.

Several days ago, he said, a man took the lives of four innocent children, including my three-year-old daughter Alanna.

He fought back tears. He chewed at his lip. He glanced down at his notes, breathed in, looked up and straight at the camera.

Others were seriously injured, he added. Others may still die.

He took another deep breath and held it, then released it slowly, in an effort to maintain equipoise.

I stand before you today, he said, to beg you for something important. In the months ahead, the suspect who has been arrested for this crime will be put on trial. I ask you, all of you, to remain vigilant during this process, he said, so that together we can be sure that this man receives *exactly* the justice he deserves.

Right there the footage juddered. Demirović split like a fragmented jigsaw. Frozen pixels gave a backdrop to the buffering symbol. The wheel seemed to spin forever. What did I expect? A million or more Australians were tapping into the same video feed at the same time I was trying. The strain of all our demands caused the footage to shatter. I watched the wheel spin on. It framed the face of the speaker. He peered through it as if through a porthole. Really, I thought as I examined Demirović, the Minister for Immigration and all his conservative cronies couldn't have asked for a better victim to put on public display. In full view of the electorate stood the refugee who'd followed the rules and won, the Muslim who'd assimilated, who'd bought into the rhetoric of aspiration and made good through decades of honest graft. In full view stood a man who didn't resent the misfortunes that had shaped his life, a man who gave back to the community that supported him. But suddenly the live feed rejigged and Demirović resumed his speech, and when I heard what he wanted to say, in the way he went about saying it, he looked to me like the inverse of the minister himself. He didn't go in for rhetorical questions. He didn't float any thought bubbles for the sake of filling the air with his voice. He didn't sound like a diplomat dictating some tepid report to the commentariat. He sounded like something else altogether, as careful and as stringent as you'd expect of a man who'd flown halfway around the planet to defend the propriety of a single word. Clipped and terse delivery. Precise diction, formal syntax. Emotionally restrained but exact in his expression, the way people tend to be when addressing an audience in a language acquired later in life. And while his words still carried an accent, it was weak enough now to leave listeners unsure about his exact place of origin.

Only yesterday morning, he said, the man arrested for the murder of my daughter was identified by name. Now we have learnt many things about him and how he has come to be here. Also, it seems, we have begun a discussion about how to handle his case. *We*: all of us. We Australians, I mean. We have very respectable writers printing columns in our newspapers, and when we turn on our televisions at breakfast we see people talking, very friendly, and listening to them I must say I have been astonished, *astonished*, to hear voices calling for cruelty that does not belong in this country.

He spat out the word *astonished* as if it had clogged his throat.

These voices are everywhere now, he said. I hear them on the radio as well. I hear them, *thousands* of them, on the internet. There are people demanding that we again allow capital punishment, especially to deal with the man accused of this crime. There are people *howling* for our government to gather up its own laws and break them in half.

He snapped his fingers and narrowed his eyes.

Like twigs, he said.

Then he forced himself to cool. He looked down at the notes on the lectern and took time to check over them. On occasion, as he spoke, he glanced at them as if plucking certain words from the page and weaving them into his remarks. In this way he enlarged his lexicon and strengthened his control of the tempo.

I have heard these things and I must say they disturb me very much. *Very* much. And so, before anything else, I believe I must share with you my troubles.

Now Demirović became more assured in his delivery, more certain of the strength of what he wanted to say. His sentences picked up cadences and rhythms that revealed, beneath his sorrow, the confident public speaker and salesman he was at heart. I began to understand why he felt capable of delivering an oration at the memorial in Višegrad, and why the people there might have wanted to hear him out.

I come to you firstly as a grieving father, he said. Of course you cannot know my grief, but now you all know enough of my story to fill in the gaps with your generous spirits. I thank you for this. I do not have the words to express how much.

That seemed to me a deflationary move, a bid for humility, as he bolstered his command with his notes and became more subtle in his downward glances.

But, he went on, I come to you also as a refugee. I come to you as someone who arrived in this country in need of charity. And it is this part of my self, my *life*, that I must share with you now.

Here he took a moment's quiet. He fell into solemn recollection. He broke his gaze from the camera and scanned the notes on the lectern, but this time he looked over them as if to make a show of reading rather than to take in their meaning. When he returned his eyes to the camera, he spoke like someone working with the unrefined materials of memory. Not as if he'd memorised sentences to recite. More as if he'd hooked up reels of footage from long ago and was replaying the film of his own life, his youth, watching it spool out in his mind to show him things that he alone could see.

When I was a boy, he said, far away from where we are right now, my native country was torn apart by its politics. I mean by its political regime. And my experience in *this* country tells me that many people born here find it difficult to *really* imagine what that feels like to live through. The outline is well known. The crimes of the government have been widely reported. Anyone can find the details very easily. But there is something that many people misunderstand, especially when they blame the war on a dictatorship. It is that the regime did not lack the support of the people. Not at all. In fact, it *adored* the people, and many people adored it in return. There was an armed resistance that many rejected. There was an organised opposition that many condemned. The *passions* of the people led them to do these things. The passions the regime provoked. My family suffered horrors, my country suffered horrors, and the horrors were the work of a regime that spoke to the passions of the people on the ground. And the worst of it is that the horrors weren't always *crimes*. The regime did not ignore the laws of my country. It played with them. Yes. Like toys. It made adjustments around the edges. It used the laws to give itself permission to do awful things, day by day a little more, until atrocities, even *genocide*, became acceptable. So the regime fed the passions of its supporters simply by obeying its own laws. That is how millions of survivors like me have ended up doing things I've done too many times. Mourning the dead, again and again. Fleeing in fear and begging strangers for mercy.

Demirović rapped a knuckle on the lectern and wet his lips.

I hope, he said, I hope my meaning is clear, though I know my words are not. Men in powerful positions encouraged ordinary people to be *angry*. Then they drew on the anger to twist the law to their liking. If you want to know what destroyed my homeland, yes, you can think of dictatorship, and munitions, artillery, all those things, and yes, you can think of the siege and the snipers, the familiar images of the war. But *this* behaviour is to blame above all else.

And it is more terrifying than everything else because it is the true weapon of the masses. It doesn't cost anything. It comes free, from people's hearts, when powerful men speak the right words. It never runs short of supplies, so the struggle against it never ends.

Demirović, looking into the camera, suddenly seemed to look straight through it. He looked out at me from the screen of my laptop with the same expression I know I've turned towards people who have incurred my rage. He looked at me the way a man becoming livid intimidates a person he has targeted as a victim, as if the victim is no longer a person at all but an incarnation of the fire that blackens his innards. I saw him alight with the burning desire to lash out, to strike at the source of the injustice he'd suffered or just to rage against the fact of having suffered it. I saw something I understood. Then, abruptly, I saw him force himself to quench the flames. He swallowed, hard, and looked into the camera again as if perturbed or ashamed of the secret self he'd exposed to the lens.

Twenty years ago, he said in a voice of studied calm, I was sent into exile by anger. It was an anger that destroyed good people. It was an anger I hoped I'd never see again in this life. But recently I have felt it stirring right here, at home, since I returned from Europe. And I must say it is an *infectious* anger that I feel inside myself as well. So I come to you now *in* anger, yes, and with a personal stake in the case that has made so many others angry. You might say that makes me a man who has every right to speak angrily. To speak without control. But speaking now, with that right, I ask you, I *beg* you, all of you: let this case proceed *without* passion. We, we Australians, must demand that the man accused of this crime is treated with respect to our laws.

This last phrase, given its length, was one he read from his notes. At this point Demirović looked down and spoke aloud the words on the page. I couldn't be sure the words were entirely his. Their sentiment clearly was, but behind the sounds I could hear the input of people he must have trusted, native speakers, who'd intervened to smooth his rough patches.

The justice system of this country is a fair one, he said. We must insist on abiding by it. I understand, with all my heart, the hunger for vengeance in this case, against the man in custody. But if we satisfy this hunger, we will do violence to ourselves as a people, and, worse, we will also do violence—

He looked up from the page again and spoke now with a tremble in his voice.

—we will do violence to the memories of the loved ones some of us have lost.

Demirović stopped there. He rolled his tongue over his teeth. For the first time he looked to one side, away from the camera and away from the audience in front of him, and he lost himself in a sort of daydream. When he came back to his surroundings, he shuffled his papers and began again, but with less certainty than before.

Of course, he said, it is difficult for me to make this statement. Overnight, however, I discussed my feelings at length with my wife, Jessica, who I love very dearly—

He choked with a burst of sudden tears. They spilled down his cheeks and he raised his hand to his face to hide his trembling mouth. Strange to see that his wife wasn't with him at this mention of her name, this evident need for comfort. Strange to think that something between them might have been amiss. He heaved a great sigh and tried to continue speaking—and then, he said, I realised, I realised that—but he stopped again. He'd wandered away from his script. Whatever he was trying to say came fresh from the heart, not run through the grindstone of considered thought.

What I realised, he said, was that my anger, my anger at what I was hearing in public, had started to, to, ah, to *swallow* my thoughts of Alanna—

He shook his head in shock at what he'd just heard. Surprised, it seemed, to hear his own voice speak her name without having had to steel himself to say it. I think I knew what he felt. Thoughts of my daughter had snuck up on me like that as well, landing on my tongue unbidden before I was able to secure my nerves against them. I could see how he'd knocked himself off-stride. I could see it in his face on the screen and in the reflection of my own. When he looked ahead of him once more, he looked out at the crowd around him, the mass of bodies not captured on camera, instead of returning to the eye of the machine.

By right, he said to his listeners, parents like myself and my wife should be free to, to just sit with our grief. Just to sit with it. Our thoughts should be with the children we've lost. Our *hearts* should not be pulled in other directions by, by—

He made a flicking gesture with his hand, swiping at some invisible irritant.

—by *feral* powers out there, in our culture, chattering all around us. But I felt very on-guard when I heard those public calls for terrible things. I was in no danger but I felt, I don't know, defensive? Very suddenly. Because the things I heard reminded me, he said with a finger jabbing the lectern, they reminded me what it felt like to be under threat from a mob. They stole my attention from Alanna, he said, and that, I think, that should show you all how *urgently* we need to shut them down.

He let those last few words settle into the room. Then he returned his eyes to his notes. He seemed to try to steady himself by reading aloud more of what he'd prepared. Again I could hear the murmur of other voices behind his remarks, the echoes of whoever had told him not to ask more of his listeners without placating them first.

We are a civil people, he said. And we must prove to ourselves that we can be civil, always. For that reason, I make a request of the other parents who, like my wife and myself, now find a silent space in the homes they once shared with their children. We have met, many times before. I know all of you. We are bound together by more than the grief we are enduring now. That's why I ask you to join me in something which I hope will change the conversation around us. I ask you to recognise the murders of our children as the act of a wounded man. He may be cruel at heart, that's true, but he may also have difficulties of his own to face. We must respect this. On that basis, Demirović said, I ask you to join me in pledging, publicly, to offer him your forgiveness.

That final word resounded through the room like a clap of thunder. I didn't like the way he said it, I bristled at the blatant appeal to the rhetoric of the church, but I liked its contrarian punch; I liked what it did to the people who bore the brunt of it. Although I couldn't see the journalists on the laptop screen, I could hear them shift, audibly discomfited, like cattle spooked by an imminent storm. I felt I could hear their thoughts as well, their confusions. They were searching for a way to describe the audacity of the man's request, to describe it honestly but without denying him due respect. What they'd seen in him was a fearless show of sentiment that I knew many would consider weak, mawkish, if not outright insane, but they could never use those words to describe it while still garlanding him with the dignity he deserved. They'd walked into his public address expecting to report on a straightforward conflict between a decent man and a devil. They'd embarked on a campaign for drastic measures and they'd looked to him for guidance. Now they'd have to search for a fresh brawl. Demirović against the media. Demirović against the other grieving parents. Demirović against himself, deluded into asking for things that should never be requested. Demirović, the refugee, pledging allegiance to a fellow soul, over and above his fidelity to his countrymen, to his daughter, to natural justice. But how could you sell that story without also offending everyone who'd thrown support behind him? Panic flooded the room. It was the panic of people who'd realised, too late, that they'd created a character who had no intention of quietly taking his place in the story they thought they could write around him.

We must be *examples*, he insisted with a conviction that seemed to electrify the space he stood in. We must be the people we wished our children would become. We must possess the dignity that was stolen from them. Forgiveness is our only chance. We must confront the man who committed this crime. His name is Imran bin Musa. We must know who he is, but we must judge him by more than the worst thing he has done. In good faith we must show him the same compassion we expect from others. This will not be easy. Some of us may find it impossible. But what sort of people would we be if we didn't try?

The electricity sparked in his eyes as he peered again into the barrel of the camera.

I ask this question seriously, he insisted. I have given it many, many hours of thought. And I must say that my answers so far have caused me great despair. That's why I make this request to the families who share my grief. Together we can stand up as—

I sat exhausted at the laptop, my hands at rest on the keyboard, and watched the buffering symbol endlessly revolving. Repetition, repetition. Demirović froze on the screen again, his palms turned down and fixed to the lectern. Corrupted pixels corroded his face. His wife, his equal in mourning, remained as far from his world as mine did from me in our empty house. An anguished voice whined from the speakers at the back of the laptop. The young woman sang 'The Unquiet Grave' for the hundredth time that day. Layered behind the browser window was an icon lit up green. Two arrows curled in a circle, the tip of each one touching the other's tail. In the browser, beside the stalled footage, were the bright eyes and beaming smile of the daughter the frozen man had lost.

What did Demirović see when he looked at her now? Too easy, perhaps, to think he saw a child whose absence he'd rue forever. Somewhere in those eyes, I thought, there stirred a power that entreated him to find a way to make peace with his pain. I fancied I could hear the girl pleading with him. Not in speech, not in her sweet young voice, but through the sudden release of unadulterated meaning. I fancied I heard the girl pleading with him to try to unshackle himself from her suffering. Of course he had to hear her, too, as she lay on her back and bled out in her final moments. The gasps he heard must have been like ghosts themselves, haunting him from the time they entered his head. But louder, more insistent, drowning out those sounds, I heard him hearing her keening for release. She'd live again in agony, and she'd keep on living that way, whenever his mind returned to her. Her torment would only drag on the longer he raged against it. He couldn't have meant for his thoughts to hurt her. He couldn't have meant to make an endless loop of her dying breaths. How to break it and end her pain? He'd need to transmute her somehow. He'd need to channel his sorrows into some other form, to fashion his memories of her into something possessed of new life. If he wanted to escape his purgatory, I thought, he'd need to take a cue from Child.

Shortly after Child returned from Europe to Massachusetts, he married his long-time sweetheart and together they started a family. His visits to Britain to collect his ballads wouldn't come until later. First, approaching his thirties, he had more domestic priorities. Two daughters were born in the space of three years. Soon enough there was a third. Child and his wife named her Henrietta. Eventually she'd become her father's favourite, but sickness stole her from him early. She died at the age of five. He must have believed he was to blame, guilty on the basis of his need to be near water. He had to feel close to the power of the thin places, whatever thin places might exist in Boston. By habit he loitered around the bend in the Charles River and the foetid Belle Isle Marsh. Although I didn't know it during the years I lived there, he'd spent many a frigid dusk not a minute's walk from my apartment, traipsing through the reedy gunk of the Back Bay fens when the land was still a quagmire. Nobody sane would strike out for such places to aid their health, to invigorate the soul. The fens were cesspits of sewage, bodily waste, the carcasses of animals and the odd human cadaver. Even so, they were by far the best inland waters within walking distance of the city. That's why Child stood willingly amid their wetness and, I suppose, did all he could to attune himself to their latent magic without inhaling their fumes.

Whatever the case, he didn't do enough. He ended up contracting typhoid fever. It's a cruel illness. Lethargy, a carmine rash, a hacking cough, confinement to bed. His wife was the only one to brave his company. She kept him quarantined, kept the children well away from him, while she attended to his needs thrice daily. Recovery took him months. Even when he returned to his feet, he could at first only hobble around with the help of a shillelagh. But he must have remained infectious, at least to the young and susceptible, because he'd hardly readjusted to standing at his bedroom window when Hetty took ill with similar symptoms. She never left her bed. Her recovery never came. She broke out in scorching splotches of red. Scarlet marbled her cheeks and chest, her arms and legs, the whole of her torso. Beneath her skin her veins contracted, shrivelled up as if running dry, and her lungs began to crinkle, depleted of their moisture. She lost the ability to breathe with ease, and a body starved of oxygen loses its capacity to move. She lay supine, atop sheets drenched in sweat, and she panted faintly, faintly. Her father, feeling better each day, sat on a chair in the recess of the window and wept without making a sound.

Look at her sitting there, too, in that same spot, back in the days of her health. She flips through a book of illustrated fables. The windowpanes curve around her in a triptych of glass, each one catching the sun to throw light upon her pages. Her blonde hair shimmers gold. Her pale skin takes on a sheen. Her father stands in the doorway, wordless, and watches her immerse herself in the world she holds in her hands. What need does he have for songs of the fey folk, or tales of elfin dukes and dames, when the real thing lives and breathes before him in his home? He smiles when she looks up at him.

Sing to me, she says.

He always leads her in song when she asks him, always scours his memory for something to stir her spirits. He doesn't have all the songs yet. He has never been to Britain. He doesn't have any variants, only the standalone pieces he found in manuscripts and archives during his years of study in Prussia. But he has enough to know a number of stories to captivate the girl, and to know that there must be more out there somewhere.

He steps into the room, into the haze of the sun, and settles on a song about a ghost. He's certain she hasn't heard it before.

Look at her now as her health ebbs away, as she lies immobilised in bed. She loses the lustre in her hair and the liveliness of her youth. Her eyes are empty, no longer alert, and her hands are too limp to rise from where they rest on either side of her body. Her father clasps one hand in both his own. He sits beside her and presses her palm to his forehead and he hums a melancholy tune. As days go by, as they drag out into weeks, as she wastes away before his eyes, he sings through his entire repertoire. He sings of the three crows debating whether or not to eat the flesh of a fallen knight. He sings of a common blacksmith seduced by a noble lady and then shot in a duel when found out by his lover's husband. He sings of Robin Hood, of the Battle of Flodden Field, of the Bonny Lass of Anglesey, of Andrew Lammie and Jellon Grame and Willie o' Douglas Dale. He exhausts his reserves. He sings all the songs he knows. He feels they have the power to sustain his daughter awhile. But he doesn't have enough. Even as he sings he knows his trove is lacking. He knows he'll need more if he wants to sustain her longer. As his catalogue dwindles and her body withers, he sees the paucity of his knowledge and swears to procure the missing magic. Come what may, whenever it may, he will turn an ear to the songs he hasn't yet heard and with his hands he'll conduct their words into something that will never die. He swears to himself in her presence that he will someday collect the songs for her. In her absence he swears the same, but now he swears to his memory of her. Eventually there are no longer any hands to hold and no songs left to sing. A depression in an empty bed. A room filled with brightness that lights up nothing alive. A gap in the world that he cannot in good conscience leave unfilled. He takes up his shillelagh, takes to his feet, and takes off to pursue the music.

Look at him walking those lonely trails. Wrapped up tight in woollens to brace against the bite of winter. Shuffling through forests with his amphibian waddle, hunkering down under canopies to evade the sleet and snowfall. He steers clear of the Roman roads as much as he can. Instead he inclines to the old ways, journeying from hamlet to hamlet along the rude trails made by the stamping of generations. Think of the ache in his bones. Think of the burn in his calves. Cramps in the soles of his feet and the thud of an overtaxed heart. The drag of his satchel, the twisting and rubbing of straps and the pinch of ill-fastened buckles. Think of the sweat beneath layers of clothes, and think of how suddenly he would have shivered at the first touch of a breeze. Think of the nights he would have failed to find an inn with a vacant room, or a household with a makeshift bed in the hayloft, and the bitter nights he would have spent cowering, wide awake, amid the woodland undergrowth or using a hedgerow as a windbreak.

The clop of his boots along cobbled streets. The arch of his shoulders under thatched eaves. The knock of his knuckles on elmwood hatches. The effusive smile he'd offer in greeting, the swell of flesh around his gullet and the flash of sunlight in the lenses of his spectacles. What of the people he met? Toothless old ladies in threadbare frocks and aprons. Bald men with lumps on their polished heads, with goitres swelling their jaws out of shape. Lame children, too many lame children, toes lost to the swipe of a miswielded scythe. A young girl approaching the age of marriage, grey of hair with a shoulder askew. Another swollen with twins due any day, a double chin at rest on her bosom to peer down her nose at the stubby man. Shirtless young lads with bodies of bronze, carrying baskets of fish uphill from riverside to marketplace. Whole families trying to eke out an existence by farming a flock of sheep on barren land of mud and shale. Itinerant peasants looking to sell a herd of pigs. Highlanders on horseback, a boatman at a river crossing. A boot-black in a royal burgh. Merchants touting their wares by the sea and gamblers guzzling beer in a tavern and more, many more, than I am able to number.

When a door swung open he'd offer a grateful smile to whoever stood on the other side, then he'd beg forgiveness for intruding and he'd explain himself. He was searching for songs from the old life, he'd say, as many as anyone could remember. When those songs were sung to him, the words that spilled from his pen were given to him by illiterate people who, in turn, gave substance to the lives they'd lost. Diaphragms contracted in the thoracic cavity. Fresh breath swelled into the abdomen. Vocal cords vibrated in airstreams, and melodies and intonations were released for the appeasement of the scholar. By and large, he noticed, the songs told tales of the landed gentry, tragic tales carried by people dispossessed of their land. But there were others, too, songs about different realms of existence. These turned out to be the newer songs, more recently taking root in the culture or else adapted from old favourites. Strange things had been seen, Child learnt, since the people had resettled on foreign soil. Uncanny figures, eerie weather, odd behaviour in the livestock. Every time, Child asked where he might find the locus of all this strangeness. An old man extended an arm to point to the top of a distant hill. A woman tilted her head to gesture at a nearby grove. Children clamoured to show the scholar the way to the local tarn, and newlyweds drew maps of routes to rugged streams and burns, to pools and ponds, to menhirs, barrows, henges, dolmens. Child noted their locations. They were the thin places of Scotland, he wrote, and they were the wellsprings of songs that detailed the wily ways of the fey.

All of these things, all the people he met on his journeys, all the exhaustion he put himself through, all the troubles he brooked on the way, all of them are also testament to his love for his daughter. His painstaking migration, his harvest of songs, fed his efforts to honour his daughter's memory and to do penance for having carried her illness to her. Imagine what he underwent. Read it into the books he produced. You have to discern, between the lines, all the miles he traversed, all the setbacks he faced, all the stumbles and pangs, the doubts and the loneliness, the uncanny solitude of the single traveller in deserted glens and vales. Only then do his thousands of pages seem even vaguely able to bear the weight of his grief, invested with a significance to equal the magnitude of his loss.

Now look at him stepping into a tavern in one of the wynds off Edinburgh's Royal Mile. Dense white mist again. Another freezing downpour. Shards of ice pelt over the stones, intermingling with driving rain. At a table in a darkened corner, he takes refuge with a pint. Give him this moment of respite. Look at him peering closely at his face reflected, blurred, in the murky pewter of his mug. He holds the handle tight. As he tenses his fingers the veins in his wrist stick out. Let this call to mind the countless times he held the hand of the ailing Henrietta. She'd lie awake for hours, her body convulsing silently as she tried not to trigger a spell of brutal coughing. He'd clasp her wrist and see her veins grow bright beneath her skin, and he'd press her palm to his forehead as he leant in to give her the music he knew she needed. *Though pleasant is—this winter night*, he sang,

I feel
some drops
of rain …

Look up now and see the face reflected not in pewter but in matte gunmetal. Look at the grip on the handle, stainless steel, and the eyes dimly mirrored in the surface. Those eyes are also witness to a vision of an infant girl. Five years old with long blonde hair and a complexion to match the snow outside. She wears a T-shirt and slacks and a pair of sheepskin slippers. She lies on her side and curls up in the foetal position. Her hair spills out across the mattress. The tips of it touch my pillow. Look at her lying there, eyes closed, awake but retreating into a world of her own. Listen now as she sings to herself, in a voice like the tinkle of bells, softly, softly, singing on,

I never had
but one
true love,
    in green woods
    he lies
    slain …

Behind her I can see the bars of the cot we'd bought before she was born. We'd removed one side long ago to latch the cot back onto our bed. *I'd do so much—for you—my love,* she sings, and tenderly I reach out to rest a hand on her face and suddenly the singing stops and she opens her eyes to look at me.

What? she says. What are you doing?

I want to not break the contact, the touch. I relish the warmth that seeps from her skin and into the tips of my fingers. Again I marvel at the reality of it, the reality it seems to hold.

Why are you still in this bed? I say. You're way too big for this bed now.

She lies there cramped and curled, knees drawn high to her chest. Not ill, though. Only playing.

I wanted to sleep here like I used to, she says.

I don't know what to say. I feel I've come face to face with a miracle and I don't want to trouble it for fear I'll make it dissipate. I only want to savour it.

I'd do so much, I sing, *for you—my love—*

As any—maiden—may, she sings with a smile. Then she draws breath as if to sing the next lines, but before she can release the music I press a finger to her lips and sing the words, intone them, by myself.

I'll sit and mourn, I sing, *upon—your grave—a twelvemonth—and—*

You're singing, said my wife.

I sat upright in bed. A bleary head, a hammering heart. Sheets pulled up to my chest. Fully clothed but heavy in the limbs, as if I'd been sleeping all day. My wife stood in front of me, right where the cot had been. She folded her arms across her chest and looked down at me. You were singing, she said. In your sleep.

I didn't know what to say. I struggled to clear my thoughts. In the end I said, Why couldn't you just let me sleep? and I lay back down.

My wife pointed across to the window. I turned to follow the direction of her finger. Beyond the glass, darkness had swallowed the forest. Clouds obscured the moon and left the snowdrifts the colour of soot. I guessed it was midnight or near enough. Then I saw what my wife meant for me to see. Standing on the windowsill, on my side of the bed, was the canister of ashes. I must have moved it from the kitchen table. The keepsake. The urn.

From beside me, my wife spoke in a tone of exacting calm. I couldn't see her directly, still turned slightly away, but I saw her doubled reflection in the glass of the window. There are simpler ways of saying you don't want to take the ashes home, she said. Actually, there are simpler ways of saying most of the things on your mind. I don't understand why you have to make it so complex.

Well— I began, but I didn't finish, didn't even have a sense of where that sentence might go. I watched her reflection turn away with a hopeless shrug.

I don't know why you can't just come out and say it plainly, she said as she moved to the bedroom door.

Come out and say what? I said. Too late. She'd already left. I swung my legs over the edge of the bed, took to my feet and followed her.

In the hallway I saw her boots discarded by the front door. A faint brown ring encircled them, a puddle of snowmelt gone dry. She'd been home for hours.

What do you want me to say? I said.

I shadowed her as she entered the kitchen and flicked the switch on the kettle. In the snow outside the glass door, I could see, her boot-prints sketched a dotted line to the edge of the trees and into the forest. She kept her back to me, reached out for an empty mug, and with her free hand she pointed to one side, towards the kitchen table, where the laptop sat with the screen upright and brightly lit.

You spent the whole day writing all that? she said.

Well— I began, but I didn't have a sense of where to take that sentence either.

The kettle began to chuckle.

I mean, look, she said, turning to face me as she leant against the kitchen bench. Clearly you have your way of seeing things. That's fine. I don't—

She stopped, reconsidered, walked back that line of thought and started over.

I can't deny you your viewpoint. I won't. What I don't get is why you're letting yourself stew over the things you think you're seeing and taking them to, to such, you know, taking them to such depths of detail, I guess, like what you've got on the computer.

None of that was for you to read.

I know. I do know that.

Billows of steam rose up from the kettle and the burbling sound that spilled from the spout forced my wife to raise her voice.

But I came home and heard the music, she said. This song, over and over, this woman singing some awful dirge. I've heard it before and I hate it. I only went to the computer to turn it off. Then I saw the document you left open, which I assumed you didn't mind me reading, and once I started I couldn't stop because—

The kettle clicked off. The last of the steam drifted up and dissolved above us.

Why? I said.

Come on, said my wife.

No, really. Why?

Because it's all about me, isn't it? Basically. Ultimately. It's about your life with me.

No, I said.

Yes it is. Of course it is. How can you honestly say it's not?

It's not about you.

Well, she said, it is and it isn't. Right? She plucked a teabag from a tin and dropped it into the mug. She picked up the kettle and poured the hot water. I mean, she went on, there's this character in your story who shares my place in your life. *My wife, my wife.* You've got those words on every page, don't you?

She stopped pouring and set the kettle aside.

But really, she said, I can't see any resemblance between this character and me. She's like a stranger wearing my skin. I don't deny that what you've written about her is accurate, at least from a spectator's perspective. She's like someone who says a few things I've said, does a few things I've done, but she's got nothing at all going on behind the face she shows you. I don't mean she comes across as dumb or, I don't know, what's the word? Duplicitous. That's not what I'm getting at. What I mean is she's a shell. She's, you know, she's all surface. You've not put in any effort to make sense of why she does what she does, says what she says, wants what she wants, you know? She comes across as vapid because you haven't tried to understand her. You haven't. In fact, the only person you've actually tried to understand is that poor man in Australia and even then, when you crawl into his head, you can still only see yourself. The things you and he have in common. The parts of his situation that chime with yours. Like he's just a proxy for what you want to say. Talk about narcissistic. But, whatever, I don't care. I know you. I know you need to write it all down to sort out your thoughts and take a breather. I knew you'd do it sooner or later. I just think you need to think it through again. There's nothing of *this* person, of *me*—she thumped her chest with an open palm—nothing from *in here* to fill out the woman you think is living my life. That tells me you're missing a big part of what's going on in this house. There's a hole in the way you see what's happening here.

She arched an eyebrow as if expecting me to challenge this, almost as if daring me.

I said nothing in response.

For example, she went on. All those cards you sat down with in the hallway on our first night back. Congratulations and condolences. You remember those? How many did you ever respond to? Forget meaningful responses. How many did you acknowledge receiving? Zero. That's how many. I'm the one who's spent untold hours contacting family and friends, even distant family, even friends we haven't seen in years, and thanking them for reaching out, letting them know we appreciate their sympathies. I've sent *countless* cards in response, and emails and text messages, and I've made phone calls and I've made promises to get in touch with all the people I haven't had the energy to talk to yet, and what have you done? You've been sitting around and wondering, just *wondering*, what I've been doing behind closed doors. Sitting around is fine. I can't tell you how to cope with what's happened to us. But sitting by yourself and making judgments about what I'm doing, when in fact I'm doing my absolute best to make contact with people who only want to *offer support* despite the absurd distance between where we are now and where they live—

She stopped.

I made a move to speak but she spoke over me.

No, wait, she said. Let me backtrack. I don't want to get into the details. None of this matters. None of the particulars matter now. What matters is that there are things I think you're not conscious of and they're warping your sense of what we need to do. I don't mean to criticise you for that. I know what you feel and I know how that feeling closes you in on yourself. I get it. But what it means for me is that I'm not really here. You can't *see* me. You just, you *feel* something obstructing your own expressions of grief, someone *competing* with you for, I don't know, for the *authority* to reshape our surroundings, to *mould* our world into what each of us thinks it should look like now.

She picked up pace as the sentences spun out, and ended up short of breath.

I'm here, she said. I'm *here.* I'm a person. I'm not some weighty ornament dangling off your tender feelings. I'm me. I'm not a thing you need to clear away, I'm not blocking your recovery. I'm not a secondary thread in a story that belongs to you. Look at me. There are things I *want.* The things I want might very well conflict with the things *you* want. That's only because I'm just as entitled to want things as you are. It's not because the things I want are petty, it's not because I'm hysterical or frivolous or impulsive or whatever else you might think of me these days, it's not because I make spurious decisions, or overly sentimental decisions, about what I feel is the right thing to do, and it's definitely not because the *world* is using me as an instrument to frustrate *you.*

She fell quiet then and let her eyes fall to the surfaces of the kitchen. The floor, the cupboard doors, the countertop beside the sink. Faint steam still curled from her mug. The tea grew dark, almost black, awaiting a splash of milk.

I am every bit as immersed in the same experience as you, she added, and I have to do the things my heart is instructing me to do.

I nodded to myself. I had to acknowledge her case. I'm not sure she saw me do it. When I was certain she'd spent her words, I spoke.

Which is really to say, I said, that you want me to give my consent. You want me to say it's okay to scatter the ashes in Australia.

Even if, I thought to myself, I felt a stronger attachment to those ashes than anything else I could now set my eyes on. Never mind that the attachment was entirely illusory. Never mind that the ashes didn't even embody a child I'd known profoundly but were, at best, only an emblem of a child from a life I wished I could have lived. I wanted to cling to them. They were what I had.

Consent? No. To my surprise, my wife shook her head. No, she said. Not yet. I mean, eventually, soon, that'd be nice. But first I think I need you to take a step back. Your consent doesn't mean anything until you've looked at what you've been doing.

She picked up her mug and glanced down at the tea. She didn't add the milk. Instead she turned to the sink and splashed the tea down the drain. She set the mug aside and with both hands she held on to the countertop. She flexed her shoulders and bowed her head. She mimicked the stance Demirović had taken when the footage froze.

Do this for me, she said. Go back to what you wrote today. Read through it again. See if you can find me in there. Look at the wife you've depicted and see if you can appreciate her reasons for her behaviour. I don't mean I want you to explain them. I want you to feel them, I want you to know what it's like to have them inside yourself. Do that. Okay? Do that, and when you've done that, come back and let me know. Then we'll start talking over what we should do next.

My wife stopped speaking right there, with those words. Still, her silence set loose all the thoughts implicit in what she'd said. She wasn't actually thinking about what we might do next. She was thinking about now, about how there can't be a *next* if the *now* is broken. She was thinking about the fact that when her husband looked at the now, he saw a life lived by two people but fully formed for only one. If he went on seeing it that way, I understood, we wouldn't even have a next. We couldn't because we'd no longer have an *us*.

BIN MUSA

A wad of letters scrunched through the slot in the door. From where I stood in the kitchen, I looked down the hallway and watched them fall. Envelopes slapped the bristly mat beside our riot of boots. I'd been awake through the night. A daze hung about my head. It sagged my shoulders as I took a step and shuffled forward. I thought I could stoop to pick up the mail but when I bent I realised I couldn't. I had to kneel to gather it. Fifteen or twenty envelopes, some bound together with elastic bands. I sat on the floor, back to the wall. I flicked through what I'd received and stopped when I saw an official seal.

I thumbed open the adhesive, unfolded the letter inside, deciphered the text as best I could. Something had been resolved. Somebody had capitulated. A death certificate would be notarised and issued by the end of the month. The news left me feeling somehow only semiconscious, liminal, as if I'd awoken inside a dream that wouldn't release me. My daughter still didn't have a birth certificate. The powers that be saw her as a child who'd died before she'd even lived. All they were willing to recognise was her existence as a ghost.

The front door hadn't been left ajar, but the weather-strip must've split. Icy air from outside curled under the skirting and edged into the hallway to touch the bare skin on my arms. Still holding the letter in one hand, I pushed myself up off the floor to unlock the door and swing it open. Snow spilled over the lowest part of the frame. Sweeping upwards from the nearest edge, like a mountain rising skyward from its foothills, tracts of powder undulated away from the house, high enough to conceal the road that hugged the property line. A single set of boot-prints showed the way the postman had waded through mounds of white. Now I understood why he'd delivered so much mail at once. He must've been avoiding our house for days because we hadn't cleared a path. All this snow hadn't fallen overnight. It had been building in increments even before I went to Interlaken. But I hadn't left the house since I returned, so I hadn't picked up a shovel. I guess the postman's resolve to avoid was no match for my anomie. He'd given up, knee-deep in snow, to offload the mail he'd accumulated while waiting for me to move. Probably, I figured, I should step outside and set to work. At the very least, I needed something to do with my hands.

Your shoulders bear the burden first. Then your toes and the arches of your feet. The earliest ache comes from flailing about. You have to flail because powder tumbles, slips off the blade as easily as rain. Shovelling it is like trying to stockpile mist. Your shoulders bow as you bend down and to the side, then flex as you pick yourself up and turn the other way, and in the repetitions of those canting, pitching motions, hunch and heave and hunch again, you'll have shifted almost nothing from the space you want to clear. Perhaps enough to fill a bucket. Sometimes barely enough for a bowl. The rest will have spilled to either side of where you stand, working against your aims and building into banks you'll have to dig at later. By this point you'll no longer feel your toes. Your heels and ankles, sunken in snow, will have started to burn, and the lining of your boots will rub a film of sweat from your soles. But this discomfort marks a turning. As you press through it, press on, you kindle a warmth in your abdomen. It spreads through your torso, traps itself in layers of clothes, then thrills through the rest of your limbs. From arms to hands and freezing fingers gripping the shaft of the shovel. From thighs to calves and downward, downward, to soothe aching feet submerged beneath the white.

But it doesn't last. The labour takes the body to its limits. You don't really have a choice. You've got to reconnect with the outside world and this is the price to pay for it. The trouble is that the powder isn't the only snow to be cleared. Once you've worked through the finest of it, you'll reach a layer of something stronger. Fragmented particles pressed together and sculpted by the wind. Easier to pile onto your shovel but also heavier, more dense, compacted by the airflow, and harder on the joints in your arms as you fling them away. Beneath them are the grains that at some point softened in the sunshine and then froze together again. These are heavier still, and denser, too, even harder on the small of your back, your upper thighs, as you squat to split them apart with the blade. Next, if you haven't drained yourself, you'll find a snowpack shielded by ice. This you have to stab. Raise the shovel high and pierce it, if you can, with all your strength. It'll take a few blows to crack, a few more blows to shatter. Then it's easy to break into chunks you can pick up with your hands and hurl aside. That's if you're still capable of bending down to take them.

By this time the ache will have returned and started to cripple you. It migrates from your shoulders and feet to devour your body, your torso, closing in in a pincer manoeuvre, drifting down your spine to sting your back at the same time that it rises from your heels into your knees, your hips. Altogether this gruntwork, this gruelling maintenance of order, is as much a part of the Alpine winter as icicles melting in sunshine, the hush of a hike through the forest, the swish of skis on a downhill run. It's the countervailing force to those pleasures, I guess, and one that compels you to purchase your pleasures using the currency of pain.

But that's overkill, isn't it? Easy enough to write those things when you've got the headspace to think them through. Easy to take things too far. *Currency.* What was my pain actually worth? The problem was that I'd spent the night awake, on edge, torn between combing through the thicket of text on the laptop and awaiting the splurge of details promised by events overseas. I thrust the shovel into the powder, churned, and swung. A twinge in my rotator cuff. My mind remained fixed on Imran bin Musa. I'd found his face captured in an artful, soulful portrait, headlining the broadsheet websites, when my wife retreated to bed. Beneath the picture, a banner of text printed his name and followed it with a colon and a question: WHAT IS HIS STORY?

Everyone knew the basics already. His flight from war-torn Fallujah, his smuggling into Australian waters, his detention on Christmas Island and, later, Nauru. Everyone had in fact come to know a lot more than the basics. Details had trickled out here and there, flickering from the press conferences that had blitzed the media the day before. He hadn't fled directly to Australia. He'd reached it after setting out from someplace on the coast of Java. Then, too, he hadn't fled directly to Indonesia. He'd crossed the Strait of Malacca to reach it from Kuala Lumpur. That's where he'd first made contact with the UN High Commissioner for Refugees. The relevant offices there had records of his claim for asylum. The topsoil of the paper trail enabled reporters to reassemble his route. He hadn't followed the lead of so many others, down to Basra by car, smuggled through Iran, dropped off somewhere in Pakistan and forced to head for Asia on foot. Apparently he said he'd left Iraq from Um Qasr. That was the port, south of Basra, where he'd chanced a ride on a merchant ship that took him through the Persian Gulf and gave him passage to Karachi. Somehow he'd journeyed overland from there to the east of India. Too crowded, too dangerous, to risk running through the heart of the country. First he'd crossed and re-crossed the border with Pakistan all the way to Lahore. Then he'd roamed the province of Punjab, followed the Ganges into Uttar Pradesh, and held to the edge of the Himalayas the entire length of Nepal. Mostly on foot, I imagine. Mostly at night, keeping to backroads, passing through villages that fell silent at sundown. The distant lowing of tigers. The quibbles of macaques in the trees. Sometimes he'd speed up, stowing away in trucks or on freight trains, but only when he had the strength to risk it and the luck for the risk to pay off. Eventually he must have stumbled out into the Siliguri Corridor. Bhutan to the north, Bangladesh to the south. He'd pressed on to the east, to the hinterlands of Myanmar, then he'd managed to hop the border into Chiang Rai in the north of Thailand.

That was apparently where he'd first been met by people smugglers. A crude network swept him south over the Golok River and into Malaysia. There he made himself known to the authorities. He volunteered his details, his name and nationality, and he gave the bare bones of his story in exchange for food, a wash, a bed beneath a roof. But everyone who read his story in the aftermath of his crime knew exactly what he couldn't have known while he was living through it. Kuala Lumpur was a holding pen. The authorities had no interest in him and no resources to process his claim for asylum. His story wouldn't get him anywhere. Once he'd told it, it would halt. His papers, duly submitted, would be left to languish in a drawer somewhere. The system had screeched to a standstill and so had he. Official records said that upwards of one hundred thousand were still awaiting processing, and tens of thousands of other arrivals hadn't even registered. Reports in the press told stories of people wasting their lives in limbo, waiting decades for responses to their claims, twenty or thirty years begging on the streets, vulnerable to attack and exploitation and at the mercy of the elements as much as the whims of enigmatic powers. Who would countenance any of that if they had a chance to change their fortunes? Who would not go to formidable lengths to regain control of their life? Why would Imran bin Musa wait out the end of his quandary? The only way things would start moving again was if he took to his feet.

He lingered in Kuala Lumpur for a little shy of a year. His name appeared in the records of various charities and NGOs. He'd made enquiries into how to appeal the stalling of his case, how to expedite the processing. When nothing worked, he sought out the last people who'd been able to help him get from one place to another. They were there for anyone determined to find them, underground but always on the lookout for a catch. That's how Imran bin Musa ended up as contraband on a trawler, and that's how, at dawn one summer's day, he fell into the hands of police on a beach in North Sumatra. What would a poor and terrified young man from the rubble of Fallujah have made of the fructuous forests, the pebbled beaches, the indigo waters of equatorial Asia? Or would these wonders have failed to awe him after everything he must have seen on the journey that took him there?

I speared the snow with the shovel, jammed the blade in deep. The shaft stuck straight up from the powder. I'd barely cleared enough to be able to see, over the cusp of a mound, the edge of the nearby road. The blood in my feet felt as if it had frozen. My neck and my deltoids stung and my vision warbled. To force myself to focus I ventured calculations. Karachi to Chiang Rai via Lahore and Nepal, and through Myanmar, had to be something like three thousand miles. Hoofing it at three miles an hour, a thousand hours in total, walking maybe ten hours a day, added up to more than three months living wholly biologically, reducing oneself to an organism, seeking only food and shelter and basic security and answering only the demands of the body. I couldn't conceive of the ache of all that. My own body wasn't big enough, didn't have the range of experience to be truly sympathetic. I leant against the shovel and wanted to punish myself, to scourge my energies far in excess of their capacities, in order to better know bin Musa's baseline readiness to face whatever was lying in wait for him. And his currency? When he needed help to move forward, not even from place to place but just from moment to moment, how did he offer payment? His few belongings? Theft? Favours? Submitting to rape? What more?

I wasn't visited by some epiphany there in the snow, some revelatory understanding of how dramatically my difficulties paled in comparison to his. I felt the difference between us before I knew the details of his life. I felt it more profoundly as I read about him at length in the early hours. Just the fact that I could read about him, that his story was proffered to people like me to consume without harm, to be made aware of events in lieu of living through them, was in itself proof of the inequality between us. It was also a reminder that, when it came to our currencies, our ways of paying for the indignities we had to go through, I was and would always be in debt to someone in his position.

Worse than his thwarted escape, however, was the repeat of what he'd faced in Malaysia. Arrested in Indonesia. Handcuffed, conveyed to a precinct prison, transferred to immigration authorities. Delivered again to the UNHCR. Ordered again to tell his story. Compelled again to lodge a claim for asylum and then cut adrift and abandoned, again, in purgatory. Relocated to a processing centre in Medan. No choice but to wait there for his claim to be evaluated. Could take years. Maybe decades. Might never happen at all. The centre was big enough to house one hundred people. The authorities had crammed in more than four hundred so far. Medan was where people seen as problems were dispatched to disappear. Call it a monument to the fact that there's nothing innate about a person's existence. It's not a truth in the world, it's not something you possess. It's a creation of other people with the discretion to confer it on whomever they please or revoke it whenever they wish. If they don't want you to exist, you won't. You may be a material creature but you might as well be empty air. Medan was bursting with so much human vapour.

The authorities demolished all the bedroom walls. The inmates slept in bunks in an enormous communal space. Everyone had to share mattresses, two detainees per bed. In monsoon the rainfall caused the groundwater to rise. Flooding soaked the mattresses and swelled the walls, clogged the gutters, left splodges and fractals of mould and mildew in its wake. Damage to the ceiling forced people to sleep beneath tattered tarpaulins. In this steaming pit of flesh and fluids, dysentery and tuberculosis and malaria stewed. Without a reliable sewerage system, the water supply was tainted by vomit and diarrhoea. You could keep your head down and stay there if you didn't mind gambling with your future, hoping with all your soul that someday someone would see fit to set you free, but even if you were willing to stake your life on that, every day still involved waking up to misery and placing a bet on whether you'd even survive until nightfall. So, again, why wouldn't you run? There wouldn't be a *you* anymore if you didn't try.

I dropped the shovel into the snow and stopped to take a breath. Blazing cheeks and blistered fingers from gripping the handle with woollen gloves. I peeled off the gloves, pressed my hands to my face, wiped sweat from my forehead and drew in the cold, sharp air. With my back to the house I looked over the snowdrifts. I'd barely gouged a pathway through them. When I turned around again I saw myself bend over, hands on knees, to hold the air in and then slowly let it out. Lifting my head a little I could see my reflection once, twice, overlaid, in the double-glazed window of the room intended for my daughter. Through the reflections I could see the bars of the wooden cot I'd stashed away. Through the bars I could see the toys and trinkets I'd piled high. I'd put it all there on our first night back at home. I'd closed the door behind me and hadn't dared return. That room had been a repository for too many dreams to keep count of them all. Now it was only a storage space for the detritus those dreams had become.

Not only dreams, I realised as I hovered at the window. Worries, too. Cares and concerns. I remembered a day at the end of autumn when I'd become suddenly apprehensive. I'd walked out the front door, on my way somewhere, and instantly I realised I hadn't thought of what it would mean to give my daughter a bedroom at the front of the house. Her window would almost look out to the street. What if somebody wanted to snatch her from us? How easy would it be for some stranger to jimmy open the lock and steal off into the night with her? Panic rushed through me, sent my heart into palpitations, speckled my throat with beads of sweat. I asked my wife if we shouldn't swap the two rooms around. She and I could take the front room and give our daughter the room by the forest. A safe little nook, a cosy refuge. My wife pointed out the obvious. My panic was paranoia. We lived in a village of a few hundred people. Everybody knew everyone else and strangers rarely showed up. Nobody would steal a child. I'd just been overcome by a flash of a father's most powerful instincts. Protect and defend, protect and defend. The two commands resounded through me like the tick-tock of a metronome lodged in my solar plexus. Fortify a space for the safety of those who depend on you. I'd received the command from myself, at some level beneath consciousness, and the urgency to act on it had given me a rush.

I reached for the shovel again to clear the snow outside the empty bedroom. From Francis James Child, somewhere in his songs, I'd heard tell of a man who'd crept into the nursery of an infant boy and bled him dry. I'd heard it first, in fact, on an antique recording, an old man's voice crooning ballad ninety-three. The voice cracked and fractured as it reached for the high notes. The recording popped and fizzed with the sensuous flaws of vinyl. *The doors were all bolted—and the windows all pinned*, sang the man,

except one
little window
where Long Lankin
crept in …

He is a fiend, this man, Long Lankin, and a shapeshifter too. In variants of the song he is known instead as Bold Lambkin or Balankin, or Bloody Rankin, Bald Lantin, Broad Limkin, False Lammilankin, Cruel Lincoln. But, in every version, he is known to the lord and lady of the manor as a hobgoblin to be cautious of. Disaster strikes when the lord's business takes him to a distant town. Before he leaves he warns his wife of the dangers that surround their home, dangers concealed and camouflaged beneath the material surfaces of the world. *Said the lord to his lady—as he mounted his horse*, we're told,

Beware of Long Lankin,
who lies in the moss.
Said the lord to his lady,
as he rode on away,
Beware of Long Lankin,
who hides in the hay.

He orders his wife to bolt the doors and make sure all the windows are locked. He orders her to secure their manor *and leave not a hole for a mouse to creep in.* But then, of course, she forgets to latch the window beside which their son lies asleep, and Lankin seizes his chance to turn his malice upon the boy. *He pricked him*, writes Child,

and he pricked him,
all over
with a pin,
and he held out a basin
for the blood to run in …

A dreadful tale, a hideous image, but one with a sentiment I understood in my bones. I couldn't deny it. Lord Weary was the name of the dead boy's father. His absence was a warning to fathers everywhere, even to fathers centuries later. Not that being beside a child is enough on its own to guarantee safety. You can fail to answer your instincts without even knowing it, fully convinced you're doing exactly what you're bound to do.

I pressed on along the edge of the house, where a gritted path lay buried under snow, and I took to demolishing the banks against the stonewall foundations. The shovel chuffed softly into the finer stuff, scraped against the wall each time I compacted what I'd built up. In other versions of the story of Long Lankin, the villain had started out as a mason of enviable repute. *Lankin was a mason good—as ever built with stone*, it's said. *He built Lord Weary's castle—but payment got he none.* But the truth is that Lankin had been on my mind all day, leaping into my thoughts when I heard the news of Imran bin Musa in the early hours. As the tune played out in my mind again, bin Musa's face was the one I saw. Heir to Long Lankin's bloodlust, perhaps, but heir to his pain as well. Beyond his escape from Medan, easy enough under cover of night, he'd set out on the journey that would take him to Australia.

Nobody had yet reported the details of this part of his story, but I'd heard enough in outline to guess what he'd gone through. A blindfold. A place beneath a canvas tarp in the cab of a flatbed truck. A beach with softly crashing waves, far from the bustle of the docks on a port. A man speaking stilted English. A dozen other voices, a dozen other men with blindfolds, a dozen terrified faces when the blindfolds are removed. A dinghy without a motor, only a pair of oars. A journey over the waters to another boat offshore. A bigger boat with a mast and rigging, a winch, a net, a sputtering engine, the choke of diesel fumes. A carrying capacity of fifty. A hundred wayfarers on board, men and women and children from Sudan and Eritrea, from Syria and Yemen, from Iran and Turkmenistan and Afghanistan and Sri Lanka. A hundred stories every bit as harrowing as bin Musa's. An audience in the darkness, silently watching the new arrivals disembark the dinghy. A wooden gangway and a ladder. A tentative step, careful not to slip, then a foot and then two feet upon a firmer surface. A hush throughout the crowd as the dinghy disappears. A cry of gulls overhead, a chortling as propellers chop into the waves. A voyage to a place that everyone knows not all will see. A journey towards a life that some on board will never live.

At the corner of the house I stopped again and looked over the path I'd made. I'd cleared the snow outside the front bedroom and the living room. The concavity, soft at the sides but hard at the base, stretched away to my right. To my left was the edge of the forest, the yew, the trees outside our bedroom, and, nearer to me, the glass door to the kitchen and the window above the sink. I looked through my own faint reflection. I could see my wife inside. I guessed she'd been woken by the scrapes against the wall. She sat at the kitchen table with her back to me and held her head in her hands. I guessed the letter from the authorities lay on the table in front of her. Her shoulders made stuttering movements. She looked as if she was holding herself to try to keep from breaking apart. I leant the shovel against the wall and stepped back into the snow. Nothing to do but stand there and watch her. Nothing to feel, I realised, but the obligation to witness. Not in the same way I'd felt obliged in hospital, during the delivery. Not as a way of supporting her, connecting with her, extending part of my self into her sphere. Just because she was there, alone, and I was in a position to see. Surveying your surroundings, beholding all things and all people in your presence as if they are distant objects: is there a word for that state of mind?

Probably the boat would've been at sea for just over a week. Each day, one third of the passengers would've received a ration of food. Usually only a handful of rice, boiled before the boat left the dock and hardened into a solid mass. Probably the potable water would've run out halfway to Christmas Island. Probably a few of the children would have dehydrated and died. The elderly and the ill as well. They would have received what officials referred to as burials at sea, placed in hessian sacks and cast into the churning wake of the boat. For a week or more there would have been nothing but water and sun and shocking blue sky. Perhaps an unfamiliar bird, squealing overhead, and high above it the white contrails of planes bound for distant parts of the world. Then, at last, someone would recognise land. On the horizon, a strip of green. Next, of course, someone would see a naval frigate. A dull grey giant with a huge white number painted on its hull. The diesel engine would be cut. Patrol boats would descend from the sides, plashing into the water with officers on board.

In a different time, under a later policy, that frigate would have towed the boat all the way back to its port of departure. For Imran bin Musa, however, the boats that sped towards him must have brought some slight relief. They'd ease up alongside the vessel he'd boarded. They'd have space enough to accommodate the weak and weary. They'd take people to safety, to shore, to solid land. Brilliant golden sand, rippling in the heat haze. Clumps of scrub and beach grass, the sweet smell of a salt water breeze. Probably Imran bin Musa suspected what he was in for. Months more detention, bunks and inedible food, constant sweat, overcrowding, another indefinite wait for his claim for asylum to be processed. But probably, too, he felt something upon reaching Australian territory that he hadn't felt on any other soil he'd trudged across. Too optimistic to call it hope. Call it instead a new attunement to possibility. Call it a new sense that anything at all could happen now. Not the old, persistent worry that one wrong move could set off any chain reaction of horrors. Something different. A new arc in the story he was living. An arc whose direction he couldn't foresee even though he had to hope it would lead to a resolution.

What came to light overnight was that the authorities at Christmas Island weren't ultimately responsible for the direction he'd ended up taking, the course that led him to violence. Soon after his detainment, Imran bin Musa was transferred to Nauru. Apparently he met a woman there. None of the news reports named her. All of them suggested she'd been in detention for some time. I took up the shovel once more. I took a step forward, towards the window, towards my wife with her back to me, and with the shovel in hand I started clearing the last of the powder from the side of the house. I flung it about with abandon. I battered it with the blade, smashed it down, smacked it firm, then lifted the compacted segments high and swished them to the side of the path. I flailed about with scattershot motions, desperate just to end the ache, random, haphazard, wayward with all the confusion of a man bereft of an object on which to concentrate his rage.

The shovel broke into the next layer of snow with a sound like shredding canvas. My knees and back sang out as I bent to shuffle the snow onto the blade. I hauled it aside with a pining in my shoulders and the grate of sandpaper in my swelling lungs. Sweat all over my body released an odour that wafted up through the collar of my jacket. Still, I knew, I'd have to keep going. Back along the path I'd cleared in the powder, back to the corner and around the front of the house to continue scraping away. I broke into the snow again and heaved.

I'd taken my place at the laptop the previous night, intending to read over what I'd written about my wife. I didn't doubt that her complaints were valid. I knew she was right. I just needed to see for myself the granular details of my unfairness towards her. But the words on the screen began to warp. I couldn't concentrate enough to let them hold their shapes. An atmospheric tension kept me wired. Something out there, far away, was fast approaching. I could smell it like a distant storm. Something about Imran bin Musa. There was a vacuum somewhere in the stories I'd read about him and I could hear something on its way to rush in and fill the space. The mystery. Not why he did what he'd done, as if he'd hoped his violence would help him achieve certain ends, but why he'd had the notion that he should do something like it, something so inexplicable. Not a motive, not a rationale, not a cause for his crime. The *other* why, the subterranean why. The cause for the state of mind that made his crime a possibility. The source of his rage. The push.

Whatever it was, there had been a sharp drop in the likelihood that the cause could be attributed to some ideology. At one in the morning in Switzerland, the Australian papers reported that the government had retracted its bid to charge bin Musa under the anti-terrorism laws. So the authorities knew he wasn't a terrorist. They must have known something else they weren't sharing. They must have known, too, that some third party was preparing to go public with something big, something seditious, something that would explode in the faces of the people in charge if they didn't start running from the blast radius.

It wouldn't be true to say that I withheld judgment on bin Musa just because I wanted to. The truth is that when I looked at what I knew of his life, he'd earnt the right to circumspection; he warranted second thoughts. He hadn't just gone through more suffering than I had. He'd gone through a bigger world. But having travelled so far, seen so much, experienced so many things that I couldn't convincingly imagine, wasn't it the case that he'd become a man who could survive almost anything? What final provocation, worse than his years in the wilderness, could have driven him to his crime? Media voices were asking how he could have done it, of course, but they were asking rhetorically, posing the question to express their horror, rather than seriously considering how he came to be capable of it. If he could endure everything he must've encountered between Iraq and Australia, what comparative pettiness, what suburban irritant, pushed him past his limits?

An hour later the Fairfax papers flagged a scoop. Then they plastered Imran bin Musa's face across the top of their websites and replaced their day-old question, WHAT IS HIS STORY?, with something subtly different. This time they asked: WHO IS THIS MAN?

The man turned out to be a father. There had been hints of this beforehand. As soon as his name became public there were journalists from all over the country on the hunt for his home, for any loose-lipped friends and family, for any neighbours willing to sketch a picture of his daily life. A council housing tower, an old lady interviewed halfway up the stairwell, a group of young blokes playing football in the parking lot. Yes, yes, everyone who lived there knew who he was. They'd seen him around, they said, and they'd seen the girl as well. So he was known to have a daughter. She was six, maybe seven years old. Her presence thickened the textures of his story. He'd made his way to Christmas Island by himself. He'd been sent to Nauru by himself after that. Strangers were his only company, no relations by blood or marriage. With his claim for asylum approved, he'd been in Australia for only five years. How could he have a daughter who was older than his freedom?

My body whined in particular places where the pain was so fine-tuned that it stole my attention from the general discomfort. The skin around my navel stretched and strained each time I bent at the waist. The ligaments at the back of my neck and the muscles in my throat and jaw pulled taut, agitating beneath my skin as if trying to split me open. I made a new effort to build the rhythm I should've built at the start. Bend, dig, dispose. Repeat.

I couldn't picture the woman's face. I couldn't bring myself to do it. I don't mean that in an ethical sense. I didn't feel I'd be crossing a line if I tried to imagine her and describe her features. What I mean is I didn't know enough about her to describe her in a way that would touch on anything truthful. Right from the broadest facts of her appearance, like whether she was Syrian or Somali, or Sri Lankan or something else entirely, down to finer points like whether or not she wore a headscarf, whether she was slim or plump, whether she looked her age or younger or as if she'd burned through a lifetime during her years in detention. All I could picture, really, was a pair of wide, brown eyes, eyes that projected an unbridled eagerness and hunger for an embrace. But I knew they didn't belong to her. They couldn't be the eyes of the woman Imran bin Musa met when he arrived on Nauru. They were the eyes of my wife on the day I first saw her. Nothing special about the way we met. A pub that doesn't exist anymore, lots of unfamiliar faces, loud live music and inaudible conversation. Thousands of couples, maybe millions, would have met this way. But her eyes were exceptional. They had to do the work of attraction that speech couldn't handle in such a hectic place. The eyes I saw in my mind could not have belonged to anyone else. They were all I could fully recall from our earliest moments together without having been lost to the witherings of memory. Those eyes and the way they looked at me, *saw* me, urged me to reveal my self to her.

She'd risen from the kitchen table and disappeared into the house. I turned the corner and started moving back along the front wall, towards our bedroom beside the forest.

Of course I could still remember what happened after we met. We slept together that first night. I took her back to where I was staying. But I only remember the essence of the facts. The years have dimmed the specifics. My next clear memory is of a doubling of daylight, then a hand, then a breath. I'd been renting a room in a boarding house in Sydney's inner west. I woke before she did, felt her warmth beside me, watched her for a while. She slept on her stomach, oblivious to my presence, in the bed I'd paid an extortionate rate to use as my own even though I could in no way think of it as mine. On the adjacent wall, my landlady had hung an old oval mirror. The curtains that covered the window beside the bedhead fell open slightly. A shaft of sunlight shone through the gap and extended a line along the wall. When it hit the mirror it glanced off at an angle and lay across the sleeping woman's back. I rose, moved slowly, tried not to disturb her, placed my feet on the floor and picked my way around her. I stood beside her, still dazed from waking, and with care I let my hand rest on her back and felt her breath. I felt her breath move through her. I felt it make her large before she rushed it back out and reduced herself again.

There's no word for what struck me as I stood there. You can't call it love. It wasn't that. Beneath my fingertips lay a person, a human being, fully herself, fully her own, with an existence independent of my care and my control. Whatever relationship we'd just struck up could end in an instant, as soon as she woke, or it could last a lifetime. Nothing of what would happen was really up to me. What is the word for the feeling that follows awareness of facts like those? The future had a horizon, but within that horizon anything and everything now seemed possible. I had no way of knowing what would happen to me, to us, when her eyelids fluttered open, when she returned to herself, and I bathed in the radiance of the mystery. I felt in contact with the pith of something impossibly larger than even my largest conception of who I might be. But would she hate to find me writing things like this? Even when it's about her, it's about me. I can't escape my own orbit.

And Imran bin Musa? And the woman he met on Nauru? There's no obscuring the filth and terror of that place. An island made from seagull shit. A defunct sports stadium converted into makeshift housing for desperate arrivals. Not enough fresh water and not enough shelter for everyone inside the gates. Designated sectors for habitation, hygiene, recreation, food consumption. Humid air and a horrid stench trapped in buildings that never admitted a breeze. First of all, among the people, endemic loss of short-term memory, typical of solitary confinement. Then theft, abuse, rampant rape and self-harm. Sedatives turned out to be the government's solution of choice. Daily doses of sleeping pills. Zombies queued up at the canteen after mealtime to receive the handful of capsules that would become their only means of coping with perpetual incarceration. As the efficacy diminished, week by week, the medical ward became overburdened. It had been designed and funded to deal only with things like tropical rashes and insect bites. Now it was bombarded with hunger strikes, attempts at hanging, nooses fashioned from bedsheets, overdoses of medication, skulls smashed repeatedly against walls and barricades. These are the actions of people whose futures have been curtailed, cut away from a present of indefinite inertia. When those two bodies came together, flesh against flesh, breath intermingling, was their union really just another way of escaping the grinding stasis of their days? Was it only impulsive, an opportune means of release, a tribute to bodily instinct in a moment of shared desperation? It seemed impossible to me that two total strangers could meet one another in a place like that, that cesspit, that chamber of horrors with so many other tormented souls crammed in all around them, and bring into being a relationship of intimacy and compassion. The environment would prohibit such a thing. Animal hunger and total despair had to be what drove them together.

So the girl he ended up raising was conceived behind razor wire. News reports linked to academic studies with grotesque statistical findings. At about the time the girl was born, eight hundred children were held in offshore detention and almost a quarter of them were there on Nauru. Researchers who arrived to observe them found that none of them referred to one another by name. Even among themselves they were known by the numbers the authorities had assigned them. Three letters, three digits: FLN661, JDK239, alphanumeric codes deprived of selfhood. Worse than that, most of the children had stopped speaking, or else they'd never learnt to properly speak in the first place. They wet their beds as a matter of routine. They made no eye contact with the outsiders and rarely with one another. Each of them retreated, recoiled from the world, to huddle ever deeper inside an invisible chrysalis. Many of them retreated for good, irrevocably abandoning their lot. The authorities had recorded more than one hundred cases of attempted suicide by children who hadn't yet reached their teenage years. This was the sort of childhood faced by the daughter of Imran bin Musa. This was what she spent her first two years around. I couldn't believe it was something he would have wished for a child. I couldn't see her conception as anything other than accidental. To think that it might have been intentional was more than I could allow.

At the window of the second bedroom I stopped again and saw myself in double. This was the life I wanted, in my own safe and unimaginative way. A life of walls and windows, of solid domesticity. Having it, now, fed my sense of propriety, my earnt right to live as unexceptionally as I pleased amid my basic creature comforts. Walls and windows, food in the fridge, a sofa, a bed, a laptop. I was the kind of man for whom there was no question about whether I would or wouldn't watch the birth of my child. Many men still don't. My father didn't, nor my father-in-law. But there were things I never doubted of myself. I would secure a patch of earth for my dependents, a place to live and a career with a good chance of prolonging my fortunes. My life would be the foundation upon which they could build theirs as they chose, and so of course I would be there to watch the growth of the family for whom I had prepared the ground. That was the way it would happen. From the very beginning, as we made our early plans, my wife and I had agreed this much and surrounded ourselves with the structures to make it so.

Holding the shovel upright with one hand, I took my free hand to my throat and unwound my scarf and slung it over my shoulder. Sonograms. Maybe amniocentesis. Checkups and scans in accordance with antenatal protocol. I remembered it all. I'd been there in the hospital with my wife. I'd watched it unfold. I'd honoured my word. The labour, too, and the delivery. Could bin Musa say the same? Had he seen the things I'd seen? Far from being willing, had he been permitted? He wasn't married to that woman. He wasn't related to her by blood. He may not have even been recognised as the father of his child until after the girl arrived screaming into the medical ward. Did he stand with his back to the wall and observe the birth as I did? Did he have a chance to watch contortions wrack the pregnant woman? I plucked the scarf from my shoulder and scrunched it into a ball to toss aside. I wrapped my fingers around the shovel again and felt its weight in my hands. Why did those scenarios spring to mind with question marks attached? Something in my picture of him didn't quite add up. Why did I doubt his willing presence at his daughter's birth? Why did I equivocate on the likelihood of his wanting to see? Because, I suppose, it didn't fit with my sense that he and the woman had been desperate in their contact, so casual and urgent and lost in the moment as to remain otherwise unbound.

I felt the weight of the shovel in my hands but I didn't return the blade to the snow. I stared at my double and tried to think through the scenario by working backwards from what I knew. Imran bin Musa had raised a daughter in a council housing flat at the edge of the airport. He'd been resident there, as her legal guardian, for the last few years of the five he'd been free. On Nauru, he'd been given every imaginable chance to simply abandon her. If he'd wanted to do so, he could've walked away from the woman, pretended they'd never met, denied that he'd fathered her child, and eventually started afresh by himself in Australia. Instead he chose to stay close to the girl. He cared about her enough at least to pivot his new life upon her needs. If he chose to do that for five years straight, five years of single custodianship, why would he not also have chosen to stay close to the woman? Wouldn't he have had to answer his instinct to care for the girl at that time as well? But if he chose to devote his years to the girl from her birth until his arrest, how could it be that he felt only fleeting affection for the woman? Why would he give so much of himself to the offspring of a grubby fling that meant nothing to him besides an outflow of pent-up energy? And if their contact wasn't momentary, if there was a deeper significance to it, if she meant more to him than sex, then what exactly had drawn the two of them together? Authentic attraction? A genuine meeting of minds? Lust that grew into something greater? Sympathy? Tenderness, even love? And what did the girl become for him then? More than a hungry mouth to feed? An embodiment of hope for the future? A focal point for a new sense of purpose beyond himself? Was Imran bin Musa actually capable of feeling things like those? And if he really turned out to be capable of them, not only feeling them flash for an instant but sustaining them for years at a stretch, then how did he become the man who slit the veins of eleven children and two adults with a sawtooth blade? How did he devolve into that creature?

Questions.

I crunched the edge of the shovel into the last of the particles. I twisted it and flung the snow aside and piled it up off the pathway by the window.

The problem with Long Lankin, I realised, wasn't that he wronged Lord Weary in some indiscriminate way. He was a mason of good repute. *He built Lord Weary's castle*, it's said, *but payment got he none*. More than that, he begged his lord to pay him what he was due. *O pay me, Lord Weary*, he cried, *pay me my fee*, but Weary pleaded poor to him because he *maun gang o'er the sea*. But Lankin persisted, *pay me, my lord—O pay me out o' hand*, and still Weary claimed that he couldn't pay up *unless I sell all me land*. Not that that could justify any part of Lankin's crime. But still he built a home for a man who wanted a dwelling to shelter his kin, and the only reason he would have done it was to provide shelter for his own. Rob a man of the chance to do that, to shore up the very elements of his family's well-being, and repercussions are bound to issue from his loss.

WHO IS THIS MAN? The Fairfax broadsheets answered the question at half past three in the morning, just before lunchtime in Australia. Their reports filled some of the gaps in what was known of Imran bin Musa, but that was the least of what they did. They also paired their findings with an uncensored copy of an official document, a letter that bore the insignia of the Government of New South Wales. Much to the ire of a government spokesman, muckraking journalists had obtained it by means they wouldn't reveal.

Early November the previous year. Almost time to knock off work. The mercury had reached new heights. Heatwaves in the middle of spring are impossible to prepare for. You haven't had time to acclimatise and you don't appreciate the force of the blast until it hits. Thirty-eight, thirty-nine degrees in inner Sydney, a minimum of forty and inching even higher around the suburban belt. That's the kind of heat with the power to debilitate. It's the kind that lacerates and awakens the worst in people. You can't move under the weight of the sun. You persist through the heat by riding it out and pretending it can't stop you.

Imran bin Musa had an appointment to make at four o'clock. He'd applied for a job and he'd been offered an interview. For nearly five years he'd worked in Randwick, carrying out maintenance and janitorial duties at that day-care centre. It didn't offer enough hours and didn't bring in enough money to afford him a better life. It gave him only subsistence wages that locked him into council housing for the foreseeable future. Why not shoot for something better? More prestige, more cash. Nothing wrong with ambition. He'd been a teacher in Iraq. He figured he could at least land new work as a teacher's assistant. Now a school in Liverpool had asked him to come in for a chat. The problem was that the panel wanted to see him after the school day had ended. His daughter's day-care finished at three and he didn't have anyone who could take her off his hands.

Before he picked her up he bought an overpriced bottle of water from a convenience store. He promised that once they arrived in Liverpool he'd only be gone half an hour, forty-five minutes at most, and he'd keep the windows down a little so she could have some air. But he couldn't find a car park in the shade. He also didn't have any way of filtering the glare or covering the windows. Then to be sure that she'd be safe inside the car, he locked the doors before he rushed off in an effort to better their lives.

The letter put the outcome very plainly. It came from the Department of Health and Human Services. It mentioned that an incident had occurred on 6 November. It made reference to a written complaint that Imran bin Musa had filed the following day. It stated that authorities within the department had recently completed an inquiry into the claims he made; that the inquiry had also reviewed the claims and counter-claims made by officials obliged to act in accordance with departmental policies, guidelines and best practice; and that the findings of the inquiry affirmed the validity of the following three points originally submitted by senior departmental staff:

First, that Imran bin Musa had purposefully and of his own volition locked his daughter inside a vehicle belonging to him, significantly imperilling the health and wellbeing of the child at a time when the temperature stood at slightly over forty degrees Celsius;

Second, that the condition of the child in the car had been reported to police and to staff at the Department of Health and Human Services; that the authorities had arrived at the car and supervised the child in the absence of her father; and that their intervention warranted a subsequent investigation of Imran bin Musa's accommodation arrangements and ability to provide for the health and wellbeing of the child at their place of abode;

Third, that this investigation found Imran bin Musa's circumstances insufficient to guarantee the health and wellbeing of the child, and that custody over the child ought therefore to be transferred immediately to the Government of New South Wales under its remit and obligation to safeguard vulnerable children as peremptory wards of the state.

Did the authorities respond in the right way? Maybe. Maybe he really couldn't take care of his daughter adequately. Does it change things to learn that he'd never before had a complaint against him? Or that his complaint against the authorities was concluded and dismissed without any means of appeal? Does it change things to acknowledge the double standard? I mean the allegation, on the part of the state, that by taking steps to improve his situation, this man was putting his daughter's wellbeing at greater risk than the state itself had done when it kept her imprisoned on a faraway island from the day of her birth.

So the girl was removed from his care. Just for a while at first. He'd finished his interview at the school, slipped through the gates and crossed the road, only to find a spray of shattered glass around his car and the vehicle obscured by a crowd of suits and uniforms. There must have been awkward conversations. Details requested, scratched onto notepads. Someone acting as the voice of concern, someone else to ensure that everyone followed protocol. Someone to break the news to the father, he couldn't take his daughter home, she'd need to go along with so-and-so. Also those detained as witnesses, the first passersby to glimpse the girl through the window, the woman who'd tried to speak to her, the man who'd phoned the police, the officers who'd smashed the window to gain access to the car. Someone supportive, too, with appropriate credentials, to help the girl's father keep himself together when he understood what they meant to do. Each of them raising a hand to their brow to shield their eyes from the force of the sun. They promised an expedient process.

The girl would be kept in care for only a couple of days. In the meantime they'd arrange for someone to inspect the flat the father shared with her. He would've been ordered to hand his keys to one of the constables. He wouldn't have been permitted to move to take the girl into his arms. Someone else's hands would have reached for hers. Someone else would have had to find a language and a tone to let her know what would happen to her, to tell her she needn't be afraid even though she must have been.

Questions, then. Questions about the future that awaited them. No, he couldn't accompany her to wherever she was going. No, she couldn't go with him to gather some belongings from home. He'd have to return to an empty flat, a flat in which his whole life had once again entered a state of always pending progress. Pending potential charges, pending investigation, pending the conclusions and recommendations of the inspectors. Then the devastating outcome. The imposition of systemic controls to keep him from his daughter. The struggle to understand exactly what was happening. The inability to imagine how the girl might be living, how she'd physically inhabit a place he wasn't able to picture, surrounded by sights and smells and sounds he couldn't anticipate, in the company of people whose faces he'd never seen, who existed for him only as names on official documentation.

What did he do when left to himself? Did he pace? Did he wring his hands? Did he cry? Did he try to resist? Muscles tensed, a palm cupped over his mouth. Could he sleep? Could he eat? He didn't stop going to work, I know that. One of the newest reports included quotes from his senior colleagues. None of them had noticed anything strange in his behaviour. No visible change in his habits. No idea that something extraordinary had riven his life outside the daycare centre. My guess is that he kept his head down on the advice of his lawyer. He had to have consulted one in order to appeal the actions of the state. He filed his letter of appeal within two weeks of the inspection of his home, within two days of receiving notice of the outcome. In mid-December, three weeks further on, probably taking shape as some departmental lackey's final item of business before the start of the holidays, a copy of the letter that now appeared online was sent to Imran bin Musa. With his workplace closed for a week he had time to stew over the letter's implications. At some point he had the notion to procure the knife, the thought that he should hold on to it. Then he returned to his duties in the new year and did what he did to bring himself to public attention. The letter gave his actions a mathematical simplicity. His act of murder, no longer an act of terrorism, looked like nothing more complex than a deranged quid pro quo, an awful distortion of archaic justice that upped the eye-to-eye ratio from parity to more than ten-to-one.

At maybe four in the morning I sank in front of the laptop and watched connections emerge between the scattered dots. Imran bin Musa made sense. He didn't stand shrouded in mystery. I could draw a line directly from his history in Iraq, in South-East Asia, on Christmas Island and Nauru, to his actions at the day-care centre. It passed through his resettlement in Australia, his attempt to improve his circumstances, his simple predicament and his bad luck, a lack of childcare on a freakishly hot day, and it extended from there to his altercations with the state and the implacable bureaucracy. That's when Long Lankin first sprang to mind. I heard very faintly the feeble, fractured voice of the man whose rendition I most admire. *Lankin was a mason good—as ever built with stone*, he crooned. *He built Lord Weary's castle—but payment got he none.* He'd done what he was supposed to do to ensure the safety of his family. He'd cleared the hurdles obstructing his way, exactly as he'd been ordered, but when he didn't receive his dues he decided to take them as he saw fit instead of sanctioning the debt. All he wanted was what belonged to him by right. Failing that, it seems, he'd exact a brutal recompense, a wrong that would make him feel less alone in his loss even if it couldn't offset the wrong that riled him.

But who could sit there as I'd been sitting there, deep in thought, exhausted, breathing life into the outline of a man imprisoned on the far side of the planet, without making an effort to do the same for the woman in bed on the other side of a nearby door? The screen went dim with disuse and sat me before myself again. Understanding? Misunderstanding? I'd layered the news headlines over the top of the document I'd written, but I didn't need to see my words to know that what I'd written had nothing to do with understanding. I hadn't failed to understand why she'd done what she'd done, why she wanted what she wanted from me now. I'd declined to admit it. I'd felt it growing between us and I'd flatly refused to give it words. Easy to see why. With the shovel I scraped aside the remnants of the snow, the final sheet of fragmented particles, and exposed the murky ice that covered the underlying pavement. I'd refused because I couldn't reconcile her story with my own. I couldn't let her have what she wanted and also keep hold of what I felt I had to. There was no way around it. I lanced the ice with the blade of the shovel, chipping its surface once, twice, then split it open with the third blow. Fissures shot out from the wound, cracks like fault lines beneath my feet. Well, then. I looked up from the window, saw myself in the glass, and squinted through the tinting to see my daughter at play in the bedroom behind it.

I'd seen her in the morning's early hours. I'd reached for the urn of ashes, fingertips scuffing the matte, and I'd seen its surface reflect her form in the empty space behind me. I froze with arm outstretched, didn't dare let the urn escape my touch. She sat on the sofa, kicking her heels, with an open book in her lap and all her attention devoted to it. Six or maybe seven years old. A tomboy, a ragamuffin. Her hair hung past her shoulders and a fringe obscured her eyes. She swung her legs to a steady rhythm, bopping a foot against the sofa and waiting a beat or two before she bopped the other. I wanted to turn around and go to her and touch her again. I wanted to toss her in the air to hear her delighted squeal, I wanted to nuzzle her neck to make her giggle. That admission sounds silly, I know, but there she was in the room with me and all I wanted to do were all the things a father does, the playful slapstick things that really only a father can do. So I turned. She disappeared. Now, though, she'd come back and I stood still in the snow and watched her.

She crept into the empty room, the room that would have been hers if she'd lived, and sat herself in front of a chest of drawers. The cot I'd stored in there was gone. The toys, the clothes, the blankets, everything. The colours had been spruced up. The space seemed brighter now. The girl rolled open the bottom drawer and began removing the clothes inside. Skirts and singlets, socks and underwear, shirts and trousers, all of them belonging to her. I'd never seen any of them before. They materialised at her touch. She spread them out around her, each item placed in a pile according to its type. I watched her in fascination. I couldn't see any purpose to what she was doing. She just went about it, patiently and methodically, without having noticed me through the window. She immersed herself in her own little world and carefully surrounded herself with objects drawn from nowhere, revelling in their tactility. She fondled zippers and buttons and she flicked at baubles and tassels. She ran her nails across a rough patch of velcro. She traced the line of a hem, the ruffles of a tutu. Everything I saw her touch, like everything I saw in her, had taken a form I felt I could contact through my skin. Sewn or stitched together, knitted or crocheted or woven, or born as a creature of flesh and blood, brought into being thread by thread, spool by spool of substance, cells and particles harnessed one to the next, everything I could see on the other side of that pane of glass seemed to me like no illusion but very definitely an assemblage of real, solid matter that occupied real, identifiable co-ordinate points in three dimensions. It looked like a moment plucked from a life that struck me as real in all respects, incontrovertibly so, even though I knew for sure I wasn't living it.

I took up the shovel once more and shot it into the ice, splitting off chips and chunks that skidded over the surface of what remained intact. I took it up and shot it down and shattered even more, busting apart the solid block that clung hard to the path. I stomped to the side, away from the breakage, and took up the shovel and shot it down again and again. I broke the ice the way you'd assault a tract of soil to gouge out holes for fence posts, and steadily I worked my way back down the path to the corner of the house and around to the kitchen window. When I'd seen my wife there before, I remembered, she'd had the urn beside her at the kitchen table. Her trouble was that the ashes inside didn't show her the wonders they'd been showing me. Actually her trouble was that even if they did show her wonders, she'd never be able to buy into them. She'd put up a resistance. She'd refuse to see anything plausible in a child spirited up from a place subsumed by snow. Her element had always been water. Salt water warmed by sunshine, gushing through rock pools with crystalline clarity, swishing back and forth across vast stretches of sand. That's why she wanted to take the ashes home. Not to release herself from her grief. She wanted the visions I'd already received but she felt she couldn't have them, couldn't believe in their authenticity, if the child she saw was one who she knew had never beheld the sea.

Coming around the corner, though, I stopped. Shovel raised, poised to strike ice, I seized up when I glanced at the house. Again I saw my wife with her back to me. The difference this time was that I found her outside. The difference was that she stood beneath the branches of the yew. The door to the kitchen was open on its hinges. The warmth from inside the house became a ribbon of silver as it met the frigid air. My wife wore a long black cloak that hung to the backs of her knees. She kept her hands plunged deep in its pockets. She'd placed her feet somewhere close to where the grave would have been, at the base of that massive trunk, and she bent her head as if in prayer. Because I'd stopped breaking the ice she must have known I was there behind her, but she didn't acknowledge my presence. She just stood in silence, breathing in, breathing out. The fabric across her back moved out and in, out and in, with each breath taken and released. The back of her cloak. That's all she offered. She kept her back to me. I wanted more than anything else to rest my hand upon her. I wanted to feel her breath move through her again. But I couldn't. How could I have done it? I cast the shovel aside and left her, stumbling over the shards of ice along the path. When I came to the door I turned the handle and rushed inside, and I felt the warmth of the house bombard me with the heat of a summer's day.

The more thorough report on Imran bin Musa had hit the news at seven. I'd almost fallen asleep at the table only to be jerked awake by a flash, a banner proclaiming a breaking story, on one of the broadsheet websites. Audiences in Australia would've been ready to head home from work. Many would've already taken to the pub, maybe passing through before jumping on a bus or train, and many others would've been raiding the kitchen cupboards for dinner.

The woman from Nauru had a voice. Her name had been withheld for her protection, and she hadn't given consent for photographs to be taken, but she'd spoken to someone, she'd shared her story, because she'd felt the need to set the record straight. Against all expectations, she lived in the dust north of Adelaide. I'd figured she'd remained in detention after bin Musa's release, right up to the present. I mean I'd leapt to that assumption and thought nothing more of it. Now I figured that some pavement-pounding journalist had tracked her down and knocked on her door. I was wrong to think that, too. She'd reached out to the press. She wanted the country to know the man she knew, not the monster he'd become. She wanted her daughter to be able to look back, in years to come, and know that her father *was* a man and not the villain people would remember.

She'd been released eight months after Imran, she said. Initially she'd joined him in Sydney, in a two-bedroom, ground-floor council flat in Waterloo, and they'd tried their best to make things work and honestly build a life together. She stayed home to raise their daughter while he went off to his job. So far, so average. Soon, however, trouble arrived. A bullet in the letterbox. Graffiti on the door. Strange sounds at night, someone hopping the backyard fence, sensor lights blinking on in the early hours. They reported it all to the police. Then one evening a window shattered and a Molotov cocktail came flaming inside. By some miracle it didn't burst. It landed, making a gentle whump, on the thick brown carpet on their living-room floor. Without a thought, without hesitation, Imran bin Musa snatched it up and hurled it back into the darkness. It broke open on the lawn. A slick of fire flowed like liquid across the ground and left a char on the grass. The two of them feared the obvious. They'd become the targets of some local with a grudge, someone disgruntled by the presence of refugees in the neighbourhood. Such incidents were known to happen wherever refugees were resettled. But then, as the woman and her daughter went about their days, the situation became more complex and steadily more sinister.

She made overtures to the Muslim community in the area. She thought it wise to solicit support, solidarity. Straightaway, though, she overheard gossip. In conversations with people she knew only in passing, only on a first-name basis, she suffered cutting remarks and a range of implied criticisms. Within a few weeks she understood that she'd become an object of scandal. She was a woman who, it turned out, declined to wear a headscarf. She was known to be raising a child whose father she'd met in detention. She and he hadn't married. Not before conceiving the girl, not after moving in together. The conservatives among their neighbours saw them as pollutants.

They ended up changing address, but their reputation stalked them. Someone who'd lived around the corner knew someone else who knew someone else who lived on the same street as their new place. They moved again, aimed for something more discreet, but their income was painfully low and their options thin on the ground and so the same thing kept happening. The woman came to understand that the problem lay with her. A man with a daughter to raise on his own would have been seen as strange but steadfast, maybe even admirable. A woman with her history would always be looked at askance, viewed at best as a questionable influence, at worst as the bearer of a contagion who risked infecting the girls around her. She decided to put some distance between herself and her family. Only for a while, for the safety of everyone. A support group in South Australia helped her find a job and a flat, a little respite, and, if she wished, a chance to become someone new. But she kept her sights on Sydney. She and Imran agreed, she said, that they'd try again when things had settled down, when he could find a place that would give them room to breathe. That was almost three years ago. He'd been looking for new work, she said, in an effort to escape the mire. He'd been doing it for her as much as for their daughter, for the unity of their family. He loved her, she said. He was a loving man. He proved it with his actions, with his dedication to their future together. More than that, she said, he proved it with his letters.

I hadn't understood the picture at the top of the report. Only now did it make sense. It showed a woman's hand holding the rim of a round wooden table scattered with piles of open envelopes and stacks of notepaper covered in a foreign script. The woman said she'd held on to every letter she'd ever received from Imran. She said she'd received one almost every day they'd been apart. Not the brief notes that a man might dash off in a hurry just to let his lover know he held her in his thoughts. Each of these letters ran to several pages. He wasn't a man who enjoyed writing, she said, but he found he could express himself more clearly in writing than in speech. She claimed he had a flair for the poetry of Arabic, although the monolingual journalist couldn't attest to the truth of that. What could be verified was the volume of his outpourings. An estimate put it at more than three thousand pages. Woozy and sluggish at six in the morning, I tried to do the sums. Three years' absence worked out to more than one thousand days. That gave Imran bin Musa an average output of three pages per day, assuming he sat down to write to the woman every single day they'd been apart.

I scrolled back up to the picture and I paled at what it showed. At the edges of the frame, on the floor around the table, still more missives and packages rose up in hillocks and mounds. The sight of all this made my vision spin. The sheer size of what he'd written. This testament, this towering monument, to the love he felt for that woman. Just the exertion involved in producing all those letters would have been enough to prove the strength of his feelings. But then there was the depth of thought and the emotional energy. Imagine him with pen to paper. It's the end of another exhausting day. He has spent the better part of his hours cleaning up after screaming children, mopping hallways and scrubbing toilets and disposing of bags of rubbish. The remaining hours have been spent caring for his own small child, preparing her dinner and putting her to bed. Now she's asleep, it seems, and darkness has arrived outside the window. He has very few reserves to draw on for further activity. He could as easily slump on the sofa and sleep. Instead he takes care to find the time, or takes care to make it, to sit down with a notepad and pen and concentrate on what he'd say to the woman if she could be there right beside him in the room.

He dedicates his attention fully to the task at hand. First he turns his gaze inwards and attunes himself to the movements of his heart. Then he puzzles over the alchemical process of transmuting his wordless emotions into sentiments he can articulate. Finally he starts to pick out particular words, to lay them down before him and affix them to the paper, and for an hour or two or even longer he lets them flow, lets them ripple into the world through the tip of his pen. He does this day after day, every day without fail, committing himself to the habit in full faith that those words have the power to ensure that the bond connecting him to the woman will not be broken by the distance between their bodies.

Now imagine the journalist she'd approached and invited into her home. Imagine the journalist's need to reconcile all that proof of Imran bin Musa's capacity for love with the actions that would put him on trial. Imagine the journalist's pressure to blow a hole in the woman's narrative, to suggest that Imran bin Musa wasn't really the man she thought he was or the man she'd made him out to be. Maybe he wasn't so dedicated. Maybe, despite appearances, he wasn't as faithful as he seemed. Maybe he didn't love her the way he said he did on paper. How do you phrase a suggestion like that? You give it some disciplined thought, you take a sip of the tea the woman has poured you, and then you ask a question.

If it is indeed the case that he is so devoted to you, you say, why didn't he try to resolve your troubles in Sydney by asking you to marry him?

The woman reportedly shook her head. He and I are not able to marry, she said.

The woman went quiet as she delved into thought. Not thinking over what she should say, but thinking how best to word it with care.

We are not able to marry, she said, because Imran is married already.

The woman insisted that, despite the way it sounded at first, this fact was further proof of the fidelity of the man. If people would just hear her out, she would help them understand.

The journalist suggested that this revelation would reopen the question everyone had been asking now for days. Who is this man? What is his story?

Behind the browser containing her words, behind the picture that captured the words of bin Musa, I could hear the susurration of the words I'd written about myself and my wife. I'd almost say I felt ashamed to go back to those words after seeing bin Musa's, ashamed to think that mine were wanting the simple generosity that seemed to have given fuel to his, but then it was half past seven in the morning and I'd been up all night again. I didn't have the vigour to let myself feel shame, or to feel much of anything at all. I closed the browser window, skimmed a few of the facile things I'd been slack enough to write, and finally shut the laptop screen to cut the glow and bring on the dark. I sat there with drifting thoughts for maybe an hour, maybe more. Then I heard a shuffling sound at the front door, and when I stumbled into the hallway I saw the wad of letters squeeze through the slot and plop onto the floor. Eight o'clock? Eight-thirty? I stooped to gather the envelopes but ended up sitting, crushed by fatigue, and started flicking through them.

I downed a glass of water at the kitchen sink. Through the window I saw my wife still standing under the yew. After a moment she turned to come back into the house. I clunked my glass into the basin and left. By the time she'd reached the kitchen door I was already back out the front. Between the front door and the corner of the house stretched a shattered pathway. I crouched down to pick up the brittle chunks of ice and hurl them, sheet by sheet, into the snow banked up along the pavement. Strange to think that the snow had earlier seemed as strong as a barricade blocking the path, as if the house was fending off an elemental attack. Now the path and the house together seemed like wonders of solidity, both of them firm against the shifting tempers of the season.

Later on, I'd watch the overnight developments break out into a war of words in Australia. Predictable outrage came from a spokesman for the Minister for Immigration. The minister sent a spokesman to make someone else look like a fool. He'd damaged himself the previous day, when the papers had published the letter regarding the girl. He'd convened a press conference and taken to the airwaves to denounce the irresponsible public servants who'd shared the document with reporters. The problem was that public servants hadn't leaked it at all. It had been retrieved and handed over by a witness to the crime. The witness had picked it up at the scene and kept it from police, disturbed by what it said. Imran bin Musa had left it there, abandoned, on the grass outside the day-care centre. The letter, not some verse from the Qur'an, was what he'd been bent over before he went inside. He hadn't brought himself to his knees in prayer. He'd been brought to his knees by the heaviness of the words on the page.

The spokesman for the minister would try to raise new questions on the back of the testimony from the woman in Adelaide. So Imran bin Musa had a family, he'd say. Doesn't that make his crime even worse? Think of the girl in state care, he'd say. Imran bin Musa had murdered four children in response to her treatment. That didn't show dedication, he'd say. It showed malice, malice aforethought, and that's why the Commonwealth Government intended to pursue charges of aggravated assault and homicide against the accused, with a view towards extraditing him to his country of origin. It didn't matter that he might be subject to persecution in Iraq, the spokesman would say. He'd thrown away his right to permanent asylum, even if he hadn't known it at the time, when he'd fled to Indonesia after registering with the UNHCR in Kuala Lumpur. Registering for asylum and then turning his back on it, for whatever reason, was proof enough that he hadn't needed asylum in the first place. He was really just an interloper, a queue-jumper. Immigrants who committed crimes could go back to where they came from. The law permitted it, the spokesman would say, and moral justice for so many grieving families demanded it.

The spokesman, in his own strange way, would give voice to the question I turned over in my mind as I cleared the ice. The question came on the heels of the first two, WHO IS THIS MAN? and WHAT IS HIS STORY?, and assumed an ethical quality. What was this man capable of? That was the question that adhered to bin Musa, the question I heard in my head every time I saw or thought of his face. The ministerial spokesman would insinuate, of course, that there was nothing he wasn't capable of. He could cheat the immigration system, deceive the woman he supposedly loved, betray his duty of care for his daughter, take the lives of innocent children and their guardians. But the question, for me, deserved a real response, not a rhetorical one. What, truly, was that man capable of?

The woman in Adelaide had begged for a willing ear. Who could turn away?

When Imran lived in Iraq, she'd said, he'd been married to a woman he said he loved with all his heart. She'd arrived in Iraq from a village over the border in Iran. She'd entered as his spouse, receiving a residence permit through her marriage to him, and after settling in Fallujah they'd planned to start a family. Then the Americans invaded. They toppled the Ba'athist dictatorship and sent Saddam Hussein into a rathole. They brought carnage to Fallujah, they brought the conditions that led to protests, riots, an ambush and an uprising, incineration and smoke, corpses swinging from the trusses of a bridge, followed by months of military reprisals and paramilitary mobilisations. The mayhem turned bin Musa's wife into a human target. The old regime had never been able to suppress the popular hatred of Iranians, but it had at least been able to contain and deter violence against them. Now a vacuum opened up and anything could happen. The two of them decided they had to escape. They couldn't seek refuge in Iran. Both would become targets there: he for being an Iraqi citizen and she for sinking so low as to marry one. So they fled together, first to southern Iraq, then they left Um Qasr aboard the boat that took them down the Persian Gulf. Together, too, they disembarked in Karachi and escaped into Pakistan.

Imran lost his wife, the woman in Adelaide said, somewhere along the border with India, before he pressed on to Lahore. Early night, springtime. Tornadoes of moths around the spotlights at the Karachi shipyard. They'd stowed away in a cargo container. Someone on the crew of their vessel must have known they were in there. Someone let them out when they docked. Starving, sweat-soaked, deprived of sleep, Imran and his wife came across the next link in the chain of their journey. A convoy of freight trucks prepared for dispatch. They'd head to Hyderabad first and fan out from there to a range of destinations. A group of men, long-distance hauliers, gathered in the shadows to offer passage for a price. They assured

Imran the offer wasn't a one-off. Dozens of people, many of them children, already hid beneath hessian sacks and sheets in the backs of the vehicles. He could pick a truck to peek inside, if he had his doubts, to satisfy himself that this plan had already won the confidence of others.

Imran eased open an unwieldy door. In the darkness he saw countless shimmering points of white. Terrified eyes reflected the fluorescence of the docks. So the numbers were no lie. But, the hauliers told him, men and women were forbidden from travelling together. Did he feel his wife recoil when she heard that? The two of them talked it over. Neither of them could see another option for transport to someplace safer than where they'd landed. He promised her they'd be apart for only one night. They'd reunite when they reached their destination in the morning. They checked with the drivers to make sure they'd be bound for the same place after Hyderabad. Yes, they were told, of course. Yes, of course, don't worry. They parted without a kiss goodbye. He climbed into a truck full of men much like himself. She was taken into another reserved for women and children. The engines jolted to life and the trucks pulled out of the shipyard and roared north along the potted roads.

Imran bin Musa never saw his wife again. The last thing he watched her do was scramble onto a running board at the base of a roller door. Two or three hours northeast of Karachi, his truck came to a halt. At gunpoint all the men inside were ordered out and dumped at the fringes of a wetland. The women and children were what the drivers wanted. They'd only taken the men to make it easier to claim the more valuable goods. Now, I imagine, he found himself at a loss for what to do. Shortness of breath, dizziness. The ground skewed beneath him and he stumbled. I picture him hobbling around bewildered, aimless in a place he cannot name. Now, as if manhandled outside the ambit of life, he could see only the husk of things beyond himself. The people who remained part of the world were hauled onwards through their hours, through days and months, with a dogged, inexorable ongoingness, oblivious to his alienation, unmoved by his distant spectatorship of the present. He could not find a way to rejoin them there, to involve himself in life again. He could only stand back to watch affairs unfurl around him, without him.

He loitered where he'd been abandoned for several more days, a week or so, tentatively approaching strangers, whenever he felt safe enough, trying to learn what had happened to his wife. The likely scenarios must have harrowed him. Slavery in fields or sweatshops. Servitude, imprisonment, rape. An arranged marriage or else an attempted escape, an accident, death. Yet, in time, he had to move on. He couldn't dawdle forever. He had to leave her behind, wherever she might have ended up. He struck out for Lahore, the next step on the journey that would take him to Nauru, to Sydney, to a day-care centre desecrated, but even now, it seemed, even after all that, he could never forget his wife. If he couldn't be sure she was dead, he had to assume she was alive somewhere. He was a faithful man, the woman in Adelaide insisted. He was so faithful that even when he started his life over again, even as he permitted himself to step into a new and open future, he resolved not to break the marriage he'd lost because he wanted still some vestige of it to survive.

What was that man capable of? Chips of ice skittered under my feet. A blast of wind, surprisingly warm, gave me a sideways shove and fled into the trees. I couldn't bend my back anymore. I started kicking the ice aside. Imran bin Musa was capable of a resilience that my threadbare experience couldn't prepare me for. He was capable of rebuilding his whole sense of self from the rubble of serial traumas. Fallujah, Karachi, Lahore. Nepal, Myanmar, Kuala Lumpur. Indonesia, Christmas Island, Nauru. After the ashes of all those places, an arrival in Sydney. New job, new home, new family. He put himself back together. He was capable of that. Capable, too, of falling in love not once but twice in a lifetime, and not successively but simultaneously. Whatever else might be said of the man, he had a heart that was able to contain competing emotions, no one feeling suppressing the others. Even the woman in Adelaide, who had every right to be jealous of his determined tether to his wife, even she respected him for resisting the bedlam that should have ruined him, for accepting and surviving what had afflicted his calm, for sharing with her, candidly, the complexities of what he carried inside him. He was capable of so many things, many more things than I felt I'd ever be capable of. Would he then be capable of remorse for his actions? Would he be capable of showing repentance? Would he, in fact, be capable of meeting with someone he'd irreparably wronged and accepting the man's forgiveness?

No. The message came from his lawyer later in the day. After the spokesman for the Minister for Immigration had stepped aside and left the stage, the lawyer called a press conference outside the sandstone façade of the criminal court.

My client, he told the crowd of reporters, has no comment to make on the progress of his case. However, he does wish it to be known that he has no intention of meeting with Mr. Demirović.

The reporters erupted and hurled questions at the man. He raised a palm like a buddha, tranquil in the face of the tumult.

What about the parents of the most recent children? a woman asked.

No comment, said the lawyer.

I had to click back to the broadsheet websites to see what they were talking about. I'd missed the news while engrossing myself in the life of Imran bin Musa. There had been an announcement. Two of the children badly injured had died in intensive care. One of them earlier in the day, one the previous night. Both of them were boys. So four deaths had grown to six, or eight including the adult victims, and the number of mourners had swelled.

The woman raised her voice. He has nothing to say to these people?

The lawyer shook his head emphatically. My client has no comment, he insisted. That's all for now. Thank you.

He turned and walked away and didn't look back at the cameras.

But so dismissive a response seemed destined only to further inflame public outrage. Especially given the rejection of Demirović. Especially, too, given the rising toll. A man who purposefully claims the lives of children can't simply refuse forgiveness without consequence any more than he can freely roam the streets. Even when Long Lankin confesses to his crime, detailing his actions for the anguished Lord Weary, his admission and his sorrow aren't enough to spare his life. In the earliest versions of the song, Weary himself condemns him to death. But, as Child pushed on into the north of Scotland, deeper into the communities forced to the edgelands of the country, among the remnants of those that had been broken and scattered, he found the sufferings of Lankin becoming increasingly severe. In versions collected from Midlothian and Fife, the people who pledge fealty to Weary are so outraged by Balankin's crime that they seize him and strangle him on the spot. In versions collected from Perthshire and Angus, along the southern edge of the Cairngorms, they trap Lamerlinkin and burn him alive on a funeral pyre. In versions from Moray and Strathspey, they stuff Rankin into a sack and stab him and drop him into a freezing lake, and in versions from the coast that runs to the northern tip of Caithness they boil him alive in a cauldron full of molten lead. For many people only blood can possibly repay the shedding of blood. It's an instinct too ancient to expunge or quell. When the shedding of blood is not renounced immediately, when even serious repercussions fail to elicit the bloodletter's regret, when his refusals look like a mockery of the liberties that protect him in the aftermath, the popular lust for blood only grows stronger and more urgent.

Was Imran bin Musa capable of seeing the wrong in his actions, of trying to make amends for his crime? No, apparently not. But later in the day, after the path had been cleared, I thought on him in his cell and I saw his refusal gleaming with new light. Nightfall had ushered me back inside. My wife had already taken to bed. As

I leant against the kitchen door and watched fresh snow settle over the pavement, I let my thoughts drift through the space in which bin Musa dwelt in solitude in Sydney. Bare concrete walls and peeling white paint. A small barred window, close to the ceiling, which let a square of sunlight hit the door at a slant. None of the stink and squalor of Nauru, though his cell was no less cramped than what he'd been given there. Nothing, yet, to alert him to the rising toll. Silence all around him, perhaps even serenity, except for the thoughts I brought into the room. Was he unrepentant? When he sat there on the ground, back against the wall, knees drawn to his chest, head at rest on folded forearms, was he still the steadfast man who refused to unguard his emotions, refused to surrender to the relentless pressures of others? He didn't seem unrepentant to me. He didn't *feel* that way to me, he didn't radiate strength at all, he didn't seem set upon mounting a hidebound resistance to what was asked of him. He looked like someone who knew exactly what he'd done. He looked like he'd glanced back over his actions and recalled them with perfect clarity, and felt the impossible weight of them and concluded that he didn't deserve forgiveness. From the desolation of his cell, his refusal to accept Demirović's offer looked like a way for him to punish himself. The longer he could hold out, fending off human connection, the worse it would hurt and the more he'd incur the pain he felt he was due.

With a shift of the eyes I came back to where I was.

I'd returned to the kitchen table to find that my wife had opened the rest of the morning's envelopes. On top of the pile she'd left a letter unfolded for me to read. It was her way of sending me a message without speaking. The letter had been signed by the Director of Instruction and Assessment at the school we worked for. She was writing to express her hope that the two of us were faring well, she said, and to inform us that our bereavement leave with pay would end, as per our contractual arrangements, at midnight on the Sunday forthcoming. Should we wish to continue leave without pay, she advised us to call her as soon as possible to negotiate the terms. Otherwise, she said, she'd appreciate it if we could drop her a quick email to acknowledge receipt of her letter. She could assure us that we would have the full support of our colleagues and the leadership team upon our return to work. She looked forward to seeing us again on Monday morning.

LINCOLN

Fever dreams were always one of the early signs of the Föhn. First the sky would fill with clouds shaped like enormous, tufted fish, and the blue would take on the shade of a bruise as dust interfered with the light. High-pressure patterns south of the border, in the flatlands of Piedmont and Lombardy, would push a wave of heat in the direction of the Alps. Gusts of wind would funnel through the passes of Ticino, building strength on their way to the Berner Oberland, and then they'd tumble over the tops of the mountains to batter us for days on end. That was the Föhn. The atmosphere would feel as dry as a cellar warmed by a furnace. The air would writhe with swirls of flies and, in autumn, wasps. Black-and-yellow devils, stealthy and vindictive, would slip through windows to threaten you as you sat down to a meal, or tried to focus on work, or lay in bed at night, until you slapped them dead. Then they'd spring to life again, until you realised that their resurrections were another effect of the Föhn. Pressure on the skull, torrents of sweat, wavering vision and fever dreams. You couldn't trust your own eyes or the clarity of your thoughts.

The Föhn hit the mountainside at nightfall. I'd sensed its approach, its imminent arrival, as I'd taken to the pathway with a bassine broom and swept clear the last few scraps of snow. For many people a sudden migraine is another early sign of the wind, a result of the plunge in air pressure that heralds the coming gale. It struck me like an icepick to the forehead, as if some sharpness in the air had targeted me for trepanning.

After I went back indoors I downed a handful of headache

tablets. I knew full well they'd do me no good. With the heel of my hand pressed hard to my brow, I eyed the letter from the Director of Instruction and Assessment. It was still at rest where I'd left it on the keyboard of the laptop. Innocuous from this vantage point. Incendiary when I re-read the words. With my free hand I flipped it over and pinched it into a transverse fold, as if in doing so I could silence it. Then I sat out the onset of darkness feeling the heat inside the house become more intense, more compressed, as the pressure outside rose even higher and warmth gushed over the peaks. Shoes off, socks off. Bare feet helped to keep me cool. Through the kitchen window I watched the forest sway like kelp in a deep sea current, entire trees like fronds of weed waving in the black.

It took the Föhn only an hour or so to liquefy the white. The snow would never thaw fast enough to flood, too densely packed on the roof, too tightly clinging to the tiles, but it weltered into a sprawl of trickles and rills that purled over the shell of the house. Run-off squiggled lines down the panes of the windows. Droplets fell from eaves and spattered cement and brickwork. Trembling beads of water troubled the lintel above the kitchen door, plonking arrhythmically into a puddle that stretched from there to the edge of the forest. Sheltered now, and dry, but surrounded on all sides by spit and drizzle, I watched the Föhn gnaw into the winter. As snow dwindled down into water, the world around me rippled.

My wife, on the sofa, told me to go to bed.

I'd just sat down at the kitchen table and powered up the laptop. The letter, I saw, was no longer in sight, but the dark screen captured my wife's opaque reflection. I watched her where she sat, behind me, as she smoothed the creases from a sheet of paper on her knee. She'd been reading through it again, contemplating its contents, though she didn't mention it.

Now the laptop screen lit up. I clicked open a browser tab.

What are you trying to do? my wife said from over my shoulder. You've been awake for—what?—another twenty-four hours? You look addled. You need sleep.

It's the Föhn, I said. Like always. Feels like it's cracking me open.

So go to bed. Sleep through it. At least sleep through the worst of it.

I said nothing in response, pressed my hands to the table, hauled myself out of my seat and made for the bathroom. A splash of water on my cheeks, a smear across my brow, a couple of dabs around the temples. Then I returned to the glow of the laptop. The ashes in the urn remained behind the screen. I clicked through to the news.

What are you *doing*? said my wife. Why are you doing this to yourself?

I told her I just wanted to check in with the world beyond our own four walls. I'd spent all day alone in the snow. I wanted to feel connected again.

Protesters, she said.

What does that mean?

You want to see what's happening with the funerals, she said.

She was right. At that very instant the summertime sun would've been rising over the east coast of Australia and later that day, I knew, four children were due to be farewelled. Nobody could've foreseen how opulent the event would end up. There had been a public fundraising initiative to help the families lay their children to rest together, all of them in the same cemetery, in plots at seaside Waverley rather than the unkempt, unsightly grounds at Rookwood. Donations made the funerals a class act. The money was still flowing in, too, now that there would be two more burials to pay for. But with public largesse came certain expectations of gratitude, decorum, propriety. Obedience to the public mood, if not fidelity to a script or an observation of the limits on expression. So I turned to the newsfeeds because I wanted to see if something unpalatable would happen, something to challenge the common feeling. I wanted to see if Demirović had anything new to say.

Yes, I said, I do want to see. But tell me. Protesters?

I read a report that said protesters were rallying outside the cemetery gates.

To protest what? The mourners?

The whole thing, the whole situation. The crime and the killer, obviously, but also the idea of showing him clemency. They don't like it. They don't think he deserves it. They want payback all round. Police are expecting trouble.

I sagged in front of the laptop. The broadsheets had decided to freeze their coverage of the story while the funerals were underway. An editorial note on the *Herald* website used the word *undignified* to describe the idea that the media should provide real-time updates, from the moment the mourners arrived at Waverley to the moment they retreated to their homes. But the sudden aridity of the broadsheet feeds only sent me in search of new oases. Plenty of fringe outlets spurned the oversight of moderators. Plenty of quote-unquote citizen journalists rode high on trending hashtags. They had their own ideas about what was undignified, of course, but they defined the word in a way that happened not to encompass clickbait, dogpiling, or the surreptitious filming of people seeking privacy.

So what are you doing now? my wife said. Turn the computer off. You're up to speed on the news. There will be funerals and protests but nothing's happening yet. Go to bed. Come back in the morning.

No, I murmured. I shook my head. No, I'll wait it out.

What do you mean? You're staying up?

I didn't turn to look at her. Yeah, I said. For a bit.

All night?

Maybe a couple more hours.

Well, she sighed, okay, whatever. It's your brain to fry.

A little later, exhausted herself, she stood at the bedroom door and held it open for me. She hadn't announced her intention. She just rose and moved to the door. The letter, I guessed, remained behind me on the sofa. Open again, face-up, so its words could speak.

You coming? said my wife. It's time. You can join me.

No, I murmured again. No, I want to see this. But go on. I won't be far behind.

So she went. The bedroom door clicked closed.

Could she tell I was lying? Not about going to bed, but about waiting out the news. The laptop wasn't what I wanted to keep an eye on. That was just a way of occupying my hours. I didn't want to let the gunmetal urn out of my sight. I could feel it thrilling with energy on the other side of the screen. I wanted to stay close to it, within reach, to see it issue its manifestations one more time. This time, though, somehow, I wanted not to turn around to find my daughter gone in an instant as if she'd never really shown herself to me. I wanted to hold her in this world a little longer, to hold on to her and keep her with me awhile. So I curled a hand around the edge of the screen and felt the matte of the urn swish beneath my fingertips. At my back I could hear my employer trivialising my grief, the words of her letter assuming a need now to put distance between my daughter and myself. With my free hand I kept refreshing the screen, the headlines, to muffle the voice behind me and fend off sleep until the impossible happened again.

That voice was hounding me into returning to a place I felt I had no obligation to revisit. Aside from the question of whether or not I wanted to be there at all anymore, I felt a flimsiness in the grounds on which my return was expected. There was a flaw in the reckoning of onuses and allowances. I shouldn't have been surprised, really; I'd been living with the mismatch for a long time now, almost from the beginning. Towards the end of my first term in the Alps, while my wife and I were still on probation as employees, I'd found my position at the school unsettled by an unpleasantness based on similarly lopsided equations. Every week the student council would host an assembly for the entire school community. Five hundred people, faculty included, would come together in an oak-panelled hall at the heart of a huge chalet, gathering against the backdrop of the Wetterhorn and the awesome glaciers that flank it. A bell would be rung to silence the crowd and then the council leaders would moderate a discussion about the most pressing problems of communal life. Sometimes these discussions would drift towards finding solutions. More often, though, they simply offered airtime to a range of perspectives on the everyday tensions of the campus culture. The goal was a reflective, humanistic one, to prompt students to reassess their own conduct through the eyes of the people in proximity to them.

One day, one of my senior colleagues stood up to express concerns about a problem infiltrating the social sphere. He addressed the community in precise, formal English distorted by a gruff German accent. The Föhn thundered over the campus. As my colleague spoke, students with restless hands swatted at wasps and sometimes crushed them with a clap. He did his best to ignore the distractions. He had something troubling to say. He'd noticed an increasing tendency, he said, for students to denigrate one another, usually in jest, with recourse to the insult *Sklave*: that is, slave. Someone's pencil would slip from their desk and they'd have to bend to pick it up. Someone playing football would get into a tussle and tumble to the ground. Someone would spill food down their shirtfront or they'd find themselves a few coins short of the price of an icecream. In each case, my colleague said, he'd noticed onlookers laughing at the person's misfortunes and calling them a slave in the way an earlier cohort of students might have called them, with less offence, a loser. He wondered whether this insult didn't cross a moral line. Time had faded its intensity, perhaps, but its domain was unique and in need of defending.

A surprising number of students rose to justify their choice of language. They insisted that anyone concerned about it had misread the context, the tone, the playfulness of friends exchanging mock insults. Some rose not to excuse it but only to downplay its severity, unconvincingly, and a few took to their feet to side with my colleague and say how uncomfortable their peers made them feel when they used the word *slave* with such nonchalance. Teachers voiced opinions, too, unanimously condemning the insensitivity of the slur, but I noticed that they spoke exclusively in abstract terms, in terms of manners and politesse, and so, after a while, I rose to offer a contribution of my own. In teaching history and politics, in anchoring my activities in the American past, I was at that time delivering a unit on the transatlantic slave trade. I could see that the insult did an injustice to more people than those who copped it. I thought I could help the students to see it as well.

When you call a person a slave, I said, do you know how much degradation you're invoking? As I spoke I heard my words parlayed around the hall in a foreign echo. A council leader stood on the far side of the crowd to offer a simultaneous translation into German. Maybe, I said, maybe here in our cosy lives in the Alps, maybe here in a world where slavery exists in the shadows, ad hoc, we can't fully appreciate what it looked like as a system with a global reach. Or maybe the problem is time, maybe it all happened so long ago that we can't tap into it anymore and see it as something that really occurred, something that fed a whole architecture of power. But you should know, and bear in mind the next time you speak, that slavery was a very real horror that prevailed on this Earth every day for more than three hundred years, and it wasn't an accident or aberration. It was arguably the greatest crime against humanity ever committed by anyone, anywhere, and the people who committed it were men and women who considered themselves civilised.

That's when I should have resumed my seat. I should have stopped there, contented, having made my point. But when something ignites my passions I tend to dig in and double down. The succinct, after all, is the enemy of the rigorous. Inwardly, then, I could feel myself getting more and more worked up, and I fed off something voltaic in the vibe of the room.

So, I began again. *Slave.* Doesn't seem like much, I know.

The Föhn rattled the windows, rushed heat through the hall. The wasps buzzed about with fervour. The students sat still to listen to me, to the words I spoke and the words on delay. I took their acquiescence as an invitation to be emphatic.

One word, I said, one word, that's all. Doesn't sound like it's worth a lot of thought. But that's exactly *why* you need to think of it more carefully. It's part of a code devised by men who rode roughshod over their moral duties to others, to people standing right before their eyes, and then used the code to blind themselves to their own ugliness.

The wind upset a clutch of chimes outside a neighbouring chalet. They tinkled almost all at once, in tandem with the pings of alerts in a social media feed. On the laptop a tab began flashing. I inched closer and clicked it.

The cameras showed up at the cemetery gates before the protesters did, but the protesters showed up well ahead of the families. The ceremony would be private, I learnt. The entire premises of Waverley Cemetery would be restricted to the loved ones of the deceased. With the legacy outlets releasing themselves from coverage of the event, fringe figureheads cried censorship and scrambled to supply what was lacking. They ended up sourcing it from freelancers without scruples. Three or four photographers angled telephoto lenses through iron bars, capturing details of the scene from a distance. In time, when the ceremony was underway, they'd serve up glimpses of the mourners in glorious despair. For now, though, they fed tweets and status updates with snapshots of the cliffs at Bronte. Where the eastern edge of the cemetery met the open ocean, waves of white froth scoured a high stone wall. Protected from the turmoil, but not from the spray and spit, angels of shining marble spread their wings with their backs to the sea. The spikes of palm trees jabbed at the sky and reached for the saffron flare of the sun.

Then the first protesters arrived and the coverage coarsened. As the interlopers bunched around the sandstone pillars at the gates, the feeds clogged up with rapid-fire photographs and grainy footage of vox pops captured on phones. Most of the faces I could see belonged to men, although off to the sides and in the background I could also make out a woman every now and then. I'd expected most of these people to be middle-aged or older, but to my surprise I saw more than a few who couldn't have yet reached thirty.

With an air of great purpose they began unpacking placards, picket signs, posters mounted on easels. I caught a few glimpses of the pictures they raised aloft before I caught a glimpse of something swift moving through my hallway. I leapt to my feet, closed the laptop. I tilted my head to the side to peer around the corner of the kitchen wall, to look for whatever it was I'd seen out of the corner of my eye. My heartbeat thundered, once, twice, vibrating my entire body, before I realised that all I'd seen was water. A long, thin rivulet ran the length of the hallway. It spilled past the entrance to the bedroom and into the kitchen, pooling a little at each threshold, and silently flowed into the groove where the skirting met the floor.

What the pictures on the protest materials showed were the children. Faces culled from TV news reports, from the day-care centre website, from the unsecured social networks of parents and teenage siblings and extended family. Nothing I hadn't already seen. Not even the two most recent deaths were overlooked. Seven, eight, nine exuberant children. Boys and girls, different ages, different ethnicities. Different poses. A boy hugged by his mother on a stunning day at the beach. A girl cosseted in a capsule seat in the back of a car. In each case alive, very much alive, frozen in a state of disarming animation. What could anyone say to sights like those? The pictures were bracingly beautiful. They were also devastating. Their unvarnished beauty was what made them devastating. These slices of lost lives, of unassuming youngsters, hadn't been put on public display simply to convey their beauty, but to stand as symbols of beauty violently despoiled, as human emblems of goodness razed by indiscriminate death. By parading them outside the cemetery, enlarging them to formidable size, the protesters forced onlookers to see what wasn't there anymore.

I took myself from the kitchen, thrown off by the faces on the screen, and step by step I traced the trickle to its source at the end of the hallway. When I saw the door to the bathroom ajar, I saw more than a rivulet rippling over the tiles. Water had drenched the bathroom mat. Now it lapped at the base of the toilet. Beneath the roar of the Föhn, I could hear another sound, a rushing, and then I understood what had happened. I dipped my bare toes into the puddle I'd accidentally created.

What didn't the protesters' pictures depict? Everything that made those children worthy objects of the cause. The injuries and the pain, the wailing and caterwauling and the bleeding out. The death and decay. The bodies lying lifeless on the ground. You could look at the pictures and see all these things without seeing pictures of any of them. There was nothing horrific at all about the joy and glee of the children, but their faces were held high as reminders of what was lost. The pictures devastated me because they brought death before my eyes, gave it fresh and vital presence, by showing only relics of what it had taken away.

I sighed and bent above the sink. I'd forgotten to turn off the tap after I'd splashed my face. The drain had been fitted with a pivot plug, a silver disc, which sealed and unsealed the sink by spinning from side to side. The waterflow had slowly pushed it closed. The sink had filled up and spilled over and then the floor had flooded. I gave the plug a flick and opened the drain again. Instantly the water stopped cascading and started gurgling down the duct.

I stood almost ankle-deep in the flood and looked about the room, listening to the suck and slurp, thinking over what to do. I met my own sunken eyes in the mirror. My wife was right. I looked addled. I looked worse than that. I hadn't slept and I'd eaten nothing all day. I hovered awkwardly on the spot, examining myself through murky vision, like a spirit in possession of my own disjointed body. Why bother doing anything more? There was a drain in the floor. More than likely something had clogged it someplace deep in the ground, but sooner or later, drop by drop, the water would find a way down. With a sideways glance as I returned to the hallway, I saw myself, weaker and thinner, take a step out of the bathroom before the light went off.

My words had returned to me disfigured, I remember, with extra syllables bloating the vocab and sentences slanting to end on multiple verbs. The foreign echo might have carried the gist of my remarks, but it carried none of the growing urgency I could hear in my voice. When you think about the victims of slavery, I'd said, it's too crude just to picture a group of people, monumental as the numbers may be. You have to take *time* into account. You have to find a way to feel what an enslaved person lost, moment by moment, in the course of a life spent entirely in bondage. And you have to try to feel the loss as more than something that happened; you have see it also as the only thing that *could* happen, the only thinkable prospect for generation after generation of people born as slaves. That's on top of the day-to-day torment, the whips and lashes, starvation, exhaustion, and worse, far worse, than you'd care to imagine. When you use the word *slave* to denigrate your friends, you're belittling all the people who ever lived their lives like this, who were deprived of themselves, agonisingly slowly, as the seconds ticked away, until their time was simply gone. You're misusing their lives, which were *real* lives, just to get your kicks. You're taking trauma beyond your comprehension and reducing it to fuel for laughs. And do you have any idea how many people are wrapped up in this one word? How can we calculate the scale, the monstrous scale, of the crime that devoured them and their hours? You can't count the bodies. The most anyone can do is guess. Best estimates put the figure at twenty million.

I paused for a moment to think on what I'd said, on whether my listeners saw what I wanted them to see. In my silence my foreign echo resonated throughout the hall. I waited for it to catch up to me before I went on, more certain of my case.

How can you get your head around that number? You're all familiar with the Holocaust, I know. Six million Jews, five million others, all of them sent to the gas chambers with no hope of return. We talk about it like it's history's greatest atrocity. But when we talk about slavery, we're talking about an institution of cruelty that was literally twice as large. And as awful as the Holocaust was, it lasted only a decade before its apparatus was dismantled. Slavery lasted thirty times as long. At its worst, when entire families perished, the Holocaust destroyed three or four generations, from infant children up to their great-grandparents. But then, best-case scenario, a man and woman in chains at the dawn of slavery would have been the great-grandparents of the great-grandparents of the great-grandparents of the first slaves to see mass emancipation. So think of Auschwitz or Bełżec. Think of the sheer number of victims, of what was inflicted on them. Think of the unforgivable duration of the system that targeted them for persecution. Then multiply all those things exponentially and whatever number or concept or gut feeling you get at the end of your calculations, keep your attention on *that* the next time you think of using the word *slave*.

I affirmed what I'd said with a quick, definitive nod, then I resumed my seat.

The rest of the discussion unfolded as cordially as those things usually did.

When the assembly ended, however, another colleague caught my eye as she passed me on her way out of the hall. You're either very brave or very foolish, she said in a quiet voice. Have you forgotten where you are?

As we neared the exit, a senior colleague joined us. He had less patience for niceties like rhetorical questions. Ironic, he said, that a teacher of history should deprecate the histories of a hundred students in this room without even a hint of misgiving. In his indignant eyes I saw myself misshapen, a misproportioned wretch, just as my words had been when aired by someone else.

The passage back to the news from Sydney, down the hallway to the laptop, grew thick with other shadowed selves as I moved through the house in a mist. My silhouette matched my footsteps, along the hallway walls, until I sidled into the kitchen. There my doubled reflection, dark in the dim light, watched me from the window and the glass of the door to the forest. At the laptop I sat and raised the screen and for an instant before it lit up I found myself once more facing my distortion. The blur of the glass hollowed out my eye sockets, sharpened the bones of my cheeks, threw a pall over my face. In the surface of the urn, an arm's length away, I saw myself elongated, stretched out as in a funhouse mirror, dimmed and clouded as if wrapped in gauze, until I seized the canister and held it close to my chest, felt its coldness on my palms, and all but explicitly prayed for it to open itself to me.

What was the true worth of the contents of the urn? The Director of Instruction and Assessment had a perverse answer to that question. The letter she'd sent us remained where my wife had left it, unfolded, face-up, on the armrest of the sofa. Lopsided equations. The letter took the value of my daughter's life and gave it a number. Multiple numbers, time and currency. The letter churned her value through an elaborate calculus. I received a salary of so many francs per month. I worked so many days per month, and so many hours per day, and so, on an average day, I'd earn x francs and y rappen. Therefore: (x plus y) multiplied by z, where z was the number of days of paid bereavement leave I could claim, equalled my employer's estimate of the probable duration of my grief, or at least the portion of my grief that would be allayed financially, but clearly this arithmetic was bent out of shape by an imbalance between variables that can never be equated. The money could not offset the loss that entitled me to it. Yet there would be no extra payment for returning to work as normal while my grief still stuck to me. If I were to return, what would I be returning to? A place in which I felt my employer was in debt to me while my employer felt the very opposite? If I were to return, what would I be doing? Salvaging the status quo ante? But if I didn't return, if I didn't write to acknowledge the letter at all, then what? Where was I supposed to go?

I set the urn back on the table and released my hold on it.

The morning after I'd risen to address the school community, I'd received a summons to see the Director of Instruction and Assessment. I hadn't met with her in private since the day I'd arrived on campus to take up my post. She had the wizened eyes of a soothsayer and dewlaps that swayed in tandem with the pashmina she always wore. Gigantic hoop earrings dangled beneath the scrunchies that pulled her hair into a double bun. She smiled, genuinely, and waved at an empty armchair in the corner of her office. I sat and waited for her to speak.

Look, she said in an accent from somewhere in the American South. I'll be honest. We've got a problem here and we've got to solve it today.

In her hand, a manila folder. She flipped it about but didn't show it to me. She said it contained printouts of the emails she'd received from upset parents, plus written complaints from more than a few of the school's current students. Most of those who'd contacted her were Jewish. Those who weren't Jewish descended from families targeted by the Nazis. Unsurprising, really, that the school should have so many stakeholders with such painful histories. More surprising that I hadn't thought of this when I stood before the campus community and diminished the relative severity of the Holocaust.

We don't have many meaningful options here, said the Director of Instruction and Assessment. You have to retract and apologise for your comments. We'll draft a statement, you'll sign it, then I'll issue copies to parents and alumni and post it in the office.

I took some time to think back over what I'd actually said. I took a little longer to think of how to diplomatically challenge the idea of retracting it.

Well, I said, hold on. I'm not sure I've done anything *wrong*. Everything I said, you know, it's on record for anyone to find. It's not made up, it's not—

With another wave of the hand she motioned for me to stop speaking.

Look, she said. I know. I know you know your stuff and I know you're not misrepresenting the facts. But. There's a significant number of people with a deep affection for this school who have personal experience with survivors of the Holocaust, and rightly or wrongly they don't want anyone to minimise what they and their loved ones went through. They flat-out don't want to hear it and in all honesty I can't blame them.

But it's not the case—

No, no. Forget the *arguments*. You can't *argue* a response to these complaints. The blunt truth is that the people you've offended are people who have gone their entire lives with a sorrow in their hearts that they feel is unique, unique as in *incomparable*, and they've done it justifiably, too, because just look around you. Their sufferings are close to home. They don't want to feel that their sorrow isn't as incomparable as they've always believed. They certainly don't want to be *told* so, and even if they did, they wouldn't want to be told by *you*. It's not your responsibility to crusade against people's feelings. Is it?

I said nothing.

No?

I said nothing. I shook my head in submission.

Good, she said. Now let's get something written.

So we wrote the retraction and the apology and I offered my name to the words. That's power, isn't it? Not mine: hers. To have the world assume the shape you would give it in writing. To put a pen to paper and with just your hand to lay down terms for the truth to follow. That's power, of a sort: if on a minor scale, still enough for those who bear it to shift the flow of the events they're implicated in. I could only aspire to what she had. In the end, I signed as I was expected to do. I followed orders to keep my job, my visa, my place. I accepted, then, that I was in debt to my employers. I owed them loyalty for their generosity to me, for their decision not to terminate my probation immediately. This was part of the ethos of the place to which I'd now been instructed to return. Surely, though, the imbalance had shifted the other way. I felt that circumstances owed me more than the workplace policies entitled me to. After an incident of such magnitude, facing a situation without precedent for many people, how could my wife and I simply resume the mundane duties of our days? Colleagues who'd reached out to us said that work would help us take our minds off our distress, encourage us to not dwell on what had happened. But I didn't see how I could allow myself relief. I couldn't consent to it. I didn't want to take my mind off the calamity. To take my mind off it would be to depreciate, to denigrate, the value of what had been taken from me. To return to my employer now would be a marker of my generosity. That's why I felt I couldn't do it. Not even to send the email acknowledging receipt of the letter. Not even to show courtesy. My generosity had run dry. I wanted restitution for my robbery.

Events on the screen seemed construed to appeal to my anger. The protest, I saw, had begun to agitate. The crowd looked like it might even rival the gatherings of a few days earlier, the public displays of solidarity for Hassan Demirović. Chants welled up, then grew faint and faded out. I couldn't hear the words but they had a regimental rhythm. Now cameras began to zoom in on particulars. Sunglasses, straw visors, streaks of white zinc on noses and cheeks. Some ruddy faces and piercings, some singlets and sandals, but mostly respectable shirts and trousers, dresses and jewellery, clean teeth and healthy skin. Who were these people? Who were they, exactly, that they felt moved to do this, to give up their time to stand in the sun and stake out a spot to make their anger known to the world? Were they me in a different life? Were they people I would've been among this day, if instead of living abroad I had made my life in their midst? But then, I noticed as the cameras swung around, not everyone in the crowd had gone to Waverley because they wanted to protest. Some had been brought along, escorted into the spectacle. Many of those in attendance were younger people cradled or shepherded by others. Many of them weren't adults at all, but children whose seething parents were already scarlet with wrath.

Far, far from the Alps is a field at the base of a hill. Maybe it's better to call it a meadow. I went there once, during one of my periodical escapes from Boston. Throughout my years in America, whenever I was able, I'd strike out for places further away, places farther removed from the present. To begin with I'd leave home in the morning and return just after dusk; I'd take daytrips out to Bunker Hill, to Lexington and Concord, conducting cursory raids on these metonyms for minor events that had finally reshaped the world. Eventually, though, my movements began consuming weekends, then whole weeks at a time; I strayed into New York and New Jersey, to Ticonderoga and Saratoga, down to Trenton and across the Delaware. By the end of my first stateside spring, I felt myself drawn farther westward by the pine hollows and peaks of the Alleghenies, via Valley Forge, and later on, near to high summer, I answered the lure of the meadow, the boneyard, at Gettysburg.

Those hallowed grounds I found abundant with life. Tall grass fizzed with whirring insects. The gentle hues of blue flax sprouted around butterfly weed, and Queen Anne's Lace twisted up through clumps of scarlet phlox. The hill overlooking the meadow didn't seem especially high, but the battlefield itself was much broader than I'd imagined. So, I saw, to reach the hill from an encroach along the western ridge, a man would've had to cross a mile of open terrain and expose himself to enemy fire from above. That's why, half a world away from Sydney, that meadow is today a cemetery on a colossal scale. That's why I was thrown back there as I peered through the gates of Waverley, through the eyes of distant observers, and scanned the field of sunlit headstones not yet peopled by the mourners. Each headstone marked a life, of course, but seen from afar like that, in their tens of thousands, no one lost life could be distinguished from the abundance.

Upon the meadow, I remember, I'd tried to picture the men beneath the soil around me. To know the facts was no challenge: one hundred thousand soldiers in blue, three quarters that number in cadet grey. The challenge was to make the facts manifest as flesh and blood. What had they done, how had they been, in their final hours? I saw them pitching lean-tos in forest clearings; I saw them playing cards, emptying bugs from their shoes, stirring at dawn when woken by the trilling of larks. I saw some exhausted and others elated; some withdrawn to quietude, others vexed, on edge; many fearful of their fates, a scant few resigned to whatever might await them. But I couldn't stabilise their faces in my mind; I couldn't lay hold of their idiosyncrasies. Each one was blotted out by the others who crowded my vision. There were just too many wasted spirits to really look at them all. Even indoors, I couldn't picture the faces of a few children without help from the protesters carrying banners. So, I remember, again and again, no sooner had I summoned a man from the meadow than I'd watch him evanesce, vaporising into the vastness of the warring forces. And when at last the hostilities ceased, I knew, the casualties left behind would also dissolve into abstract sums. Twenty thousand dead or missing, thirty thousand injured with loss of function beyond repair. The granular details of each tragedy fogged over, faded, became indistinct, whenever I tried to draw them out from horrors of such magnitude.

Much easier to appreciate is the reality of a single loss. I knew this, I *felt* it, as I sat there in front of the laptop and sensed another man seating himself. I heard the creak of an old wooden chair. Scrolling through photographs from seaside Waverley, plunging without end into a bottomless feed, I felt my vision warp and let my mind drift far from the meadow, far from the fallen, to find a still and silent refuge a hundred miles away. I saw him there, alone in the dark, at a desk of fine mahogany. Close to him, closer still: I wanted to see the flaking of the desktop varnish, the impress of notations scrawled on papers long discarded. Close enough for his scent to reach me: I wanted to smell the camphor on his clothes, the stink of coal on his skin. On the screen I saw the sun, a stain of ochre, pressing hard upon the headstones, and in its burning brilliance I could see the flame of a paraffin lamp. I leant in close to the light and let it bathe my face and I saw other eyes. They drew near to me to show the other man his own face in the glass of the lantern. Shadows accentuated the grooves that pinched his brow, the curves and recesses of his cheeks. Bony and angular, taller than most, with tremendous legs like those of a locust in flight, he'd had to fold his limbs into himself to take his seat at the desk. Then, as the feed scrolled on and rinsed the screen in a stream of colour, I saw the man close his eyes to concentrate. To ward off his worries about his wife. She has again crawled into bed by herself and seems every day more willing to let grief bedevil her nerves. He doesn't know how to help her, to soothe her, and his not knowing is its own pain in need of relief. Here, then, in his private dwelling, he allows his own thoughts to circle around an absence: a distraction from his unease, an obsession with another heartache. From a drawer he removes a lithograph, facedown. He fingers its edges before he turns it over to look. His son. His boy. Innocent, insouciant. Just on the cusp of becoming his own person. The faint lines in his brow, the creases in his clothes. The man scrutinises these details as if to more clearly commit them to memory, as if memory alone could give the child new life.

A sinkhole of speculation like this can swallow a string of hours. For days on end I'd loosened my grip on time, seen too many nights bleed into morning, so that now, so close to him, I saw the man at the desk see the sunrise just as I did. Come the dawn, having been briefed on the casualties of the day before, he sits by a window where early light keeps him sober as he pores over the numbers.

They beggar belief every time, after every conflict. One thousand dead, eight thousand wounded; three thousand dead, ten thousand wounded; five thousand dead, twenty thousand wounded; and would an extra thousand here or there have any meaningful effect on the carnage? At a certain point, numbers of that order cease to matter. And yet the conscience won't allow the lives they represent to go unrecognised. Often now, increasingly often, the dead are only boys. The man at the desk doesn't have the latitude of the newsmen, can't make daily summaries of slaughter, won't have all the significance drained from losses that upend other people's worlds. He has bound himself by oath and duty, by his ascension to highest office, to respect each loss, each death, as its own unique and solemn disaster. He must recognise the dignity of every fallen son and, somehow, he must hold it equal to that of every other.

But how, exactly? How to feel, to recover, the preciousness of these wasted youths? How to validate it? It takes a concentrated effort of the will. It takes a dedication of thought to the elders. For me, it would take only attention. I'd swing my eyes in the right direction, peer at the screen, refocus. I'd been drawn to the parents from the start. I'd followed their movements through the unfolding of events. Now I sat at the laptop waiting for them to arrive and cross the distance between us. But he had to work to imagine the bereaved, to dignify their losses with his care. While some young men might have had only siblings or widows to survive them, most had a mother or father, or both, who'd be there at home to receive official notice informing them, as next of kin, that their lives had been irrevocably altered by what they'd dreaded the most. Month after month, battle after battle, dispatched the length and breadth of the country, those notices would almost always be delivered to parents. He knows the sickness those parents must have felt. If he can just recognise the fact of their woe, might he give weight to each lost life by placing his own sorrows in communion with theirs? He, too, knows the paralysing heartache. He has a memento with which to keep it raw. He too knows the inner drag, the slosh of bile pulling him to his knees. He holds the lithograph in hand. He thumbs the corners, lets himself admire the boy's fine features. Glossy hair, precisely parted, and lips drawn into a pout. Now he feels the lurch in his heart that means he is about to cry and he cannot stop.

He has made a habit of this, this sitting alone in wan light, thinking and thinking until the tears flow. He too. He, too, is aware that he has become unmoored since he saw his child taken from him. He has even disclosed his troubles to one of his less unctuous subordinates. Panic at three in the morning, discussing the disaster at Antietam. Do you, he asked in a moment of candour, do you ever find yourself talking with the dead? He'd seen his boy several times now, when alone in his office, only after reviving a fire in the hearth. The boy seemed to need the flames to live again. Where their glow succumbed to shadows, his form would fade from sight. Although the man had at first resisted speaking to him, supposing the surprise of speech might drive away the visitation, more recently he'd ventured some words, some questions, to ascertain what immanent things were capable of evading death. Did the boy still carry any memories of his life before his passing? Might he still hold feelings of fondness for his loving father?

The boy had offered no answer, no succour, flickering in the firelight. But rather than meeting silence with silence, the man had surprised himself by continuing to speak. He spoke, unguarded, of his private turmoil. He cast off his burdens and confessed to his son the doubts that plagued him daily: about his authority and prudence, about the justice of his decisions, about whether his love for his wife would survive their present trials. Then he saw that simply by addressing his concerns to a ghost, he'd cast doubt on his own fitness of mind. Did others who felt his grief pin their hopes on apparitions? Or did his indulgence in fantasy confirm he'd become unhinged? He'd had to consult a colleague on these matters because he could not at that moment consult his wife. By herself in bed, as usual, she'd long ago descended into her own well of pitch. All these fractures in his reality, all around him at every turn, have impressed upon him the consequences, the profound and manifold alterations, of just one loss, one absence. Now he resolves to cultivate the pain, to never allow himself to forget it, in order to superimpose it on others, to know the worth of each life whose loss will inflame it in parents elsewhere.

When advance reports from Gettysburg reach him, he careens into his rickety seat. I hear it creak as it takes his weight. Ten thousand dead in the field, fifty thousand casualties all told. The soldiers on the hilltop had followed orders to stand their ground. Their opponents had been ordered to march forth and dislodge them. The meadow, as I remember it, must have given the advance an unexpected rhythm. The terrain wasn't flat. It rippled like an earthen sea. The land rose up in waves, in a succession of rounded crests, each of which sloped into a swale so that as men marched down from the summit of one, they'd disappear behind the next. Atop the hill, reaching the apex of the highest slope, I turned around to survey the scene and tried to imagine the vertiginous panic that must have struck the stalwarts when they saw the meadow overrun. As the charge began and the enemy ranks approached them at speed, rising and falling across waves of grass, showing their faces before vanishing, the vastness of the grey formation would have atomised into many men distinguishable from one another. While cases and canisters blasted into the soil, while solid shot ordnance thudded into bodies, still there were many who ran on and crossed the meadow and I vied to see them as they would've been seen by those who did not move for them. Close, closer: sunburned skin and a peeling nose, yellowed teeth, a kerchief stained and torn. Closer still: a hand reaches down for a sword in a scabbard, chilblained fingers grasp the hilt, and suddenly there's a person right there and with a cry and a lunge, spittle, foul breath, the tip of the blade touches a throat. Face to face like that, in immediate engagement, each man, each boy, was confronted by the singularity of another, and in those foreign eyes, in the centre of his field of vision, his final heartbeat before the strike would have given him a glimpse of himself as he appeared to the world.

And yet, when I looked out over the meadow and tried to call up the fallen, I found my view of the grounds enshrouded as much by words as lives. Some time after hostilities ceased, the man at the desk had been tasked with commemorating the dead. He'd agreed to attend a ceremony before the year expired, to ennoble all the sacrifices, to formalise the burials, and in doing so he'd been persuaded by colleagues to address the mourners. Given the daily retreat of his wife, and the nightly return of his boy, and his increasingly fragile sanity, his own instinct had been to hold his tongue. But his cabinet had been persistent in extracting a concession: he'd take to the dais, as befitting his position, to solemnise the occasion with a few remarks. Now the time has come for him to find the appropriate words. By lamplight, at his desk, he sits within reach of inkwell, blotter, fountain pen. Still, sitting, he doesn't actually reach for them. He cannot make himself move.

There are many things I have learnt about the corporeal experience of grief. The thing I've come to know best, the thing I saw in myself most often during those days of torpor, is the way in which grief unabating will literally drag you down. Grief, it's often said, is something that weighs on you, a heft on your shoulders you can't shrug off. I don't think that's true. Grief doesn't impose a weight from outside your epidermis. It creates a new weight *in* you, compacting your innards until they have the density of stone. You can't carry yourself around anymore, can't move yourself in any direction except towards the ground. Impossible to resist the gravitational pull on your body. It's as if your limbs are hollowed out, and an intolerable weight pools in your feet, and from deep within it some infiltrator shoots a grappling hook into your head. The claws pierce your skull from the inside, the flukes lodge in your scalp, and then there's a tug at the other end. In the worst moments you simply sit and stare.

At best you move so slowly that you feel you're pushing your body through a fen, thick and stagnant and without bounds.

It is wading through this bog, dragged down by his inner weight, that I picture the man at the desk when he finally drafts his address. Slowly now, achingly slowly, he takes the fountain pen between his fingers. Liquid black drips from the nib. The inkwell squats at the corner of a blank page, the blotter aligns with the edge. The man holds his words in suspension. Close in, as close as possible: look closely at his hand. Weathered, callused palms, evidence of a youth spent felling trees and splitting rails. Nails cracked from too much time between his teeth. Thick, vermiculate veins, and knuckles like ball bearings beneath his skin. But he knows what that hand is capable of. A year ago he'd swished his signature over the bottom of the proclamation. With that one act, though it took only a second of his time, he gave warrant to the freedom of three million souls held in bondage all their lives. That's the sort of power I'll never come close to possessing. In any given lifetime, so few people do. And yet, and yet, even that phenomenal power isn't enough to exempt a person from the inertia of their particular grief. It can't dispel what clouds a mind in obsessive mourning.

I felt an urge to rectify things, to revise what I'd written about my wife, or else to annotate and clarify, but when I set my fingers upon the keyboard I found they wouldn't move. Alone in the lamplight, as I saw the scene, the man at the desk felt his hand grow leaden. What words could he hope to find to honour the boys beneath the meadow? I heard a groan, a complaint of discomfort, a jet of air through nostrils. I saw those eyes glance again at the lithograph. What worth is there in attempting any remarks for anyone else's misfortunes when one's own life has been cleft by an absence such as this? Paralysis seizes his hand, his arm, his entire body. Only his thoughts have life. Equanimity is a futile hope. He knows he can't appreciate the import of every lost life without preference or favour. His grief for his son will always outshine whatever pity he might feel for others. Nor can he express the import of those deaths even intellectually. The scale of the carnage strips his words of substance. It reduces them to wisps of wind that fly free of the meanings he'd make. Nothing works anymore, no matter what he does. A hundred thousand men grow dim in the glare of his heartache for a single boy, and even if they didn't, even if he could see the faces of them all, recompense for their spilled blood could never come from speech.

So the man, heavy inside, sits at his desk, a sedentary thing. Although his pen is poised to write, he only sits and watches the flame shudder his reflection in the lantern. If he watches long enough, might this flame also offer sufficient light to bring his boy to him in a thinner state of being? The room is almost silent, the night-time air is cool. Far off in the distance he can hear a soft percussion. Explosions, advances, retreats, under cover of darkness. Another hundred men will be dead by the time the cannons have hushed. Perhaps, he thinks, perhaps his boy will return to him again. Perhaps right here, in the glow around the glass. Perhaps he should stay at his desk a little longer, stay awake just to see what happens. Sleep can wait. His bed can wait. His wife, in bed, can wait as well.

The weight inside the mourning parents made them move like beasts of burden. I didn't need any film footage to see how it dragged on them. The first few pictures made it clear enough. Heads bowed, shoulders rounded, they looked as ready to collapse into themselves as stars depleted of inner fire. I recognised some of them from the pictures I'd seen on the train from Interlaken. There was the woman who'd broken down, shrieking, as a policeman embraced her. There was the husband and wife who'd clasped each other tightly in the pages of the newspaper. There was Hassan Demirović, a slim figure in a suit and tie of perfect black, and there, too, was Jessica. They didn't stand together. They didn't walk together. She kept a few paces ahead of him. He trailed a short way behind her and far behind the rest of the mourners. In one new picture, he stood alone on the path while everyone else walked ahead. He looked as fraught as I did. He looked as sleepless and grim as I felt. He stood and watched the others withdraw from his presence. A bewildered soul who'd stumbled into a universe all his own, wondering how to slip back into a more familiar one. If only he had a helping hand, someone willing to stop and look for him, to reach out to him and lead him away from himself.

I closed my eyes and tilted forward in my chair at the kitchen table. The table vibrated to the drumming of my fingers. Eyes open, I reached for the canister of ashes beside the laptop. Cool to the touch, not rough but resistant. I held it in both hands. I cradled it close to my chest. Nothing had come of it yet. Does something slip away when you hang your hopes on an apparition? Is it better to say that whatever is lost is in fact relinquished? Is there a dash of willingness, acquiescence, to the letting go? I assumed that my wife, in bed, had fallen asleep. I assumed she'd grown accustomed to my absence. Maybe not, though. Maybe I kept her awake by keeping myself awake and away from her. In one of the pictures I saw when the screen refreshed, Hassan Demirović had sunk so deeply into his own inner space that he didn't notice the hand extended towards him from a distance. His wife, now at the edge of the crowd, had turned back and gestured at him and waved for him to catch up. The photographer had frozen her with her fingers flexed in a beckon her husband hadn't seen. What strength did it take for someone to lead a man out of the world he'd barricaded himself inside? Strength enough to drag him? To lay hands on him and haul him to freedom, even against his will?

Thirty-nine, I've come to realise, is the song of Child's that means the most to me. The extended hand, the liberating touch. The thought of it, in Waverley, strummed the first chords of the tune in my mind. For a long time I understood thirty-nine as a song about muscle, brute force, the fearsome brawn of a man whose temper isn't stable. In retrospect, I've come to see that it's actually about the opposite. It's a song of frailty and vulnerability, a song of collapse and a cry for compassion. In my favourite rendition, it is sung by a wistful mezzo-soprano, accompanied by a countertenor who also fingers a lonesome guitar. In their duet, their voices interweave, ducking and hiding from one another and then uniting and rising together, true to the interplay of the characters in the song. The plucking of the guitar evokes the turning of leaves in sunlight, oak and ash, true to the setting of the story.

In Scotland's southern uplands, where the Yarrow meets the Ettrick Water, there's a forest known as Carterhaugh. I went there once as well, a year or so after leaving Boston, when I wondered if I might stake my life in some other part of the world. At the time, though, I was less interested in the places I went than in the company I'd started to keep. Hannah was someone I thought I could fall in love with. At least I had some vague hope of a future together. I mean only to admit that I cared for her more than I cared for my surrounds. I had no notion of the song that took Carterhaugh as its setting. Close to the forest, with a view over the canopy, there was once a manor house, a sort of provincial castle, with a room in a turret belonging to a young beauty named Janet. Confined to her quarters by her overbearing father, Janet sits by her window to admire the sumptuous view, and then, to distract herself from the pangs of her solitude, she begins to sew a dress:

Janet's locked
    in her lowly room,   sew-
        -ing her   silken seams
    but longs to be
    in Carterhaugh,   a-
        -mong the   boughs
            and leaves;
and Janet's locked
    in her father's tow'r,   sew-
        -ing a   slender thread,
    but longs to be
    in Carterhaugh,   a-
        -mong the   roses red …

She drops her needle—to her feet, we're told, *flees—on nimble toes,* and plumbs the depths of Carterhaugh, *as fast—as she—can go.* But then she plucks a crimson rose—*a rose, and only one*—and in a dervish of dust and foliage, a maelstrom of blinding light, a sudden storm of broken branches and crackling bracken,

there appears
the sprite—
    Tam Lin
        —saying,
        Dear maiden,
        leave alone!

In some versions of the song, the man is known as Tom Lyne. In others, Tamlyn, Tamblin, or Tim O'Lane. I know of just the one version that explicitly calls him a sprite. The other versions only imply his true nature through his hostile reaction to the plucking of the flower. He is a forest dweller, a guardian of the green. A being of fickle presence, he darts here and there to hide in the branches and seek refuge in the undergrowth. Can you see him leaping out from the darkness at that lonely young woman, materialising before her as she holds the stem of the rose between her thumb and forefinger? He arrives on the scene as a terror from elsewhere, an otherworldly predator prepared to feast on defenceless flesh. He squints, scowls, shoves his face in hers and berates her:

What makes you pull the rose, m'dear?
Why won't you leave it be?
What makes you walk
through Carterhaugh
without consent from
me?

What follows these words is a puzzling exchange, puzzling because of how readily Tam Lin shows another, more desperate side of himself. Janet stands her ground, remonstrates the sprite, and suddenly his vehemence subsides and he reveals his vulnerabilities. Janet summons her inner strength and snaps at him in a display of defiance, and then, perhaps chastened by her, perhaps fearful of her hidden power, perhaps recognising in her the strength of spirit he needs to see in anyone who might help him, Tam Lin relates to her the tale of his misfortune. *The forest is not—yours to own*, she says,

I'll pluck whate'er I can,
and I'll pass through
howe'er I please,
and not bow down
to any man—

Then Tam Lin *takes her by the sleeve*, and Janet *starts to wail*, so he *draws her near* and *whispers, Dear—*

let me

unfold

my tale—

and he holds her tight, his fingers biting her wrist, and whispers to her of his troubled past and the future he fears will befall him. She is close enough to see the stubble on his chin, to smell his pungent breath. She is close enough to see the throb of green veins at his temples, the clench of arboreal fingers like the roots of a toppled tree. He was, he *is*, a man, he insists, of human stock like any other. But now he stands before her, he says, clothed in ethereal raiment, *for when I was a younger lad—me father bid me ride*, and hardly had he mounted his mare than *awful woe did me betide*:

It fell upon

a winter's day,

a cold day and

a snell,

as we were come

to Carterhaugh,

that off me horse

I fell,

and as he tumbled to the floor of the forest, from out of nowhere sallied forth a horde of fey folk on horseback. Tall and pale faerie knights sat astride their steeds, riding at a gallop beside their squires, all of them in flowing gowns of lurid, preternatural white, and at the heart of the company cantered the radiant fairy queen. The boy had scarcely seen her, transfixed by her lustrous features, before she tilted to one side and seized his arm and swept him off the ground, snatched him from his father, and spirited off to a thin place with him, *took him to her land to dwell.* Now, he says, he flits hither and yon, wavering betwixt dimensions, *and I've a tale of fear to tell.* What he needs is the extended hand, the hand that will lead him out of his morass. He needs the gaze of recognition, not just to be seen by another but to see for himself that another has seen him.

Away went the picture of Demirović turning aside from his beckoning wife. A swipe replaced it with a view of the mourners assembled before a celebrant. The proceedings had begun, at last, though the distance from which I observed them was at odds with the longing for closeness I heard in my head.

Tam Lin enlarges himself, invades Janet's space, overrunning her field of vision. His skin exudes the scent of wet soil, the spice of freshly fallen leaves. His complexion has a translucence to it, as of a protean creature deprived of continuous presence, and yet, when he speaks to her, the warmth of his breath brushes her cheek. He says he worries that to remain in this limbo is to condemn himself to eternal torment. For six full years, he tells the damsel, he has served the fairy queen and her people as the protector of the woods, empowered to ensure that the verdure isn't vandalised. But now, he says, he quivers, he trembles, at the thought of an approaching occasion. Scarcely three months hence. The night of Lughnasadh. Gourds, a grimoire, a reality in flux. Every seventh year, he says, at around this time, the fey folk who have taken him pay a tithe to the powers of darkness. They convene in ceremony to cast a spell and conjure a portal, to hurl a living soul into the maw of the underworld,

and me so bold,
    and ripe in health,
I fear, this year,
    I'll lose myself—

and with his confession sputtered out, choked down at the final word, Tam Lin jolts, totters towards the mystified Janet, and drops to his knees and holds her and weeps with his face pressed into her gown. The poor maid knows not how to move. For a moment she is paralysed. The man, the sprite, sheds tears in terror and shows no sign of stopping. What is Janet to do? What else but what her instincts command? Offer comfort to the wounded. Alleviate their suffering. Do whatever it takes to bring them the peace they crave. So, then, according to the words of the song as Child saw best to preserve them,

Janet takes him
by the hand, leads him
by the sleeve,
and she lays
the fellow down, among the boughs
and leaves;
and Tam Lin takes her
by the waist, upon a
mossy bed,
and he lays
his lady down, among the roses
red …

The forest outside thrashed in a rush of wind. As the snow on the yew tree melted I could picture droplets plonking off the needles, but the Föhn blasted the branches so hard that they flung the runoff at the kitchen window and scattered rain across it. I stood at the table and stretched myself to wakefulness. I bent an arm over my head and pulled on the wrist, shook out both arms and then bent the other and pulled again.

On the laptop, I saw, the orations had begun. I watched, as the cameras watched, from a distance that made words indistinct. The mourners formed a scrum of black suits, black dresses and shawls. At length the mother of one lost child emerged and turned to face the rest. She spoke for some time, in a murmur, then concluded and returned to her place in the crowd. When she finished, another parent, a father, took a step forward. He started to speak, tentatively at first, then found his rhythm and went on for a while.

At the funeral in the meadow, on the edge of winter, the first man to speak spent two hours addressing the shivering dignitaries. I understand the impulse. There's a certain cast of mind, or an inflection of the heart, that leads you to feel you can fill the void of an absence with the quantity of your words. If you can just go on a little longer, say something a little more precisely, make sure you've given consideration to every conceivable detail, maybe you can beguile the world with a spell that negates the reality of your loss. With a hiss another blast of the gale spattered the window with more rain. I turned aside from the silent orations to watch the droplets trickle down the pane, to watch them drip and huddle along the sill.

Even granting the outlandishness of the premise, suspending disbelief in sprites, I often find the abrupt union of Tam Lin and Janet attracting my scepticism. Janet was maybe sixteen years old. Why would she willingly offer her virgin body to a strange man, an uncouth savage, a sprite of potential ill will, wholly for his benefit, to comfort him and quell his tears, with no thought for her safety or her wants? I can only account for her change of heart by thinking her uniquely receptive to the spirit of Carterhaugh. I remember the way I'd seen the forest when I went there as a younger man; I remember it as a refuge from real life, a zone of pure potential. Anything could happen there. That was the sense it emanated. I remember walking hand-in-hand with Hannah, two innocents skirting a stand of hawthorn, and how easily we'd glided into a more serious state. Glided, yes, as if drawn deeper into the air of a place where possibilities grew as readily as any thicket of trees.

The dog days of summer. Balmy in the sun, cooler by several degrees in the shade. The sweet smell of hazel, the whisper of birch in a breeze. Squirrels scurried after conkers on the forest floor. Hannah wore a pale green shift and a dark green shrug, let her long hair hang loose across her shoulders. Sunshine fell upon her like gold cascading through the leaves. There wasn't another soul in sight. Anything could happen in a place like that. You could fall into someone's arms. You could do it because you've been hungering for it or just because it felt right at the time. You could withdraw into the trees and free yourself from the turmoil around them. You could cast off a life you felt pressured to flee and fly towards a place that held the promise of a new one.

My cheeks burned with heat as the wind hit my face, flushed cool as the gale pelted me with water. I'd opened our back door to the forest, swiping aside my reflection, to step into the wild night. I'd watched Demirović speak and finish speaking in a matter of minutes. Cameras captured him from a distance, though their microphones were too weak to make anything audible but the waves. On the screen Demirović mouthed silent words at his daughter's graveside. He read from prepared remarks that drooped in his hands. The other mourners gathered round to listen to things outsiders would never hear. Hardly had he begun before he stepped aside. He folded up his notes and slipped the paper into a trouser pocket. With every move he made he became the embodiment of an echo, the echo of the meadow and the man who struggled to summon his words at the ceremony there.

The man himself had grown careworn and churlish. Colleagues told him he looked ghastly, as much a cadaver as the boys he'd commemorate. He'd seen himself in the glass of the lithograph, in the window of the train, in the lenses of his spectacles, and he couldn't deny his decline. In the end, though, he'd haled up the strength to speak. To what purpose? Two or three minutes of waffling. Nothing of any real substance. Neither he nor anyone else could charm the world with hallowed words, he said. Nothing spoken there could possibly add to or detract from the brute significance of the lives now interred in the soil. He said these things in a voice drawn thin, reading aloud from hasty notes, as he yielded his mind to thoughts unhitched from the saying. In contemplating the grieving parents, he'd thought on the hopes they must have once held. How many unknowable wishes had been obliterated with those bodies? He'd thought on the hopes that he and his wife had held for their own son, all of them lost when typhoid took hold. Nothing ambitious. A respectable life. A useful trade, a liberal education. That he might know his forebears; that he might find someone to love. All of it, all of it gone. And where had it begun? Where had it all come from, to be invested in that body? A hand on a rounded belly. The tenderness of skin to skin. The intimacy of such moments. The kicking the man could sometimes feel. The way he held his touch as if by force of will he could muster up all his dreams for the unborn child and release them through his palm, supercharging the life to come with as much potential as he could envisage. Didn't every parent do that? Wittingly or not. Wilfully or not. When all those men, those smothered boys, were yet to become part of the world, hadn't their parents done the same? Skin to skin, full of hope. All that hope, the whole almighty reservoir of it, now just another casualty of war. And words? What use was a word when you had a body to contend with? What power could words ever hold in the presence of so many bodies?

He denigrated his words with his papers in hand, scribbles referred to and read aloud. Then he fell silent and shuffled aside and folded his notes into a pocket.

I imagine he stood still, bemused and a little perplexed, when an admirer approached him afterwards to ask for a copy of his address. I imagine him as a man too humble to grant the request, demurring with a blush. Later, too, having returned home, I imagine him sharing this story with his wife. As if he couldn't believe that anyone would want to preserve his prattle. As if something so fugitive could be worth posterity. With a glance at his wife he solicits her agreement. But the woman, I imagine, replies with upturned palms. Perhaps you *did* have something to say, she says. How in heaven's name should I know? You haven't let me read it. Then she watches him shrink into himself, slouching in a suit that hangs loose about his limbs, and regards his concerns with as much care as she'd give a passing breeze. Something appropriate was said. What do the words really matter?

Remarks at an end, Demirović, too, resumed his place beside his wife, slinking back into the crowd as others stepped up to speak. The pictures that fluttered online let viewers pry at the couple through paparazzi eyes. Jessica seemed to regard her husband apathetically. She didn't hold his hand. She didn't even let her shoulder brush against his. Impossible to look at them and think that at some stage in their past, barely four years ago, those two people had treated each other with tenderness in private moments. Another belly swollen, full of the promise of new life. A hand against the curvature, the warmth of his palm on her skin, to feel the kicking inside. To make contact with a new life, exceeding the biological sense of the phrase. To reach out to a person beyond touch and beckon them to communion.

As Child records it, that's also what sends Janet back to Carterhaugh and into the arms of Tam Lin. Jump ahead some months. Enough time for her figure to have changed. She's spent her days among her waiting women. She's been noticed avoiding the gentlemen of her father's court. These past weeks have been tense. She fears her father's outrage. She's been trying to change her clothes to cover up what she can't any longer conceal, until one day her father approaches and pulls her aside. It is with this gesture, I imagine, that Janet not only knows what the old man is about to say, but anticipates her only means of escape, the terrible harm she must inflict on herself to be free of his possessiveness. Then he holds her close and, *in a growl both harsh and wild*, he makes known his concerns and says,

Alas, I see
you've grown
with child …

But, of course, the callous brute cares nothing for the unborn infant, nor for his daughter's wellbeing. He cares only about his bloodline. He demands that Janet tell him who she has been consorting with. He demands to know the name of the child's father. His manor is overstuffed with men who proclaim allegiance to him. There's a man in every room who might have seduced his daughter, or been seduced by her, and secretly conceived an illegitimate heir. *Is your man a man of worth?* he asks. *Is he a man of fame?*

O, who among
my loyal sirs
shall owe the babe his name?

But Janet scoffs at the thought that she'd condescend to bed her father's underlings. She tells him she wouldn't deign to receive their propositions. She insists that, if she is with child, *then I alone—must bear the blame*, and she turns from her father, quits his presence, thinks upon the sprite in the forest, and resolves not to reveal their secret: *she shan't—say his—name*. Then she retraces her steps to Carterhaugh, *flees—on nimble toes*, and in a reprise of the opening lines she runs *as fast—as she—can go*. But she trips and falls *among the weeds*, scrambles *among the thorns*, and in madness she thrashes about, snapping branches from trees and wrenching brambles from the earth, and as she begins to coil vines around her arm there's another whirl of dust and magic amid the greenery,

and there appeared
Tam Lin—
again
—saying,
Lady, *destroy no more.*
What makes you pull the briar rose?
What makes you shred the leaves? —

and with those words, I imagine, he stops, falls silent, and stares in awe at the distortion in Janet's figure as he realises what has come of their tryst. His expression collapses. His eyes begin to water. He realises what the arrival of the child has driven Janet to do. She has looped the vines around herself because, in her own chaotic way, she is trying to fashion a noose to fix to an overhead branch. He can't allow her to go through with it. *Why seek you now—to hang alone*, he asks, *when I have got—a babe—with thee?* But Janet is enraged, furious at her own indiscretion, and in a temper she scolds and sneers,

I *will* pull the rose,
Tam Lin,
and I will shred the leaves,
for I will *never*
bear the babe
that you have made with me—

and yet, before he can speak to contest her, she says she'd devote herself to her child, she'd love him and care for him, cradle and caress him, soothe him in his times of distress and laugh with him in joy, and she'd nurse him *through the winter nights* and *all the summer's days*, if only, *only*, she insists, locking her eyes on the helpless sprite, *were he born to—a gentleman—and not—a slave—of fey*.

Is Tam Lin wounded by her words? She calls him a shadow of a soul. She calls him a nothingness condemned to insubstantial life, a mockery of a man. Does he even hear the insults? If he does, he takes no offence. He gives her words no weight. He shrugs them off and barrels forth. His thoughts zip around in a craze as he runs through the possibilities, the ways he might persuade Janet to spare her life and, at the same time, to save his own and the life of their child. *Let me step—into your arms*, he says,

for now we two are kin,
and hold me tight,
and fear me not:
I'll prove
a gentleman …

But first, he warns her, as he seizes Janet by the wrist and without forethought rests the palm of his free hand on her abdomen,

first I'll change
before your eyes—

and he begins to unburden himself, to confess his most shameful secrets, to caution her about his inner darkness, about the beasts he conceals in his heart, and as his words spill out and gradually cohere into a proposal, a plan of action, a way for Janet to rescue him, a way for him to protect her, he holds her hand against his chest, hard, so that she may know the human form he longs for her to recognise. On the laptop screen, Jessica Demirović kept her hands flat against her sides. Her husband stood beside her and bowed his head and did not reach for her. But a hand with fingers gnarled was lifted from the surface of the desk, taken up in the hands of another and held, turned over, examined. Creases and cracked skin. Deep lines on the palm. Immense power with the potential to reshape lives by way of a gesture or a word in writing. And in the other hands? A gentleness, a softness to the touch, a spirit of compassion both offered and sought. I pictured those hands together and imagined, in bed, my wife, alone, with her hands curled beneath the covers. Then I saw Hassan Demirović holding hands with Imran bin Musa. The sight appeared in an actual picture, a crude caricature, on a cardboard sign brandished by a protester outside Waverley Cemetery. A bright red circle enclosed the two men and a red line slashed through them. In sloppy lettering above the illustration were the words NEVER FORGIVE.

In most of the media I accessed, the cameras kept the signs and posters in focus and pushed the angry faces to the limits of the frame. I found one live feed, however, which cut to a woman, mid-sentence, as she hectored the lens and her viewers.

—*my* kids, maybe, she said.

She had the face of a muppet, skin like a boiled tomato and a lower lip that swallowed the upper.

I mean, it's ludicrous! she howled. Not even considering the children we're burying today, tragic as the situation is, we've *got* to think about who's next and we've *got* to be prepared. Could be your kids, could be my kids, could be *anyone*'s kids. I just look around at these kids today, kids at day-care, kids heading off to school, and I worry about who's next. Don't you? Shouldn't we all?

She threw her arms in the air as she spoke and appealed to bystanders for support. None of the other protesters pushed her away from the camera, but they jostled together in a fractious sort of camaraderie as the burgeoning crowd took on the feeling of a fray. The woman pointed into the lens as she became more insistent.

There are kids out there right now, she said, who are *marked* and they don't even know it. There are people out there with *plans* for our children and they will stop at *nothing* to have their way, and so far as I'm concerned those children have already been failed by the system and they're basically already dead. And that's tragic, and it disgusts me, and I'm taking a stand. I've got to. I couldn't call myself a responsible parent if I didn't. If we don't do *absolutely* everything we can to protect our kids, then what have we become? Who cares if it means we ship some criminals back to where they came from? For the safety of *my* kids, I guarantee you, there is *no* price too high, there's *no* price I won't pay, and it's time we all—

Unfolding. That's the jarring word, the word I get stuck on, when I think back on how time moved around me that night. I'd say I sat quietly and watched the funeral unfold if only the experience had been a lucid one. Better to say the funeral shuddered, came to me in spasms. Photographs flashed up every few minutes, conveying events in thin slices of time and washing its flow into the spaces between one snapshot and the next.

The crowd of mourners congregated around an open grave. Initially a legion of black clothes gathered respectfully at the edge. Then, minutes later, a division emerged. Hassan Demirović cut a lone figure on one side of the plot. Most of the other parents stood as if arrayed against him on the far side. Between these two poles were a handful of strays. Jessica Demirović still kept her distance from her husband, but put twice as much distance between herself and the larger group. Two or three mourners had moved into her vicinity, hovering just behind her. The scene, as shown, could have been an effort to replicate a battlefield in miniature. An enemy trench had cleaved apart a company of soldiers and already a minority was set to go renegade.

At the first image of the first burial, the actual turning over of soil, I had to look away. My body moved of its own accord, the way an animal moves when startled. I swung in my chair, turned ninety degrees, and I didn't know why until I'd regained myself and no longer felt my eyes stabbed by the light of the screen. The trace image of a coffin floated about in front of me, overlaid upon what I could see of the kitchen floor and the hallway. The barest glimpse, an instant's awareness of it, had been enough to drag me back to that parlour on Lake Brienz. The peach-coloured walls and salmon carpet and the tiny coffin on the conveyor belt. I sat and waited for the vision to vanish, or to be replaced by the sort of vision I wanted, needed, to see. Nothing more took form.

After a time I turned back to the screen. Demirović still stood alone, now further away from the other mourners. The grave had been filled with fresh soil. Everyone else had started to move to one of the other sites. He lingered alone on a footpath and stared at the empty space ahead of him. He looked like he'd halted at the unexpected arrival of someone else, as if steeling himself to approach a person who wasn't really there. Obviously that's not what he was doing. That's me looking at a picture of him and wondering what he'd become involved in. That's me knowing the meaning of his expression and his stance, recognising my own bearing in his posture and his daze. In him I saw myself as others might've seen me in solitary moments. I'd almost say I stepped into his body, a spirit taking possession of a host, as his carriage struck me so familiarly that I felt I could slip it on like a well-worn garment.

When you stand like that, when you stare like that, when you let go of yourself in that way, you appear to the world as one enraptured by a ghost. Maybe you see it in the hallways of an empty home. Maybe in the light of a candle, maybe in the shade of a tree in a seaside cemetery. When all the remarks have concluded and the crowd has begun to disperse, you can see the same thing in the meadow. A fine rain begins to sprinkle the scene, laying a glisten on the grass. The speaker, having spoken, stands upon the dais and dreams. What does he see when his eyes glaze over? Perhaps the ghosts of the dead. Ten thousand men begin to drag themselves from the soil. A few rise up from the graves in which they've been laid to rest, stepping forth as if hauling themselves out of bed in the morning. Many others keel and crawl from the ground they happened to fall upon, the dirt and mud in which they'd been left to decompose. They muddle together, blue mingling freely with cadet grey, and then they begin to wander the field like sojourners biding time until given a signal to march. Weary eyes watch them trudge on, trudge past. They are meandering, itinerant, adrift.

Perhaps, too, the disfigured living are with them in spirit. From the periphery of the meadow, from behind the hills, fifty thousand soldiers press in on the edges of the speaker's vision. Some limp along with shrapnel lodged in thighs and calves. Some on crutches stumble, a leg blown off at the knee; some sway with an arm that ends in a stump. There are men whose faces have melted away, the skin burned back to sinews, like the work of a painter smearing a portrait not yet dry. There are men with cataract eyes, with tendons exposed, with only fragments of jaws. There are men whose bodies have been taken to pieces and then reassembled, it seems, by some power unfamiliar with the human form. Yet weariness isn't enough to let the onlooker turn away. You can't just dismiss a miracle like a manifestation, no matter how harrowing it may be.

And perhaps the dead and maimed are joined, in turn, by the living who are doomed to die. The Earth will turn tonight, he knows, and come the dawn the words he has spoken, every last one of his ennobling remarks, will have made not the slightest redress nor forestalled the deaths of all those who still unwittingly await their fall. Nothing of what he has cajoled into speech will prevent even one more man from dying. I imagine he stands there in that meadow, on the cusp of winter, drizzle eating away at the open air, surrounded by those thousands of ghosts, watching them pass before his eyes, and he dreams up tens of thousands more, men and boys he has never seen, soldiers who are at that very moment alive, unharmed, safe in their homes or at least encamped on their way to some future engagement, and when he sees them and hears in his head his own words, he cannot feel anything but impotence, futility, and shame that his hands should have wielded only a fountain pen.

I found my palms pressed tightly, tensely, against the surface of the gunmetal urn. I couldn't say when I'd picked up the urn or how long I'd been holding it. On the laptop screen I saw a stream of yet more pictures. The mourners, captured in profile, thinned out into a line as they trudged towards the third or fourth graveside. I glanced around the room for any signs of another presence. I pressed my hands so hard to the urn that I felt as if I was trying to shape its contents into some embodied form. I didn't imagine I was alone. As I set the urn back on the kitchen table and bent forward to bow my head, I saw those gnarled fingers grasping the edge of a desktop and I saw them move to slide open a drawer. Inside the drawer, the lithograph. The boy. The parted hair, the pout. The fingers tenderly raise the picture so that, with all the gentleness of his soul, the father leaves a kiss upon the forehead of his son. He holds the picture to his skin, holds it as tight to himself as I'd been holding the urn, and when he opens his eyes I imagine he peers into the darkness of his office in search of what he'd hoped would visit him again. This time, though, there's nothing to see. He returns the lithograph to the drawer. Then, joints aching, one hand flat on the desk, he heaves himself from his seat and, as if snared in a dream, ambles to a cabinet by the window. There he sees his face reflected, faintly, in the glass door. He reaches inside for a tumbler, catches his eyes in the decanter, pours a dram and downs it in an instant. In my throat I felt the burn. I set the glass beside the laptop and bent in my seat to take up the bottle I'd placed on the floor.

On the screen Demirović bent to lay a bouquet of white flowers on a mound of soil. In the next picture he pressed a finger to his lips and his eyes met mine directly as he stared into the lens of the camera. When that picture changed to another he held hands with Imran bin Musa again, on a placard outside the cemetery gates. Behind the protesters a pair of photographers pointed long-focus equipment through the fence. Had Demirović been looking at them? Had he been looking towards the placard? If he saw it, would he see himself in the caricature? There he stood as a man pulling a murderer out of the depths he'd sunk to. Is that what he'd become? Someone who'd plunge so low? Who, then, would descend to pull him out of his own descent? Who could he possibly reach for?

Intercede. Intervene. Force yourself in like a wedge between me and my fate. That's the plea Tam Lin makes to Janet. That's the beating heart of his plan. But how? He admits with dismay that there can't be an intervention right now. He is imprisoned in Carterhaugh by a spell that prevents him from escaping through the thin places. But when the fey folk prepare to make their tithe, he says, they will have to repeal the spell if they intend to cast him into the pit. The barricades will be lowered. That's when Janet should help him flee. But *how*? she asks. She can't fathom it. She doesn't know where he is in his own skin, she doesn't know where he might be when she could come to his aid. She needs to be told what to do. He needs to reach her first, to show her how to reach him. Lughnasadh is approaching, he says. The fey folk will make their tithe. They'll hitch him to his horse and ride him to the pit, then they'll take him down and make incantations and hurl him, alive and screaming, into another world. But, he says, there's a crossroads near the fateful site. Janet can hide in the undergrowth and ambush the procession. She'll see him riding a stallion the colour of milk. She should run forth with a dagger in hand and cut the cords that secure him to it, and once he is free they can take flight into the shadows.

The greatest danger with this plan, he says, is that the fey folk will curse her with a failure of nerve. Magic, he says. They'll deceive your senses. If the horde should espy us together, you'll be bombarded with spells, inundated with hexes. Sparks of unearthly power will crackle the air and you'll see me change before your eyes. I'll metamorphose from a man into some new monstrous form. First I'll be a lion bold, clawing at your throat in want of blood. Then I'll become a wild wolf, slavering at you with the stink of rotten flesh on my breath. Lastly I'll shrink into an angry adder, coiling slender around your waist and striking your heart with a venomous bite.

But you must remember this, Tam Lin beseeches the quaking Janet, you must swear you'll remember this. No matter the form they force upon me,

if you,
my love,
would win,
then hold me tight,
and fear me not:
I'll prove
a gentleman …

Have faith, he says, have faith in the integrity of the soul beneath the skin. Have faith that there is a constant beneath the terrifying variables. If the young woman didn't have faith, of course, there wouldn't be a song.

Now Lughnasadh approaches and darkness covers Carterhaugh. A crescent moon drapes the trees in white. Leaves on vines and branches rustle as the air grows cold. Janet steals into the forest and proceeds softly, with trepidation, along a clandestine path to the spot where Tam Lin told her to hide. Starlight gives her skin a lustre. Frost tries to settle on her bare arms but melts away as she quickens her pace and her pulse. She holds a protective hand to herself, to feel for her unborn child. With her other hand she holds the hilt of a dagger stolen from her father's armoury. At last she arrives at a crossroads, her own faint path intersecting with a wider one, and searches for a place to vanish. An old oak looms above her, a behemoth of a century's standing. She cowers behind the trunk and waits, tense, straining to listen for something beneath her own hurried breaths and the crackle of the wind-whipped woods. Then it comes. She goes rigid to hear it clearly. A mesh of sounds. Distant commotion. Perhaps a quarter-mile away. The rhythmic, regimental thudding of hooves, the steady murmur of voices in conversation and then, surprisingly, in song.

Suddenly something tramples the path ahead of her. A shake of the snout, a twitch of the ears, a snort. Closer than Janet's senses had led her to believe, the horse is a barbed and brambled thing, spiked with broken branches and holly leaves and thistles. Mingled with the musky scent of animal hide is a fine perfume and the tang of beer on a belch. Then the horse lifts a leg, stamps its hooves in mud, and Janet finds the fey folk riding right before her eyes. She catches her breath and holds it. At first one, then two, then three abreast, a trail of twenty or thirty. Heraldic banners, escutcheons, broadswords, pikes. Their passage couldn't take more than a minute but, as they enthral the young woman, the flow of time seems to bend around them, much the way a river parts around an immovable rock, and every second slows and stretches out to the length of a life.

Finally, at the rear of the procession, Janet sees the hapless sprite. His stallion, white as milk, stands out from the herd of brown and black, and Tam Lin has been lashed to it. Hands bound to the pommel. Steadily he approaches. Janet takes a breath. Step by step, he draws near. Now in range, now within reach, Janet leaps from behind the tree and in a single movement swipes the dagger across the fetters and Tam Lin tumbles from his mount.

They run. He clambers to his feet, she races through the trees, and together they flee as shrill voices swarm around them. They run, they run, and then there's a flash of light, the sound of air sucked into a fire, a dazzling burst of magic, and Tam Lin is undone. Tendons twist in his arms, teeth elongate, hair spills into a mane, and salivating jaws snap at Janet, but she runs beside the beast, steels herself against her terror and does not run away.

Another burst of magic, another metamorphosis. A snout, a lashing tongue, a pair of pointed ears. A sprint through the trees, a snarl at the woman in flight, and jowls retract to expose the chops, to sink teeth into her flesh, but even so she doesn't collapse, doesn't detour, resolves to stay the course with the animal at her heels.

Another burst, a shifting of shapes. Follicles of fur are shed, revealing scales, and eyes narrow down into slits. A hiss and slither, a drip of something sinister from fangs, and a forward thrust that misses its mark as Janet darts out of reach and then trips, stumbles, falls to the forest floor, and turns to see her pursuer striking towards her.

A crackle of electricity, the sound of something shredding, and breaking through a reptilian skin the man, Tam Lin, sinks to his knees, trembling with fever, sweating, weeping, disoriented. He looks up, whirls around, finds himself surrounded by forest, finds the young woman standing awestruck before him. He is naked. He is free.

In front of him is an open hand. The young woman reaches for him, to lead him out. He is safe. He is wanted. He seizes her hand. She enfolds him, we're told, and shrouds him in her cloak, a steadying hold on his shoulder,

and then
she takes him
home …

At her touch, her fingertips to his collarbone, he turns, just enough to see her, and he smiles. Then he reaches around with his own gnarled hand to rest it upon hers. She leans over him where he sits and drops his notes onto the desk.

You read it? he says.

I had a minute or two to spare.

And?

She sighs. I suppose you'd like to hear me say I think it's poetic?

You don't?

Sententious, maybe. She deepens her voice and intones: Four score and seven—

Stop it, he says with a smile.

Yes, yes. Very well. It's poetic. But then again, speaking as your wife, what I find most remarkable about it isn't the poetry at all.

No?

No. It's the exhaustion.

She slips her hand out from under his and moves away from him. She stands beside his desk but turns aside and doesn't look at him. She clenches both her hands at her chest, pinning her shawl with her forefingers.

It reads to me, she says softly, like the work of a man who has driven himself into the ground. He has grown thin because for too long he has been trying to shoulder the burdens of too many other people. He has very nearly gone mad from trying to find the words they can't find for their own sorrows. But he can't speak for everyone, and he knows it full well, and this speech, this *noble* speech, is his exhausted admission. Eloquent indeed, but exhausted. He has nothing left to give. He has scraped his heart dry and now it is empty. What can he say after this, after he has told his people there's nothing more to be said?

With pursed lips she begins silently to weep. Her husband bows his head. If he'd cared enough to reimagine events through her eyes, he knows, he'd have a better grasp of the frantic thoughts that have etiolated her into this, this phantasm of herself. But he didn't, so he doesn't. He tries to pay penance for his failures by seeking consolation in the one face he knows he'll never find it. On the desk beside the notes is the lithograph of the boy.

You have done enough, she says. She tries to control her voice beneath her tears. You must know that. You have done enough. Everything you have done and given. All your prayers, all your thoughts, even the ones you've not spoken aloud. Everything you've written. Everything that has come into this world from somewhere deep inside you. It is *enough*. You have proven your worth. You have proven the worth of everything you seek to sanctify. You are entitled to rest, you know. You deserve a reprieve.

I heard her say to him everything I wished I could hear said to me.

Come to bed, I heard her say. Please. It's time.

He sits at the desk and drums his fingers against its surface.

I'm so tired, she says, but I can't keep my thoughts still without you.

He looks up from the desk, looks to his wife. He catches sight of her at a slant. He can't see her face, only her back and shoulders, her hair knotted into a bun and clothed in a fine black net. What does he see when he looks at her? When she says these things to him? Does he try to see through her, to peer into the thoughts that run in endless loops? How much did he really know of her fever before she spoke of it just now? He'd deduced her troubles from her comportment, her daily dithering, but what depths of mind had he really plumbed to read her preoccupations? The truth is that he hadn't turned his talents to the task. He'd so immersed himself in articulating abstractions, the unvoiced thoughts of a multitude in distress, that he couldn't face the frenzy inside the head of someone closer. He hadn't tried to put himself in her position, to see himself through her eyes, to see what she needed from him rather than what he might give to others. Now, though, he could see it. As if her skin and bone had gone transparent to show him the lightning flashes of the storm inside her skull.

Come to bed, she says again. She turns to him now and implores him with wide eyes. What are you waiting for?

He shakes his head, no, and chews at his lower lip.

What are you waiting for? she asks again.

With thumb and forefinger he lifts the lithograph so she can see it. Into the light from the lamp on his desk, he angles the face of their son.

Yes, she whispers. But what are you *waiting* for?

She means from the future, from the next moment and the one after that. She means to make him determine what he hopes to extract from time that has not yet passed.

What do you think is going to happen? she asks.

Outside the window the dawn was giving the forest its first touch of colour. The Föhn had kicked up dirt and dust from the melted snow, had filled the air with particulates that stifled the intensity of the light. The trees showed up as masses of shadows backlit by ambient beams. The runoff had hardened into stubborn frost, nacreous and speckled with broken leaves and windblown soil. The assault had not yet stopped. Branches creaked and water dripped and all the air around me filled with the rush of white noise. But it had eased, become less a barrage of roars than an omnipresent rumble, and an incipient peace had come to rest upon the house. Between my palms, still, I felt the surface of the urn. I placed one hand on the lid as if to unscrew it and peer inside, to see what it contained after it kept its silence, but I stopped myself. I returned it to the kitchen table. It sat there now as a monument to the happening of nothing at all.

On the screen the broadsheet websites had made a banner showing Hassan Demirović locked in an embrace with his wife. Nothing about him suggested reticence or desperation. He didn't seem to be holding her out of a duty to offer comfort, or a need to receive it, or to pose for the media, or in an attempt to restore something they might have lost. He held her tight, crumpled her clothes, clutched her to him at the same time that he let the mass of his own body press against hers. He looked as if he had released a weight from inside himself and let his being fall, as if invisible shackles had been removed and he could actually touch her again. In my mind's eye I could see Imran bin Musa hungering for exactly this kind of touch. Not from inside his cell but before he ended up there, before he ever picked up his weapon and committed his crime. It was a touch that through its intensity, its tightness, seemed to offer release. It was an embrace that suggested a collapse and a relinquishment, a giving way to powers greater than oneself. It made him look free.

When I entered the bedroom I found my wife still asleep. She lay on her side with an arm beneath her pillow. She'd kicked off the blanket as the Föhn had taken the chill from the room. Gently I sat on the edge of the bed and then, keeping my movements as slow and subtle as possible, I lay on my back beside her and looked up at the ceiling. I watched the swirling paint grow white as daylight snuck in around the drawn curtains.

Okay, I said quietly into the air.

I let a moment's silence pass, let the word become real for me, before I spoke again.

Okay, I said. Australia. Okay.

On the pillow beside mine, I felt my wife shift into a waking state. I turned to one side to watch her as she came back to herself, as her eyelids edged open and the whiteness of dawn swam before her. Eventually her searching eyes found me there. Without a word spoken, with just the movements of tiny muscles around her mouth, she seemed to ask me if what she thought she'd heard from me in sleep was true. If I really meant it.

I nodded just slightly. I said, Okay.

I think she thought I'd assented, yielded, because at last I'd come to feel the need to let go of what we'd lost. Actually, though, I understand now, I'd given in to her wishes because I thought it might be the one way to hold on to what little we two still had.

PART 2

EQUINOX

SHANE

Only in times of crisis have I taken to the beach. Retreated, I mean, or fled. I know that the beach is an idyll for many people. A crescent of sand, warm underfoot, and an expanse of immaculate sea. Big, bright skies and cooling breezes, soothing waves rushing over the shore. It's a paradise of almost boundless space. Walk the length of the sand to a distant headland, clamber over rocks to reach a neighbouring bay. Step into the water. Dive as deep as you're able. Swim out as far as you can. Feel yourself move in three dimensions. There's a kind of weightless freedom you can't find anywhere else. I understand all this. For me, though, the beach is a place of last resort. It's the precipice of anyplace I can inhabit. Being there leaves me feeling I have nowhere else to go. Whenever I've taken to the beach in crisis, I don't mean I've gone there expecting time out or relief, or a chance to unwind before picking myself up again. I've gone there because I've been at the mercy of forces more powerful than I am and I've exhausted all other options.

That's how I ended up in that house on the coast near Aberdeen. Half an hour south of the city, far from anywhere you'd call a town. I'd fallen ill, contracted a virus. I'd shrugged off the early symptoms, as usual, having no reason to believe the worst of what ailed me. Then things got so bad I couldn't dismiss it anymore, I basically couldn't move my limbs, and I learnt that my evasions had given the illness an advantage over my recovery. Burnout, lethargy, chronic fatigue. I lost a lot in the time that followed. I lost time itself, passed out, woke up in a hospital bed a week after I'd last been conscious. I lost my job and almost all my meagre savings. I lost my moorings and my bearings. I lost my sense of why I was in the place I'd ended up, of what I wanted from the things I was doing there, of who I thought I was and who I was trying to be. My doctor released me back into the world with a warning that if I didn't carve out space in which to rest and recover, to devote myself patiently to reviving my capacities, I'd burn out again and end up back under medical care. This was at the start of spring, just as Fallujah began to decline and Blair and Bush were planning more boots on the ground. British soldiers would be there by year's end, including soldiers from Scotland, with boys from the Highlands at war alongside Americans and the mercenaries of Blackwater. Who knows? It's possible that one of their bullets thwacked into a wall and spat out the rubble that convinced Imran bin Musa he couldn't stay in Iraq.

I spent a few weeks hunting around for options. None of the people I'd come to know, at such a distance from where I'd grown up, had the room or the time, or the money, to help me pull myself together. Then, at a loss, I thought of Hannah. I hadn't seen her in more than a year. I didn't expect her even to take my call. In fact, though, she did more than answer the phone. She offered me all the help she could. Shelter in her tiny flat, a sofa to sleep on at first, and then, after pleading with her parents, a stretch of time by myself in her family's beach house. She saw me off at the train station and promised she'd check in with me every other day. She told me to rest up, to enjoy the air and the scenery. At the last minute she told me I should also keep an eye out for the neighbours. My train was about to pull away from the platform. All she managed to say was that I should call her to let her know if I ever saw the husband. She promised she'd explain more if I did.

The coastlands of the Mearns turned out nothing like what I'd pictured when I thought of beaches. Sheer cliffs cut into stretches of moor and pasture, plunging straight down into sea. Where the rockface was less precipitous, softening into ground you could walk on, the sand was grey, not gold, and unrelenting crosswinds clumped the grains into large, rough mounds that spiked my soles with reeds. Mostly I kept myself boarded up, indoors and out of the elements. Floor-to-ceiling windows in the living room opened onto dunes that surrounded the house like ramparts around a fort. Standing close to the glass, squinting through the salt that spattered it, I could watch the waves thundering onto shore and I could ponder, beyond them, the dull cataract of the North Sea.

I gave a lot of my time to the shelves that bowed with no shortage of books. The library was unmistakably the treasure of people bred in England but besotted with the north. Too much Walter Scott, too much Robert Burns. But then, somewhere in there, I found *In Search of the Thin Places of Alba*. I don't remember reading it. I must have looked at it, of course, because it sprang to mind when I came across the words to 'The Unquiet Grave', but I can't actually recall it. Knowing the songs as I do now, and knowing number one in Child's index, I imagine I put it away after a glance at the opening pages. The first song tells of three maiden sisters *somewhere in the north*, living in a cottage they share with their mother. It begins with verve, moving along at a spritely tempo, but then, in the recording I like best, the singer, a woman, shrugs off the lightness to become almost doleful, heartsick. *One evening late*, so it goes, a young man arrives at the house and asks if he can lodge for the night. What follows is a veiled attempt on the part of each sister to win his hand in marriage. *The eldest sister—let him in*, we're told,

and locked the door
    with a silver pin.
The second sister
made his bed
    and laid his pillows
        'neath his head …

But the youngest sister, *fair and bright*, keeps him company *all through the night*, and *when the morning comes to be*, she asks him: *Sir—will you marry me?*

The man says yes, eventually, although of course there's a catch. Wordplay and riddles and tests of the young woman's wit. Not that I would've had the patience for his frivolities on the first reading. I imagine I snapped the book shut and tossed it onto a table. I guess I left it somewhere I could pick it up later and read on in a senseless haze, sinking a selection of songs into the trenches of my memory. It's only when I've looked back on those days, in the years since I left the beach house, that the rhythms of the song have tinted my understanding of what I saw there. Part of that has to do with the place itself, the rhythms of the sea, the siss and boom of the waves. Part of it has to do with what I came to know of the man whose name, I learnt in time, was Shane.

True to her word, Hannah reached out. She made an effort to call me after I'd been away a couple of days, and then she called again a couple of days after that. Her voice held in it something more than courtesy or the fulfilment of an obligation. It sounded as if it held genuine concern. She wanted to see if I had everything I needed, if the house was providing the relief I'd hoped to find. I didn't have much to say on either occasion. I told her what I'd been reading, which of the books had sustained my attention and which of them had depleted me. I spoke of things I'd seen outside, of skuas snapping at gulls and foam congealing on sand. Other than those trivialities, though, I had nothing to report. I could see the neighbouring house from the living-room sofa. It nestled behind an intervening dune, ducking down beneath the rise, but I had a clear view of the kitchen window and a portion of the balcony. Once or twice, I told Hannah, I'd seen lights left on. But no, I had to admit, I hadn't actually seen the neighbours.

That changed one evening when the winds died down. I lay on the sofa, resting, in the hour or so before dusk, when I caught a muffled voice outside. I sat up. Through the window I saw a woman walking the dunes. I couldn't make out her face or her features, but from the way she carried herself as she crossed the unsteady terrain, shoulders back, all composure, she seemed to me one of those middle-aged people who take pains not to lose the trimness of their youth. She didn't straggle or stumble. She stood tall, maintained her balance, moved with purpose. She wore cargo pants and a tight-fitting black shirt, no shoes as far as I could tell, and she kept her hair pulled back in a ponytail. She strode with her hands in her pockets. With roaming eyes she searched the ground for something I couldn't see. Her companion followed literally in her footsteps. He emerged from behind the dune a few moments after she reached the top, plodding with great deliberation and making every effort to plant his feet in the prints the woman left. He seemed to be a younger man, chunky, lumbering, and wholly focused on his movements until he reached the woman's side. She spoke a few words to him and then the two of them bent over to rip up fistfuls of marram grass from the sand. They spent a while on this task, each of them building up a bundle of dry reeds, and when their arms were full they trundled down the side of the dune and struck out for flatter ground. There they set about a different task. As twilight approached, a shear of dark blue on the horizon, they dropped the reeds onto the beach and began arranging them into what looked like geometric shapes. Darkness had come and covered their work before they were able to finish, before I'd been able to see what those shapes were supposed to be.

All of a sudden the man charged across the sand, churning it up with his heels, and made for the neighbouring house. I noticed some lights on inside. After a few moments the man returned to the beach. This time he led another person in his wake. He walked with one arm out behind him, grasping the outstretched hand of a figure that seemed able only to shuffle forward. I couldn't see much of the newcomer, just a few details as the man led him into the soft light that lit up the sand around the house. Hefty shoulders, a hump to the back. Bald and somehow broken. When the two of them stepped into the shadows, now halfway between the house and the arrangement of reeds, the man came to a stop and shouted. Farther off in the darkness, the woman sparked amber into the air. The switch-switch of a cigarette lighter, spent, or nearly so. Finally a flame sprang to life. I watched it descend to the sand and light up the reeds in a crackling frenzy. The blaze raced over them, snapping at the sky, until first one and then both shapes burned clear and bright. They made a number: 44. The woman and the boy began to sing 'Happy Birthday'. When they reached the part where the song calls for a name, the woman sang 'Shane' while the man sang 'Dad'.

In only a minute the fire had died out. The reeds had become charred flakes. The breeze swept them away and spiralled smoke across the sand. The woman joined Shane and the other man as they returned indoors. In their absence, the beach fell quiet again. A couple of hours passed. I turned off all the lights around me, ready to go to bed for the night. But just as I made to draw the curtains in the living room, I noticed movement by the water's edge. People. Two of them. I didn't need good light anymore to make out who they were. Intermittent clouds, a scattering of stars. The moon was still a few days from full. Its atmospheric glow cast a sheen across the sea. Shane kept himself steady with one hand on the woman's shoulder. She stood still and waited for him to raise a foot, to reach around with his free hand, to yank off his shoe and then switch his stance, to drop his weight onto his bare foot as he tried to pull the shoe off the other. When he could stand without assistance, holding a shoe in each hand, the woman flicked off her sandals and easily swept them up.

Slowly, moving with baby steps, the two of them began to walk along the beach. She made an effort to keep to his pace. They did not hold hands. Shane drifted into the crashing waves and walked ankle deep in the water. The woman stuck by his side but did not step into the water herself. I watched them for a time. The waves gushed over his feet and back out to sea, leaving a streak of starlight on the sand, then spilled forward again to swallow his toes, his heels, his shins. Just before the couple turned away, I saw the woman pause.

She raised an arm to point towards the stars above the horizon. Shane stopped as well and looked to the sky in an effort to follow her lead. But he looked straight up, I noticed, craning his neck to peer at the stars directly overhead. The woman let her arm drop and simply stood there, watching him, making no move to correct his line of sight. He seemed unable to see what she'd urged him to see, and as he tottered about unsteadily, now haphazardly scanning the dazzling sky, he looked to me as if he couldn't really see the beauty overhead at all.

All the screens zapped off at once. They'd been showing breaking news. Before they went blank I'd glimpsed a couple of shots from a story on what looked like an airline disaster. An illustration charting a flight path interrupted by an x, shaky footage of distant wreckage spewing out black smoke. I lingered beside my wife where she sat at the boarding gate. She clutched the canister of ashes, pressed both palms against its surface, and held it in her lap with her head bowed over it, eyes closed, in prayer or meditation.

The security staff had given us trouble when we'd tried to carry the canister through. They'd instructed us to open it. They'd peered in and eyed the ashes sceptically. I worried we wouldn't be allowed to take them with us. My wife looked harried. She hung her head. I tried to explain, in English, that we'd followed the law to the letter. We'd lodged a customs clearance request. We'd declared the ashes well in advance. We'd waited weeks for the approval of the paperwork. We'd weathered those weeks like monks, tight-lipped, back at work, focused on meeting rote responsibilities, and almost silent in each other's presence. Customs clearance arrived via post and we'd booked our flights only when we were sure the formalities had been settled. Signatures and official stamps. A new number, not a name, to put a bureaucratic label on our daughter. Then a senior officer intervened. He waved us through but gave us a scolding. He said something about packaging guidelines, about responsibility, about making sure we always read the fine print. I didn't understand it. My wife would've understood, but I'm not sure she heard.

Delayed for so long at security, we rushed straight to our

departure hall. As we navigated the maze of the terminals, moving briskly, I was conscious of being in the place, but not quite on the very ground, where Hassan and Jessica Demirović had received the news of their daughter. In my haste I looked around in search of any telling features, any background details I'd recognise from the picture I'd seen on the train, as if the space I'd entered held the stain of what I knew had happened there. But we were in a rush and nothing of what I saw seemed remarkable. At the gate my wife took a seat and held the canister tight. I watched the news until the signal was lost. I glanced around at other boarding gates to see if any screens were still in service. All of them were dark. The feed had been pulled. A blunt way of shielding airline passengers from breaking news of an aircraft accident. Didn't work. People had seen. Murmurs were going around. Terrorism, someone nearby whispered to a companion. *Again.* Flew it straight into the mountain, just like that. Can you imagine? Eerie, though, to see all those flashing screens plunge into silent black. Eerie, too, to board a plane knowing why we'd not been allowed to watch.

Thirty-something hours later, the seatbelt light blinked on. Then the overhead speakers crackled with the order to open the window sashes. The sun over Sydney poured into the cabin and seared my eyes. When the blitz of white receded, the world rippled back into view. I pressed my forehead to the pane beside me and eyed the metropolis below. Equinox, long past the worst of summer, but still the city seemed to have been gifted, or afflicted, with at least one more day of temperatures close to forty degrees.

I tried to get my bearings from above. Hard to tell from that height whether Sydney was all edges or all interior. Wide bays and spits curled around glassy waters, and inlets and coves danced with slivers of light. High-rises nestled together where land pressed into the sea, townhouses crammed in along promontories. Beyond all this, suburbs spread like a blight across the Cumberland Plain, gobbling up the continent far into the haze and smog. Such were the scorch marks of the slow explosion that had incinerated the first peoples of Port Jackson. Beneath my feet the engine rumbled the cabin with a respiratory hum. Outside, I fancied, I could hear the sizzle of hot sand at Bondi and the roar of the surf at Wanda Beach. I could hear the chatter of sunbathers twinkling with cream, the squeals of children poking jellyfish with sticks, the grumbles of rotund retirees in tight togs. I saw cancerous moles blotching burnt skin, shards of pippis between bare toes, bluebottles washed up on the shoreline, a swollen pufferfish dead in the shallows.

When the plane dipped a wing to circle once more before descending, Waverley Cemetery came into view. I saw the wrought-iron gates, the headstones, the monuments. I saw council housing towers overlooking Botany Bay and wondered which of them had once sheltered Imran bin Musa. I saw Anzac Parade carving a clearway through the city, stretching from Surry Hills down to La Perouse, and I wondered which of the streets branching off it was the site of the shop run by Hassan Demirović. Could Demirović hear the plane overhead from the comfort of his home? Would bin Musa see the contrail in the sky if he chanced to gaze up through the window of his cell? And what had the two of them seen when they'd sat where I was sitting, coming into Sydney for the first time and looking over it from above? Actually I imagined they'd been more impressed by what they couldn't see. No systemic violence. No smouldering buildings. Nobody mown down by gunfire. Peace.

At that height I wondered if I could see the intertwining of their lives. The tangle of motorways and thoroughfares and suburban streets connected the space assigned to the prisoner with the space occupied by the man who walked free. And as the plane continued coasting, I found myself unpicking the ways in which their lives might also have tangled with mine. I glanced down at Surry Hills, zeroed in on the nest of buildings that once held the pub where I'd met my wife. I scoured the harbour for Balmain and Rozelle, sites of the weekend evenings we'd spent hopping from venue to venue in search of music we enjoyed. Berry Island, a favourite picnic spot in the cooler seasons. Glebe Foreshore, our vantage point for fireworks on New Year's Eve. Customs House at Circular Quay, my place of precarious employment, and Lidcombe, where my wife's grandfather, a widower for many decades, had resettled after he turned his back on apartheid-era South Africa.

An aerial view of the city made it look like a blemish on the sun-blasted land, pockmarked with countless places of sentimental value that make up the scenery of life in familiar surroundings. It sweltered beneath the plane in a vision as distinct as I could imagine from the tarmac strewn with snow, the billboards glamorising chocolate and fine timepieces, the champagne and oyster bars and the climate-controlled hush of the airport at Oerlikon.

Every particle of my body tensed in the heat that poured through the window. Every molecule wanted to be away, to get away, from the blast furnace of the sun. The reflex came from the elements I was composed of. I wanted cold and wind. If I had to be in sight of sand and water, I wanted to be back on that beach in the Mearns. After I'd reported to Hannah the things I'd seen, told her of the man and the woman together under the stars, she shared what little she knew about them. She'd only ever met the woman, and only once. She said her name was Kerry. They'd had a chat on the beach, exchanging pleasantries about their lives, although she'd sensed a desperation in her that she couldn't account for. The woman had to be pushing forty, Hannah told me, but she wore a bikini to flaunt a figure that made Hannah, still in her twenties, jealous. Yet, Hannah added, despite appearances, Kerry's attempt at small talk amounted to concerns about ageing, crow's feet, sunspots and sagging skin, and she baldly confessed that she felt old beyond her years.

As for the husband, Hannah said she'd never seen him herself, only heard about him from her parents. *Seen* was the word she used, not *met*, as if he was a spectacle to be sought out and gazed upon. But what she knew of him was that he, too, had retreated to the beach in crisis, had been the one to lead his family there, as a way of escaping the heat of a previous life, of being always and forever soothed by cool air and the sounds of the sea.

Hannah gave me the surname of the couple.

Look them up, she said. You can find them on the web.

My wife clutched the canister of ashes beside me. She tensed her shoulders and locked her elbows to keep the ashes steady as the plane tossed us about. Stomachs dropped when we fell onto the tarmac. Bodies swayed with the bump and skid. After the plane had docked and we were free to disembark, we slogged through border control. Then my wife assigned me to gather our suitcases and deal with quarantine. She didn't have the wherewithal. She proceeded ahead by herself, carrying only the ashes.

I need to pause here. When I look back on these days, of all the images to haunt me, that's the image that most often returns. Her back to me as she walked away and her possessive, protective grip on the urn. She didn't know at the time how I would betray her trust. She didn't know how I'd insult her dignity. To be fair, neither did I. I didn't know I had the intention. But I had it. I see that now. I had a will to drive everything into the ground. To take what she wanted to hold, to end what she hoped to prolong. We landed in Australia and we didn't know, then, that we wouldn't leave together. I'm sorry I couldn't have been sincere in my way of being with her. I was in crisis. I'd been brought to the precipice.

I had to wait twenty minutes for our luggage. At the carousel I watched Sydney surreally harmonise with Switzerland. Screens were stationed around the hall, returning me to the news I'd caught before we took off. Tracts of wreckage strewn across an Alpine landscape. Fuselage and shrapnel, but also, miraculously, the recognisable debris of ordinary lives cut short. A red beanie. A black handbag. Somebody's shoe, a video game console. Somebody's cardigan, knitted, turquoise. All this along with the broken parts of the plane and investigators in flak jackets picking through the disarray. Then our suitcases came around and I caught up with my wife and we trekked to the exit.

Her parents met us at the arrivals gate. An awkward reunion beside a pot of fragrant bougainvillea. My father-in-law, tall and weather-beaten, stretched his lips into a smile without showing any teeth, and in jagged motions he moved close to wrap his arms around me. From his tension I could tell he really only wanted to hold his daughter. She and her mother stood locked together, pressed hard against each other, both with tears streaking their cheeks and dampening their shoulders. My father-in-law reached for his wife's elbow to guide her away and when she stepped back she turned to me. Stout, garishly lipsticked, with big hoop earrings and powerful perfume, she came to me and threw herself at me and wept. My father-in-law took my wife by one arm, held the canister of ashes in his free hand, and leant in to plant a kiss on her forehead.

My in-laws owned a two-door compact car with barely any room behind the front seats. The four of us squeezed in, luggage stacked so high it blocked the rear window, and then my father-in-law sped off for the sandstone chasms of Sydney.

Strange days stretched out ahead of us. My wife and I would start off staying at her parents' home. We'd take a couple of days to adjust and then my parents would fly down from Brisbane. My in-laws kept a granny flat in a corner of their backyard and they'd offered my parents the bed. Finally, congregated, the six of us would scatter the ashes. Afterwards, we'd spend a few more days in Sydney before we'd split up again. My wife and I would farewell her parents, then fly north with mine for the Easter break. We'd fly out mid-April. Now, though, late in the day, shadows of steel and glass crept across the city and laid darkness on the streets. We came to the edge of the CBD and inched into the nightmare of rush hour. Chauffeured by a man whose stinginess was the stuff of family legend, we picked a path through Woolloomooloo to avoid the toll roads to the expressway. The car slowed to a crawl. My wife let her head rest on my shoulder and tried to doze. My mother-in-law reached out to turn on the radio and catch the last few reports at the top of the hour.

—difficulty after the funerals, Mr. Demirović—

No, said my wife. Off.

I was surprised to hear his name on the news. It had been weeks now since he'd last had a profile that captured media attention. After his appearance at the memorial service, his story had gone static.

—claims he sought the meeting because—

My mother-in-law obliged and with a push of the button cut the newscaster's voice.

I didn't say so, but I would've liked to hear more. Two days deprived of civilisation, I felt as if all the world was further ahead in time than I was.

I only want to hear the latest, my mother-in-law complained. That flight in France. While we were driving in to pick you up they said it was probably the captain who did it. Can you imagine? Not even a hijacking. The man behind the controls. Awful. They'll retrieve the black box soon, you watch, and then it'll all come out.

I don't want to hear it, said my wife.

Terrifying. Absolutely terrifying. All those families.

Not right now, said my wife.

Eyes closed, she tilted her head away from me to rest against the window. Sunlight splashed over her face as we crept out of the CBD, stuttered with a strobing effect as we drove beneath the girders of the Harbour Bridge. Port Jackson stretched out around us, beneath us, calm and smooth and dotted with ferries and speedboats that scratched whiteness across the cobalt surface of the water.

Take a good look out there, my father-in-law said with pride while keeping his eyes on the road ahead. What a day. Unbelievable.

At Crows Nest we turned towards The Spit and crossed the water again to head for Manly Vale, Curl Curl, Dee Why. Speeding on through Seaforth and Balgowlah, time began to unwind around us. When I caught sight of the places I once used to visit with my wife, the flow of things shifted into reverse. We'd taken to hiring paddleboats at Sandy Bay the summer my in-laws went to New Zealand and we looked after their house. We'd powered over the pristine waters of Shell Cove and brunched most days in a café at the marina across the strait. The marina slid back behind us as we drove along the bridge, and into view came Clontarf Beach and the stretch of sand and scrubland leading to Grotto Point. Early in our time together, during what turned out to be our courtship, my wife had taken me there to show me the ancient engravings overlooking Washaway. Rock art and the remnants of a midden. She'd hoped to win me over to my new city, *her* city, to show me things I'd been deprived of growing up in the squalid corners of Brisbane. Later on I'd urged her to come and camp with me one night near the cliffs at Dobroyd. Off track, in the open air, beneath a night sky alive with pinpoint lights. No tent, no canvas, no sleeping bags or pillows, only the naked earth and a thin blanket to keep us warm. We talked about making a fire but we didn't follow through. Our two bodies nestled together against the cold. We'd go there again years later, decked out in suit and gown, to pose for wedding pictures. An outdoor ceremony beneath a marquee at Reef Bay, confetti exploding over us like sea spray at the lookout. We still had the prints at home, although I couldn't say exactly where.

I turned away from the beach to face straight ahead while we drove through the coastal suburbs. In Fairlight were the places we'd go when we realised we'd become a proper couple. The galleries and theatres we'd check out when we were feeling stylish. The fish-and-chip joints where we'd pick up a dirty meal when we felt comfortable acting like dags. Further on, near Manly lagoon, was the spot beside the water where we'd often spend weekend afternoons with friends. At first our friends were the friends my wife had known before I'd found her. Then, as time went on, we gathered mutual friends, friends who'd only ever known us as a pair. I still didn't feel an affinity for the country, but I could see, or remember, that we'd made our lives here as nice, as amenable, as we could.

Now we drove on into a tangle of memories, passing by countless reminders of the way things used to be. We glided through places that had long ago become the stuff of our spur-of-the-moment exchanges and reminiscences in Switzerland. Do you remember where we went on the day that—who we bumped into when we—what happened that time we were at—and what she said when it started to—or why we met them there instead of? Yes. No. I'm not sure. I can't quite. I might be confused. Maybe. Do you mean the same weekend we—but wasn't that where—or am I thinking of that other occasion? The answers to those questions, the times and places they pointed to, thickened everywhere outside the windows and whipped past the car like the clouds that had engulfed the plane we'd stepped off.

On Pittwater Road we snagged a red light. My father-in-law had a habit of cutting the engine whenever he had to wait for the green. With a choke the grumbling that had followed us across the city fell quiet. The stillness was broken only by the swishing of the cars that sped through the intersection up ahead. My wife, I saw, had fallen asleep. My mother-in-law swiped at the screen of her phone, scrolling through the news. On the far side of the road stood a row of shabby shops. In a window over there I thought for an instant I could see the smiling face of Alanna Demirović. I forced my eyelids to flutter, tried to force the illusion away, then took another look through the glass. I still saw Alanna Demirović. Surrounding her, in smaller photographs, were the faces of the five other children who'd died. Above her, in large handwritten letters, were two words: NEVER FORGET. The pictures and the words had been stuck to a placard. The placard remained fixed to a tall wooden stake, the better to raise it above a crowd. Remnants of the protests at the cemetery, I supposed. The remains of an anger that I guessed had cooled. The colour had faded somewhat. The pictures were curling at the edges. The shop looked to be a laundromat full of coin-operated machines.

Not a staff member in sight. Someone had taken advantage of the space to keep their message alive.

So did you follow the news on that sorry affair? my father-in-law asked, catching my eye in the rear-view mirror after he'd looked across to what I'd seen.

Only from a distance.

Lots of angry people, he said.

I guess that's to be expected.

The lights changed and we jerked forward. The movement dragged the smiling girl out of sight. A line of palm trees swept into view and whizzed past as the car picked up pace.

Somewhere out there, I realised, was her negative image. Elsewhere in the thick of the city. On the streets, the footpaths, in the full force of the sun. Indoors with the blinds drawn, cosseted in a muggy room, plodding towards the end of the day. Given the way she'd been treated, taken in by the authorities and granted anonymity by order of the family court, that's where I imagined her. If she wasn't still a ward of the state, probably she'd been assigned to a foster carer who knew how to be discreet. Seven years old. How much did she comprehend of what her father had done? How much had she been shielded from? How much had broken into her field of awareness? What of the people around her, the people who encountered her daily? Had they come to know who she was, how she connected to the crime? Would she ever know the truth? That last one was the question that nagged at me as we sped along Pittwater Road. For this girl I foresaw a future so arranged by the authorities as to divest her of all traces of her past, her family, for her own wellbeing. I saw a future so organised as to force her to start over, to rebuild herself from the bottom up. How could she reach a more advanced age, twelve years, fifteen years, eighteen years, and learn then about what her father had done, what he'd destroyed in revenge for her mistreatment, and not feel that her hands, too, were stained with the blood he'd spilled? She didn't ask for any of it, not from her father, not from the state, but she'd been tarred with guilt by association and cast aside in the public eye like so much collateral damage. Nobody had printed pictures of her face. Nobody had memorialised her at a protest or in a shop window or anywhere in the press. She'd been shoved into the shadows and kept there, and there was no way that anyone could in good conscience bring her into the light, and yet, and yet, all of this, the destruction and the mourning and the responses to disaster, stemmed from that girl and her father's singular concerns for her future.

Shane had managed to keep his son out of the media spotlight. He'd given his family a remote existence specifically to preserve the privacy of his son, to hide his boy from prying eyes. No less than for Demirović, no less than for bin Musa, his child, that lumbering man, had been the rock upon which he'd driven himself to ruin. He hadn't managed to avoid attention himself, though it had left him long before my path crossed with his. That's what I learnt when I listened to Hannah and looked him up online. I learnt about his life, about its abbreviations, and I read my knowledge into what I saw the following night.

A clear sky, no wind. Moonlight on the sand once more. Husband and wife returned to the waves. I stood at the living room window, in shadow, and I tried to focus.

Kerry faltered. I guess she gasped. She'd been leading Shane along the shore again. Now her sandals fell from her fingers and she released her husband's hand. She raised her foot and seized it, angled it around to scrutinise the sole, and pursed her lips as she probed with a finger at blood. I pictured a shard of seashell, about the size of a fingernail, sticking out of the hole it had sliced into her skin. As she stood and tended her wound, I noticed Shane lingering, listlessly, an arm's length away from her. I realised then that he was tending a wound as well. He seemed to be holding his hands together, almost wringing them, and he cast his gaze around in something like agitation, away from his wife, towards his house further up the beach, above him at the sky overhead. All the while he pushed and prodded with thumb and forefinger the skin warped around his left elbow. Just beyond the elbow the arm ended in a blunt cicatrix. Radius and ulna broken halfway to the wrist, sealed in a patchwork of scar tissue. He grappled at a misshapen nub.

How did they navigate the simple things of living together? Not even the give and take of a marriage, just the first things of daily interaction. If he were to smile at her, I wondered, would she recognise the expression on his face? If he were to reach out to her on the sand, how could she know whether he meant to help her or whether he needed help?

He'd been bent over the telephone booth near noon on his twenty-second birthday. A silver cord spiralled out of a bulky box to connect to the handset. He'd held the receiver to his ear and heard the chirp of the dial tone. Did he hesitate to make the call? Did he wonder whether he'd wake the sleeping boy at the other end of the line? Beads of sweat crawled down his back, the length of his spine, like bugs beneath his fatigues. The desert dusted the rubber of his boots. He scuffed at the sand with a heel and heard it swish. He hadn't pictured himself being here, back when he signed on the dotted line. Early eighties. Thatcher was making trouble. He'd signed up for this gig as a way of avoiding the real conflict, at a time when diplomatic tensions were becoming denunciations at the colder ends of the Earth. But then the Israeli tanks had blustered into Lebanon, and Britain dispatched its grunts to an international peacekeeping mission, and so here he was, with his wife and son far away, and five minutes to call home was the best his commanders could give him.

When Kerry picked up the phone, I suppose, she wished him a happy birthday, told him she missed him, asked if he was safe, if he got along with his colleagues, if he felt the language barrier obstructed his work with the locals. He asked after the boy, I imagine, quizzed her on his health and growth and what new things he'd learnt, whether his burbles and mumbles were turning into sentences yet, and he'd asked after Kerry, too, how she was coping in his absence, whether she had the help she needed or whether it was all too much. Not that he enjoyed the privilege of privacy or the time to go into detail on any of this. When their conversation ended he returned the receiver to its cradle and for the last time in his life he used his left hand.

They'd met at university. Only one class each week. This they revealed in passing in an interview with the *Guardian*. They didn't say more than that, but the timelines of events implied the trajectory of their marriage. Their relationship, I inferred, spilled over only briefly into the pub and quickly into the bedroom. Illicit, a spontaneous thrill, perhaps a first for both of them. My guess is that neither one held any deep interest in the other's ambitions, and neither dreamed that their affair would survive the end of term. But then there was a rupture in the way things were supposed to work. A missed period. A test at the doctor's surgery. Suddenly they found themselves on the way to becoming parents. In the process, they also found they'd lost the parents who'd raised them.

Shane came from the working class. His parents were still trapped in it. They lived on a council estate in Gilmerton, outside Edinburgh. When he'd earnt the grades to study in Dundee, they'd scraped up enough to send him there and get him out of the place he'd been raised. He'd had to take weekend work to make ends meet, signed on to train in the army reserves, but day by day he was writing himself into a story he could control. When Kerry shared the news with him, he pushed for an abortion. Neither of them should have to risk the futures they were creating, he said. But Kerry came from a Catholic family, respectable, middle-class, and she wanted nothing to do with abortion. Too scandalous, too morally compromising. She went to her parents for help. Humbled, on her knees, but pregnant to a boy she hadn't married and barely knew. They sent her away. What next? Shane hoped his parents could do something. He returned home to a storm of insults. His father called him an imbecile. His mother couldn't accept that he'd thrown away his fortunes on a fling. They had no resources to offer. No money, not even goodwill. Only disappointment and vitriol.

Kerry and Shane retreated to his ramshackle bedsit in the backstreets of Balgay. He held her close and couldn't think of what to do. *Sir,* I imagine she said, desperate to break the silence, desperate to find some way forward, *Sir—will you marry me?*

They were wed, in a hurry, with little romance.

Then the antenatal tests started to flag anomalies. Problems with oxygen levels in utero, with the circumference of the head. The palm of his hand to the curve of her belly and expressions of hope for the best. Birth. A boy. Complex needs. Down's Syndrome. A malformed thyroid. A degenerative condition they couldn't pronounce and problems with respiration, oxygenation. Diagnosis. Diagnosis after diagnosis. All the hopes the parents held, all the possibilities they'd dreamt of for their child, shrank away in the presence of his fragile body. Did they hope for anything at all anymore, abandoned to care for him by themselves? When all you really want is for a child to live another day, another week, is it right to think of that as hope?

They knew they'd have to try again. A need for social support, a need for financial support. Another round of pleading with parents. Shane's still had nothing to offer. Kerry's wondered if the boy's deformities weren't a form of punishment for her insolence. There were no good decisions to be made. Shane made the least bad decision he could think of. He put his studies on hold and stepped up his commitment to the reserves. Full-time, a reliable salary. No inclination to fight for a bunch of islands of no use to anyone but the penguins. He stepped sideways in the ranks, into peacekeeping, assured by his superiors that nobody anticipated action anytime soon. What a fool.

The growing pulse of a migraine pushed him to wake in his hospital bed. The thudding of blood, the beep of machines, the drip of fluid through tubes. A gag on something stuck down his throat, a wince at something jammed into a vein in the one wrist he still had. Voices not in foreign tongues. Doctors trying to extract recollections. Did he know his name? Did he know where he was? Bandages tangled his limbs like vines and his body was covered in bedsheets he couldn't kick off. Did he remember what had happened? The whip-crack of a faraway bombardment and the cackle of gunfire nearby. As if with an exhausted heave, hot wind rippled the cypresses outside his window.

So. A roadside explosive. A bomb stuffed into a sack of garbage. Seventeen others dead. They'd borne the brunt of the blast. Shane, at the phone booth, had been further away. One of the doctors said he'd been lucky, all things considered. The structural damage had come entirely from the shrapnel. His left hand had been severed, his left eye pierced and lost. The fire had caused only superficial injuries. Did this mean he'd recover? That's what Shane wanted to know. What it meant, the doctor told him, was that none of these injuries would impair his functioning in the world. That was an evasion of the question. Over the following days he understood why the doctor had dodged the facts. When the explosion had knocked him out, his clothes had gone up in flames. He'd fallen into the dust, unconscious, and he'd lain there to burn. His hair, he learnt, had been singed off, every last strand of it, and his skin had been ruined beyond hope of repair. He learnt this from an orderly who spoke to him of what she could see, spoke his new body into existence, before he'd regained enough vision to see himself again. His lips had blistered so badly that they'd melted into the rest of his face. His nose and left ear had been stripped away entirely, leaving behind only wide, exposed orifices that sank shafts of shadow into his head.

Eventually nurses folded back his bedsheets and unwound the bandages. Eventually they brought him a mirror, gave in to his demands for one, and in between a change of the dressings, they allowed him to see, in fragments, what he had become. His scalp was bare. The left side and the front of his face were flat. His nostrils and ears had become holes surrounded by crusts of scar tissue, skin torn to rags and stitched back in place like a quilt. Worst of all was the skin stretched over his forehead and scalp, and down over his chin, his jaw, his throat. The flames had peeled it away in shreds, torn it from the tendons that bound it to bone and muscle. What remained was something crustacean, a grotesque reconstruction of a person, hot pink where strips had touched and reconnected, blood red where the fire had cauterised them. Skin rose and fell in waves across his face and down his torso, his chest and back, his arms, beneath the sheets to his groin and legs. It buckled where one strip overlapped another. It yawned with a scarlet sheen where severed strips had healed too far apart.

Obviously I have no words for his pain, for the physical experience of it. All I can conceive of, really, are images, and even then only from outside his body. Kerry couldn't come to visit him at first. She had to take care of the boy at home and, in any event, she'd never be allowed to land in Beirut while the conflict held. His commanders transferred him to better care in Tel Aviv. She arranged to leave the boy with a neighbour for just a weekend. She touched down at Ben Gurion and raced to her husband's bedside. He barely stirred. She stood by him and tried to take in the damage. She hadn't planned for a child. She hadn't planned for a marriage. Even by this point in her life, she was growing accustomed to watching her possibilities atrophy around the hardships she was obliged to accept. But what did she see when she saw him for the first time? All the little pleasures she might have been able to pursue, receding from every one of her hypothetical futures to be locked away, now inaccessible, inside her husband's scars. She would be confined with him, indefinitely, in a sterile shared existence that neither of them wanted.

As the healing skin hardened around him, it encased him like a carapace. It firmed itself with the pinches and indentations of melted wax returning to solid form. In this way it gave form to a face that would become, very briefly, a symbol of opposition to British involvement in conflicts abroad. I found pictures on the internet, records of Shane's dalliance with a coalition of activist groups in London. Pacifist campaigners wanted to cease all involvement in the Middle East. They hoped to bring the peacekeepers home. Until they found Shane, they'd had no shocking images to energise public support for their cause. Faraway desert landscapes, wounded men wearing keffiyehs. Stalled tanks, morose soldiers. These were the visuals they'd relied on. Now, though, they had a human face to make a visceral appeal against foreign adventurism. Now they could advance their cause by triggering a viewer's instinct to recoil. Shane consented to his involvement. He agreed to have his picture taken. He still had a son to support. He needed money and the coalition had a budget. In the pictures I found online, he sat in his hospital bed like a pale, dejected ogre. In the simplest, bluntest terms, he had a face that made him look no longer human.

Of course he attracted attention from the Ministry of Defence. Nobody there wanted him to be the poster child for the agitations of pacifists. But they couldn't be seen to threaten wounded servicemen with legal entanglements, so they took the path of least resistance and paid him a lump sum. Enough to buy a house on the beach. Enough for him to meet his basic needs, and those of his wife, with extra help from a modest monthly pension. Enough, too, to see that his son was properly looked after. Enough, then, to set him up so that he could at last remove himself from view, retreat from those who'd watch him.

Stepping into my in-laws' house, I stepped out of the flow of normal time. I bungled a couple of suitcases through the door and bent over mine to steady it. When I stood up and looked around, I felt the flow of time slacken and loop back into the past. My in-laws hurried about me. I was dimly aware of their movements. My wife wheeled her carry-on case inside. Her mother shuffled into the kitchen to put the kettle on. Her father moved to the back door to call out for the dog. But all this happened slowly, or to a tempo not synchronised with mine.

Shane and Kerry moved to the Mearns a couple of years after the blast. I see him reunited with his son. The boy, slow and silent, shrinks from the gambolling monster who approaches him with open arms. Kerry tries to show him there's nothing to fear. She puts her arms around her husband and feels, beneath him, inside him, the echo of what he used to be. But it's a staged performance, a set of cues for the boy to follow. She didn't truly love her husband before he went away. How could she begin to love him now? She could only tolerate touching him through layers of clothes. There could be no caresses. Even just brushing against his bare skin made her revolted and angry and lonesome.

I looked around the house. At first I couldn't find anything that had changed since the last time I'd been there. The front door opened up right onto the living room. My in-laws hadn't so much as hung a new picture or purchased a new rug. The same black coffee table, scattered with the same opaline coasters, sat square between the same television set and the same old hideous grey vinyl sofa. A staircase to one side led up to the bedrooms. On the far side of the living room, just behind the sofa, a breakfast bar formed the outermost edge of an open-plan kitchen. The same family photographs clung to the fridge, the same familiar snapshots of my wife as a girl and of the day we wed. *Sir—will you marry me?* That's the young woman in the song, but that was my wife as well. I hadn't been the one to propose. I hadn't had the faith in a favourable response.

Watching Shane as I had done, from a distance, I'd been struck by the way he moved. Clearly he moved as a man who'd had to relearn how to walk, who'd learnt to treat his body like an antique timepiece, an assemblage of interlocking mechanisms, which he had to crank into action, by force, even to attempt a task as simple as crossing a room. He seemed to no longer know how to take the measure of himself, of his proportions, relative to his environment. No surprise, in a way. I imagine he would've watched himself disappear from his own life. Photographs on the mantelpiece, the bedroom wall, the kitchen counter, all removed over time, put away in a cupboard, by a wife who couldn't bear to have them around anymore. Photographs in which the camera had caught him the way he used to be. Wedding reception. Delivery room. Enlistment ceremony. Irrecoverable moments. One day, I suppose, he woke up to find that his own home contained no traces of his former self. Every day after that, he'd wake up with the sense that he'd become incapable of bringing his true identity to the surface of the world. It was locked inside him now, not even visible in those solitary moments when he stood before the bathroom mirror and, looking deep into his one remaining eye, he'd see, looking back at him, whatever you wanted to call that thing. Not Shane.

Beside the sofa, on a tiny hardwood table, sitting atop a doily, was a docking station for a pair of mobile phones. That's what really snagged my attention. It was the one thing that wasn't the same. The landline I remembered on that table was gone. I held myself at the threshold, the door behind me still open, and I looked at the unsightly device. Right there by that little table was maybe where my father-in-law had taken the call from my parents. At any rate, his phone had started ringing. He'd already received the picture I'd sent from the hospital. Now I could see his face as his world broke down and reshaped itself. He scooped up the phone in expectation of further details, greater joy. But through the speaker he heard my father's voice. Not my wife's. Not even mine. So his smile disappeared. What words would have come down the line? We've just received news, something's happened, the doctors are, it's all so goddamn, what to do, we can't believe.

Let's say he held the phone to his ear and scanned the room in stunned silence. The walls. The sofa. His entire environment, the bland comfort of it all, was wholly unmoved by the violence of the rupture. Still, in a way, he'd been blessed by not knowing. The world in which he was a grandfather had existed longer for him than it had ever existed in fact. He had preserved it, dwelt in it awhile, as I stood halfway round the planet watching it collapse. But then the explosion reached him. My father spoke, softly, and everything erupted.

I accepted the tea with every intention of letting it go cold. Accepted the offer to placate my mother-in-law. She had to take care of us, had to show that she wanted to take care of us, had to be shown and reassured that she *was* in fact taking care of us. She insisted on tea despite the heat. I took it from her with an apology, said I needed to lie down awhile, just to gather my wits, to reel in my thoughts from their mooring in a time zone on the far side of the planet. I trudged upstairs to the guestroom that had long ago been my wife's bedroom. My wife said she'd retreat with me. She wanted to unpack. She followed at my heels. I tried to keep the teacup steady. With one hand she dragged her suitcase behind her and let it whack against each step. With the other she held on to the canister of ashes.

In the guestroom I set the tea on the floor by the head of the bed, then I lay on top of the duvet, freshly turned, and listened to my wife unpack. She opened a window to let in a breeze that carried with it the faint snarls of the sea. That sea, not so far away, would in time become the recipient of her offering, her scattered tithe. The canister she placed on a console table beneath the windowsill. She unzipped her suitcase, yanked at a drawer, creaked the wardrobe doors, jangled coathangers and flapped open folded tops and skirts. She deposited toiletries in the en suite bathroom her parents had built after she'd left home. Everything smelled of patchouli and menthol. By the time I came back to myself, though I didn't think I'd fallen asleep, I could see that the tea had grown cold. A skin of brown milk had stiffened over its surface.

I'd been out of Scotland for about a year when I heard from

Hannah for the first time in six months. All told, I'd spent four weeks at her parents' house before I felt enough like myself to move elsewhere, this time south, to try to jumpstart my life at a remove from the hauntings of the past. She asked me how I was holding up. She said she'd fallen into a new relationship, something serious this time, and said she'd decided to return to her studies while pulling beers at night. Anyway, she added, after the chitchat dwindled, I had a mind to call you because do you remember the kid? At the Mearns? I never learnt his name.

The kid?

The boy. The son. You remember?

I remembered. He had the broad figure of a man, so I hadn't thought of him as a kid, but I remembered. Something of his shadowed form swung about, flopped side to side, in my mind's eye. He hacked his breaths and his mouth dangled open as he moved with leaden steps across the sand. I'd even seen him clearly once, when he'd gone into the kitchen late at night to fetch a glass of water. The lights leapt on and caught my attention. His expression, from a distance, was entirely blank. His eyes were droopy and vacant. He filled the glass and drained it in one unbroken scull. Then he switched off the lights and left.

Well, said Hannah, I heard he died.

I didn't know what to say. I felt an unexpected something in my chest.

After a moment I said, When?

Three or four weeks ago. But I only just found out yesterday. From my mum.

I don't mean when, I said. I mean, how?

Well, she said, he had that condition, right? You remember?

No, I said at first. Then something tugged at my memory. Wait, I said. You mean that thing. Something to do with his blood.

Blood oxygen.

What was it?

I can't recall the name.

No, I said. Right. Okay, I think I remember.

What I remembered, really, was that I'd been too involved in unearthing the drama of Shane's life to have paid much attention to his son. I'd only seen the other man as an accessory to Shane's story, a pretext for his actions and decisions. I hadn't thought of him as his own person. He seemed so dependent on his parents, so removed from his own mind, that I didn't know how or to whom I might extend my sympathies. But it was true that the news reports had mentioned his ill health and poor prospects. Something to do with a degenerative condition that made it ever harder for his respiratory system to filter impurities from the air, to extract the oxygen for circulation through his body. This came on top of everything else: the complex needs, the Down's Syndrome, the thyroid, one or two other problems I couldn't recall. Still, I'd assumed, or I'd been led to understand, that the family had some way of treating the condition. Money for drugs and machinery. Access to medical specialists. Enough to help him through the worst of it. Enough to not cut short his life.

Four weeks ago? I said to Hannah.

Three or four, yeah. But like I said, I only just found out. Apparently there's a plan to put a headstone beside the house. Council wrote to my parents to get consent.

They're *burying* him there? I said.

No, it's just a memorial thing. He's already been cremated, from what I heard. The idea is just to have something there to remember him by. Y'know.

Well, I said, I mean, that's awful. What can I say? So premature. It's tragic.

Not that the news of the man's death left me reeling. Not exactly. I had that feeling in my body, something like the axial tilt of slow vertigo, but what sprang to mind, what set upon my thoughts like a raptor descending on its prey, was concentration, focus, by force of confinement. Relentless logic. Mathematical in its precision. I'd seen Shane on his forty-fourth birthday. He'd been injured on his twenty-second. He'd placed himself in harm's way for the sake of his son. The ruins he'd been reduced to were the fuel for the life his son had lived so far. They were what made his son's survival possible. Now, I realised, those ruins had been with him, had *been* him, for more than half his existence. He had spent most of his life in that shattered state. The balance of his experience had caught up with the way he was seen by the world, and the beneficiary of the price he'd paid to survive was his son. He had degraded himself for the integrity of the sickly boy. He'd reduced himself to fragments so that someone he loved wouldn't fall apart.

That *was* love, wasn't it? The real thing. The authentication of it. He'd wrenched himself through the agony of each day for the sake of that boy, that young man. He had every right and every reason to end his own life, to end his pain, but he didn't do it. His hours of persistence, of endurance, of just living on, testified to something profound inside him, some feeling for his son, by which he must have convinced himself that his own pains were worth withstanding. That they were the price he had to pay to hold on to something precious. That they bought him something he couldn't live without.

I might've seen this more easily if I'd spent less time at the window and picked up the book I'd dropped on the table. It's all right there in the very first song, for those who have the composure to listen. In retrospect, when I revise my memories of the beach house, I open the book again and I devote my attention to the early pages. I hear, too, the jauntiness and then the plangent tones of the singer I've come to adore. The young man agrees to take the maiden's hand in marriage, but only on one condition. *Yes*, he says, *I'll marry thee—if you can answer—this for me:* and with that insistence, delivered not in jest but in earnest, he reels off a list of riddles. *What is greener—than the grass?* he asks,

and what is smoother
than a glass?
and what is louder
than a horn?
and what is sharper
than a thorn?
and what is deeper
than the sea?

and, he asks, forfeiting rhyme in the last line of his questioning, *what is stronger—than the waves?* and he falls silent and awaits the young woman's reply.

Outside the window, the sea growled and sighed.

The young woman is a capable person. She is wiser than the merry trickster she has fallen for. The answers come to her easily and she recites them with faith in her talents. Each one is an abstraction that belies the sensual qualities he has attempted to give it. Envy, she says, is the answer to his first enquiry, a defect of the heart that shines *greener—than the grass*. Flattery, she says, is the answer to the second, a false social grace that is *smoother—than a glass*. Rumour, she adds, is the third answer, a pernicious force *louder—than a horn*, and the fourth is slander, a source of pain much *sharper—than a thorn*. To the second-to-last question she answers, Regret. Regret is *deeper—than the sea*, she sings, and then she arrives at the young man's last riddle, which she deflates with a single syllable.

Love, she says:

Love is stronger
than the waves …

The words rang their refrain through my head. Love is stronger than the waves. Love is stronger than the waves. But whose love? And did it matter? Shane's son was dead. The waves thundered on. His wife had never felt love for him. Still the waves thundered on. I had my wife in the guestroom with me. I watched her take the canister of ashes from its place on the console table. I watched her resettle it respectfully, almost ceremonially, on top of a whitewood dresser at the foot of the bed. The dresser was decorated with another doily, this one made of faded silk, which gave the gunmetal urn a nauseating cast of puce. I could feel in my chest the weary pounding of my heart. I could hear, outside, the tireless pounding of the waves. I knew which was the stronger force.

The next time Hannah called me, I told her what I'd seen. Two figures at a distance. Too far away to recognise, in the flesh, all the details I'd seen in the photographs I found online. But I wanted to see him, I realised as I spoke, to see how he inhabited his body, how he moved in his skin. I wanted to meet him face to face and make him real.

Hey, said my wife.

I looked up from where I lay on the bed to find her hand on my shoulder. Maybe I had been asleep after all.

Hey, said my wife. Come outside with me.

At some point she'd closed the window so that only an inch remained open. Outside, I saw, the sky had darkened. It had lost its scarlet tinge and turned grey. But the air was sweet with the aroma of bottlebrush and it still felt sticky and warm.

Where to? I said.

Just the beach.

The muscles up and down my spine tensed at the sound of the word.

What for? I said.

I winced as I turned over on the duvet, onto my back. The ache and twinge of thirty-odd hours cramped inside the cabin of a plane.

She didn't answer my question.

Just come, she said, and held out her hand to help me rise.

Downstairs the news blared from the television. My wife went into the kitchen to fill a bottle of water. I lingered in the living room and waited for her to join me. My in-laws sat on the sofa and watched the screen intently. The newscaster said the European aviation authorities had confirmed the crash was caused by human activity. But, they said, it appeared that the co-pilot, not the captain, had been the one at fault. He'd locked the captain out of the cockpit, taken control of the plane, flown it straight into the side of a mountain. One hundred and forty-four passengers were dead, including two Australians, plus an airline crew of six, including the man responsible for the disaster. At this stage, though, it was too early to ascribe a motive to the crime. My in-laws watched with interest but without investment, as the news moved on to a story about the reburial of Richard III. The bones of the king had been found years ago, encased in asphalt beneath a supermarket car park. Now Leicester Cathedral had orchestrated an opulent send-off, a televised event complete with celebrity guests, to make amends for centuries of neglect. I watched my in-laws sitting together in staid silence, taking in the pompous proceedings, only breathing, quietly, and I heard in my head the echo of what I'd heard in that men's room when I called them to deliver the news. Only breathing down the line, white noise with minor fluctuations.

My wife walked to the front door, drink bottle in hand, and held the flyscreen open for me. I stepped out into the warmth of the dusk and, by instinct, following a route familiar to my inner compass, I started off for Dee Why Beach.

A sensor light outside Shane and Kerry's house had woken me. I'd fallen asleep on the sofa. This was a couple of days after I'd told Hannah what I'd seen. I inched up from the sofa to look outside and saw, backlit by the glare of the bulb, the stumbling form of Shane. He wore a hoodie to cover his head, but there was no mistaking his posture. He seemed to be hauling something cumbersome down the sandbank between the houses. Some sort of giant contraption, some enormous mess of angled limbs. Only when he had straggled to the edge of the water did I realise what it was. He unfolded a tripod and went about fixing a telescope to it. He planted its feet in soft, wet sand, and once or twice the waves sloshed around it. The sensor light blinked off, threw darkness over him. Above the beach the night sky yawned, lavish and wild with stars.

As we approached The Strand, the sand and sea came into sight. Bathers still dotted the beach. Some sat in chairs to soak up the last of the rays, some had only just arrived to set up picnics against the backdrop of the sunset. But before I could make for the waves, my wife took my hand and led me away. Let's go down the headland, she said.

I tensed again, knowing now that this was no spontaneous change in direction.

The path we followed twisted round the rock pools and clung to the base of the cliffs. To my right rose a tower of stratified sandstone, layer upon layer, piled high and topped with scrub. To my left the sea surged up and sprayed the air with bursts of salty haze. Water slopped over the slabs of stone underfoot. We started to lose our traction. I reached out behind me to hold my wife's hand, to help her rebalance, before we pressed on. Then we came to the uphill stretch and climbed above the swell. As we strained towards the clifftop, a southerly wind punished the headland. It carried with it the pong of seaweed gone rancid in the sun. From on high, out to the east, the waves looked less ragged, more serene and stately, even artful. Some gargantuan hand had picked up a squeegee and streaked shapes across the water. Lines of little whitecaps scudded over the blue in odd, misshapen mosaics. The quarter-moon rose above it all, pale pink in the last of the sun. Here and there the first few stars had emerged.

Shane believed he had the cosmos in his veins. At least that's what he'd once said to an interviewer. He'd always dreamt of the stars, he said. Poring over the night sky had engrossed him as a child, and when he'd landed a spot at university, even if only at Dundee, he'd set his course by the stars and signed up to study astrophysics. An ambitious choice for a boy from North Lanarkshire. Stellar populations were what he'd fixed his sights on.

He never had the chance to complete his degree, never had the opportunity to write his dissertation, but now, I saw, he'd ended up in a place where as often as not the skies were clear enough even for someone like him, with his vision so badly impaired, to put his eye to a telescope and gaze upon celestial bodies a billion light years distant from his own. He could still admire and submit himself to wonder. He could still feel awe.

Shane bent over the eyepiece, contorted his figure to peer in and stargaze without tumbling to the ground. There he was, in front of me, a captive to the sky. I knew I couldn't just sit and watch him from a distance. But I didn't want to disturb him either, didn't want to approach him and rip him out of his reverie. I shrugged on my coat and pulled the hood over my head. I slipped out a side door and onto the reeds that shivered in the breeze. Skirting around the neighbouring house, I dropped down the dunes to the waves and doubled back to face Shane. He stood ankle-deep in the water, a lumpen figure in shadow with his eye still pressed to the cylinder, still geared to the stars overhead. I made my way towards him, steadily, timing my steps with the swish and suck of the tide.

At the headland the waves boomed over the rocks like mortar lobbed into a war zone. *Love is—stronger—than the waves.* I heard the words in my head again and again, again and again. *Love is—stronger—than the waves.* These were the sorts of waves that gave those words their meaning. They had the murderous strength that you'd want something precious to exceed. A love any stronger than those waves would be mighty indeed. My wife led me up to the summit of the headland, picking a path over the stones and through the low-lying bushes, until we emerged atop the outlook with the drop of the cliffs at our feet. Stretching away from the cliffs were the sands of Curl Curl Beach, bordered by the road that led to the next lookout at Freshwater. At the base of the cliffs whitewash charged at scattered boulders and fringed the blue of the sea, dark as a contusion. When I looked over the edge I could see my vague reflection far below. Rippled and indistinct, blotched upon the roiling waves, drawn thin at a distance, but mine.

Had Shane heard me approaching in the darkness? Had my feet chewed into the sand too loudly during a lull in the crashing tide? As I approached him I saw a seething wave kick up phosphorescence that lingered on the shore, that sparkled around his toes, before the water receded and took the magic with it. All of a sudden, though, Shane stood upright and turned to face me directly. I froze at a distance and looked at him. The sea swept in again, then swept out again, then swept in once more before I realised that even though he kept looking at me he couldn't see me distinctly, couldn't be sure he was actually seeing a person. His one good eye, I noticed, ran the colour of quartz. His other eye was made of glass. I held myself there in suspension, waiting for more waves to break, waiting long enough for Shane to believe again that he was on the beach alone. I stayed as still as I possibly could with the sea alive all around us, and silently I recoiled in horror at what I saw.

I don't mean that I recoiled at the horror of his appearance. It's true that he was hideous for me to look at. He stood like an insensate being, almost livestock, overweight and bow-backed and bald beneath the hood he wore. It troubles my conscience to write those words, to reduce him to comments so crude, to do it knowing I'd never have the guts to say these things aloud, but there's no more accurate way to express the revulsion I felt when I saw him. His scalp glowed pale white in the starlight. Beneath the sheen were shocking hollows, cavities, where his nostrils ate into the middle of his face and his mouth slung open in a gawp. His skin was mottled, scribbled over by the web of lines that stitched it back together, sometimes too tightly, sometimes too loosely, where the flames had corroded it. He heaved short, deep, difficult breaths, like a man forever with smoke in his lungs, and he stared into the darkness in front of him, or into the blur of his vision, as if accusing the shadows of working against him, to see if he could discern me, to make out the shape of what he'd only heard.

What I mean, really, is that I recoiled at the horror of what I saw in myself when I saw him looking for me. I saw a fraud performing a predetermined role, blindly fulfilling Hannah's intimation that this person, this man, wasn't worth knowing, was only worth gaping at. I didn't have the eyes to see him as another man might, a better man than me, a man who knew the costs of war as more than an abstraction, who'd maybe even see beneath the scars a cause for envy. Shane, after all, still had his son to cherish. But what I saw instead was only more of myself as I appeared to others. I saw a voyeur. I saw a human being behaving as merely a pair of eyes intent on turning everything they beheld into an object for appraisal. I saw a person so obsessed with seeing someone else in the flesh that he couldn't perceive the self beneath the surface. What I was too blind to see, I realise, was the love in him that I didn't acknowledge until so much later. I wish I'd looked closer, spoken aloud, connected with him. I might've seen how his capacity for love was the architecture of his body. Not his scars. Not his disfigurements. The bones that held him upright were animated by his love for his son. That love flushed through his veins. His flesh was its residence. He was made of the stuff. But instead of speaking to him, I froze even firmer where I stood. I didn't dare move because I didn't want him to see me as I was. Being found out was the least of my fears. Being recognised for what I'd just done was what stuck me to the spot.

At last, as a new wave uncurled on the sand and licked at his toes, Shane shuffled aside and again bent over his telescope. A succession of waves churned towards us then, smashing rapidly over the shore, and I took the chance, the noise they offered, to muffle my movements, to walk back towards the beach house. But as I passed by Shane, quietly, treading carefully, I saw that he wasn't bent over his telescope at all. He was just bent over. He used the telescope to prop himself up as he stared hard at the ground. At what? At the wreckage of the waves, at the luminous shimmers and sparks around his feet, at the way the lights in the water moved like a starfield drawn across the sand. The sea breathed in, breathed out. He'd halted, transfixed, to wonder at it. I trudged up over the dunes, through the reeds, and in my retreat I heard my breath match up with the tide.

Later, in bed, unable to sleep, listening to the distant waves at Dee Why, all I could hear was more breath, more breathing. I'd returned with my wife to my in-laws' house as dark settled over the suburbs. We found my mother-in-law on the sofa, once more scrolling through the news on her phone. The co-pilot, she said. He did it deliberately. Can you imagine? He wanted to kill himself, only himself, but he took all those people with him.

The black box had been recovered and the cockpit recordings analysed. The co-pilot had a history of depression and suicidal ideation, both of which he'd concealed from his superiors. When the captain left the cockpit for a moment, the co-pilot locked the door and took control of the plane. The flight path was reset to steer it straight towards the slopes of the Massif des Trois-Évêchés. A controlled descent. A gradual drop in altitude. It lasted for eight gruelling minutes. Everyone on board could feel it. The captain knew something was wrong. He returned to the cockpit door to find it locked. He knocked, then banged, then started shouting for help. People could sense themselves falling through the air. Some passengers ran to assist the captain. They tried to prise open the door but they couldn't. The co-pilot knew they'd never reach him. He sat in the cockpit and listened to the bangs and cries, the screaming and wailing, on the other side of the door, only a breath away from him, but he forced himself to remain unmoving, to stay on course for the crash, to remove all those people from the world despite their pleas for mercy, so that he could end the misery of his days. He wanted it so determinedly that he sat in the cockpit for those eight minutes despite the clamour. The black box had recorded only the noise of the uproar in the cabin and, inside the cockpit, steady breathing. The authorities retrieved it in hopes that he might have dictated a suicide note, given his reasons for taking so many lives. He didn't. All he offered posterity was his respiration, controlled and rhythmic throughout the descent. His pace never changed, never picked up. He sat quietly and breathed, ready to cut off his future, leaving nothing to the world but the sound of air drawn into and expelled from a body aimed at annihilation.

When I'd reached the beach house again, I saw that I'd been seen. On the balcony of the neighbouring house, with lights on in the kitchen behind her, Kerry leant against a railing and watched me slip back inside. I closed the glass door behind me and held it in place with both hands. I pressed my forehead against the glass and felt my face burn red. She turned away from the house and once more looked down the beach to where her husband remained, alone. She went on watching him in secret. I watched her through my reflection.

At the edge of the cliffs I'd wondered whether she'd still be spending her nights there. A blast of water beneath me had exploded into froth and scrubbed out the distant image of myself. Crisis. The precipice. As I turned aside my wife had tried to catch my eye. Would Kerry have stayed at the Mearns with only Shane? Would she still watch over him now that their son was gone? Or would she have left him to try to become the person she really wanted to be? In the end, my wife caught my eye by force, by taking my hand in hers. Wild wind raced over the cliffs and flung her hair about. Then she shifted our roles. She balled her hand into a fist and opened my hand so that I cupped the back of hers.

Here, she said. Right here. This is where I want to do it.

She held her fist upturned, as if to release an insect she'd imprisoned. Then she flexed her fingers and opened them to reveal her empty palm. The invisible ashes, snatched by the wind, exploded into the air and twirled skyward out of sight.

The conveyor belt jolted forward. The tiny coffin, sealed shut, ducked through the arch in the wall and trundled towards the inferno. I couldn't now believe I'd let it go.

Do you think it's okay here? my wife asked me.

She actually asked me that. She didn't pose the question as if she'd already reached a conclusion and wanted me to approve it with a token statement of my thoughts. She wanted to know if I truly did feel that this was the best place to scatter the ashes.

A few words, she said. A little memorial occasion. Here. Do you think that's right?

Here? I said.

I had no feelings about it either way. If the ashes were to be scattered, any place was just as fitting and just as wrong as any other. But I didn't say this. I didn't shake my head. I didn't shrug derisively or make any show of the contempt I wanted to indulge. I think I sort of half-smiled, half-nodded, unobstructively.

My wife turned back to the ocean, the wind, the rocks.

Let's take time to find some words, she said. I'd like to say something before we do it. I'd like to give our parents the opportunity, too. And I'll call your mum, if you like; I'll bring her on board. It'll work—won't it?—if we all take tomorrow to think about things, write down a few remarks. Then your olds fly down the morning after, and that's when we'll come back. Take them to my parents' house from the airport, drop off the luggage, drink some tea, coffee, get refreshed, then everyone, together, right here. Do you reckon that'll work?

I murmured without commitment. I knew my wife would take it as agreement.

She looked out to sea for a time, then turned slightly towards me, just enough so that her words, softly spoken, wouldn't be lost to the wind. She said, Thank you.

I didn't know what she wanted to thank me for. For having yielded to her in Switzerland? For not starting new battles in Sydney? Maybe for having genuinely come around to share her views, her wants, at least as far as she could tell. For being so quietly conciliatory, for sticking so firmly to the sidelines of her scheme, that she believed the release of the ashes would release me from something as well. So, then, for my performance.

She said, Thank you. Really. It means the world to me.

X

Was it the voices that woke me? My father-in-law rose from the sofa, reached towards the coffee table, fumbled for the remote control. Sorry, he said. Sorry, sorry.

He aimed at the television and reduced the volume to a murmur. I watched the blue bar swipe across the worn face of Hassan Demirović. He appeared in split-screen with an interviewer on what looked like a lightweight current affairs show.

Too loud, said my father-in-law, too loud, I'm sorry.

He pressed another button. Closed captions sprang up.

There, he said, that's better.

He returned the remote control to the table but didn't return to his seat.

Sorry, he said again.

But the volume hadn't woken me. I'd awoken to the vibrations. In my sleep I'd felt the voices through the wall. The screen sat one floor below the pillow I'd laid my head on, and the wall behind it rose up to abut the headboard of the guestroom bed. A rumbling that ran through the bedframe had stirred me. Voices, disembodied, hurled themselves at a structure that conducted them to me. My body ached to sleep on, not caring how many hours had passed, not caring if I remained out of sync with the local time for weeks to come, but the vibrations didn't let up and the thin shroud of the curtains couldn't blockade the room against the sun. There wouldn't be any going back.

When I rolled onto my side, I found the sheets beside me cold. But no wonder I'd slept beyond my wife. Memory clanked its gears, reanimated the night's events and the feeling, if not the duration, of the hours I'd spent awake in the dark staring at the gunmetal urn. Willing the blackness to speak to me, straining to discern its whispers, and eventually, slowly, so as not to disturb my wife, rising from bed to let them loose. I unscrewed the lid and looked in. The ashes were nothing. They were fine and grey, like silt: they were nothing more than exactly what they seemed to be. All the same, I felt a pull, an injunction to movement, to protect them from loss or dispersal. I forced myself to turn away and leave them, to return the lid and return to bed and let events run their course. How long it took me to do that, how much time elapsed between looking and letting go, I couldn't say for certain. In any case, newly awakened, I forced myself out of bed and I dressed and roughed up my hair. I supposed I'd join my wife and her parents for breakfast downstairs. When I came to the living room, though, I found only my father-in-law. He told me my wife had gone out with her mother. He said breakfast was long over. I glanced at the clock on the television screen. It was nearly midday. I'd assumed that Demirović had somehow landed a spot on the morning news. Actually, I realised, he'd been demoted to a talk show with a timeslot leading up to lunch. It was one of those gaudy productions pitched at stay-at-home parents and bored retirees, fuelled by stories of scandal and sentimentality.

My father-in-law hesitated at the entrance to the kitchen. Coffee? he said. I bet you could use one.

Yeah, I said. Thanks.

Bloody jet lag, he said as he left the living room. I usually need a week to get over it. Minimum. He strode to the kitchen, towards the kettle, and left me alone with the screen.

Demirović looked slight. He looked shrunken in a loose brown suit, like a cast figure slowly sinking into bas-relief. He looked as if he'd let his hair lengthen and curl at the ends, in a way that made his face seem smaller than it used to be. He glanced aside when he spoke as if he didn't quite know how to answer the questions he was asked.

Meaningless words chuntered over the bottom of the screen, ums and ahs, wells, you knows.

Context came to me slowly, an ad hoc bricolage of disconnected clauses. The lawyers had chipped away at the procedural blockades and orchestrated a bureaucratic workaround. Later in the day, Demirović would at last be allowed to meet with Imran bin Musa in the prisoner's cell. Permission granted. Twenty minutes in total. His lawyer had hashed it out with the counsel for the defence, and the two of them had taken their agreement to the Director of Public Prosecutions. Approval had been issued the previous day, with only twenty-four hours' notice given before the visit.

Even so, the interview was a mediocre affair. The interviewer was interested only in Demirović's *feelings*. Feelings were the nectar she knew her viewers craved. After months of campaigning, after all the begging and pleading, after so many attempts to reason with the authorities, how does it *feel* to know that your labours have finally paid off? How does it *feel*, now, following the groundswell of public support and then the backlash, the protests, the assault from the commentariat, the fizzle into the ambience of the daily discourse, *now* to be vindicated, *now* to be triumphant? How does it feel to look at the hours left on the clock today and know they're ticking down to the encounter you've been fighting for? Understandable questions, I suppose. Feelings are precious things, preciously guarded, and the interviewer's job was after all to crack open her guest's hoard of treasures and strew the spoils to her audience. Within minutes, though, she drew taut her loose line of enquiry and pressured Demirović to consider, to really envision, the imminent encounter.

Okay, she said, but after all this, what do you think you'll *do* when they let you into his cell? You'll walk in there and you'll look him in the eye and meet him face to face. We all know what he did to you and your family. What do you want to do?

Demirović went silent for a time.

Over my shoulder I felt the presence of my father-in-law again.

A stirring of light on the walls gave away his approach. He came forward, I guessed with a cup of coffee in each hand, and paused by the breakfast bar. He didn't speak, didn't interrupt. He stood and I felt him watching me watching Hassan Demirović.

I suppose, Demirović began, I suppose, well, I would like to say something to him. Something, what's the word? I'd like to make a gesture of peace. Firstly, of course, I'd like to call attention to the pain he has caused. I won't deny that. This pain is beyond repair. He must be made to hear it. But I must also let him know that what he has done is not beyond forgiveness, you see. So I will tell him I forgive him. I will say those very words, as I have vowed to do. At last, I will be able to say that I forgive him for his sins.

Okay, said the interviewer. But then what? I think everyone here in the audience, and everyone watching at home, understands that you'll have a chance to do what you've been promising for many weeks. But you'll have *twenty minutes* with this man.

Yes.

So then what?

Demirović stalled. He cleared his throat and said, Well, I suppose, yes, I would also have the opportunity to ask him, to probe into. He stopped. His eyes darted one way then another. One second, two seconds, three seconds of silence.

The interviewer let it simmer.

Four seconds, five seconds.

Dead air.

Six seconds. Seven seconds.

Finally Demirović returned to himself and went on making it up as he spoke.

I might ask him about his motives, he said.

He hadn't given a moment's thought to what he'd do once he'd granted forgiveness.

I might ask him what he believes awaits him, he said, if, as a man of faith, he knows that his soul will one day be judged by God.

He hadn't thought of what he wanted to get out of the confrontation other than the fact of getting it in the first place.

Then again, he said, it's possible that the most important thing to, ah, to pass between us is, is not—

He flailed a hand.

Not something that, that *flows*, from me to him, but, ah, something *else* that I can, I can *extract* from, from—

He shook his head.

Beneath him the closed captions splintered into gibberish.

Actually it's not true to say that my father-in-law stood behind me. That's an interpolation. My memory puts him there but I can't be sure that he actually was. His presence in that moment comes from later on, that night, when the two of us discussed the matter and I understood what he'd read into my outlook on it. Nothing whatsoever to do with me. Something I might have an opinion on as a distant observer, an opinion with no more gravity than my thoughts on the prospect of a snap election or Australia's odds at trouncing England in a Test match. But the things he'd say later enraged me. The disingenuousness of them. Their pretence of innocence when dealing with matters of life and death. The way he cast them towards me as if only angling for passing conversation, idle talk. The rage that flared from that was a rage that returned, recursively, to colour my memories of what Demirović said and the thoughts that spun out from what I heard.

Demirović shrugged and with a dismissive wave he swatted at empty air as if to shoo a bug. He made the gesture with his left hand. Despite the speed of it, the flash, I noticed he no longer wore a ring on his finger.

Look, he said with a sigh. Maybe you're right, with what you're getting at. Maybe there's more to the meeting that I haven't given enough thought. Maybe it's true that I'm going into this for my own peace of mind. Maybe the most important thing that can happen today is that I get to see him in the flesh and see that he is, in the end, just a man. Not a monster. Nor an innocent person broken by a punitive government. Just a man.

He shrugged again and bowed his head.

Just a man, he said. And, you know, he's been on my mind for a couple of months now but he's been kept out of my sight. I'm happy to have a chance to change that, finally.

Right there is where the day's indignation took root in me. Was Demirović delusional? Was he just presumptuous? Whatever the case, he prized his own gifts too highly. How could he think he'd see anything other than what he expected to see? He'd invested so much in his encounter with Imran bin Musa that there was no way he'd be able to see things as they were. So they'd stand in the same room together. So what? At this point, their characters were cast in iron. Whatever passing graces might emerge from the meeting, there'd be no oxygen left in that cell for genuine empathy, reciprocal understanding. The only thing Demirović would see was a creature of his own creation. An accessory to the event, not a participant in it. Not a man with his own life. A repository for a grieving father's beliefs about the propriety of absolution. Was this another one of those things that Demirović hadn't thought of yet? Did he think his audience would simply let it slide? Or was it the case that he knew but didn't care, didn't want to let his knowledge freeze him into inaction?

In recent years, I've tried to live in accordance with certain principles I swear by. Each of them now feels to me as much a fixture of my self, integral to the fabric of my being, as any of my limbs or bones or my internal organs. I adhere to them faithfully. I'd no sooner break with them than submit to an amputation. And yet, I realised there, with Demirović stalling on the television screen, of all the principles I hold, only one impinges on territory that could plausibly be called spiritual. Put the right words in the right order and you draw down the power to restore what is broken. There it is. It's the same principle that animates any prayer or incantation. It's the pith of any plea for intervention from elsewhere, for otherworldly forces to rectify transgressions, to redress injustices, in effect to reverse the flow of time. On reflection, too, it struck me as much the same principle that sustained Demirović, spurring him on towards his audience with bin Musa. In him, again, I saw part of myself. That said, he seemed to have placed more faith in his own capacity for empathy, and the innate power of what he might say to another person, than in the powers of a deity with a sympathetic ear.

Because I am not by nature a spiritual person, this principle comes into practice for me only in very particular ways. When I'm aware I have done damage to some delicate equilibrium, when I have broken someone's trust or imbalanced a relationship, when I alone am responsible for straightening out a misconception, the right words in the right order lead to apologies and explanations. Not one or the other. Always both together. Circumstances will change their proportions. Sometimes a thorough explanation of my intentions might make an apology seem slight. Sometimes the opposite is true. In every case, however, one without the other is impotent and both are needed to make amends.

That's why, I suppose, a week or so after I'd buckled and signed a statement of regret which I knew was insincere, I still felt dogged by the suspicion that things around me were fractured. I'd been moving through my days with trepidation, as if picking a path amid the rubble of a building in slow decay. My relationship to the students I'd offended wouldn't recover without effort. Their grasp on the facts I'd tried to lay out needed guidance, a course correction, but also, more than that, I felt an imperative to reaffirm my own integrity, my commitment to the things I *knew* to be the case. I couldn't continue in silence. I couldn't let my silence be read as a validation of the objections raised against me or an approval of misunderstandings. I definitely couldn't let it be read as a tacit acceptance of my error of judgment. With the apology having contaminated the air around me, I felt I had to address my complainants and explain myself to them, to reassemble myself, to show myself as I was and not as I had been led to appear. I had to revoke, I had to reverse, and then I had to rebuild. The right words in the right order were what I had to find.

At my request, my invitation, half-a-dozen students had agreed to meet me, informally, in a chalet at the edge of campus. Three girls, three boys, all seniors. Mostly young adults, in fact, since only two were not yet eighteen. More importantly, five of them were Jewish, including the on-again, off-again couple who served as joint leaders of the school's Jewish Club. Jakob came from a village in rural Hesse. Naomi came from wealth in upstate New York. Of the other two girls, Renáta, from Prague, was the lone European; Tamara was a third-generation Israeli. Of the other boys, only Eric was Jewish, an American slacker from a part of Boston within walking distance of where I'd lived. The sixth student, another German, had a very different background from his friends. Luca's great-grandfather had been a diplomat in service of Hermann Göring. Since the end of the war, the old man's escapades had been a source of shame for Luca's elders, and for decades now the entire family had been investing its fortunes in forms of atonement. Luca's enrolment at this particular school was part of a dynastic effort to make amends.

Clearly the situation wasn't likely to be comfortable for anyone. Anticipating tension from the start, I'd searched for a venue I hoped could defuse it. A residential building. A rec room in the loft. No labs, no classes, only dorms and breakout spaces. None of the architecture that gave a school its hierarchy, nothing that would goad me into a position of default authority. I needed to lower my status. I intended to invite the students to call me by my first name. I wanted us all just to sit together and *talk*. So: a pair of sunken sofas instead of straight-backed chairs, a mess of beanbags, a kitchenette with a kettle and teacups, crumbs from the cakes the younger students devoured during recess.

When I first planned the meeting, I'd pictured myself alone in that room, at ease, preparing my words, putting them in order, while I awaited the students' arrival. A window opened onto a vista looking straight down the valley at the Wetterhorn. I'd stand there to gather myself, I thought, and then, at the sound of the opening door, at the rising chatter in the stairwell, I'd turn to greet the students and smile and thank them for coming. I'd let them make hot drinks, even Ovomaltine. I'd open a packet of ginger snaps while the water boiled. I'd bring zopf from the kitchen as well, still warm, and they could pull it apart and smear it with chocolate while we talked things over. I'd at least try to make the occasion a little more relaxed than I feared it could be.

But my plans dissolved as soon as I reached the top of the chalet. I found the door ajar. Inside, already, the students were waiting for me. The room felt suddenly cramped, compressed. Tamara and Renáta blocked the view of the valley, leaning on the windowsill and conversing in low voices. The other four had crowded onto a single sofa, two on the cushions and one on each armrest. They looked up at me in unison when I stepped inside. I found myself out of puff from my trek up the stairs. Hand to my chest, I tried to catch my breath. Through the door behind me a waft of unexpected warmth snuck into the room. Someone on the floor below had just stepped out of the shower. I swung the door closed against a cloud of vapour and as I moved I felt the students' eyes on me. I sensed the lingering spirits of a conversation I'd curtailed. What had I intruded on? Except for the two girls at the window, the others appeared to have huddled closely, swamping the sofa, to take a look at a book I noticed now in Jakob's hands. A hardback volume with a cover of dark green cloth. Jakob held it tight.

Well, then, I said. Hi. Wow. You're all on the ball today.

Steam rose from mugs on the carpet and cups cradled in warming palms. A packet of paprika crisps leant upright, already opened, against a wall.

Just kicking back, said Eric. We weren't sure how you wanted to play this, exactly.

Right, I said. Well. Let's see.

I'd wanted to play it, so to speak, by making a bygone reality vivid for them. I didn't want them to feel *maligned* by anything I'd said at the assembly, or anything I'd go on to say here. I only wanted to help them apprehend a blunt, discomfiting fact of history, that the awesome scale of one atrocity might indeed overwhelm another, and at the same time to not *be* discomfited by it: to not see it as somehow diminishing the histories more personal to them, to not see their acceptance of it as a betrayal of their heritage. I said, Okay, and lowered myself onto the vacant sofa, opposite the students on the other. I suppose I hoped to arrive at an accommodation of sorts, a coming to terms, which I thought I might guide them towards, if only I could have them see the textures of lives thrown into shadow by the passing of the centuries. To that end I said, Let's start here, and I called into view a hole in the world. There's an emptiness left behind, I said, when, without warning, a person is taken. Raiders arrive, or bounty hunters, and a human being is extracted from the lives of those dearest to them. There's a gap where they used to be, as if the air has moulded itself around the contours of an absent soul. Can we fill this empty space? I asked. Then, with all the composure I could muster, I felt out words that might invest me with the power I sought.

First, I said, we need to be clear about *who* we're trying to see here. I feigned a collaborative effort to involve the students in my quest. From their place at the window behind me, the two girls drew near and returned to their peers. Tamara, desultory, dropped into a beanbag; Renáta remained standing, propped against a wall, and shoved both hands into the pockets of her hoodie. I waited for things to settle, took the tenor of the room, then continued speaking, steady, unperturbed. Can we *feel* this person back into being? I asked. Can we refashion someone taken away, suddenly gone? If we can see them *alive*, I said, we can better acknowledge the value their life possessed. So I sketched out images to reconstitute a stolen body: of wrists bound by shackles and chains, of jawlines abraded by iron collars, of lips blistered from exposure to the sun. I sought, as ever, the slantwise ingress, the sidereal progression, to fade the familiar into the foreign, to not make it exotic or outlandish, but finally, for what? I was cut short. The students curtailed me.

Yeah, okay, said Eric while I was still mid-sentence. But the thing is, you don't have to do this. It's like, we know. We know this stuff already. Don't we?

He sat on the armrest nearest the door and scanned the room for consensus, searched out the eyes of his friends. Nobody spoke to back him up, but nobody dissented. He returned his gaze to me, looked at me with an expression I read as verging on incredulity.

You gave us the stats in the assembly, he said. So, like, what is there to prove?

I don't want to *prove* anything, I said, I just—

My words came to a stop. They fell back into my throat. My

thoughts raced ahead to uncomfortable places, to branded flesh and prodded fibres, to sinews and muscles appraised and valued, to the fortresses and barracoons of Elmina, Luanda, Île de Gorée, but my own abrupt silence distorted my mental trajectory and dragged my focus back to the here and now. I caught up to myself with new awareness of my folly. This was no way to help anyone understand anything. I'd taken an unknown element, a human being become a lacuna, and started bombarding it with experiences, hurling them at it erratically, as if pelting it with fistfuls of mud just to see how much would glob on, gain purchase, to approximate the shape of a slave who turned out to be, at base, no more than an instrument: finely drawn but finally crass, not knowable as someone real because not anyone *specific*. Now, I saw, all I'd really done was impress on the students more of my own presence, my ego and my concerns, soiling a hypothetical person with suppositions that finally pointed right back at me. The words I'd chosen only threw light on their speaker. So much for meaningful illumination.

Okay, then, I said. I guess that means I'm not really sure why we're here.

I took a moment's pause.

I mean, if what you're saying is that you all sort of agree on the facts, then—

I looked around for someone to betray their intentions.

Is it that, just because I'm a teacher, you felt obliged to attend? To accept my invitation? Is that why we're here?

A quiet voice spoke up and said, No. A clipped accent, Eastern European. Renáta stood at the edge of the group and with a single word she commanded the room. We thought, also, that maybe *you'd* like to know why, ah—

She halted and took care in choosing how to phrase her complaint.

Why your comments at the assembly felt to us like an injury.

Even with facts being facts, Eric added as Renáta withdrew.

Well, I said in a huff, on guard, now this feels a little like an ambush.

Eric laughed and said, Uh, no. Nobody's under *attack*.

Well, but you've been conferring. Before coming here. Just as I'd pictured myself in that room, I realised, they'd been painting their own picture of how things would unfold.

Exchanging notes, that's all, said Luca. We thought: why not?

Well, why? Fill me in. What's the idea, exactly?

The idea turned out to be there in that book, barely beneath the hardback covers. Jakob idly fingered its edges, thumbing its blunted corners and patches of worn cloth. The idea was to give me a sense of why my words had riled them, even when they accepted my numbers. I'd urged them to be awed by a starscape at midday: no matter how great, how vast the constellations I'd have them see, their sun burned so bright that it blotted out everything else. The idea was that I hadn't reckoned with the power of proximity, the pre-eminence of things at hand. Each of the students had their stories, preserving dozens of tales of family they'd never known despite a connection by blood. Each of them carried within themselves accounts of dispossession and diaspora, of starvation, malnutrition, asylum, of relatives lost or disappeared, incarcerated or interred, killed outright or driven to take their own lives.

But in telling their stories they told me first of *things* in their family homes. They catalogued the things they left behind each time they came to the Alps, the known world they'd return to at the end of each school session. They spoke of bric-a-brac and furnishings, often drab and commonplace, which anchored their stories to the world they'd grown up in, the world they knew by sight and touch. A cracked plate was, for one family, the only item retrieved from the shards of Kristallnacht. A dented candelabrum and a brass cigar cutter were heirlooms prized in place of an uncle who hadn't escaped Dachau. What I have only lately come to appreciate, to understand in a visceral sense, was what they wanted me to feel even then, what they tried to convey to me despite my lack of experience. Absences don't just amount to sudden vacancies of space. They deposit traces of perished souls in the objects that linger on. The flotsam of a life cut short still hosts a spark of human presence, and that presence is a lived concern of those who would salvage the *things* that survive.

Naomi showed me a series of pictures on her phone. She'd asked her mother to send them. Things from her home in Saratoga, from the archive of family treasures her parents tended to with care. Letters dating to the 1950s, handwritten pages with words scratched out. Apparently an elderly matriarch couldn't bear to look upon certain names anymore, but she could neither bring herself to burn the notes nor leave them undefaced. Tamara spoke of photo albums in her parents' wardrobe, none of them dating from before the war, and Eric described a ceramic bowl, locked inside a display cabinet, full of tarnished rings and bracelets marked with sentimental engravings. Luca had nothing to share and remained as quiet and watchful as I did. He only spoke up when he felt it right to call on someone else to speak. More often than not, he was among the respected few who served as interpreters at the weekly assemblies, and so, now that the others seemed to have fallen silent, feeling as if they'd each made their case if not quite exhausted their stories, Luca was the one to turn to Jakob, the boy from Hesse, and say, with an encouraging nod, *Sagst ihm.* Go on.

Jakob arched an eyebrow. Then, lips pursed, he held the book out to me.

When I took it from him I found in my hands an old, water-damaged copy of *de Bello Gallico* rendered in High German. I expected, then, to hear a story somehow spun around it. Someone unknown to him had once been a scholar of antiquity. Someone had been dismissed from an academic post, or else aspired to study the classics but never had an honest chance. Someone, perhaps, had gone into exile and left this behind and never returned. Gone where? Zürich? Further, London? But I didn't think it right to ask, to venture aloud my guesses at the significance of the book. I just frowned at Jakob and said, Well?

He made a sort of wince. Then a tension flickered through his jaw and he turned aside, looked away from everyone, and said, I am feeling, ah, let me say this: *missgestimmt.* Will someone translate? He winced again and said, Not *upset.* Something else, different.

Grumpy, said Luca.

Not quite, said Jakob. Like an instrument in the wrong key.

His choice of simile surprised me. By reputation he was a serious, studious young man, nearly twenty years of age, admitted to the school on a scholarship thanks to his clear intellectual promise and his family's modest means. Taller than most, myself included, and slender, too, with short hair and a habit of dressing formally, always in collared shirts and pressed trousers, he had an intensity to his appearance that conveyed his dedication to his ambitions. For years he'd committed himself to mastering the Swiss Matura, one of the most difficult secondary qualifications in the world, passing exams in eleven subjects and having recently declared his intention to major in mechanics and applied mathematics. He didn't strike me as the type of person who'd have any patience for music, or, indeed, for expressing himself figuratively. He sometimes came across as so stern he seemed contemptuous of anything without clear utility, anything even faintly frivolous. And yet, he confessed, at this moment he felt like an instrument in the wrong key.

Out of tune, I said. Maybe the word is *distempered.* At any rate, I understood the vibe. I could see it in his face, in the torque of his posture.

He looked back at me and said, softly, Maybe that's it.

Okay, I said. Do you want to tell us why?

He shot a glance at the book and made an offhand gesture, a finger raised and a flick of the wrist, to indicate that I should open the cover. I did. On the frontispiece, in the white space between the title and the colophon, someone had penned an inscription in tawny ink. Four lines of text were signed off with a pair of florid initials, *E.F.*, followed by *Dez. '38*. I drew a deep breath and let it out slowly. Obviously the text made no sense to me. I looked up from the page and sought a cue from Jakob. He kept his eyes on the book.

I can't read this, I said.

It's not important, really. A few remarks between friends.

Addressed to?

My twice-great-grandfather.

From?

Enrico Fermi.

I shook my head and said, I don't recognise the name.

Now Jakob looked to me with what seemed like genuine surprise. Truly?

Should I?

I thought you would.

In fact I should have. Now I've come to know. I can see him easily these days, these restless days of roaming ever northward. He appears to me insubstantial, pale, as the light begins to fade, half-reflected in the window of a railway carriage crossing the Alps. The lenses of his spectacles catch the last of the sun. The glow of a winter's dusk gives his baldness a warm patina. Then, as the carriage embarks on its ascent of a mountain pass, the world outside goes dark and the train rocks through banks of rising snow. The man studies his sallow image and tries to imagine himself, as he presently appears, already accustomed to the new life he is embarking upon. He fancies himself happy, or at least at peace, untouched and untormented by the rupture with the self he has cast away. From the seat beside him his wife reaches out to take his hand. They are nestled, warm, in a private booth for a family of four. Opposite them, their son, a toddler, stretches his legs as he lies down with his head in the lap of his older sister. The girl begins to drift off, too, as night enfolds the train. Back in Rome their house would now be dark. All the belongings they left behind, all the accoutrements they relinquished, all would remain unlit, in shadow, like objects in a museum closed to visitors, without anyone home to enliven the rooms. So much jetsam abandoned in their haste. What few things remain in their possession? Two cases of clothes, stowed in a different carriage, and personal trappings in the valises beneath their seats. That's it. That's the sum of their shared world. And in the man's valise: the book.

Your grandfather knew him well? I asked Jakob.

My twice-great-grandfather. His name was Joachim. Just Achim, for friends and family. He and Fermi, they studied together in Göttingen. You know where this is?

Hesse, I'm guessing.

Near enough. Lower Saxony. They were colleagues.

Both Jewish?

Not Fermi, no. But his wife was, so his children were as well.

Right, but it makes no sense. This is 1938? And he fled *north* from Rome? Why cross the Alps? Where to, Austria? In December. That's after annexation.

He had papers.

For what?

Passage to Stockholm. He was on his way to collect the Nobel Prize.

I squinted at Jakob, sceptically I suppose, then at the handwritten words in the book. Hunched *m*s and *n*s, and *k*s and *t*s that kinked out at strange angles. So this was the cramped style of a certified genius, sloppiness excused by intellectual supremacy.

What'd he win for? I asked.

Well, said Jakob, now feigning a nonchalance at odds with the solemnity of what he was about to say, this is why I thought you'd already know. You know much about America, yes? That's where this honour took him. To conduct research for Roosevelt. There is a story I've heard. Seven years later, in New Mexico, Enrico Fermi was the one man who lay down on the ground while all his new colleagues remained on their feet. The desert. You know it? He lay on his belly, very flat, stretched out on the white sand, very dusty, so he could listen instead of watch. The other men, they kept their eyes on the horizon, but Fermi lay down and turned an ear to the ground. He wanted to hear it and feel it in his body. The rumble through the earth. The *power.* Yes? Twenty thousand tons of TNT, energy in *millions* of megajoules. Like an earthquake in the air. Impossible to imagine.

Jakob smiled a little. That was the smile of a student enamoured with his chosen subject. Last I heard, he'd won a place at the technical school in Zürich on a six-year degree in engineering. That was the kind of mind he'd been gifted, and with which he dwelt on that explosion. If he could truly conceive of the subject of his words, of such pure and malicious *force* shredding the silence of the sun-blasted desert, I'm sure he conceived of it dispassionately, mathematically, first and foremost as the masterly solution to some labyrinthine equation. Its destructive capabilities would have been a secondary concern.

Trinity, I said.

He nodded and said, Trinity was Fermi's third child.

No, no. You're mixed up here. You're talking about Oppenheimer.

No, said Jakob, now with none of the nonchalance of a moment ago, now with the firmness of a displeased authority challenged on his specialist knowledge. Oppenheimer was at Göttingen as well, with Fermi, with Achim. This was in the twenties. They worked with many men who went on to achieve great things. They were the ones who created the field, you know? Quantum mechanics. Heisenberg, Wolfgang Pauli, Paul Dirac. Others, too. They were all there at the same time. How many Nobels between them? Max Planck, also. He'd already won. But Fermi was the first to move to America. He went to Chicago. You know what he did there? Under the streets of the city—really, *really,* in a laboratory underneath the concrete, the footpaths, the roads—he became the first man to split the atom and *control* it. You understand? He created the self-sustaining nuclear chain reaction. Imagine. A mushroom cloud could have swallowed the whole of Chicago, *all* of it, but it didn't because Fermi wouldn't allow it. Again Jakob smiled. Fermi got his numbers right, he said. Then he gave the numbers to Oppenheimer, and that's how Oppenheimer built the bomb.

I clenched a little at the thought of it and the plainness of the words. Okay, I said. Okay. And for this Fermi won the Nobel? But Jakob shook his head, no, and I realised I'd spoken too early. I hadn't got *my* numbers right. I'd skewed the course of events.

Fermi won in '38, said Jakob with a nod towards the book, for his early work on nuclear fission.

Ahead of his real achievement, then.

Yes, but not too early. Just in time to save his family.

All right, then. Tell me.

In the end, I learnt from Jakob, the telling of the story had fallen to Fermi's wife. Her name was Laura Capon. She'd been the one to answer the phone on November 10, 1938, first thing in the morning. A voice with an unfamiliar accent asked her to confirm her husband's identity and to inform him he'd receive a call from Stockholm later that evening. After supper, while waiting as instructed, he'd tuned the radio to the news and together they'd listened, wracked with angst, as the commentator summarised the laws enacted that day. According to Laura's account, written during her husband's final weeks, the airwaves trembled with a voice that was hard, emphatic, and pitiless. Jewish children were to be excluded from all public schools. Jewish teachers had all been dismissed from their posts. Jewish lawyers and doctors could henceforth practise only for Jewish clients. Jewish firms would be dissolved and Jewish citizens were all to have their passports rescinded. This was in fact the second round of anti-Semitic laws inflicted on Italy. The warning shots had been fired months before, in July. Laura and the children had been on vacation at the time, cut off from the news in a village in the Alps. Fermi had stayed in Rome to focus on his research, but in August he'd shocked his family by turning up, unannounced, at the door to their chalet. Mussolini had just released his so-called manifesto on the races, distinguishing a range of lower species from the true Italians, and in September the first round of laws mandated a mass dispossession. Laura Capon had been entreating her husband for years to take up one of the many offers he'd received to work in the United States. He'd turned them all down politely, unwilling to forfeit the familiar comforts of Rome, but now he wrote back to recant and plead for a place. He and Laura resolved to leave Italy as soon as possible. When the call came in from Stockholm, then, they found their opportunity. The prize would buy their family a privilege not afforded to others, to accept the honour and travel north, to attend the ceremony and never return.

Achim went to Stockholm, too, said Jakob. Fermi invited him to visit. Also others from their years in Göttingen. But that was the last time Achim travelled outside Germany. When Fermi refused to return home, he caused an international scandal. His escape drew the attention of the SS to his friends. Achim had already lost his laboratory privileges at Göttingen. Then the Reich put him under *Schutzhaft*, you know this term?

No.

Protective custody, said Luca. Not allowed to leave the country.

If he had a chance to leave, said Jakob, the SS thought he'd follow Fermi. So they locked him inside the borders. But then he had no more to lose, so he started speaking out.

Explicitly? I said. Against the regime?

Against its techniques, said Jakob. Against *force*. He was a pacifist. A loud one.

And?

And so they came for him one night and sent him to Sachsenhausen. That's where he died. He was shot. More than once.

I let out a long breath I hadn't realised I'd been holding in. I said, His descendants?

Swiftly Jakob rose from the sofa and held out a hand to retrieve the book. I passed it to him. He flipped it over and opened the back cover to show the flypapers. My great-grandmother was seven years old, he said. He tapped a finger on a smudge of ink, a black stamp imprinting the name of the school above the words SPECIAL RESERVE. This is a library book now, he said, because it was given to this school by my great-grandmother. A gift for, ah, I don't know the word in English. I will say *Erkenntlichkeit.*

As a token of gratitude, said Luca.

Gratitude, said Jakob. Yes.

At Göttingen, he explained, there was a man, a colleague of Achim's, who had once been a teacher at this very school when the first students were still in the Odenwald. After the SS raids, however, this man sought to reconnect with the philosopher who led the school, and from then on the two men kept a secret correspondence. He tracked the movements of the philosopher in exile, followed the progress of the students from village to village across Switzerland, and so, when Achim disappeared, it was he who appealed to the philosopher to find a place at the school for Jakob's great-grandmother. To *save* her, you know? said Jakob. She came to this school when it was in the Jura. She finished the year the students settled here in the Berner Oberland. And when she died, an old woman—

Jakob clapped the book shut and returned it to me.

When she died, he said, she gave this school a gift to show her gratitude. The gift Achim received from Enrico Fermi, the night Fermi won the Nobel Prize.

As I held the book I felt my fingertips burn.

What was I supposed to make of all that? I confess, after long deliberation, I find Fermi inscrutable. No doubt the fault is mine. Mathematics was his true language, much more so than Italian, but I've only ever had a barbarian's grasp of it. The day after I met with the students, Jakob came to me in private. He brought me Laura Capon's account of her life with Enrico Fermi, along with facsimile copies of pages from Fermi's notebooks. When I scanned Fermi's jottings I saw integrals and derivatives penned with the utmost care, numerals with none of the awkward swerves of his inscription. I saw the gentle arcs of parentheses, the confident strokes of fraction slashes, the lacelike loops of gamma, delta, epsilon. I saw, in the artistry of his script, his reverence for his materials. The precision of his pages, the exacting style of his penmanship, made clear to me that all those strings of symbols, all those coefficients and polynomials, were actually the purest distillations of this man's deepest thoughts about the world in which he'd found himself. He'd strip-mined his years of ruminations and given the most profound of them a form as firm as a diamond cut and polished, and every bit as unyielding, expressing each facet of his innermost truths in terms that couldn't be tampered with. If my entanglement with those students had made anything clear to me, it was that my amateur dabblings in mathematics were ill-advised, at best, so that Fermi's mind, set down on the page, would never truly be mine to know. Possibly, though, the fault lies only at a tangent to my shortcomings. Maybe he's inscrutable because he chose to be that way in life. Maybe he was merely cold of heart, or made cold by his circumstances, and all the cold equations he left behind are perfectly intelligible as the life's work of a man reluctant to share his human warmth.

Here is what I know about him. He took the call from Stockholm, was greeted by a voice that awarded him the honour of his life, and before he'd even said farewell and returned the receiver to its cradle he'd reimagined the event. The glory of it, the prestige, the grandeur, the things he should have been revelling in, were all less important to him than the opportunity it presented, the chance to make a swift escape from Europe. Let me grant him some bitterness. It has to be a bitter thing to reach the pinnacle of one's labours and yet value it opportunistically, not for its own sake. But let me also grant him hope, and dedication, and love. He did not seize the opportunity for himself. He didn't give up his life in Rome for his own gratification. He did it for his two children and he did it for his wife. His actions speak of the stirrings of his heart, of the people who *really* moved him. But if that's true of his actions in flight, and in the weeks leading up to his escape, it must also be true of his actions in the months after Stockholm, newly arrived in Chicago, and in the years that followed, in the course of events and the chain of decisions that led him to White Sands.

What did Fermi see when he crossed the Alps in that train and left behind his life? What visions played before his eyes? He let his wife take his hand in her own. He looked across, lovingly, at his children asleep on the opposite seat. In Rome he'd packed their belongings, he'd been the one to select which clothes and toys they'd hold on to, as even now he guarded them from any awareness of what was going to happen. No farewells to friends. No final visits to cherished places. What else, what more, did he keep inside himself? Could he imagine, even then, the unstable elements encased in shells, the split of the atom, the twin blasts and the blinding light? He didn't build the weapon. He didn't even supervise it. A team of engineers pieced it together on the orders of other men. But he could foresee things in detail. He'd envisioned meeting old friends in Stockholm; he'd imagined reunions precisely enough to bring one man a certain book, specially chosen for him, specially inscribed to speak to his concerns. How far, then, did his foresight extend? Could he dream up faces he'd never seen, the faces of the unknowable people caught beneath a flaming sky? Could he anticipate the thousands, tens of thousands, instantly incinerated, every particle carbonised, scorched out of existence in a split second and dusting the rubble of war like so much soot? Could he foresee the fallout that would sicken generations yet to come? It's implausible to think he didn't try. In his reckoning with numbers he was prodigious. Those thousands had to have been there in his calculations, even if only as spirits, as he went about finding a formula to extract carnage from an atom. So, then, he appears to me as a man of insatiable vengeance. I see him on that train, wearing a mask of exceptional calm, now awake alone in the dark as his wife, too, submits to sleep. I see him knowing full well the destruction he will bring to others, I see him committing himself to it with an awful serenity, and I see him convinced that it is just, it is *warranted*, in view of the violence wrought on his peace and the threats against those whom he loves. I see a man with a mind of godlike capabilities, and when he is moved to displeasure I see him as inclined as any god to use his power to smite.

Jakob resumed his seat. He lowered himself onto the sofa in thought of the ties that bound his family to the place in which we'd met. But I was still taken with his sketch of Fermi, the escape to the north, the encounter with old friends, and I wanted to know what a man like Fermi might have said to someone like Achim when he felt able to speak freely. I opened the book again to the inscription at the front and I passed it to Luca.

Do you think you can translate for me?

He scanned the words and chewed his lip. It's bad, he said. Bad handwriting and also the grammar is strange. But I think maybe—*denken an, trotzdem*—maybe it says something like, *Think on this, my friend.* Ah, *nevertheless*, or *despite it all*, ah, *today*—

He read ahead in silence for a moment. Then, I noticed, he frowned and raised his eyes from the page to seek a response from Jakob. He looked puzzled.

Jakob couldn't hide a knowing smile.

All right, then, said Luca. *Think on this, my friend*, he said, taking care to enunciate his words: *in spite of everything, even today, with our living breath, we return life to Caesar.*

I glanced across at Jakob and watched the smile widen.

I said, You look like the only one here who has any idea what that means.

Well, then, this is it. What's the word for what I did when I had the house to myself? When I had the urn to myself. What I did with, or to, the ashes. What's the correct preposition? I unscrewed the lid and cradled the urn in my hands. I took a step back from the dresser, the doily, and sat on the edge of the bed. Then while one hand still held the urn, the other hand slid in. First I let my fingertips rest lightly on the surface, feeling the powder against my skin, but after a moment I pressed down and watched my fingers sink, watched the dust swallow my nails, my knuckles, and part to make way for my palm, my wrist. What's the verb for this? I didn't dip my hand in the ashes. I immersed it. *Plunge*, perhaps, or *submerge*. But luxuriously. I eased it in, gently, gently, sensitive to every nuance of what my fingers were passing through.

My father-in-law had found me staring down at the sludge, the dregs, at the bottom of my cup of coffee.

Refill? he said.

I shook my head. No, thanks.

He held out his hand for me to pass him the cup.

I'll do it, I said. I took the cup into the kitchen. He stayed where he was, in the living room, and called over to me.

We're all set, he said. I've got the granny flat ready for your folks.

He meant he'd straightened the sheets on the bed and vacuumed up the dog hair.

Great, I said. Thanks. They'll appreciate it.

I put the cup in the sink and heard the tinkling of keys.

No worries, he said. So, then, it might be time to give you some space.

I came back into the living room to find him by the front door.

I'll let you sort yourself out in peace, he said. Leave the dishes, I'll look after them later. Take a shower. Freshen up. Get yourself on an even keel. The girls'll be home soon.

I nodded and said, Okay.

We thought we might have a barbecue tonight. Last chance, maybe, before daylight savings ends, while the weather's still ripe for eating outside. But I'll have to go buy beer.

He opened the door and patted his pockets to be sure he had everything he needed.

Sounds good, I said.

Any other requests?

Nothing particular.

White wine, too, he said. All right. I'm off. See you in a bit. Then the door swung shut with a bang, and the space I could claim for myself burst open all around me.

Nothing of where I was seemed tangible anymore. It had all the feebleness of a mirage, the worn material of lives that didn't intersect with mine. I was estranged from it all in the most pointed sense of the word, a stranger from another land. I felt like a ghost not quite able to touch the reality around him, or else like the only living thing in a space that had become ghostly in my presence. I guess that's why I had a hunger to make contact with something, something I knew to be my own. Faint grey powder so soft and fine that at first it was almost imperceptible, barely more matter than air. Only as my hand searched on did the ashes take hold of me in turn. I reached towards the base of the urn and felt the powder gather, building up in a layer that coated my skin and filled my pores like dust from chalk or crumbled bricks or lime. I hadn't reached into the urn to seize the ashes, certainly not to scatter them, but when I reached in the ashes reached out and clung to me.

I turned my hand beneath the dust, twisted at the wrist, and curled my fingers and flexed them and slowly began to sift. I'd imagined, long ago, having to search for just the right words, in just the right order, to reach the students I'd summoned by bewitching them with visions of movements like these. I thought I'd speak to them of chain gangs in captivity, bound to board a merchant vessel, marched at gunpoint along a sparkling stretch of coast. I thought I'd contrive for them a stumble, a fall upon the sand, fingers twisted into talons, hands clawing at fugitive grains snatched by the wind and taken to sea. I'd pictured myself in that room with them and anticipated their resistance to my words, their doubts about my case and my self-defence, and so I'd planned on appealing to them with sights that already sparked their sympathies. Cynical, yes, carefully plotting my manoeuvres, I'd prepared to embroider images purloined from Primo Levi: emaciated bodies amassed in shallow graves, set alight with blazing torches held to pitch, reduced to flakes of char swept into the sky. But then came *de Bello Gallico*, inscribed: a stimulus for Jakob to bewilder me with talk of Fermi's formulae, of elementary concepts I couldn't hope to grasp.

Perhaps those exchanges had brought to mind my wife holding open her hand atop the cliff. Or perhaps the sight of her hand had stirred memories of the encounter while I slept. Either way I sifted the ashes, twirling my fingers through their depths while barely troubling the surface, and all I wanted was to hold them tight and keep them from her reach. Not that I thought of backing out, retracting my consent to let them scatter. I wanted to hide them somewhere. I wanted to lose them somewhere. At one and the same time I wanted to respect my wife's wishes to let go of the ashes and also to impede her, to rescue my daughter from the wind. I felt my wife wavering at the periphery of my vision and I didn't see how I could bring her back to the centre. I wanted her to know all this without having to tell her. I just didn't want the ashes gone. I didn't want to see them given to the waves.

But, then, the meaning of *gone* was as unclear as everything else. Enrico Fermi, in my mind, sat in silence on the northbound train and watched his reflection grow almost solid as the darkness deepened beyond the window. In Göttingen, Jakob had told me, Fermi had made his reputation thanks to an intellectual party trick. He had an uncanny ability to derive orders of magnitude from minimal data and inferential calculations. He perfected it throughout his life, much to the awe of others, running the maths in his mind to demonstrate astonishing things. The approximate number of piano tuners in a city the size of Chicago. The approximate volume of all the pebbles on the bed of Lake Michigan. And, famously, this fact: anytime anyone draws a single breath, anywhere on the planet, there's a probability of ninety-nine per cent that they'll inhale at least one molecule of the air expelled by Julius Caesar, in his final gasp, as the conspirators closed in and Brutus brandished his blade.

Jakob tried to gauge my response with wide-eyed enthusiasm. Did you know this?

Sounds pretty fanciful.

It does, yes. But the numbers don't lie.

My grasp on the numbers was infantile. One man, one breath, recycled through the millennia. Revived, reinvigorated, even now, even today, in billions of other bodies. That's as much as I could hold in my head.

Actually, said Jakob, the mathematics is quite simple. You begin with the lung capacity of an average adult male. From that, you calculate the number of molecules he would inhale. Easy. Then you calculate how long it would take for those molecules, *exhaled*, to return to the atmosphere with an even distribution—

Without a sense of the actual figures, I worried I'd be lost.

If the atmosphere contains *x* molecules of air, he said, and of these a given man exhaled *y* molecules, then the probability that I will inhale—

No, I said. Sorry. Just wait. With a heave I struggled up from the sofa and retreated to the window. Wait, I said, just wait, giving instructions even as I turned my back on the students. My train of thought had split from Jakob's, had instead continued trailing the words that propelled his logic. The words on the page. The writing of them. The Alpine pass at night, the children asleep in the silent booth. Laura Capon drifting off and the serenity of the rocking carriage. The snow outside. The runaway calculations. The retrieval of the book and the nib of the pen, the ink, the inscription. The state of the man, outwardly stoic, about to cross, as calm as can be, into a crisis of moral compromise.

Was that where I'd taken myself? My fingertips reached the bottom of the urn. My nails scraped the gunmetal buff. I held tight to a fistful of ashes. Even so, I didn't have the strength to do what I wanted the most. I wanted to compact them again, compress them, squeeze out every last subatomic space between them, undo everything they'd had done to them and mould them into new life. I didn't just want to keep them from dispersal. I wanted them to become more than what they plainly were. I wanted to see more of the life that had once moved through them and gave them motion.

I saw her in my mind, a mewling infant, one day old, with faded ink on her foot and a face of the utmost calm, but I wanted to see her with me in the world again. Instead I saw only dust, only lifeless particles, which gave me no satisfaction whatsoever, even though this was all that remained of something immeasurably precious to me. I saw them also as a reminder that even at this stage in my descent, even as I dropped into the moral gutter, and even as I felt disgust at the sight of them, I still had things I couldn't bear to lose and their loss was imminent. Coarse and paltry as they were, I wanted to sit there like that, my hand in the ashes, and let my wife walk in to find me as I was. I wanted her just to leave them be, to understand that I wanted them to be left. Knowing that she couldn't, wouldn't, I realised that what I actually wanted was for her to leave me. That was it. Not in a rage. I wanted her simply to no longer be around me. When I stirred the ashes with my fingers it was the loss of her presence, the way I *wanted* the loss of her presence, that mingled with the dust. By now, I knew, she'd be on her way back to the house.

Is that what Shane wanted, too, when he stood by his dying son and watched him breathe out his life? I could see him there in the bedroom stacked with specialist equipment, watching the vital signs as they lagged and slowed. I could see him raising his eyes as Kerry stepped into the doorway. Not to say she wouldn't be all concern, all anxiety. Only to say that in my mind her husband wants her gone. Not to leave, not to disappear. To be gone. Just to not be there, to not be a reminder of a loss that hasn't happened yet but already haunts him through her presence. As the dying man breathes in, breathes out, a fog creeps over the windowpane. His shallow breaths are enough to keep him alive, for now, but they forsake his parents to the agony of waiting, constant waiting, waiting and waiting for him to make the crossing that will finally divide them from one another.

At the window I'd let out a sigh, looking across the valley to the Wetterhorn, and I closed my eyes to concentrate on what Jakob was trying to tell me. Run it by me again, I said. *Slowly.* So he did. He obliged me. An inhalation. An admixture of molecules. Oxygen and nitrogen drawn into the trachea of a tyrant, charging through the bronchioles, into the alveoli, then discharged into the bloodflow about to be ended. My thoughts snagged on the tip of the knife between the ribs, the puncture of a lung, the splutter, the spittle, the fading warmth of a dying gasp stolen away by a breeze. My thoughts swept up that breath on the Föhn, buffeting its elements across the Tuscan hills and over the sprawl of the Padan Plain and up, up, into Ticino, through the warren of the passes, to fall upon the sides of the mountains I could see when I opened my eyes again.

Shane, I imagine, holed himself up in his house and didn't leave. The boy breathed his last. The logistics were sorted out. The soldier shut himself away. Call it a form of private penance. He had to share the space with Kerry. He denied his skin the cooling breeze. The house, his shelter, became his scourge, his tomb. Ample room to move around, to be by himself, to spend time alone, but everywhere he went he could see her or hear her or feel her there, the woman who reminded him of what he'd been and what he'd lost, who filled his vision with ghosts of the boy he'd saved by making a ghost of himself.

When I turned from the view of the valley to face the students again, to find them already watching me, my thoughts, I realised, had outrun my awareness and made the students appear to me as other than themselves. In them now I saw something I'm sure Fermi meant for his words to reveal, to prompt his one-time friend and colleague to see. Gone were the people in that room. Gone as well: their names, their expressions, all their surface features, leaving before me only miasma, a host of hazes, as of chemical fumes, assuming vaguely human dimensions. What was this stuff, the stuff of their being? Volume without mass, matter without bonds or compounds, but instead something like sediment, like a granular residuum, churned up to drift and twirl through the vacuum spaces of organs and tissues and veins invisible to me. If there was any truth to Fermi's words, *with our living breath, we return life to Caesar,* then, I reasoned, that truth had to hold up exponentially as well. Why stop one's thoughts at the breath of one man? In the course of a single day, we'd breathe in the breath of every person who ever lived, and who had, in their time, inhaled the breaths of all who'd come before them. We'd also breathe in more of the stuff of life, in molecules borne on the air. Tears, once shed, would evaporate. Blood, once spilled, would coagulate. Flesh would decay and then dissipate, and so, I saw, just to *be,* to live and survive, to eat and drink, to breathe in, breathe out, would be constantly to take into one's body the particulate remnants of all the dead. It would be to accept them, to hold them, to expel them and then accept others: to incorporate them, to carry them inside oneself, as I saw them now carried by the students in the chalet, as Fermi had once wanted his friend, Achim, to see.

So, Stockholm. The nib, the ink, the inscription. The ceremony, the banquet. The honorary lecture and the medallion. A reunion after many years. A handshake, an exchange of smiles. Pleasantries, perhaps. Congratulations. Commentary. Commiserations and sorrows. Then, in a private moment, *de Bello Gallico* changes hands. If Fermi knew where he was going, and why he had to flee, he had to have known what fate awaited those forced to abide the rotting of their homelands. A few collegiate reassurances, a hand on the other man's shoulder. Achim is as tall and thin as his great-great-grandson, as serious and scholarly, as neatly dressed, as reserved. He shrinks under Fermi's touch until the lauded physicist offers him an understated gift. Green cloth. Pages as yet uncut. He eases open the cover and reads:

> *Think on this, my friend:*
> *in spite of everything, even today,*
> *with our living breath,*
> *we return life to Caesar.*

The inscription has the ring of a farewell, unwelcome but unavoidable. The choice of book raises a spectre of where this farewell will finally lead. Plumes of smoke spew into the sky, the length and breadth of the continent. Fermi would have known. I assume Achim knew as well. These were men of culture. They would have understood that when one gave another a gift, the object itself, carefully chosen, had more import than the gesture. Did the students have any idea? Beyond the euphony of the title: conquest, displacement, families fed to the flames. With that book in his hands, with that inscription before his eyes, did Achim understand that Fermi meant to take flight, to secure for his family the safety that would elude Achim himself? Did he have to conceal his awareness, raise his eyes from the page and put on a visage as stoic as his companion? Still a young man, a young father, his face has lately taken on a jaundiced tone and his hair, although not grey, has begun to thin. He peers at the words as his vision blurs and so he moves in closer, closer, to pick out the farewell behind the entreaty as a bird would bend to peck seeds from grass. Dry mouth, dry lips, a tremble and then a resolve. Even as I see Achim maintaining appearances, forcing a smile, mumbling gratitude, I see his eyes stung by sudden tears.

Was Shane able to cry? I've wondered that for a long time. Were tears possible for him anymore? One eye blasted out. The other eye glossed over. His face blown apart and soldered together again. I picture him lying on his bed in a house dispossessed of one life. I picture a tear sliding down his cheek, scudding through the gutters in his skin. I picture Kerry beside him, awake and staring at the ceiling. I picture Laura Capon in that private booth in the snow, speechless, as with her gaze alone she caresses her sleeping children, letting her body sway in time with the clanking of the carriage. I picture Enrico Fermi, too, watching his wife reflected in the dark, as salt water wells in the corners of his eyes and he throws himself into the monstrous mathematics that will finally define him.

From Stockholm the book returned to Göttingen. The hands that held it were shackled, the recipient apprehended, the pacifist interred. He had a wife and daughter. The nib, the ink, the paper, and tears in the woman's eyes as she writes to her husband's friends and colleagues for help. Her appeal finds its way to a man who cherishes his memories of the Odenwaldschule. In these fraught times he maintains his ties to the old idealists across the border. The nib, the ink, the paper, and tears in the eyes of the prisoner's daughter as her mother sends her to a place of greater safety. She presses the book into the girl's hands and presses a kiss to her lips. She leaves her with a token of her heritage and a reminder, *think on this*, of a sort of survival.

All of this is to say that I lifted my hand from the ashes when I felt my own tears falling. Whiteness covered my fingertips, caulked up the lines in my palms. Shane. His boy. How could he have ever sent the body to the furnace? A boy that size would have taken hours to burn. Heat so high it tops a thousand degrees, obliterates the heart and brain, the lungs, all the internal organs, releases gases into the air as it eats into skin and muscle and bone. Then the remains are sent to the cremulator, ground down and pulverised, and what you're left with, what's returned, is a body blasted apart. It had occurred to me to wonder, while I kept my hand in the ashes, which parts of my daughter I might have been touching. Had her own fingers made contact with mine at the same time that I cradled her head? But it occurred to me, too, that questions like these were fallacies. When you're handed the ashes you're not left with the parts of a body, a body in pieces. You're only left with a few. So many have been vaporised and oxidised, vanishing into elements, filtered out during cremulation, that it's wrong even to think of the ashes as the remains of a person truly conceived.

Now take a man whose own body had endured its own discomposition. How could he willingly send his son to the flames? If I'd been baffled by it when Hannah told me Shane's son had died, I was doubly baffled when I looked on his death in hindsight. Even putting aside the method of cremation, how could a man like Shane, a father, grieve for his child without holding on to the body? Demirović had held on to the body. I wished I'd intervened to hold on to the body. How did Shane not feel the same need? Bewildered at first, I asked myself this question in a rhetorical sense. Then, as I turned it over, I began to ask it sincerely. What peace was known to Shane that wasn't known to me? Had he done something to seal his grief without fixating on a burial? How so? What did he do?

I flexed my hand and returned the ashes to the dresser. But then I left the urn uncapped, placed the lid beside it on the doily, and went downstairs to see if I could find a vase. Why is it not okay to want the worst for oneself, or, if not to want it, at least to know what it is and move towards it anyway? Why does this mindset persist, this mindset in which even people in the most dire situations will always, unremittingly, want what's best for their interests? Why assume that those people will always take measures to avoid pain and seek peace? In extremis, that mindset decays. You know you've arrived there when you start closing down your own escape routes, destroying your own best chances of getting out.

With a last glance out the window I saw a house ablaze. Silver birch and mountain ash. It burned where it stood on a rise in the valley and it came to me, I knew, from the opening pages of Jakob's book. Not the inscription, but the text. Rewind the decades, the centuries. Stuff the smoke back into the chimneys, let the char reconstitute bodies. Pull every last particle of air from the breath of everyone who ever inhaled it and return it to the atmosphere. Reverse the flow of time so the wind can reclaim that final, desperate gasp and return it to the throat from which it fled. Unhear the cry, *Sic semper tyrannis!*, then watch the blades restore blood to the tyrant. He rises to his feet, bids farewell to his assassins, relinquishes his seizure of power, retreats across the Rubicon. He went there in the first place, north of Rome, crossing the river to reach the Alps, because the houses were burning. Because the people who lived in them had no choice but to burn them and flee. If Jakob had looked beyond Fermi's words, he'd know. If he'd read on past the inscription, even just one page, he'd recognise the people by name. They called themselves the Helvetii. They were the tribe of Celts who are recognised today as the first people of the Swiss plateau. They were, in the truest sense, the indigenes of the ground on which we met, and all of them were gone. Foreign assaults on their territory had pushed them onto unforgiving soil. They wrote to neighbouring tribes to petition for asylum, to beg for resettlement, and they were denied. They didn't simply uproot themselves and leave. They wrote, they applied, they sent emissaries and ambassadors. They pleaded for safe haven somewhere. But all their pleas were dismissed. What meaningful choice did they have? There's no withstanding the whimpers of malnourished children or the cries of the elderly as they starve. There's no abiding the constant threat of enemies raiding supplies. They had to move, they couldn't return, and so, before they evacuated the plateau, they struck sparks against their dwellings and gave their homes to the flames. Their survival as a people, their integrity, they staked on relinquishing everything they'd ever been.

I knew this much about them as an assortment of facts, but I could never reconcile the facts with my experience. How could a person incinerate their own place of safety? What despair, what loss of all hope, could incite someone to build the flames and hold them to the structure? What did it matter if these were people of sackcloth and tunics, torcs and lunulas? Woad and bronze, chainmail, chariots: these artefacts of bygone ways play no part at all in my life, but even so, beneath the ornamentation, I'm sure I can feel with these folk the pain, the simple pain, of holding a torch to the status quo. In La Tène, at the western end of the Alps, an abundance of art and sculpture, swords and shields, had returned to the world almost three thousand years after these people submerged them in Lake Neuchâtel. In Hallstatt, to the east, excavations in a government mine turned up hilts and armlets, and situlae, from a thousand years before that. In Zürich, a wealth of ceramics. In Bern, hill-fort foundations. The people of these places, unknowingly doomed to Caesar's conquest, were at the centre of a culture that sprawled out from the forests east of the Danube as far west as the windswept Hebrides. Their bond to the land was an ancient one, beyond their living memory. They wouldn't have severed it willingly, or easily, without misgivings, without grief, without distress or remorse. I imagine, inside them, brute devastation as they turn from the flames, the houses ablaze on the hills, and trudge away into a hostile world.

Devastation, a long arc, was what yoked them to those of us gathered atop the chalet overlooking their land. Legionaries and mercenaries had moved like a scythe across Gaul, cutting down families, decimating oppida, eliminating entire tribes, in a firestorm that raged from the Berner Oberland to Britain. The Helvetii had been the first to fall. Then the Aedui, the Sequani. Eventually the Cantii of England, the Dumnonii of Cornwall, tribe after tribe until all that remained were soul-stricken druids in ragged white robes howling curses at the invaders from the beaches of Wales. These were the people whose diaspora, under imperial incursions, culminated with survivors confined to Ireland and Scotland while the conquerors reshaped the ways of the tribes they'd subjugated. So cultures began to shift. To pin down their place in the cosmos, to map out the mysteries of things, to fasten the very stars to their land, the survivors had erected thousands of rings of stones. The rings, when abandoned, became for later peoples gateways to other worlds, the thresholds crossed by *aes síth*. To withdraw from the reach of invaders along the coasts and on the inland plains, these people took to the uplands, sought solitude in the heather. Adopting as their deity the conversing of the elements, a god of utter indifference to human affairs, they became known to pious outsiders as coarsened pagans, as the heathen. Rewinding the centuries as far as I could, these people were at some point evidently *mine*. But affinity is not continuity. The chain that connected me to them had been cut long ago. I had nothing like what the students in front of me held on to. When the Celts had been corralled into the farthest reaches of the world, when the Rubicon had again been crossed and almighty power assumed with military force, later commanders had sent their men eastward and mounted another diaspora, this time against Judea, whose endpoint across the centuries led me right back to that chalet, that loft, that book, that inscription.

For all the particulate matter I'd seen in the students a moment before, I looked anew and saw in them astonishing integrity. I saw the integrity of their stand against me and, more, I saw that it came from the continuity of their belonging to a people wrenched apart, dispersed. I wanted that integrity. I have wanted it for so long. But, in wanting it, how could I possibly surrender, release, what I held in my hand, what also held on to me? I saw the ashes rise to my wrist. Beneath them I felt my fingers clench. Did I really believe in the integrity of my daughter? Was I actually committed to not letting her disperse? However hopeless my cause, however belated my change of heart, could I say in all honesty that I did not want to let her go, or would those words only come at the end of my efforts to find better ones and bring them order? If I didn't want to let her go, if I *truly* didn't want it, how much was I prepared to risk to keep her as intact as I could? How much to keep some part of her with me? What was I willing to stake? What was I willing to relinquish to hold on to her?

This is what I did. I found a vase in a cupboard under the kitchen sink. Wafer-thin glass, fluted at the top, with a long stem leading to a bulb for the water, it seemed designed to display only a single flower. I took it upstairs to the guestroom and steadied it on the dresser doily. Then I reached into the urn again and scooped up a fistful of ashes. I held my fist over the vase and slowly spread my fingers. A stream of ash slipped out and plashed into the spherical base, as graceful as sand sinking through an hourglass. Once more I reached into the urn and took ashes in my fist, held them over the vase and carefully released them. This severance, this violation, was agonising. But it was also the only way I could see to rescue my daughter from complete obliteration, the only way to retain some talisman that might bring forth her spirit again in years to come. So, then, with another clutch, until her ashes filled the vase, trying not to let them spill, not always calm enough to succeed, I steeled against the agony and took her from the remnants of herself. This is what I did. Deceptive and duplicitous, and desperate as well, this is what I did. Is there a word to name it? I held the torch to the status quo. I cleaved the remains of my child in two, some to be scattered, some retained, neither part ever to be reunited with the other. I did it for reasons that didn't accord, though they moved me in equal measure. I did it because I had to, because doing so was as close as I could imagine to doing *right*. But I did it also because, once more,

I found myself in a place that awoke my atavism, and my calculated inclination was to do the worst.

Hassan Demirović staggered into the cell. Staggered because the footage wasn't fluid. The voiceover on the nightly news explained the situation. Filming was not permitted in the prison. Only Demirović had been allowed to see Imran bin Musa in the flesh, trailed by corrections officers who'd observed their encounter from a short distance. A single photographer, appointed by the government, had been permitted to document the preparations, but not to follow the visitors inside. The first picture, then, showed Demirović stepping towards the door. The screen whisked the picture away and replaced it with another. This one caught him midstride at the threshold, extending his hand towards a figure out of frame. With another swipe he disappeared and the cell door closed. In my mind's eye I tried to see bin Musa on the other side. He sat behind a table, beneath a ceiling light, with a small barred window above and behind him. I imagined him wearing the expression of a bewildered youth. Wide eyes, a downturned mouth. Freshly shaved with short-cropped hair. His was the face that Demirović had for so long wanted to put himself in view of. It was a face the visitor otherwise wouldn't look at twice. What had he finally found in it? Without seeing the face for myself, would I ever know?

That afternoon I'd been pulled out of my stupor by an engine in the driveway. The engine cut and car doors slammed. I had no idea how long I'd been sitting on the bed and staring at the ashes through the glass. Beneath my feet I felt the front door open and swing closed with a bump. Two voices at the base of the stairs. The rustle of plastic bags. The lid screwed back onto the urn. The urn went into place on the dresser. The bottom drawer of the dresser slid open. I squatted above it and put the vase inside. From beneath the urn I extracted the silken doily. I scrunched part of it into a sort of wadding and stuffed it into the flute of the vase, then wrapped the rest around the glass and nestled it all among folded bedsheets. The drawer slid closed and swept the pilfered ashes from sight.

Downstairs my wife had already gone to the kitchen. Cupboards open all around her, the fridge door yawning wide, she'd piled the bags on the countertops to empty out the shopping and put the new things in their proper places. I went to offer help but her mother intercepted me at the breakfast bar and feigned shock when she saw the state I was in.

Good Lord, she said, you slept a while. Feeling more rested now?

I've been up for a bit, I said. Woke up around midday.

I eyed the clock on the kitchen wall. It was nearly three.

What about a shower, then? said my mother-in-law.

My hair stood out, scattershot from a restless night, and I hadn't changed my clothes. I nodded and rubbed my eyes with a knuckle in a pretence of ongoing weariness.

Right, I said. Maybe now's the time.

My wife called out from the kitchen. Early dinner tonight?

Your dad said a barbecue.

Early, though. Say five-thirty?

She scrunched up a fistful of plastic bags and shoved them into a cotton tube that hung from the handle of the pantry cupboard.

Right, I said.

She closed the cupboards around her and closed the fridge. Then she moved to the back door, the glass streaked with smudges from a moist snout, and she slid it open to give the dog a treat. This is what she did. These are the things I watched her do. What I saw in her motions, her ease, wasn't quite the attitude of someone you'd call carefree, but it was at least the attitude of someone whose troubles didn't include even a suspicion of my conduct while she'd been gone. Nothing about the way she carried herself suggested a performance. Why would she need to perform her mood? She had nothing to conceal from the people around her. She could afford to do these mundane things. But with my fake surprise at the lapse of time, my fake shame at having my mother-in-law see me in my jet lagged squalor, I stood there by the breakfast bar, holding myself in position, eyeing the clock, turning to trudge upstairs to the shower, carefully controlling all my movements to affect a lackadaisical air, and I ended up feeling like a puppet whose strings were being pulled by some larger version of myself. All the mundane things I did in front of my wife and her mother were bricks in an edifice I built to block their view of what I'd done while they were out.

Demirović staggered onto the screen after all the plates had been cleared. Outside, in the garden, the charcoal in the barbecue simmered into powder. By the back door, the dog ground her teeth on a T-bone stripped of meat. In the kitchen the dishwasher hummed and the kettle, freshly boiled, clicked off in a puff of steam. My father-in-law had gone to make some tea. My wife and her mother shared the sofa and sat watching the news. Demirović's meeting with Imran bin Musa scored all of a minute's coverage, headlining only the second-rate stories that followed the first commercials. The reporter said the meeting had lasted the whole twenty minutes. There had been no disclosure of what the two men talked about, and the pictures didn't even make it clear that they'd meaningfully conversed. All I could see, when I thought on the encounter, was Demirović seated at the table while bin Musa sat opposite him and waited for to him say what he'd planned. All I saw as the report wrapped up was one last photograph of Demirović emerging from the cell. He kept his head down, his back to the door, and seemed almost to be searching the ground for a path to follow as he walked towards the camera. My father-in-law eyed the picture when he returned to the sofa and offered me a cup of tea. I took the tea from him and looked at that last picture and felt an impulse, an irrepressible *need*, to hurl the cup at the screen and shatter the face of the man who'd staked so much of himself on a vacuity. Twenty minutes. Twenty minutes of what? Not a thing that was of any use to me.

And that was it. The news moved on. An explosives detection dog who'd been trained by Australian forces in Afghanistan had gone missing seven years ago and today miraculously returned. That was all there was. Three or four pictures from outside a cell. Evidence of the fact that an encounter had occurred but no hint of what it had entailed. Dim lighting, drab clothes, washed-out colours, framing restricted by the access policies of the prison. This was the sputtering end to a story I'd watched unfold in pictures of shock and grief, rage and sorrow, delirium and dislocation that exceeded all conveyance in words. This was the big climax. This was where everything else had led, from the first scenes of agonised parents outside the day-care centre to the crowds that swelled the streets in solidarity with Demirović, from the glowing pictures of the grieving man's daughter to the investigation into the perpetrator's history, from the clamour outside the cemetery to the embrace between mourning parents and then, suddenly, the absence of a wedding ring. This, all this, led up to dull pictures of a dull man doing dull things in a dull place.

Viewers wouldn't care. That was the reality. That's why the broadcast seemed so comfortable with paring back the report. Tempers had cooled since the attack and the funerals. People had moved on to other outrages, other occasions for public mourning. A year earlier, there had been an outpouring of sympathies for more than two hundred missing, believed dead, when a flight from Kuala Lumpur dropped off the radar somewhere over the Andaman Sea. Now all sorrows flowed towards the Massif des Trois-Évêchés. A year further on, two years, three years, there would be other atrocities to stoke the passions. Vehicles driven into pedestrians in Nice, in Berlin, in London. Concertgoers blown apart by bombs in Manchester and Paris. Gunmen picking off victims in Orlando, in Las Vegas, in small-town Florida. Australians would watch it all from afar. They'd join in the global displays of fellow feeling for the survivors, then they'd let their attention float freely to the next attack, the next calamity, and they'd react to that one in much the same way. They were sightseers. They were spectators to a parade of captivating stories, entranced by each one and then suddenly not. Even when a story arose on their own shores, everyone but the people involved in it became swept up in more vital events as soon as they broke out.

I wasn't spared from the spectacle any more than anyone else. In mid-December, a café in Sydney had gone into lockdown when a crazed man, a refugee from Iran, took eighteen customers hostage and engaged police in a standoff that lasted sixteen hours. But when the police decided to raid the premises, the planned arrest went awry. The man killed one person. Police officers killed another by mistake. Only after two people had died was the man taken down. Four other people were seriously injured. The entire city was in shock. I hadn't noticed any of it. Not the drama itself, not the days of analysis and public grief that followed, not the weeks of recriminations and debates over legal reforms. All of this had formed the context for the public outcry triggered by Imran bin Musa and I had entirely missed it. Mid-December in the Alps, I'd had more urgent concerns on my mind. I'd caught up with the masses only when a fresh outrage came around, and even then I'd latched onto the one that spoke most directly to me. A week before bin Musa's attack, a mother in Cairns had drugged seven of her children along with one of their cousins and stabbed them all to death. Days after that, in Maroochydore, another woman was arrested for poisoning one of her grandchildren, smothering a second, and trying to kill two more by locking them in a room and setting it on fire. Neither of those stories had attracted my notice. I'd followed the story of Imran bin Musa mostly because Demirović's involvement found me where I lived. No doubt, though, there had been memorial events and the mobilisation of crowds in Queensland as well, and no doubt they'd tumbled out of the spotlight when bin Musa stole it. But the spotlight had long ago been stolen from him in turn, and so a crime that once incited people to flood the streets, to set up vigil, to editorialise, to fulminate, now no longer warranted more than sixty seconds of airtime just a couple of months after the fact. Not even on the day that Demirović offered bin Musa forgiveness, the very forgiveness that made those people so incensed in the first place, and certainly not on the basis of what the story still meant to me.

Obviously I felt the pang of something cut short. I could only see the situation as a betrayal. Not a betrayal of my investment in it, not a betrayal of the stake I'd claimed, but a betrayal of everything that had been at stake between those men, and everything that remained at stake as the case against bin Musa went to trial. I didn't want to see just a handful of stills of Demirović outside bin Musa's cell. I wanted to know what happened in that room and what was felt throughout those twenty minutes. I wanted Demirović and bin Musa to be hooked up to pulse monitors, I wanted peaks and troughs, fluctuations, oscillations, a second-by-second graph of their moments of queasiness, of indignation, of forced calm, of hesitation and confusion. The photographs deadened the encounter, the enlivening face-to-face, and flattened it into an event to be noted but not felt at all. I tightened my grip on the ceramic in my hands and forced myself to sit there and swallow, suppress, the bitterness that swilled inside me at the sight of such a pathetic end to the ordeal I'd zealously followed from afar. I knew it wasn't true that the encounter had been a dull occurrence. The pictures made it dull, they'd blunted its sudden turns, its intensities, and drained it of exactly what made it worth understanding.

Focus, close focus, can distort as much as clarify. When the students cut me short, fractured my single-minded discourse on the minutiae of something I thought they'd misunderstood, that's what drove them to intervene. When shown to them in all the blood and agony of its fine details, slavery had appeared to their eyes as a horror too granular to resolve. With my stubborn insistence that they see it in its every particular, if I'd continued I would have only drawn them away from immersion in the past, down a path towards a pointillist panorama viewed too closely to be taken as anything real. They'd seen me doing the inverse of what I saw on the screen. The news report took an exceptional event and flattened it with a focus on tedious things. My fixation on the traumas of an enslaved existence only sapped the pain from where most of it really accumulated, in the constant, baseline sorrow that pulsed through the drudgery of passing days.

At one point Jakob came close to putting his finger on that pulse. In telling me briefly about his great-grandmother, he'd used a word that Luca had translated as *integration*. He'd described her as a woman who lived with the pain of her younger years by integrating it into the fabric of her hours. He spoke of this pain as if it was something to be managed, to be worked with, to be allocated a quantity of one's spirits while one conducted one's daily affairs. But I baulked at sharing his view of it, at surveying the sweep of one's years from a distance and erasing their distinctions, tamping down their formative terrors until they dimmed into the background noise of a lifetime. I couldn't do that any more than I could content myself with sitting on the sofa, sedentary, beholding bland snapshots of a man as he emerged from an encounter that was, for him, an epic event.

I can't even, I just, I really don't know, said my mother-in-law. I really can't understand how that poor man could do something like that. Any parent would be forgiven for losing their mind in that situation. How did he keep himself together?

On the screen the news changed topic again, but her thoughts had been held by Demirović's visit to bin Musa.

Awful, she said. Just awful. How could you control yourself?

Jakob, I'd suddenly realised, had managed exactly that. He'd exercised self-control, integrated his distresses into his serious demeanour, right before my eyes. I'd seen the tension flicker through his jaw. He'd turned aside, he'd winced. He'd dropped that word, *missgestimmt*, and then evaded the subject. It took me a while to catch him. We'd gone on speaking, of Achim, of Fermi, of the girl who'd bequeathed to the school her father's gift of *de Bello Gallico*, and as Jakob sketched out her adult life my thoughts, too, had snagged, had spooled around my resistance to something he said: *integration*. How does a person adjust to the constant ache of upheavals such as hers? How do you not feel an urge to lash out and pursue recriminations, even haphazard, even random? Or is the urge only suppressed? I thought of Fermi in exile, the rift with his old life as he moved to protect his family. In his soulless formulae I saw recriminations of awful forbearance, of deliberation, painstakingly assembled for years after he fled, and executed on an order of magnitude incalculably greater than the losses that led him to board that northbound train. He hadn't lost as much as he could've. He hadn't lost his family. He'd lost enough to make him aggrieved, but his children and his wife hadn't come to the harm that came to others. He'd been roused to act, to protect and defend, to strike, simply by the threat of harm, by the spectre of potential losses. But if his wrath somehow speaks to the intensity of his sorrows, what can be said of the sorrows of someone who could feel the same wrath and swallow it?

Well, said my father-in-law, maybe that's what real forgiveness looks like.

I couldn't tell from his tone if he was being serious or shooting for sarcasm.

But just imagine, said my mother-in-law. In the same room. Keeping yourself composed, from the looks of things. Wouldn't you want to strangle him on the spot?

Imagine. That's where Jakob took the discussion, carried it over the following day when he gave me the book by Laura Capon and the facsimiled notes, and I broached the subject with him. Out of tune, I said. You told me you felt *distempered*. I asked you why, but you never gave a reason. In that room, with those students, I'd planned on going further than I did. I'd hoped to convey the *fury* of enslavement, to have the students feel themselves inside the skin of a person stirred by a rage that would one day escape control. I'd thought to speak of auction blocks, plantation life, punishment by whip; of decades lost to bestial labours, of humiliation and degradation and finally, fuelled by fury, a rising up in retaliation. I'd aimed for Prosser and Vesey, and Turner, these men who'd spurned the notion that they might *integrate* their pain into their days, who'd instead been moved to desecrate everything they could set their hands upon. I had no idea, until the next day, how totally Jakob at least would never have entertained any part of what I didn't say.

Missgestimmt, he said. Yes. That is the way I feel whenever I try to imagine Achim, and when you spoke out at the assembly you made me imagine.

Imagine what?

Imagine if he'd lived, how many lives he might have saved.

I stared at Jakob in an effort to stand where he stood, to divine his meaning.

Well, said my father-in-law. But he let himself fade out and silently conceded the point.

Well, I said, like an echo. Who can say what anyone would do in a situation like that, except maybe those who've suffered it themselves?

I kept my eyes on the television screen but I felt my wife turn towards me and stare. I felt a burn of some emotion flush my throat and my face.

I mean, I said, it's not impossible to think that if someone loses something they can't get back, and everyone else carries on as usual, they'll be angry and confused and they, you, y'know, won't know what to do with themselves. Or what not to do.

I felt my wife still staring at me. I sensed my mother-in-law staring, too, and putting a protective hand on her daughter's arm.

Not that I agree with the things people do in that state of mind,

I would've said if I'd spoken on instead of shutting up. Not that I think I could follow in their footsteps. But I get the solipsism. The abandonment. The way the world at large won't validate what you've lost. I get that something sticks to you and you don't have a clue how to get it off.

Now I turned to my wife and in my head I heard myself babbling on.

I don't know, I would've said if I'd been able to find the words. I don't think the passage of time wipes anything away. I don't think I'd want it to. I think, if anything, the opposite. When your sufferings are stretched out over the course of a life, I think you have to take them cumulatively, looking at them altogether, because that's how life is lived. Not in retrospect. In moments successively slipping by, where your losses are reborn every instant.

My wife stared at me. I stared down at my hands on the desk. The students stared at me as I retreated to the window. I stared out the window at Shane. Kerry stared at me. I stared at Demirović. He stared at Imran bin Musa, who stared up at the bars of his cell. Beyond them, somewhere, was the daughter who'd been taken from him. Beyond them was the woman who'd entrusted her to his care. Beyond were all his losses. The bars themselves were a constant reminder that the losses would be his to endure for all his remaining years.

I stared at Jakob as he took my presumptions about his sympathies and turned them inside-out. If you want to calculate numbers, he said, try calculating how many people have suffered because of what Fermi gave to Oppenheimer. When I told him I'd made an effort but reached the limits of my powers, he asked me to try to imagine the things he'd had cause to imagine. Imagine how the numbers might have differed if only Fermi had had a stronger conscience, clearer moral lines. Imagine if Fermi had enjoyed the counsel of an old friend, a pacifist committed absolutely to the cause, who might have been able to persuade him, or implore him, not to let his formulae devolve into anything more monstrous than an idea. This thought, Jakob said, was at the root of his distemper. He didn't *mourn* Achim. He'd never known him personally. He knew little about him besides what he'd shared with me and his peers. But he'd bridled at the corruption of my tallied numbers, my failure to reckon with the ripple effects of the lives destroyed by the Holocaust, as if the reach of each of those lives was confined to the shell of a single fallen body. I stared at him at a loss for words, bar a simple thanks for the books, as I tried to figure out how he'd managed, so adroitly, to hold his passions in the balance. He couldn't conceal the vibrancy of his admiration for Fermi's achievement. He hadn't even made an effort. He'd worn it nakedly, his rapture, as he thought on the beauty of the equations, their sophistication, the elegance of their complexity. But he radiated indignation at what the numbers had wrought in the world, the harvesting of elements to be dropped from the sky as engines of indiscriminate carnage. He saw Achim as a bulwark against the brutality of Fermi's sublime concepts, a force of resistance and reconsideration, and if he grieved for his ancestor at all, he grieved for him *through* his distemper: distemper at what more was lost than a single life, at the lost *possibility* of a man whose survival might have spared countless others from losses immeasurably greater.

I stared at my wife, who stared at me, and who saw in my eyes what I'm sure she read as a raging fire even though what I felt inside me was the burning of a starscape. Grief and anger are inseparable, I wanted to insist aloud, because grief and love share the same lifeblood, the same spirit. Each of them balances the other like an element in a perfect equation. Grief, in fact, *is* love, *pure* love, for something you've irretrievably lost. If you try to adjust to the loss, if you overcome your grief, you have to forfeit the love, or dilute it, or let it dry up. If you don't want to lose your love as well, and if, like me, you're made of the stuff, then you must never allow yourself to break free of your grief. For a time, early on, the world around you will reflect your sorrow. But then the world will change. It'll adjust, it'll forget. It will carry on as before. And if you can't figure out a way to replace what you've lost, literally to find or build some *thing* in the space left vacant by its absence, you don't have many options. Because your loss is irretrievable, because you've been deprived of something you can never get back, the only way to honour your love in a world that cares nothing for it is to deprive the world of something else, to rebalance the scales by subtracting something whose magnitude equals the grief that will not leave you. Look at it in this light, then, and anger that seems inconceivable, even reprehensible, becomes an embodied act of a love rendered impotent, an adoration robbed of someone to receive it.

That's how it seems to me anyway, I wanted to say. I sat on the sofa, nursing my cup of tea, while my wife narrowed her eyes at me as if to have my unspoken thoughts transmitted silently to her. But, I went on wordlessly, I'm bound to see it that way, aren't I? I'm not a believer in a world beyond this one. I've long considered myself a heathen in every sense of the word. I don't think there's anywhere else you can put the losses that haunt you. No quarantine. Acts of closure don't compartmentalise these things, relegating them to some manageable space. They erase them from your consciousness. They scrub them out, detail by detail, until all you've got is a memory of a thing that no longer has the power to move you. The only way to honour the memory is to allow yourself to be moved while it still burns hot.

BRYANT

My father-in-law looked up at me and winced. He forced his face to hold the expression. He meant it as a show of sympathy. I'd eased downstairs in the dark, careful not to make a creak, and padded towards the kitchen until I saw the light already on. I froze. I'd woken with a burning throat and no idea of what time it was. I'd gone to get a glass of water without expecting anyone else awake. He sat at the breakfast bar, head bowed over a newspaper, and raised his eyes when he sensed my tentative approach.

He held the wince a little longer, then he let it drop. Your body clock must be haywire, he said. I feel for you. I really do. I remember what it's like. Back before Christmas. Like someone had scooped out my eyeballs and was forcing me to stay conscious.

The clock on the wall showed that it wasn't yet eleven. I'd been asleep for less than two hours and woken up feeling as if I'd slept a day. I woke up dried out, too, like I'd had a week of the Föhn. I ran my fingers through my hair and forced a series of rapid blinks.

I only came down to get a drink, I said.

He rose from his stool and waved towards the empty space he'd made.

Sit, sit, he said as he moved to the sink.

I sat in the seat where I'd later sit beside my wife and bring all this to an end.

The dishwasher had just clicked off. My father-in-law pulled open the door and released a cloud of warmth. He took a glass from the tray on top and swung it under a tap to fill it. I watched the water gurgle to the rim and watched the glass move in my direction. My father-in-law left it on the breakfast bar for me, then took a step back to close the dishwasher.

Thanks, I said.

The dishwasher door clicked shut but my father-in-law lingered by it.

Abruptly he rapped a knuckle on the fridge.

Remember that trip? he said.

Among the pictures held with magnets was a strip of photos I'd taken the summer after I met my wife. I'd quit my hopeless job and she'd arranged a few weeks off work and together we'd jumped into her car to follow the highway around the eastern half of the country. The southeast coast, a long detour to Tasmania. Then back to the mainland, racing through the Red Centre, before some time in the tropics and a return to Sydney. We came home with pictures of pretty much what you'd expect. Lots of beaches and rock formations. The Twelve Apostles, the Remarkables, Uluru and the Devil's Marbles.

A knuckle rapped, again, against the fridge, against a selfie we'd snapped by the waves at Eaglehawk Neck. My father-in-law made the movement casually, as if all he'd wanted to do was call my attention to the whole strip of pictures and remind me of the glories of the country I'd left behind. In retrospect, though, I've come to see that he made this gesture with all the affect of the wince that greeted me. His purpose was to make me see that selfie, to take note of where we'd posed for it.

Later on, after I'd thought through the things he asked me to consider, after I'd made an effort to meet the challenge he set me, the first thing I'd been able to see was a boy. Watery light spilled down an empty corridor. Behind a door a toilet flushed. Then the door yanked open and the boy ran out. All I saw: his back, a red shirt, a head of curly brown hair. All I could tell of him was that he was quick to run and maybe would've only reached my waist. It's possible that this was all I wanted to see of him, all I could make myself see, even though I must have seen his face on a placard on my screen. Is that restraint, a mark of respect, or is it an aspect of the withdrawal through which worse things occur? I see, then, a hand nearby, poised to seize, and suddenly the boy is gone, just gone, as if somehow revoked from the world, vacating his allotment of space. Gone. Gone where? Search about to see. There, fallen, into himself. Small and frail, inert, facedown.

Demirović had been given a lower corner spot in the middle pages of the newspaper. Imran bin Musa was nowhere to be seen. The paper was a morning edition. The photograph hadn't come from the prison. It had been taken the day before, probably around the time my wife and I were preparing to land, with Demirović standing, posing, outside the day-care centre. I scanned the text. The council had decommissioned the facility, I learnt. The plan was to re-develop it. Demirović, however, had begun collecting signatures on a petition to build a memorial there, a place of quiet reflection.

I lifted one edge of the newspaper to turn it in search of a simpler story.

My father-in-law pressed a finger against the paper to pin it down.

I raised my eyes from the words and in my mind's eye I saw the nib of the pen, the ink, the inscription. Then facsimiled notes, formulae, in the hands of a distempered young man, and a body, prostrate in the dust, ear to the ground, white light with ferocious heat.

So, look, said my father-in-law as he dragged another stool from under the breakfast bar and eased into it beside me. There's something on my mind I thought I might take up with you. Something about what you said earlier. With a raise of his chin he indicated Demirović. When *he* came on the telly, he said, visiting the other bloke in jail.

Later on, when I thought back over the conversation we went on to have, when I raked through all my memories from the newspaper to the selfie to the words he spoke, I took myself back to the sandstone shell of the café. They'd decommissioned that one as well, turned it into a memorial of its own. Getting there had been its own ordeal. Only ten miles from Eaglehawk Neck, but twenty-odd years and a world away from the shootings. A sign at the entrance to the grounds politely requested that visitors refrain from speaking of 1996. The whole atrocity had been streamlined into a year, stripped down to four innocuous numerals for those who couldn't bear to revisit it. Past the sign, things were even worse. Everything I could see rang false. Manicured gardens. Ferry rides to the island. Informative maps and audio tours. Guides speaking in murmurs, surreptitiously, to visitors who gathered round to hear the gory details, shaking their heads, ruminating or at least making a show of serious thought. All of it had been divorced not only from the past of its native peoples, and not only from the past of the convict era, but also from the past that I and others carried in living memory. The violence had been contained, sealed off in time and space, and the wider arena had been prettified again in an appeal for the tourist dollar.

You could be forgiven for overlooking the café, thinking it nothing more than the site of an unfinished demolition. It had been gutted. Only part of the skeleton remained. Bricks and gravel and not much more. I'd walked around it slowly and roamed through what was once the interior. Where the tables used to be I found a garden full of flowers, all of them thriving in sunlight that shone through the open air formerly blocked by a roof. When a fresh wind moved over the ocean, I remembered, the waves lapped faster at the shore of the bay nearby. Looking into the glass of water by my fingers, I saw the softly rippling surface of the reflecting pool. Somewhere around the pool was where the first two victims had been taken. They'd travelled a distance to be there, jet-setting south from a sultry, steamy homeland above the equator to a spot from which there was now no soil between them and Antarctica. Husband and wife locked into a private world by a language no-one around them understood. At a table they sat together, perhaps picking at the last crumbs of the teacake they'd ordered to share, and then. That's it. They didn't see their end approaching and nobody saw them go. Lives extinguished with impossible ease. Here and gone, suddenly gone, dead before their bodies could even slump. What was the last thing they saw? Maybe, at best, an indistinct motion in their peripheral vision. A force without a face, a movement without a form. Something like a swarm of wasps wheeling around an invisible centre, a core of empty air. Or maybe only the table, the glossy white surface, the backs of each other's hands, the sunlight through the windows. And then.

The sound of the shots makes a man at a nearby table leap to his feet. Opposite him another man and a woman rise. In panic they all realise their tables are too close together for them to escape the reach of a destructive thing that can rob them of their lives by standing still and pivoting. It stands still. It pivots. A young man finds the muzzle, double-barrelled, staring at him. He ducks, collapses, drops to the ground just as something explodes, and as he tumbles beneath the table a heat where the bullet grazed his scalp tells him he is still alive. The woman he loves, who sits opposite him, gasps when she sees him fall but she herself is gone, just gone, before the man hits the floor, before he feels the heat. She doesn't have time enough to sense the threat behind her. She is gone without knowing even the presence of what has erased her. He knows she is gone only when the blast is followed by the skid of her chair as her body drops onto the table above his head.

My father-in-law ran his fingers along the top of the newspaper. Here's the truth, he said. It's been preying on me, so I have to get it off my chest. The truth is that you're right. You can't know what someone else is going through, inside, when from the outside you can see, plain as day, that they're facing things, hardships, that you've never had to confront. You can only contemplate what you might do if you were in those circumstances. What I mean to say is that you're right about me and you. Where we stand. I can't know what you're going through. What you've gone through these last few months. God knows I try to guess. But I can't, can I? Not really. But that's not news to either of us.

He pursed his lips and shook his head to himself.

But what I can't imagine, he said, is that you've gone through something that lets you now feel comfortable with some strange bedfellows.

That *some* sounded an alarm in my head. It had the tone of rapping knuckles. Eaglehawk Neck and Port Arthur. Thirty-five dead, twenty-three wounded, followed by the laws that ended gun ownership in Australia. Imran bin Musa hadn't killed with a gun. The bodies at Port Arthur were the reason. The constraints on his violence resounded against the last time his sort of havoc had broken out unconstrained. In a way, they hitched the man himself to the last person who'd been able to wreak havoc in their absence.

My father-in-law eyed me to make sure I understood his implication.

You can't make such strange bedfellows in good conscience, he said. Especially not in this country, not in these last twenty years. You can't go making excuses for what those sorts of people have done. Doesn't matter whether you actually believe your excuses or whether you're just, y'know, taking them for a walk. You *can't*.

Have I been too invested in telling of things I never saw? Too quick to indulge in sensational details where I should have been more sober? I mean here, now, in retrospect. There's a vividness to some of what I've written, and a revelry as I've tried to crawl into other skulls. Why is it not enough for me to see a summary of a crime and arrive at a judgment against the perpetrator without picturing the event in living detail? The crime is incomprehensible. That is the basis of the judgment. But even incomprehensible things are not beyond the ken of the people who bring them about. I don't mean to indulge in perversity. All I want is to understand how impossible things become possible for some.

What I've come to see, I think, is that there are certain things that can't be done, courses of action that can't be pursued, in a state of mind that devotes attention to the doing. Vividness and revelry give a gloss to things that have already happened. Conducting the deeds themselves, in the heat of the moment, actually demands a distance from them, a forsaking of one's place in the zone of immediate experience. You can't take from the world indiscriminately if you don't recuse yourself from it first. Then, once you step back from what's in front of your eyes, someone or something else gushes into the void, into the body you've vacated, and for the time being you're divested of who you really are. That I never plunged over the cliff comes down to the fact that I couldn't, can't, divest myself of myself. Every sentence of this book is a testament to the truth of that. If you manage to do it, though, you're able to watch the events you enact as if they're things that merely happen, facts that bloom without cause or consequence. Of course, that's not to say you're absolved.

So let me lay down here a phrase that lodged in my thoughts long ago. Call it the glare of selection. It's a glare in both senses of the word. It's the glare of another person fixing their eyes upon you and it's a glare of such menace that you have to shield yourself from it. It's a glare that says you have been chosen. It's the glare of someone who knows more about you than you know about yourself, because that person knows what awaits you in moments to come. That's the person who has selected a destination, your future, which you can only wait to approach. The glare alights upon a woman cradling the son she has nursed for little more than a year. The woman freezes in terror and waits for what will happen to happen. Abruptly the glare is pulled away. Beside the woman her husband has thrown a tray of food in the air. In the instant of distraction the woman shoves her son to safety beneath the table. The glare of selection wavers, swivels, alights upon the first man to have risen from his seat. He feels the burn and raises an arm to shield his face and says, No, no, not here. Then there is a shot. He drops. He is gone. Those are the facts.

My father-in-law rehearsed for me some lines from an old debate. Rehearsed them as if they were new. We've been here before, haven't we? he said. We've seen this sort of horror so many times now, he said, and I've got to be honest—

He cut himself short. He sighed, then took time to give his thoughts consideration. He let a few seconds pass by, maybe half a minute, before he started over.

Look, he said. The truth is I don't know. I mean, I *honestly* don't know. I don't want to talk about what ought to be done to the people who perpetrate these, these atrocities. I'm just a guy. Who am I to have the answers? But I know what I feel, deep down. I've felt it for a long time, and I know when I felt it first.

He tilted his head back and looked up at the ceiling. He drew in a breath through his nose, held it, released it slowly. He kept on looking up.

We were pretty badly prepared for the birth, he said. Must have been five or six months into the pregnancy and we didn't have any of the kit we needed. Bassinet, stroller, PJs, all that. We were sort of going about things as if it was all still hypothetical, y'know? Like an entertaining adventure. The reality of it hadn't set in yet. And whenever she started kicking around we'd put our hands to the spot and feel her powerful little legs and smile at the newness of it, not thinking of the outcome.

It felt odd to hear him speak of my wife like that. In her absence. As an unborn infant. Reducing her to a pronoun, lacking even a proper name. But I let him speak uninterrupted.

Anyway, he said, I know you remember what that's like, that skin-to-skin feeling that's really, you know, a touch between two people and a sensation of a third. Anyway. It was during one of those moments that I felt myself change.

He made a twisting motion with a fist over his heart.

I don't recall if we were in bed or on the sofa or what, he said, but I remember we were lying down together, side by side, and I put my hand on the part of the belly where I could see some movement, and those feet were kicking furiously, and I remember feeling that they were pummelling into me, through my palm, a new, a new—

He ran his tongue over his lips and puffed his cheeks with a mouthful of air as he looked at the ceiling and tried to capture the words.

A new sense, he said, that I could no longer afford to not care *absolutely* about the wellbeing of that tiny life I'd created. It came to me and it pounded through me like someone was banging it out on a drum. Protect and defend. That's it. Protect and defend. You know what I mean? That feeling, I know you must've felt it, that feeling of being the only person who stands between a child and whatever in the world would do them harm, and not being able to be *ambivalent* about it. Or to equivocate. Or to tolerate it, or be conciliatory, or—

He dropped his rheumy eyes from the ceiling to catch mine again.

I just can't imagine, he said, how anyone who has felt that feeling, even if they've felt it only once, could ever go back to acting like they'd never felt it at all.

Now I saw his purpose. He wasn't really fishing for my reflexive agreement on contentious issues. He was drawing a boundary around his daughter to spare her from whatever it was that had tarnished me.

And, he went on, I'd defy anyone who has felt that feeling to sit down and really think through what it means to take a child from this world. Or even to imagine the scene and watch a child taken by someone else.

He pursed his lips again. This time he nodded a little.

I'm going to hazard a guess, he said, that you haven't really tried to do that yet, to look at those kids up close, and I think there's a reason for that that you don't want to see.

A bullet to the back of the head takes an elderly man who'd just retired. Another bullet tears through two bodies and takes the man's brother along with the friend beside him. A third man turns his head to the ground to avert the glare that burns at him, and an instant later he is taken as well. Shrapnel explodes from the weapon and strikes an old man and his wife, another man and two middle-aged women. A jaw shatters when a bullet breaks through bone. Not even ten seconds have passed since the first two shots were fired. The children who will be taken there, that day, have not yet been sighted.

I didn't defy my father-in-law solely by an act of will. While I can't disavow responsibility for my own troubled thoughts that night, he issued a challenge with his words of caution and I found myself rising to it. Or perhaps it wasn't a challenge as such; perhaps it was something more, an imperative, which he was right to say I hadn't answered yet. In time, then, I came to see the corridor, the polished floor, the boy revoked, and now, nearby, the open entrance to a playroom from which I can hear laughter. Another boy jumps through the doorway, jumps into the hall and spins around to howl with glee at the friends who have stayed inside. It's a taunt. It's part of a game. Then his bright red shirt grows dark and a flush seeps out of his skin. He falls like a scrap of discarded fabric. Suddenly, from inside the playroom, a girl darts towards him and skids to a halt. A woman's voice calls to her in a tone of concern that becomes alarm. Alanna, she says. Alanna! The girl does not turn but is spun on the spot and then her eyes meet the glare. That's it. What was the last thing she saw? The face of a man she saw every day without any knowledge of what he concealed inside himself. Now he wears an expression she's never seen on him before. Not rage, but dispassion. Not fury: withdrawal. The face of a man who meets her eyes but doesn't see the life in them, a man who sees only cold equations with which to balance his losses.

And I just want to say, said my father-in-law, that what you're doing with the ashes is the right thing. It is. Even if, as I said, I can't know what you're going through, I want you to know it's right. Taking time out to come back over here, to make something ceremonial of it. It's important to do that, I think. To help you let go.

Not only to let go of, of *her*, he said, but to let go, you know, release yourselves from whatever—

He stopped there. He didn't name his subject. Instead, he jabbed the tip of his index finger into his chest and kept it there and held my gaze.

I drained the last of the water but held on to the glass and held on to what I'd done.

But I don't think it's important for the usual reasons, said my father-in-law. Most people would say it's important to let go because you can't keep on living your life if you're stuck in the past. That's true, but I think you've got more at stake. You two. The both of you.

He leant in closer to make sure he had my full attention, or whatever dregs I could raise from the depths of my exhaustion.

I won't lie, he said. I think you two should think about coming back here.

In my gut I felt the same old bubblings of rage I'd felt in Interlaken.

What I mean, he said, is maybe you don't need to let go to keep on living your life. Maybe, he said, maybe you should think of it as also letting go of the life you've been living. Maybe this, all this, this scattering of the ashes, this being here, is the chance you need to say farewell to that life and work together to start building something new.

That day was the day I did start to build something new. In an earlier age, perhaps, morality or theology would have inhibited me. But I didn't have a deity breathing down my neck. The decision was mine to make and I made it. There was nothing colossal about it. It was made, one decision among many, and it could as easily have not been made at all. These days, then, when I sit down to write, I write from the life that began back there, near midnight in my in-laws' kitchen. That's not to say that it looks anything like a life at all. It's an austere place to be. But it also looks nothing like the life I was living then, nor, worse, the limbo between that day and the day I returned to the Mearns.

What sent me back to Scotland wasn't what had drawn me there the first time. Not illness, not an old lover. Not nostalgia either. It was crisis. I needed the beach. I'd seen a picture on a screen. It flashed up when I checked the news on my phone during an idle moment in a supermarket queue. Gentle white waves simmered over shiny sand. Facedown in the sand was a boy. He was fully clothed and prostrate, both arms motionless at his sides. He wore a red T-shirt and dark blue shorts. He still wore both his shoes. He'd arrived on a beach on the coast of Turkey at the end of a brutal summer in the Middle East. Five years of civil war in Syria. A string of victories for the soldiers of Islamic State. Millions of people displaced to neighbouring countries and farther afield to Europe. The boy's parents had found a boat bound for Greece. The boat did not withstand the waves. Now the water rushed in to lap at his body. Only once before had I ever seen a child so clearly, confrontingly dead.

I don't remember anything else of the day I saw the picture. All I remember of that day is the picture itself. The child lifeless on the beach. The child. The beach. The photographs zipped through the global bandwidth and, between transmission and download, built a digital monument to the life whose loss they captured. The world was predictably outraged for a time. This was the image that would win support for a response to a humanitarian catastrophe. The moment of its circulation would be the moment people could no longer ignore the human face of, well, whatever. The outrage predictably faded.

My father-in-law had risen as midnight approached. He advised me to try again to get some rest. We'd agreed to scatter the ashes come the morning.

You look like you could use a refresh before we head out, he said. Then he took himself to bed and left me alone at the breakfast bar. But I'd lost the need for sleep. His words had whipped up a storm that whirled inside me. The strip of pictures. The rapping knuckles. The *some* he'd thrown in before *strange bedfellows*. I'd been there, on the spot, to walk through the ruins. I'd seen the ghosts rise up around me. More than that, I'd been to the true wellspring of the slaughter. Years before my wife and I went anywhere near Eaglehawk Neck, years before we'd even met in that pub in Sydney, I'd set off alone for the far side of the world and unexpectedly, accidentally, I'd entered the village of Dunblane. There was the site of the blast, in faraway Scotland, that found its report at the bottom of Australia. From there one calamity gave rise to something worse, inspired a burlesque of its own grotesque self, when an altogether crueller force carried its echo to the penitentiary.

I'd been heading to Perth when I came to Dunblane. Seeing the name of the place on the sign instantly pulled me from the present and hurled me back to my adolescence, that day in 1996. I'd come home from school, turned on the TV, and found every channel given over to the events in Tasmania. I'd been spellbound by the emerging story, the first rough reports from Eaglehawk Neck, after the handcuffs, before the media briefings, when so many of the details were only terrible rumours, back when it wasn't so easy to watch these things play out in real time. Then, that night, I saw his face. Who could ever forget it? The softness. The effeminacy. The blond locks down to his shoulders. Pale eyes and pink lips, the barely angular curve of the jaw. Who could forget the stance? Lean, lanky, in a jumper two sizes too big. Slack and apathetic, rounded at the shoulders. Back when he still had a solid form and a name you could put to his person. Back before the nation relieved him of his integrity, denied him the power to hold intact his constituent elements. Back when he had a voice, querulous and naïve, and when, in speaking for himself, he'd told the officers who questioned him that he couldn't say exactly why he'd done the things he'd done but, for sure, he'd had in mind the recent events in Scotland. A man, a gun, a primary school. One teacher, sixteen children. He'd heard about it on the news. He'd heard the news speak to him.

Remember how he'd stalked the grounds less like a human being than like some restless, roaming warp in the wind? When I walked his path, though he'd long ago been contained and confined, I'd felt him still there, still moving, a presence like an atmospheric disturbance or an electrostatic charge still crackling through the air. I'd watched him bend the space and refract the light around him, so as to become a seer who could not himself be seen.

At a table close to where his first victims lay, I'd seen a woman watch as his glare seized her daughter. The girl was fifteen years old, old enough to be her own person, but like a child she leapt into her mother's arms for safety. The woman, her body become a channel for pure instinct, dived on top of the girl to shield her from the shotgun. Her spine split apart and the boom ruptured both her eardrums. She wouldn't know until she came to, in pain, that she'd lost her child. A human shield is a delicate thing. The bullet had ripped right through her body to hit the girl in the head. The last trace of the world the girl had known, as her mother held her tight and pressed her face to her chest, was the scent of the woman's cardigan, fabric softener, faint perfume, fear. That protection was everything the woman could possibly give her, but even everything wasn't enough.

A man beside a window collapsed. The glass exploded and scattered over the tiled floor. His wife, close by, felt blood at her throat as the bullet broke apart. She raised a hand to hold herself but then she was taken to pieces by a blast at point-blank range. She hit the ground. Only thirty seconds had passed since the first shots had been fired.

Deep in my chest I felt the stirrings of that reptilian thing. Its slumber had been disturbed by the place I'd landed in. It twisted around inside me, bringing with it a surge of anger as it spiralled through my innards. Sometimes the thoughts that would awaken it in places as quiet as that one, that kitchen, came from my own being, from a mood of desultory contemplation. Sometimes, though, they came from some other realm outwith me, inundating the calm and shattering it with a bombardment of recollections. I couldn't look away from the things my memories made me see, not now. How could I have done it and still hoped to sleep at night? How to banish those people from my mind for the sake of my own inner peace? Their lives, their fates, deserved to be remembered. I couldn't accept that what was taken from the world that day didn't warrant my time.

I'd moved along the edge of the reflecting pool and looked up, across the water, and watched the bodies fall, one after another, in a barricaded room whose walls I'd projected onto the spaces where they'd once stood. There. The gift shop. Shelves of colonial tack, plastic cuffs and leg irons, rotating racks of calendars, postcards, magnets, keyrings. A man on his knees starts to rise to his feet. His head and arm break open. He falls although the shot has not taken his life. Terrified, panicked, people rush for the doors to the car park only to find them locked. Imprisonment and claustrophobia and no possibility of escape. In these confines the fear that seeps from every pore of every person fills the air like noxious gas. Suddenly the girl behind the till goes down. She was due to sit her final exams at the end of the year. The bullet drains the world of everything she'd ever done, everything she'd hoped for, every sense she'd ever had of the life she might yet live. All those abstractions are dragged from her body to dissipate in less time than it takes for her to fall. What is that if not annihilation? What other word can capture that extra dimension of loss, that wilful obliteration of things that might have been?

It is annihilation, too, when those I try to see won't emerge anymore, or can't, when I'm not able to call them forth, so that what is lost remains at last beyond my reach. The day-care centre. No faces but for the girl's I knew already. No details but the surfaces of things. No actions, only aftermath; no focus, only withdrawal. Nobody else for me to attend to, though many more were present at the scene, because here the wave breaks, the breath expires, and when I see the girl in the hall I have to step aside. What am I, now, that I can't go any further, any nearer? To not look closely is, to me, effectively to look away, deny attention, and dishonour by aversion. But that's what annihilation *wants*, isn't it? Not just for lives to be stolen: for lives, once stolen, to be irrecoverable, to suffer unseen. So where's the triumph in the seeming respect I pay the other innocent dead? My cowardice makes me want to push back, to push on, but my thoughts, back then, began to falter. Time broke into bullets. Events shrank into sentences. A woman who averted the roaming gaze went down. A man collapsed at the feet of his wife, felled by a wound to his temple. Another woman who tried to flee took a shot to the back of the head. Annihilation, cold and absolute. You couldn't bring it to bear on actual lives, could you? What would it take for you to reach the point where you could? That swill of nausea in your gut, that viper in your heart? An inability to allow the world to continue unaware of what you've lost. Then perhaps only a means and a thinning of your conception of your future self.

So there you are, with snow outside, in a carriage that rocks in the dark like a cradle. As the calculations spin out in your mind, variables and constants, streams of functions, conditional expressions, suddenly you're struck by the breathing of your sleeping children. Air sucked in, snored out, by a boy and a girl oblivious to your presence. Syncopated. Contrapuntal. The sustenance of life and the endless return. It seizes you and gives you pause. For a moment you lift your eyes from the pages of your notebook. Can you imagine the countless others, the innocents who will, in time, bear the physical force of your abstractions? Can you feel the power in the pen you hold, in the ink, the nib, the notations towards destruction? You could incarnate magnanimity if you wanted to. You could stop. You could take pleasure in keeping your calculations confined to your own thoughts. You could let generosity flow through you, into your fingertips, and lay the pen to one side in full awareness of your capacities. You could luxuriate in this state, this interstice, in which all those people out there in the world, and so many more yet to be born, have no idea that you are here on this quiet train devising a means of taking their lives at inhuman speed, and you could suspend yourself there, withhold your ire. You could allow them to retain what you might revoke. Why not conduct your affairs with the dignity your power affords you? Then again, why try? Where is the dignity afforded to the family now in flight?

Or you could hold your instrument poised above the envelope on your desk. Outside, the war rages on and your boy lies ill in bed, ravaged by the typhoid that will take his life. Can you hear his rasps? Inside the envelope are handwritten pleas from fifty men condemned to death. They all deserted the companies they'd been conscripted into. They appeal to you for clemency, for absolution, citing matters of conscience, citing cowardice. You hold your hand above the envelope and with your pen you scratch onto it a single word: PARDONED. That's enough. That's all it takes. That's your prerogative and that's power, absolutely, concentrated and subject to whim, exactly the sort to attract an ambush and a gunman's admonition: *Sic semper tyrannis!* But this power need not be spent on malicious deeds.

You know this well enough already and you live the knowledge, day to day. For those who will survive you, every spring renews the knowledge. The lilacs in bloom, the star in the west, the hermit thrush in song: when your assailant brings your days to an end, your people will mourn your magnanimous heart and from among them a poet will take your memory, divest you of your name, and invest your soul in his verses, in these emblems of the season, so that you may revisit the world with the ever-returning spring. That, too, is power. Restraint can earn you goodwill, adoration, posterity. Where power could as easily degenerate into cruelty, to withdraw it is an expression of love. You can choose to exert your authority by giving reprieve to the desperate. You can dedicate yourself to the betterment of your world.

Or you could if you weren't fuelled by fury. If you had the force of mind to stop and think. If you had an old friend whose conscience, whose convictions, would lead him to make you take pause, to reconsider. If you hadn't been electrified into your calculations by blind injustice, by rage at the rising threats to those you love. With your wife and children asleep around you, you sketch your plans towards your claim on power. Or you sit at your desk and weigh the worth of a plea from another man. He's been sentenced to death for recapturing ninety freed slaves. No good. Let him hang. Your wife will come to you, of course, and plead on his behalf. She can't stand the fact that you've been vested with such sway over other lives and she can't accept it when you don't use your influence to save them. But you'll look into her eyes and you'll say, No. She'll beg you. She'll insist. Very well. You're a reasonable man. You send her away with the promise that you'll give the matter greater thought. That's just to console her. You sit at your desk and you say it again to yourself. No. Not when your own boy lies dying, nearly dead. Not when such injustice stalks your life. Who will wield a power sufficient to save your child? Who, if not you, if not God? Why should some other delinquent be spared? You hold the pen above his plea. You could save him with a signature. The power tingles through you. The power of knowing the world yet to come because it will take shape by your hand. That's some small satisfaction. Relish it. Don't act. Just sit.

That's what I did. I sat at the breakfast bar and waited for daybreak to taint the sky outside. I sat beneath the kitchen lights and stared across at my reflection in the glass doors, the window of the train, the well of ink beside the fountain pen. I can't spell out the peculiar pleasure and displeasure of wielding that sort of power. I wielded it in the knowledge I held over the people asleep in the bedrooms upstairs. I wielded it in the knowledge that I'd felt out my limits and found I wasn't capable of anything worse. There was pleasure in what I'd done, displeasure in knowing what I was yet to do; pleasure in taking control of myself, displeasure in preparing to lose it again. I affirmed my own presence, met my own reflected eyes, and tried to see myself as what I'd resolved to become. Self-possessed, for better or worse: my own person. Then I rose and arched my back and began to pace the kitchen.

One man inside the café, who'd been hiding where I'd been standing by the reflecting pool, finally thought he'd found the moment to make his escape. But when he moved he attracted attention and the barrel swung towards him. He said, No, he said, No, and crimson overcame the arm he raised to defend himself. There was a man whose neck was savaged, whose throat was shredded. There was another who lay over his wife, covering her quivering body with his, and when a shot cracked his spine and blood burst over the woman she caught her breath and held it and she forced herself to freeze, forced her muscles to go rigid, as she tried to hide among the corpses in order not to surrender her life.

Chaos in a litany of facts. Particulars pulled up online, at the end of day, then interlaced with what I recalled of the spaces I'd walked through. In the car park, with the strangers in the gift shop left behind to cower, a bus driver in uniform caught a bullet in the back and fell. His legs collapsed under him and he crawled to safety, across the gravel, to hide beneath the engine of his vehicle, where his blood flowed out. A woman's kneecap ruptured. Another's cheek was streaked with scarlet. There was one who crouched behind a coach. Except for the blur of motion on the bumper, she didn't even see what overtook her from behind. As crowds began to flee towards the jetty on the beach, they attracted the gaze, the glare, and so the bodies over there began to fall. An elderly woman fell with a shot to the shoulders. Her husband had been running beside her. Then he had to run on alone. Close to him another man suddenly couldn't move his arm. A bullet lodged in the muscles, buckshot mangled the skin to the elbow, and the heaviness dragged him down.

I bent over the breakfast bar, hands on my knees. I bent over and I thought of those people, the people I'd thought of when I walked among the ruins, and I knew then as I know now that there's no way to give them what they deserve. Nor would there be a way to turn to the man who took their lives and do justice to him or have it done. There was only loss and grief and those who survived and the force behind the atrocity.

On board a coach, a woman had lain on her stomach to conceal herself. She'd placed herself under a row of seats and couldn't stand, couldn't move. She thought that's where she'd be safest. Then the door scraped open and she found the barrel of the shotgun in her face. Did she look into its depths? Did she close her eyes or look away?

Outside, the first light of day started to suck my reflection from the glass. The sky to the east took on the faintest shade of darkling blue.

The coach door slammed shut. The gaze roamed around. A man who saw his wife shot dead crawled to her and held her. When he reached her he heard shots close by, heard bullets screaming past, and then he heard a voice. It spoke to him, addressed him, saying, No-one gets away from me. The barrel of the gun approached him and took aim. The trigger clicked back but at the last instant the man ducked and the bullet only clipped his neck. He fell beside his wife. He feigned going down. He heard footsteps crunch through the grass and fade away. He held the hand next to his as the blood escaped her body, and he must have known that he was then and would forever be a man alone.

With midnight come and gone, the date beneath the masthead anchored the newspaper even further in the past. Two days had now elapsed since the story on Demirović's memorial petition. The lag between the happening and its report had grown, not shrunk, as I moved closer to it. I looked down at the picture, beneath my fingertips, and pored over the face of the man outside the building. He was soaked in sunlight, which cast his expression in uncanny shadows, and he stared hard into the camera lens. Then, seeing him there, I did something else. This is what I did. With both hands, I took hold of the edge of the breakfast bar and I closed my eyes. I pressed my forehead down onto the bench, onto the crinkling newspaper. In quiet thought, posed like that, I decided I didn't want any more pictures before my eyes. I decided I wanted only eyes themselves, the eyes of others. I did my best to scout out the possibilities open to me in that moment, possibilities for what I might do now, henceforward, and finally, feeling my way among them, I arrived at a decision.

Straight lines south to Manly Wharf. Most of the sky was still black. The darkness was broken only by the curtains of orange dangling from streetlamps above the bitumen. Early morning in Australia has always held for me an air of menace. Hard to shake the sense that you're always being watched. Stepping into the light for safety is the least safe thing you feel you can do. You want to stick to the shadows, become a shadow yourself, take the darkness for camouflage and sneak past whatever threats lurk outside the bright spots. But if you want to follow the path, you don't have a choice. Into the light you go, a blitz from overhead, then out. This despite the absence of danger. Few cars on the roads, no other people on foot. Shuttered shops and semi-detached houses with all the curtains closed. For most of the journey the only signs of motion, of life, were sounds. Waves were crashing to the east and loud breaths spilled from me as I sped on. Half-formed utterances, barely articulated, to chip away at the quietude. *There was—in the—with a—* Whispers to trace the boundaries of the nothingness, to mark its open spaces with words that functioned like ellipses.

I came to the dock just as the first ferry was setting off across the harbour. A ticket window fronted a booth big enough for a single person. Inside sat an old man in a fleece. When I saw him rugged up, I realised I'd underdressed for the crossing. Too late. Cash in hand got me a ticket aboard the next boat, a private hydrofoil that serviced a newly outsourced route. The decks were wet with sea spray. I nestled myself in a vestibule on the starboard side, my private leeward shelter. As the diesel engines rumbled beneath my feet, the ferry sputtered away from the wharf and slowly around South Head to Laings Point, in sight of the places where people were known to jump. I changed boats before Vaucluse but decided to stay outside, braced against the wind at Point Piper with both arms clasped around my chest. Disembarking at Double Bay, I stumbled onto the jetty, frigid, still holding tight to myself. *Came to—and thereupon—*

Apprehended. That's the police terminology. That's what you hear every time some somnolent official speaks to camera. A suspect has been apprehended. What it means is that somebody, some lower officer, laid hands on someone else. Someone, unknown and faceless to me, applied force to bring another someone to a halt. That second someone was not diffuse, not mercurial, but firm, fleshly. He'd fled the scene in a stolen car, took more lives as he escaped, then he'd become confused, misplaced his ammunition, shot randomly at passersby, and drove into a confrontation with police. His name, we learnt, was Martin Bryant. That unremarkable name, appended to him in public, drained him of his outsized power, his undiluted malevolence. He was just a lonesome man-child known to his family as Marty.

Later on, in custody, he'd be able to speak for himself as well. This, I mean, it's wrong, isn't it? he'd ask the men who detained him. I shouldn't be in here, he'd say. I really shouldn't be in here. But they've got him now and they can hold him forever and they'll never let him go. And yet, and yet, when I saw the memorial, I couldn't dismiss the feeling that someone in authority had accidentally set him free. I mean they gave him a different presence, more expansive. They unlocked him from his identity, sundered him from his species, unbonded the atoms of his body so that he burst outwards like a pathogen, hanging around the site of the slaughter like an infection of the air. I know they didn't intend to give him omnipresence. They intended only to honour the innocent dead. They'd named the victims on a commemorative plaque, a gesture of recognition, to restore to them the dignity he'd tried to take away. They'd intended, at the same time, to consign him to absolute silence, to refuse to acknowledge him by name or to detail what he'd done. They'd tried to make him marginal, even invisible, even gone. But their actions backfired. Instead, on those haunted grounds, I saw and felt him everywhere, all around, with the awesome presence of one too great to be contained in a word. I felt, as I walked on, as if I was breathing him in.

Straight lines again en route to Centennial Park. Sea salt embittered the air. Engines complained as commuters prepared to meet their morning obligations. Suburban streets were littered with broken palm fronds and the crisp leaves of sycamores in decline. Gumtrees hushed in a breeze and overhead I could hear the fracas of urban possums in a scuffle. I followed powerlines to arterial roads, past gated villas and consular buildings, past low-rise redbrick flats and bungalows of rotten weatherboard. I navigated by attuning myself to the clank and hum of trains departing Bondi Junction, by following the musky scent of mown grass browned by months of heat. As I walked I caught glimpses of aircraft to the east, coasting above the Pacific, then banking around to make a descent over Botany Bay. They came into view intermittently but at a steady rate, mostly from points north. One of them was at that moment carrying my parents down from Brisbane. If they hadn't already landed, they'd at least be in sight of the city.

The abeyance of the dark brought out joggers and dogwalkers, childminders pushing strollers, and, a little later, sporadic groups of students in uniform, boys wearing yarmulkes on their way to college. As I remember it, however, the people who caught my attention most often were less intent in their movements than any of these. There's a certain type of person, almost always a man, whose habitat is the predawn gloaming and who takes flight when dawn becomes day. Clad in worn coats, patched at the elbows, these people follow footpaths with their eyes cast to the kerb. Those who inhabit the twilight, who wade through it as if submerged in its fug, imbibing its soporific air only to wheeze it out, are men who loiter on corners, idly smoking, seeming unable to gaze any farther than the tips of their cigarettes, or men pushing open the doors of grimy all-night diners, tramping inside wearing clodhopper boots to retreat from the world at a table for one. You see these men without really seeing them as they shuffle past on the street or stand listlessly on a train. They've been cut loose from the drift of events around them. They're dyspeptic, astringent, sclerotic. They're still here but almost not. They murmur meaningless shards of sentences. *When the eve—'twas a morn—O, then—* Or maybe I've transposed too much of myself onto the souls I saw as I walked the streets. Randwick, the outskirts of Kingsford, down into Maroubra. The first day of something new. I wouldn't say I became a man like one of those. I wouldn't yet say I've become such a man. I haven't occupied those gloomy hours long enough, or often enough, to have my veins run through with their spirit, to fill my lungs with their air. But I passed these men and I saw them, awake if not alert, driven home by full daylight, and I suspect I let myself get caught in their currents, eddying with them in their directionless drift.

I found a greasy spoon already open. I scraped an aluminium chair along the lino floor. I stationed myself at a table by the window and looked outside. Across the road, the shops were still shuttered with corrugated roller doors. A nail salon, a butcher, a hardware supplier. Others equally bland. Up and down the street the roller doors gave a disgruntled front to the entire strip. Except for the butcher, none of them looked like they'd open for trading for a while. I nursed a coffee and waited. I filled the empty time with fragments, attenuations, *It happened on—It led—It was*, such as filled the ballads in those places where a variant was known to have existed but could not be recovered. Stock phrases to adumbrate an absence, to sheathe a space belonging to something inarticulable. Here's one of my own: I had nothing else to do. I had no other place I should be. Obviously that's not true, but I sat there, looking out the window, and I kept myself intact with as much energy as I could rouse, and the way I managed to do this was by repeating to myself that one line, that lie, that I had nothing else to be involved in, nowhere else to show my face.

The problem I'd felt in the café was that even though the building lay in ruins, and even though it was barren of ornamentation, it drew into itself traces of events that had in fact orbited it. The worst of the things that deserved remembrance had occurred nowhere near the reflecting pool. Turning eastward to look through the café's shattered walls, I could see the ferry wharf a couple of minutes' walk from where I stood beside the water. That's where most of the people who fled the gunshots had gone when the gaze retreated from the café to the car park. But there was one woman. She cradled her daughter in her arms, held her close against her thumping chest. Ahead of her ran her other girl. Together they dashed over the grass, stumbled onto the road, as fast as they could move, and then from behind her the woman heard an engine in low gear. She slowed, turned to find a car pulling up nearby. The driver's door swung open. The woman stopped and called for her elder daughter to go to the vehicle with her. She must have thought the driver was some kind soul, come to rescue them and speed them to safety. But in the car was a weapon. The weapon drew even with her. With it came a commanding voice. The voice ordered her to drop to her knees. She obeyed, in tears, and held her younger child close to her body while out of the corner of her eye she watched her older daughter escape. When the barrel touched her temple she fell upon the grass. Then the weapon swung to the child, bawling now beside her mother. The girl on foot hid herself behind a tree near the water's edge. The steel had grown hot from all the shots already fired. The girl would have felt the burn of it when it pressed against her neck. That's it. Three more bodies on the ground. Here and then gone, just gone.

In the end, I realised, I couldn't take myself further than that, deeper into details. If I'd defied my father-in-law, if I'd imagined what he would not, I still arrived at a sight beyond which I couldn't proceed. Wouldn't. Didn't have the stamina to see more, up close, in the moment of its occurrence. I sat alone by the window looking out to the shuttered shops, thought back on myself alone in the dark in my in-laws' kitchen, and found my thoughts leaping ahead of the heartache, vaulting over further bloodshed and into a world reshaped by it. I saw, I needed to see, an apprehension. Figures in the doorway, children in distress. Police arrive and encroach from behind. Firearms drawn. Under arrest. Clenched fingers release the knife. What have you done? Crash to the floor. Hands on the body. Apprehended. The jab and brace of an elbow, a knee against the coccyx, a buckle, a fall. Arms bent back, wrists bound. There's a child out there in the world, beloved. There's a woman as well, far away. The voices don't hush. What have you done? A face collapses. Tears spill out. There are stutters and chokes. There is no glee. Remorse? Misgiving? A surge of grief? These, too, can be felt, could have been. Can that be remembered? Can it be allowed?

Later, during the inquest, an eyewitness would speak of the things he'd overheard where he'd been hiding. In the last few seconds of that mother's life he'd heard her not only weeping but begging, speaking through her cries and tears, trying to reason with the fury. She'd pleaded for the lives of her daughters. Not her own life. Her life could be taken. But with her last words, literally with her final breath, she'd given voice to the only thought to coruscate through her. Protect and defend. Protect and defend. That's it, that's all. Over and over again. No time to equivocate, no power to honour the impulse. Only words. Only imploring. She pleaded for the lives of her daughters and with those pleas her life was ended. She gave fully of herself, or begged to be allowed to give, as ineffective as her begging turned out to be. She must have known it would happen that way. She faced her own death, direct and imminent, but the only fear she acted on, the last fear she acted on, the motivating force behind her final moments, was her fear of what would happen to the children she loved. Can that be remembered, too? Memorialise it if you know how. Strip a café to its foundations or find something else for the purpose. You might as well try to memorialise a heartbeat.

It's here and gone before you can catch it. Even if you could reclaim and preserve it, its frozen form wouldn't tell you a thing about what it was worth in life.

I guess the day had ticked on to half-past nine or thereabouts by the time the roller door went up. Cars and buses filled the roads with traffic. The sky above the strip of shops had warmed to white with a blue tint, a thin scrape of cloud catching a dazzle of sunlight. My wife, I assumed, would have woken to find me gone. My in-laws, too. They'd be wondering where I was. I hadn't left a note, I didn't take a phone. I'd given them no way to contact me, no way to know my location. Soon enough, if they hadn't left home already, they'd have to head to the airport to pick up my parents without me. In hindsight I'd say that, by going renegade, I'd taken the first step into a life, the life, in which my movements were of no importance to anyone else. I'd trespassed into the company of those men. Anyway, I sat and watched a burly man saunter over to the lock on a roller door. My heartbeat sped up when I saw him, but calmed when I realised he wasn't who I'd come to see. He was neatly dressed in uniform, a yellow polo shirt tucked into navy trousers. From a pocket he took a key, then he bent at the knees and hauled up the roller until it clattered into its shelter. Its absence revealed two floor-to-ceiling windows, darkened by closed venetian blinds, with a glass door between them. The man unlocked the door and went inside to work.

Demirović didn't show up until almost ten o'clock. Two, three, four other members of staff, men and women in the same neat uniform, hurried into the shop at intervals, then finally Demirović arrived. I saw him in the flesh. At first I saw just the back of his head, his curly hair, as he pushed his way in. Only when he held the door ajar to peg it open, ready for trading, did I see his face. After pulling the cord on the blinds to reveal the whitegoods in the window displays, he turned and disappeared into the shop. At that point I lost sight of him and slouched in my chair, expelling a breath I didn't know I'd been holding. He was so commonplace, so far removed from anything remarkable. He was nothing more than a man going to work one fine morning at the end of March.

Then, instantly, he and I were breathing the same air. Obstacles, intermediaries, filters fell away. Gone was the distance between continents, and gone, too, the screen that transmitted his grief to me, the cameras that captured his image for me, the suburbs that kept his whereabouts from me, every space or surface that had once stood between us. There was the window of the greasy spoon and there was the window of the whitegoods store and then there was nothing, nothing at all. We heard the same sounds. The same light fell on each of us. We had at last come to a place where our experiences were synchronised.

When I look back at all this now, I realise, again, that I'm not sure how I made my way across the street. How I got from one place to another. In all my memories I'm either sitting or standing, sedentary and stupefied, in a space I occupy like a stone, as if I've always been there. Later in the day I'd look back on the morning and I'd realise this. I'd sit on the edge of the bed in the guestroom of my in-laws' house and I'd see how I'd frozen up, dumbstruck, surrounded by fridges and dishwashers and flashing screens, in the hubbub of Demirović's workplace. Later, too, much later, I'd drop into the reeds on the dunes at the Mearns, sit on the sand and stare senselessly at the sea, and I'd see myself on the edge of the bed as I thought back over my ennui in that store in Maroubra. What would plague me in those still and quiet moments was exactly that, the stillness and quiet. The fact of my being in a place, being so still and quiet, with no recollection of going there or taking my leave or being in transit to somewhere else. Darting through different points in time and fast traversing the stream of minutiae that gives time its body, thickens its flow.

Before all that, of course, I'd be berated for my absence. I'd slip back into the house, sordid from a sleepless night, and I'd find everyone in my face. My mother-in-law would take the lead, accosting me for distressing her daughter and showing up like this, hours later than agreed, unkempt, unapologetic, delaying the sombre plans. Then my wife and her father would echo her complaints. The three of them would surround me like sharks around a solitary swimmer. Where have you been? What were you thinking? Do you know how worried, don't you think we deserve, why didn't you, why wouldn't you— My parents would hang back a little, their consternation offset by confusion and concern for my wellbeing, before they'd step in to defuse the situation, suggesting we all just prepare ourselves to go. They already wore their formal attire, appropriate for the occasion. So did my in-laws, so did my wife. All of them had endeavoured to dignify themselves. They weren't wrong to be upset. It was irresponsible of me, and disrespectful, to leave the house for so long, at such an hour, without having told them where I was going. I knew this much, of course, but I heard it from them anyway. They had to make known their displeasure with what I'd decided to do. *Decided*, they said: as if I'd concocted a plan instead of answering an urge, following a notion, the way a hound follows a scent it catches on the wind.

Somehow I ended up in the en suite shower. I let the water scorch me. Downstairs, I knew, my in-laws and my parents were waiting for me to finish, to dress myself, to join the group and scatter the ashes as planned. My wife had come upstairs to speed me along. Through the torrent of the showerhead I could hear her in the guestroom, opening the wardrobe doors and closing them and pulling out and shutting drawers. But the noises that filled my ears were lost to the sounds I could still hear in my head. I heard the low-level chatter of customers in conversation with sales representatives. I heard the drone of traffic outside, the beep of products scanned at tills, the chimes of transactions being processed. I don't remember the things that must have happened for me to have heard those sounds. I don't remember leaving the greasy spoon. I don't remember the dash across the road, the dodging of traffic, the skip into the shop. I remember only being there and facing him, seeing him in the flesh. I remember holding back, stopping a distance from where he was working, and standing there and waiting for him to meet my eye.

Hassan Demirović appeared more modest than I'd imagined. He looked like he'd been reduced somehow, had every trace of his aura boiled off his body. He held himself together at a lower range of being than the man who looked like him in all the pictures I'd seen. I kept my distance from him but made no move to hide, no pretence that I was browsing the stock as if my real purpose was to find an affordable washing machine. I confronted him in the truest sense of the word; I stood front on, facing him, and waited, just waited, for him to look up from whatever paperwork busied him and see me, meet my eyes, face to face, and say with an uncertain smile, I'm sorry, I didn't notice you there. What can I help you with?

I was struck with awe when I saw how approachable he was. There were no crowds to cheer for him or berate him, no reporters to attend to his every word. He'd been plundered of the dignity of all the gestures he'd made, from his speech in Višegrad to his public push for forgiveness, even his presence at the funerals, even his belated audience with bin Musa. The man I saw, there, then, was not a man who made dignified gestures. He was a man who kept his head down, worked hard, expected only humble things. He was an unassuming franchise owner who got along well with his employees and was pleased to receive the recognition of his local Chamber of Commerce.

But he didn't sense me. He kept to his standing desk, his computer humming beside him, and scratched ink across invoices and contracts and other documents. I watched him write. His surroundings dwarfed him. Behind him arched a wall tacked with papers and forms, flyers, advertisements. The desk almost encircled him, penning him in. I stepped closer, thinking perhaps he'd perceive, even subconsciously, the shift of shadows and warp of light. He didn't. He looked away from me and wrote, as still as a scholar bent over parchment in a Renaissance painting. His immersion in his work gave me time to study him. I could see the curls of his hair, black fading to charcoal and speckled with grey and white. I could see the olive of his skin, the stitching of his uniform, the stray thread left behind by a loose collar button. There was a dimple on his finger where his wedding ring had been. I could see the way his polo shirt hugged his pigeon chest, scrunched up into his armpits. In my head I began to hear the questions, the stream of questions, I felt I needed to ask him, put to him, hurl at him like an inquisitor in a courtroom. I could see, on the wall behind him, the familiar face of his daughter. He'd made his own tiny memorial to the girl he'd lost.

What felled me at the Mearns was the headstone between the two houses. I'm tempted to say that the place hadn't changed in the decade since I'd first been there. Really, though, it's likely that seeing the place again rewrote my memories of how it had been, replaced them with a simulacrum so that past and present looked the same. Rustling reeds topped the dunes. Beyond the bank of sand, the crashing of waves was loud and constant. This time, this early autumn, wide blue skies were sprinkled with tufts of cloud and streaked with the exhaust fumes of jets over the North Sea. The houses squatted against the wind, side by side but not quite flush. I approached the house I'd stayed in and rounded the edge of the property. Lights off, curtains drawn, entirely unoccupied. I slipped into the space between it and the neighbouring house, making as if to take a shortcut to the waves, and I climbed the small sandbank on the lookout for signs of recent activity.

As I took the first dip down the dune towards the water, I stopped and turned around to scan the scene. There was the window I'd stood at to watch the burning of the reeds, to hear the singing of the birthday song. Behind me was the spot where I'd frozen, gone quiet, face to face with Shane. At the base of the balcony where I'd seen Kerry standing, I noticed a slight concavity in the sand. It had the shape of a crater or funnel, and nestled in it, near the cusp, I saw a small, unremarkable headstone. Not a conventional memorial object. Not like something from a cemetery. More like a mound of rocks, almost a cairn, cemented together and tucked out of the way. I stumbled over to it through divots that shifted underfoot. Exerted, panting for breath, I came to it and saw on it a plaque that instantly galled me. The plaque was made of brass and studded with an inscription. The inscription gave the name of the deceased, his year of birth and year of death, and then appended these details with just two words beneath them. It said, simply, BELOVED SON.

I stood at the foot of the bed. I'd stepped out of the bathroom with only a towel around my waist. When I saw what lay on the bed, I stopped. An empty person, a man deprived of embodiment. Over the duvet my wife had draped my suit. Black trousers and a white collared shirt, a black tie, black waistcoat, black jacket. While I'd been in the shower, I'd interpreted the sound of her movements outside as a signal that I should hurry up. She was antsy to see through the plan she'd set in motion. Now, though, I understood what she'd really been doing. The clothes lay at rest on the bed with a precision I couldn't fail to recognise. Edges touching but not overlapping. Not hasty work, not sloppy. What I saw in it is hard to say. Not love, exactly, or at least not love for me. Let's say devotion. There was something devotional to it. The care with which it had been done. The patience and the respect. It looked to me as if, with a gesture made for my benefit, she'd been directing her energies to our child and consecrating, in advance, my presence at the farewell.

What galled me about the headstone was the brevity of its inscription. BELOVED SON. That was it. I'd assumed I'd find something more. I don't know what I'd expected, not exactly, but I wouldn't have gone so far north, wouldn't have gone to the trouble of the journey, much less the knowing collision with the past, if I thought I'd end up finding only those two words. They seemed not to justify the energy expended on them. They were so plain, so devoid of particular meaning, that Shane might as well have held his silence. Seeing them there made me want to retch. To have gone to such lengths, such expense, of money and time and resilience, to return to this place and find only that phrase, that piffle, that fume of sentiment. Worse, to know what Shane had gone through only to have arrived at this. The sacrifices he'd made, the tortures he'd endured, all for the sake of his son, only to find no other way of summing up his grief, or recording it for posterity, than words plucked from a cheap condolence card. How could he have invested so much in another person's life, only to lose the life and then give no expression to the depths of himself he'd lost? Standing there, thrashed by the wind off the waves, I knew I'd need ream upon ream of paper to give voice to what I'd let slip through my fingers. I could see the sheets fluttering around me like debris in a hurricane. It gave me motion sickness, it made the sky above me spin, to think that Shane had found a mere two words sufficient to unburden himself. Maybe not because he didn't know what to say, but because the better part of what he could say was something he had to hold on to in silence. Maybe those two words were just a token gesture to a hungry world.

When Demirović looked up from his work at last, I could see in his posture, his sloping shoulders, and in the lines of his face, the burden of his crusade. He saw me standing before him. What sort of man did he see? His eyes pinched into a squint. He shifted his weight and shuffled a couple of papers on his desk.

Yes? he said. Is there something—

He didn't finish the question. He shook away a cloud of confusion and looked to me and forced a smile. He had deep grooves around his mouth and the bridge of his nose. He looked like he'd not slept in days. Probably he hadn't. Still I stared at him. Better to say

I examined him. His weariness wasn't just gouged into his face but hung about his head like a haar. Did he see much the same when he looked at me? Did he see himself reflected back in my posture, my pleading eyes? That was the first thing and probably the sum of all the things I wanted to ask him then, all the questions I wanted to let out. Did he know me by my look? Did he know what I felt, what I was still feeling? Do you, I wanted to ask him, do you know what I'm doing here?

He pursed his lips and drew breath through his nose. He shook his head to himself, a gesture almost of hopelessness, then he extended a finger and pointed at me and that was when he spoke the words that broke me.

You're not the first, he said.

He let his hand slap onto the standing desk and shook his head again. I remembered, then, one of the earliest things I'd felt as I'd observed him from afar. When he'd travelled abroad to speak in Višegrad, I'd thought, he'd unwittingly forfeited time with his daughter during her precious last days, and so, as I recalled it, I'd felt a strange humiliation on behalf of him. Now, it seemed, we'd swapped places, and he felt things on my behalf. The agitation he showed in his manner was rightfully mine, not his. He knew me only as a stranger off the street. Why would my arrival make him vexed? I was the one being starved of what I craved, answers to questions that didn't have any. Pointing fingers, slapping things, making gestures of hopelessness: these should have been my preserve.

A couple of weeks since the last one, he said. So the visits, they've tapered off a bit. For a while, though, I'd see people like you standing there, like that, every day almost. From everywhere. From all over the country, I mean. Come here like pilgrims.

In my head I felt a familiar spinning sensation, a spinning out of control. I'd broadened a binary star into a minor constellation. Now it blew out to assume the vast dimensions of a galaxy.

I'm sure I stalled, swallowed hard, before I spoke to him.

How many? I asked, when words returned to me. Others. How many others?

Demirović folded his arms across his chest and frowned. I've lost count, he said.

My vision swam as I took a step towards him.

About the walk along the cliffs I can't speak in detail. Call it a cortège. Call my reeling thoughts a threnody. My wife walked ahead of me, leading the way, with my in-laws behind us and my parents at the rear. I remember the arrangement but I don't remember the motion. Suddenly I'm just there on that day, suddenly we arrive at the spot where my wife had proposed to scatter the ashes. All of us silent on our points of greatest pressure. I remember reading them into each of our bodies. My parents held one another, jointly braced for the final revision of the story they'd written around themselves, ready to watch their growth into grandparents backtrack into unbecoming. My father-in-law, meanwhile, stood crabbed and taciturn, irritable, brooding over the bitter topics he'd broached with me the night before. I felt sick, barely stable, knowing in secret the things I'd resolved after he'd trudged off to bed. My mother-in-law stood apart from him and looked at me askance, seemingly assessing how well I'd scrubbed up and deciding I hadn't met her standards. My wife took her place beside me, cradling the urn with the lid still on, fully involved in what she was doing and absolutely unaware of what I'd decided to do to us. I knew, and she didn't, that the end had already washed over us and washed out again, and we were all just standing in its wake. I knew, and she didn't, that she hadn't felt the crash of it yet, that she'd been granted another delay in her awareness of the new shape of her life, but that its force was mounting above her and the deluge loomed.

Demirović suddenly hardened, became defensive, and looked back at me the way a deer holds the gaze of a wolf. Did I seem as if I'd grown brazen?

What do you want me to say? he asked.

If I let slip just one of the questions welling up inside me, I knew I'd never control the flow. I'd deliquesce into a blubbering sop. Instead, scrabbling around for something to latch onto, something to stop my vision from spinning, I asked him a question to anchor us to what was known and answerable.

Yesterday, I said. Yesterday, when you visited him—

I'd only meant to pause for thought, but he scowled and broke in before I could go on.

You're press, he said. Are you press?

Am I what?

I don't owe you anything.

I'm not the press, I said.

You're not a reporter? You swear it?

I shook my head. I'm nobody, I said. I mean I don't work for anybody like that. I'm not, I'm not one of them. I'm not involved in that way.

He scrutinised me hard. Then, satisfied, or at least relenting, he said, Well, what is it?

It's just, I said, I've been wondering.

Yeah, I can see that. I can see it all over you. And I've seen your type before. So go on, then. He made a motion for me to continue. What are you wondering?

When you *saw* him, I said, face to face, what did you see in him?

To my surprise a smile tugged at one corner of his lips and he raised his hand again, palm up, with a swish to indicate me.

Nobody, he said. That's what I saw. He was a nobody, too. That's the truth.

Again he folded his arms across his chest.

I didn't know what to make of his dismissiveness or how to find a way around it. I hesitated, then; I worried that all my pent-up questions had started leaking out of my skin, trickling from my pores, so that all he could do was answer the questions I posed aloud while waiting for the others to breach and split me open.

What I wanted to know, at the bottom of everything, was how he managed to go on simply *being.* How he made himself cohere. How do you bear your own weight anymore? I asked him this without speaking a word. How do you wake in the morning and dress for work and go? How do you survive the day intact? How do you force yourself to live on in the story of your life as if the story doesn't now belong to someone else? To hold the breach at bay, however, I focused harder still on things that might impose gravity, things that would keep us grounded, striving at the same time to find a route beyond the facile.

Did you forgive him? I asked.

Of course, he said without a beat of hesitation.

I mean really, I said. *Really.*

I did. He widened his eyes. I really did.

But how?

He shrugged. I said what I had to say.

And?

And he heard me out, said Demirović. He didn't say much.

I sighed. I said, Your daughter? Did you?

The questions made no sense, but Demirović understood what I was trying to ask.

I talked about her, he said. I told him about her. I tried to, to make him *see.* To see what he'd done when he, when he—

He paused to gather up his resolve.

When he took her away, he said.

And what did he say to you after that?

Nothing very important. I don't think he was surprised by anything I had to say.

So what happened, then? Twenty minutes. How'd you use that time? The rest of it.

Now I caught a shift in his eyes from my face to my hands and back again. The glance belied his preoccupations, gave away something of what was said in the cell. For an instant it held to the ring I still wore on my finger. In his line of sight, the ring acquired new heat.

Why do you want to know? he asked, but not as if he expected an answer.

I made the same shift with my own eyes and saw, again, the paleness where his ring used to be. When I came back to him and saw that he'd seen me, I saw as well that the lag between our movements was brief by comparison to the lag between his mind and mine. My thoughts were aping his at a distance, ambling in their wake. I was the echo of who he'd been, the previous afternoon. We were involved in silent collusion, and so his glance at the ring, with all its significations, was a desperate deviation from what he knew possessed me now. The questions I couldn't openly ask him, questions I'd thought were mine alone to probe, clearly already harried him, and had done for some time. Don't you just want to let it all go? Don't you want to start over again? Don't you want to unwind it all, erase it, as if your life was one long mistake you might turn back and rectify? Those same questions, I saw now, had come to him from his inner voice as much as they came to me from mine, and they'd agitated him more fiercely as he'd stepped into the prisoner's cell and entered the expanse of his allotted twenty minutes. But, of course, he couldn't have asked them aloud in the cell any more than I could keep calm and pose them to him. Don't you want to unleash destruction upon a world that won't let you do what you must? That's not a question to ask a man at risk of easy provocation. So, then, at a delay, I took his cue and threw another glance at his ring finger, drawing myself away from myself and towards a subject belonging to the world at hand. In irritation, or maybe only reticence, he tousled his hair, then he gripped the edge of his desk and drummed his fingers on it.

Yeah, all right, he said at last. I asked him about his wife.

Okay, I said quietly.

Just to have something to ask, he said. To ask instead of say.

Something, he kept on drumming his fingers, something *sensible*. To get something real out of him.

He shoved both hands into his pockets and looked down at his desk.

Okay, I said. But why her? I mean, of all people.

He exhaled, exasperated, and said, She was just the first sensible subject that came to mind.

He wouldn't look at me.

I don't think that's true, I said.

At those words Demirović caught a tremble in his lower lip. He bit his lip and closed his eyes, turning inwards for a time. Then he came back, looked up at me and sighed, All right, and admitted what he must have known I'd already guessed. I wanted to know how he did it, he said. How, when everything he'd built fell apart in his hands, he managed, somehow, to hold it together, and hold it tight. Demirović made a fist with one hand and thumped it against his chest and kept it there above his heart. So what if he only held it together in *here*, he said, *inside*? He still found a way to hold on to things that I, I just, I can't. I can't anymore. I haven't been able. So I thought maybe he could show me how. Sort of.

As he spoke, the unaskable questions crashed inside me like a swell hitting a breakwall. His confession, his unvarnished vulnerability, stole all the strength from the man and sent my body into shutdown. The questions kept flowing forth only to slosh against the barricade of my skin. Of course I'd wanted to ask him exactly the same things. Can you tell me how you've come this far? Can you share with me the secret that holds you upright? Can you draw me a map? Can you be my mirror? I'd hoped to find in him at least a rudimentary model of how to regain my bearings, how to perform myself in public while pushing the things I couldn't reveal into private places. Can you show me what you look like when you lose control? Can you tell me whether you've found yourself breaking things unawares, or waking at night with your muscles tense, or only being able to stutter when in fact you're trying to speak? I screamed at him in my head and he heard none of it. He just watched me, still pressing his fist to his chest, and gave me nothing greater than his attention, his patience. I screamed at him to tell me what more he knew that I didn't know. I hollered at him to help me. Can't you help me? I asked without asking. Demirović didn't answer. Why not? I asked, I didn't. Why won't you *offer* me help?

But you know what? he said when he let his hand fall slack to his side. He looked across the desk at me as if genuinely expecting an answer this time.

He didn't have anything to tell you, I said.

That same smile came back to the corner of his mouth. Actually, Demirović said, he refused to tell me anything. He said I was asking for something he wasn't prepared to share. His wife, you know? His love. If that's what it is. He said he wanted to keep it. He wouldn't tell me a thing. Not a single detail. I asked him again, I did. I asked him man to man. But no, nothing. Not even her name.

Then Demirović fell silent, recognising too late the hole he'd stumbled into. Would he volunteer something or would he make me ask for it? Would he refuse me as he'd been refused? He seemed willing to hold his tongue. In the end I made the move. I raised a hand to indicate the ring finger missing a ring, and I put to him the questions he'd given me.

So, then, I said, how did it happen for you?

Demirović said, Very quickly.

And was it you? Were you the one to call it?

He looked down at his hand and opened it, flexed his fingers and studied them. He scanned the imperfections as if poring over the craquelure of a masterpiece.

There's nothing I can pin down, he said, in *time.* It's something that happened, that's all. It's like, it wasn't an *event.* Or if it was, it was already old by the time I took off the ring. Right back at the start, maybe, when things happened here in Sydney and we were in the air.

He shook his head to himself again. Not in agitation now, but in an effort to clear his sight. With a slight tilt to one side, he turned away from me and looked at the picture of his daughter on display behind him. Sunlight. Water. Unadulterated joy. Alanna Demirović looked into the camera and smiled her astonishing smile. She always would, forevermore. But, I noticed, just as when I'd seen her face from the car, her picture had been drained of colour and the corners had curled. This gave me more of a shock than anything the picture showed. How could her father be unbothered by this neglect? How could he be in no hurry to revitalise her memorial? He'd found a kind of peace, I supposed, or else grown resigned to not finding it. But I couldn't see how either of those was a possibility. I couldn't *believe* they were. He turned back towards me then, but once more looked down at his desk.

I can't tell you what you should do, he murmured, or how things might happen for you. I can't *advise* anyone who comes to me like this. I can only tell you that what has to happen will happen. That's all I can say, honestly. Whether or not you *make* it happen, that's for you to work out. Just, well, just understand something—

He scratched himself around the jawline as he picked out his words.

Jessica, he said suddenly. Jessica has her share of the pain, or, what's the word? She has her *angle* on it. It's not something I can comprehend. He squinted, deeper in thought. It's not something I *comprehend*, he said, but what I understand is that there's no right or wrong. There just *isn't*. And so—and so—her angle isn't up for dispute.

He pursed his lips, almost as if he'd finished. Then he found one last thing to add.

But also, he said in the tone of a question, I wouldn't say I *left* her? No. Not like that. Not in a storm. We didn't end things. It just, ah, went away: being together. I'd made things more difficult for her than they had to be. I couldn't not do that. I mean, for one thing, we'd left Alanna with Jessica's sister, in her care. That *alone* got to me so bad I couldn't, I couldn't figure out how to settle things. I couldn't fix it, the way we started to relate to each other. Too quiet. But I didn't know how else to act, for me or for my daughter. But Jessica? She wanted none of it. Which was absolutely her right. So I think what I'd have to say is, the time came for me to just leave her alone.

In retrospect I'm startled by the generosity of Demirović. He was right: he didn't owe me anything, he had no obligation to entertain another of the pilgrims come to see him, but he didn't send me away with nothing. It wasn't the case that I simply stood there and took from him the things I needed. It was the case that he let me stand and gave me his presence long enough to assure me, through his bearing, that the chaos of what I felt was known to him. I wasn't special. I wasn't unique. That was what he'd told me before he told me anything else, and yet he still went on to give me more than he had reason to. I can't be sure he knew my state of mind precisely, but he recognised something in me that needed time to subside and he gave me leeway to nurse it. I'm sure other eyes fell upon us as we spoke, but even so he didn't act to remove me from sight. He didn't call for assistance. He didn't summon security. He let me stand and offload my questions, the ones I asked and the ones I didn't, and in the midst of being with him, when I recognised, finally, the uselessness of his advice, I felt, deep inside me, something truly alive. Something that came to life solely through our facing one another. The spontaneity of the approach. The risk of the impromptu encounter. Something about the chance it involved, about not knowing what its outcome would be. Waiting to see what would happen. Waiting to see what I'd caused to happen. Something about all this awakened a feeling in me, a feeling I've never been able to name except to say that I felt newly present, at once assertive and exposed, involved again in the world and also at its mercy, and I was startled by it. That same feeling returned to me just before I watched my wife take hold of the ashes. I watched from slightly behind her, over her shoulder, as she stood at the edge of the rocks and cradled the urn. I watched her, waiting, as she unscrewed the lid, as she twisted it open to give movement to her memorial designs.

I know there are many things in this story that would be different if my wife were to tell it. She'd have details to share about the second walk along the cliffs. She'd wax lyrical about how meaningful it was to have her parents there, and mine, how fulfilling to hold the urn, poised, careful not to trip, and feel its warmth grow in her hands like new life as sunlight hit the metal. She'd also take you to the end of the ceremony and conclude this part of the story right there. She'd skip over the opening of the urn. She'd tell you about the way she took from it the first handful of ashes, cupped them in her palm, held them to her heart and whispered words I couldn't hear, words she never shared with me, then let them go, gave them to the sea, watched them taken high and low and far off to the four winds. She might add a coda about how she offered the urn to our parents, so they could follow her lead, then passed it to me so that I might do the same. But I can't end the story there because that closure, that catharsis, isn't mine and was bound never to be. This part of my story ends with a suspension. This part has to end in the breach.

When my wife looked into the urn, I noticed a stutter in her body. She seemed to turn towards me a little and then forced herself to stop, to not react. She fixated on the ashes. They'd been depleted by almost half. She didn't say anything about it, but clearly she knew what I'd done and so she must have known, even then, that something between us was over. *Have you seen—O tell me where—and then—and what would be—* Even if we hadn't spoken of it yet, even if, by failing to speak, we hadn't made it real, she couldn't have been oblivious to the implications of the lack in her hands. But she didn't act on her knowledge at all and she didn't let on to our parents that anything was amiss. She performed her role in the ending she'd scripted in her head. Hers was a brief monument to her loss, more brief than a burial, even more brief than two words on a headstone. She took the ashes and scattered them. She scooped them up in her hand and held them a moment longer, then she opened her fingers and she let them go. Her monument was here and gone. What lingered, for me, was the intervention I'd made, the way I'd disrupted her script with something spontaneous and true. What resonated was my having acted to obtrude on the settlements of others, surprising them with a demand for an unguarded response, and in the process unhooking myself from the person they'd believed me to be.

BOYD

What I've often wondered is where the motion comes from. When the heaviness drags you down into inertia, when just to flex a muscle or shift a limb is to perform a minor miracle, how does it finally break? What's the impetus, the propulsive force? No snipers on high-rise rooftops. No screaming jets releasing bombs. No muskets at my back, no whips slicing into my shoulders. No clambering into a boat, no collapse on distant shores. No flight into a mountain range and no risk of death in the waves at the edge of a foreign land. In the absence of these terrors, movement can come only from desire, from a line of desire that connects the body to some distant place where a hunger might be fed. But what would I hunger for?

In London, by chance, I rediscovered the name of James Boyd. I wish I could say I'd been thinking of him since my father-in-law rapped knuckles on that selfie. I wished that night in the kitchen had sparked thoughts of Boyd. I wished that the tempest my father-in-law kicked up would've receded earlier, fizzed out as I saw the first bodies falling, to expose for me instead the stolid face of the man. I'd seen him there at Port Arthur, a painted portrait in a hall of the penitentiary, along with his name, a potted biography, a list of his achievements in the colonies. But that's not how he came back to me. I was relieving the pangs of a new hunger, pursuing that new line of desire back to Scotland, to the Mearns, when London brought Boyd into my life.

A couple of nights in a shoddy hotel not far from King's Cross. One night to shake off the worst of the jet lag, another to compose myself ahead of a northbound train. Sunrise at six in the morning. At first light I took to the footpaths. I became one of those men. I plodded the peripheries of perfumed gardens fenced in by iron spikes. I drifted down laneways and alleys, I stopped suddenly on corners to search the very air in front of my face for ways of purging myself of energy so that, with luck, I might return to my rented bed and sleep. I'd been dragging my feet along Regent's Canal, where the towpath dips beneath Caledonian Road, when I looked up at the terraces crowding the water's edge and saw a round blue plaque affixed to a wall. London is peppered with those things. Almost every block boasts one to distinguish the house in which some venerable figure once lived and worked, or the park in which so-and-so delivered some landmark speech or drafted an important treatise. This one cut through the clag of dislocation and pierced my memories of that long-ago journey with my wife. It staked its claim to permanence in white serif letters on a background of azure:

Mr. James Arthur Boyd, *b.* 1799, *d.* 1888,
lodged herein 1839–1843
Principal Warder, Pentonville Prison
Commandant, Port Arthur Penal Colony
Tireless advocate for the improvement of the weak
and the reform of the maladapted.

But the colour scheme struck me as slightly off compared to other plaques I'd seen, mimicking their style more than conforming to it. The text was too cramped and the blue too bright. When I reached the last line, I understood why. The plaque was not an official one arranged by some historical association. It was a personal attempt to fill a hole in history:

This memorial dedicated to his memory,
9 March 1907,
by his loving daughter and descendants.

Pentonville lay up the road, fifteen minutes away on foot. Port Arthur, though, was a daunting distance. Days of travel for me, unbroken months for him. What compelled him to move there? It couldn't have been caprice. It had to have been a commitment. To what objective? To what ideal? Suddenly water chopped at the brim of the canal. Somewhere close, I supposed, a narrowboat chugging through the tunnel to Hoxton had needed a lock to swing open. The disturbance of the water's surface squiggled my outline, turned my face to tatters. There I was outside the London residence of the penal colony commandant. I could sense at my back the pieces of another life snapping into place, the architecture, the scaffolding, the superstructures I'd encountered years ago in that theatre of punishment, and what came to mind were hands held tightly between someone else's, possessively clutched, and then, in a woman's voice, the whispered words, Don't go.

When my wife and I sat together at my in-laws' breakfast bar, almost without pause I fell to studying her hands. How we'd agreed to sit together, I can't now recall. How we'd asked for privacy, how we'd dispensed with both pairs of parents, how we'd taken time out for ourselves, I lost the nerve to inscribe into my memory. How the tensions between us shifted and eased and strengthened again weren't any longer worth the devotion to details. At some point she would have said something like, We need to talk, and that would've been how I ended up opposite her. She set her hands upon a solid surface. Her hands at rest on the lip of the breakfast bar, her thumbs hooked underneath it. She arched her knuckles. I had an urge to reach for her and interlock our fingers.

Seeing her hands right there, like that, made them seem miraculous. The crosshatched pattern in the skin. The light blue veins beneath the white. The muscle filaments stitching together the strength in her grip. The potential they held for that movement, clench and flex, grasp and release, with which she'd cast our daughter to the sea. The meaning she found in doing that. The way the gesture, the open hand, had opened something in her body, unlocking a torsion that had held her tight for months. From her hands, her fingers, I let my eyes drift upwards to her face. She had a lightness to her that wasn't there before. That's not to say she smiled or softened when I looked at her. It's only to say that she didn't hang her head or let her shoulders drop as if her thoughts had grown too dense to carry. She sat a little more freely now and waited for me to say something. I slid one hand across the table and took her hand in mine. But I didn't speak. I only waited for her to begin. I didn't mind not speaking.

Let me put Boyd behind a desk. A fast receding hairline with a puff of grey in the centre of his crown. Sharp eyes and a moustache robust enough to conceal his lips. He concentrates hard on a handful of papers, trying to decipher some underling's penmanship through the lenses of a pince-nez. Let's make his desk something aristocratic. Walnut wood. Maybe oak. It sits in the centre of an office streaming with florid light. Sunbeams pour through a window and snag on drifting dust. The dust swirls around, snatched up in a gust of air, as the door swings open without a knock and a tall, thin man steps in. He has a pointed nose and a pencil moustache and a dandyish smile that plays about his lips.

Boyd rises from his seat in a show of respect.

The other man offers a flip of the hand and gestures for Boyd to be at ease.

Boyd resumes his position warily and locks eyes on his superior. The thin man strides towards him almost preening, almost leering. Tell me something, James, he says as he approaches. He rests both hands on the desk and bends to lean in close to Boyd. Tell me. Do you still dream of Van Diemen's Land?

Twenty years had elapsed since Boyd first sailed south. He'd been stationed at Maria Island, a godforsaken welt of soil fatefully shaped like a double noose. Two great blobs strung together by an isthmus, it had been cut off from Van Diemen's Land by three miles of almost Antarctic ocean. He'd brought with him, from London, the wife he'd taken there from their home in Bridge of Allan only four years earlier. He'd also brought his daughter, an infant, six months old, who'd scarcely known a summer in her native country before setting sail for the antipodes. In the end, sixteen years later, it was the girl who lured him back to London, to that desk, to Pentonville. She'd spent those years in the care of her mother. By that tender age, though, she was a debutante in all respects but her frightful location. What prospect of marriage for a woman come to maturity in the penal colony her father oversaw? Beastly hot in the summertime, deathly cold and wet in winter. The depredations of the convicts had to be faced day in, day out, and the atmospheric moaning of the place seemed always to drown out the soothings of the sea. She declared her intention to establish herself back home. She had dreams of silken gowns and sumptuously decorated ballrooms and the chiselled faces of handsome men establishing respectable careers.

Her parents consented, eventually, and offered all necessary support. A bursary for her finances, a list of contacts to vouchsafe her reputation. They saw her off on a sloop to Hobart Town, where she'd waylay en route to Botany Bay. Once she reached Port Jackson, she'd transfer to a schooner that would convey her to Southampton. But she'd been at sea for barely a month when her mother wasted away. Heartbreak, trauma. Too much for one soul to take. Before his daughter even had a chance to set foot on native ground, Boyd had been forced to bury his wife in foreign soil. He couldn't see the sense of staying in the colonies alone. Within six months the widower had secured a transfer to London to be close to his daughter again. But he never forgot Van Diemen's Land. It wouldn't be right to say he'd grown fond of the place. He'd fallen for it as soon as he stepped onshore. He rued having lost the peace it brought him, the quiet, the calm. So of course it still came to him in dreams.

We're at the breaking point we've been expecting for years, his superior told him. Transportation to the colonies is not a threat severe enough to deter the genuine miscreants from everyday indulgences in criminal behaviour. So, now, we're looking for a more comprehensive solution. We're looking for someone who can, if you like, export to the colonies some of our more successful modern techniques for managing in-house problems and so forth. He raised an eyebrow at Boyd. Port Arthur, he said. The crown jewel of the colonies. Eighteen months as deputy to Captain Booth and then he'll retire, you have my word, and when he does he'll relinquish complete control to you.

Boyd said, Oh.

You can understand why you're thought to be the man for the job?

Boyd gave only a single nod.

Of course I'll be terribly sorry to lose you here, but every time I see you, you've got that look in your eyes. Clouded by visions of a faraway land. Dreaming of the great wide sea.

Boyd forced a smile and said, Perhaps. But I haven't accepted the offer.

The other man laughed in his face. That's only because I've not yet drawn up a contract. He banged a fist on Boyd's desk, twice, and turned to open the door again. Shan't be long, he said as he took his leave. You give the word and I'll send you on your way.

The problem wasn't that Boyd didn't want to go. The problem was that he still had his daughter to attend to. He hadn't seen her suited and wed. He hadn't had a chance to enjoy the blessings of his first grandchild. He could never say the word, never sign the contract, never accept the deal because he knew that as soon as he broke the news to her she'd reach for his hands, clutch them tight between hers and say, No. Please. Don't go.

With the tip of my little finger I touched, tentatively, the diamond, embedded in tarnished gold, that crowned my wife's engagement ring. Fine-cut and imperishable, worn for many years but not worn down by them. I had, I have, no memory of slipping it on. I suppose I held her hand at the wrist, felt the flutter of her pulse beneath my touch, and guided the ring over knuckles until it nestled at the base of her finger. But that's just a guess, really, given the way it's been done by millions of other men and women. What I mean is that there wasn't, isn't, anything exceptional about what I did when I gave that ring to my wife. Everything exceptional about our engagement came down to her alone. She was the one who took to bended knee. *Sir,* she asked, *will you marry me?,* not in so many words but with a mischievous spin on the pomp of tradition. Of course, I said, of course, of course, and I went out and bought a ring and put it on her finger and then we became like everyone else. I neutralised the event, domesticated it. Now, none of what followed had been profound enough to stick in the mind. Why then should our marriage have had the power to linger in the world? Why should we have thought it extraordinary, able to withstand the shocks that had toppled so many others?

The young woman, as I imagined her, wore on her finger a ring that broadcast her fortunes to her father before she could take his hand in hers and say, I have wonderful news! I climbed the stairs to Caledonian Road as the waters of the canal lapped peacefully behind me. I saw Boyd pass by as he returned home at the end of the day. Pentonville pushed him this way and that, pushed him to his limits with its incessant noise, its groans, its clanking, its demands. He longed for a space of virgin stillness, a space in which to ensconce himself and settle his mind. He had a habit of taking the air each evening, proceeding on foot from the penitentiary to the canal, but even this was insufficient. Clopping horses, clattering carriages, the belch of factory smoke, crude exchanges between labourers on the water. Only alone indoors could he escape the pandemonium. A key in the lock, a bolt in its chamber, and then, at last, a hush. His atrium. His sitting room. A cigar. A velveteen chair. His retreat.

This evening, however, the tumult returns to him where he'd expected to find relief. For Boyd, I imagine, his daughter's news is anything but wonderful. He hasn't taken a liking to the young man he has long suspected of courting her. Let's say a bank clerk's son. Let's say the fellow had barely spoken to Boyd and certainly hadn't privately sought his blessings. I imagine that Boyd returns home with the offer of a transfer in mind. I imagine the door creaks open and his daughter rushes forth, all glee, all hope, to greet him. I imagine he sees the ring on her finger and hears her giddy exclamation, I have wonderful news!, and as his thoughts adjust to the situation, slowly, he glances into the house and sees the young man rising, with a smile, from a seat beside the hearth.

The young man makes his approach. Boyd holds steady against the doorjamb.

Isn't everything fine? Isn't this all very well? Isn't this exactly what he wanted? A man of not unrespectable breeding, at least an adequate match for his daughter. Isn't this why he followed her back to England? It's been three, almost four years since he left Maria Island. It's taken his daughter longer to find a suitor than he'd thought it would. Now his work as a father is done. Now his guardianship is at an end. Now he is free to make decisions without any obligation to consider her wishes. Now his head begins to spin. The young man approaches with a hand extended, a hand to shake, but as Boyd wavers and his steadiness deserts him the young man moves in quickly to hold him upright. The problem is the cacophony that overcomes him and screams through him and seizes his muscles. The problem is the grind and clank that rattles bones, the scrape of iron and steel that sets his teeth on edge, the gnash and grit of some great machine convulsing in his skull. The din fills the air, besieges the house he has stumbled into, breaks in through the windows and rolls out like factory fumes to smother whatever quiet might have prevailed. Isn't there a way to arrest it? Isn't there a way to make it hush? He's spent his life these past five years looking for a way. He's spent his days trying to tune silence to perfection.

This is, he says, he gasps, as the furore subsides enough for him to recover his senses, this is indeed a surprise, I can't deny it.

He wills himself to smile at his daughter.

My little Annie Gordon, he says, with her heart set on her own true love.

He used to sing a song to her when she was but a girl. He'd learnt it as a boy in Bridge of Allan. It told the tale of a young woman who declares her affections for a nobleman. He'd always sung her as a headstrong lass, though she was also quite the fool.

And, he says, this news is, in its own way, fortuitous for me as well. You see, I have some news of my own.

When he tells her he will accept the offer, she begs him not to go.

It's my chance to improve the system, he says. To build true silence into it.

No, she says, shaking her head. No. Please. Don't go.

His own father-in-law had begged *his* daughter not to leave Bridge of Allan, back when Boyd had secured his first post at the Old Bailey. But Boyd had courted by the book. He'd wooed his wife as a debutante and invested, where he could, in her father's business prospects. He'd made an ally of the man and he'd made an appeal for permission to wed with as much sincerity as any father could hope for. That didn't just give him the right to insist on relocation. It gave him the right to ask the old man to cease his protests, to consent. His intention had always been to start a family of his own in London. The dowry signalled that much. The very fact of the property he acquired with his wife was a tacit admission that the two of them would never settle in so forlorn a place as the outer edge of Stirlingshire. He and she were expected to make a mark on the wider world.

My father-in-law had simply shaken my hand with a vigorous delight that suggested nothing more than honest congratulations. My wife had been the one to inform her parents after we made our engagement official. They were happy. My father-in-law only ever said one thing to me about his expectations before my wife and I exchanged our vows. He said it while he was shaking my hand, before he drew me close to give me a slap on the back.

Make sure you make it last, he said. Just make sure you work to make it last.

Actually, no, that's not all he said. He said he trusted that in committing myself to my wife I'd made the right decision. He said it wouldn't always be easy. He said we'd have to buckle down and devote ourselves to it when times got tough, as he was sure they would someday. But it'd always be worth the effort, he said. Always. *Always.* Then he said what stuck with me most over time. Make sure you make it last. Just make sure you *work* to make it last. Now I look at my hands, at the hand that shook his when he heard the news, and what I see is the dust of my marriage slipping through my fingers.

My wife began by saying she knew I'd taken the ashes. I knew she knew. Her words weren't intended to reveal her knowledge to me. They were intended to clear a space for other words to be spoken. I held tighter to her hand, the hand that had held the ashes, as she sat opposite me and looked into my eyes and awaited a reply. All I could do was let the silence settle over me like a shroud. I met her gaze but couldn't muster speech. She tilted her head in an expression of curiosity as if to urge me to open myself. I couldn't. She took the initiative to kickstart a line of questioning. Why did you do it without telling me? she asked. Why didn't you tell me you didn't want us to do what we did? Why didn't you say something earlier? Why let me discover it for myself? Why make me feel like a fool? Why stain the occasion with this, this betrayal? She said she wanted to understand. She put those questions to me in living hope that I could help her. I had answers for her questions but I couldn't make myself divulge them. I held her gaze and inclined towards her, but I couldn't speak. She dug her fingers into the back of my hand. She wanted contact, authentic contact. She kept asking questions, kept on making so much noise, while I went into inner exile.

Boyd gave me the totem I wielded against my wife in the kitchen. I didn't know it at the time, I wouldn't know it until that plaque in London brought him back to me, but he was there with me as a man who'd devoted his life to creating what I'd cloaked myself in. His project became known as the separate system of discipline. The idea came from the Americans. It was the brainchild of Benjamin Franklin. He'd proposed a penitentiary in which obstreperous inmates were placed alone in cells that denied them contact with others. It was built in Philadelphia and still stands there today. When based in Boston, I'd set out west more times than I could count; I'd seen the complex, the walls and chambers, that had first brought the idea into being. Boyd had been there as well, once, but he wasn't impressed by what he saw. The Americans, he reckoned, had implemented solitary confinement in bad faith. Too many half-measures. Too many corners cut. When he went to Maria Island, then, he used his elevated position to purge its daily workings of any expedient measures. He didn't understand why solitary inmates in Philadelphia were still permitted to speak to one another. He didn't approve of allowing them, via lax enforcement of the rules, to shout through the bars of their cells and converse through the corridors. Every man he condemned to solitude would be held in a separate wing of the penitentiary. No chitchat. No sounds but the footsteps down the hallway as the errand boy delivered the daily meal. Eventually Boyd decided to have double doors installed in the cells. The errand boy would open one, place the meal inside, then close the door and leave the inmate to open the door on his side to retrieve his rations. Solitary confinement meant no contact even with the system's lowliest servants.

Purity was the ideal. That was what Boyd aspired to. He'd become an engineer of silences, a connoisseur of different species of silence, and now he aimed to cultivate silence at its most pristine. Even in spaces of blessed solitude, pure silence eluded him. Even alone on a beach, the waves did not fall still. Even alone on a mountain, the wind would not die down. Purity of silence required purity of presence. As if awareness of other people was a sickness in the atmosphere of the self. As if it could be filtered out by a spatial structure and the man inside the cell would be a thing refined, purged of all that was not *him*. Purged of the slime of social beings. Purged of the sounds and senses of other bodies. Stripped of all superfluous things in a room without any trace of any other souls.

That worked well on Maria Island. Prisoners would suffer the silence once, then they'd shy away from it and keep themselves in line. Especially in that solitary place, true solitude was insufferable and the fear of it maintained discipline. Upon returning to London, though, Boyd had been stationed at Pentonville specifically to implement the separate system and pursue it to its logical end. Transportation to the colonies was losing its power to deter crime. A powerful deterrent was needed at home as well. Into the penitentiary went the solitary cells in separate wings. Into the cells went the double doors. Into the keyholes in the doors, and into the gaps between the doors and the jambs, went woollen stuffing, padding, to muffle noise and block out light that could trickle in from outside. Around the walls and across the floor went great thickets of cotton, to take from the inmates even the whispers of their own footsteps as they paced their cells, to deaden the slapping of flesh on brick as they pummelled their fists against stone.

Absolute darkness. Every gap in every joint, every crack in every surface, was covered over, sealed. To be in one of Boyd's cells was to have illumination shaved away, to be deprived of all vision of tangible things. Absolute solitude. Every wish and want, every memory, every thought, would come screaming to the surface of the consciousness. To be in one of Boyd's cells was to hear nothing but the brush of skin against the fabric of one's clothes, the ceaseless thud of one's pulse and the roar of respiration. To be in one of Boyd's cells was to be plunged into oneself, left to descend into one's own body. Purity. That's what purity looks like. Not just a room bereft of others. A world bereft of a world beyond *you*.

That world is the achievement of the five years given posterity on the plaque beside Regent's Canal. The plaque first captured my interest purely by virtue of the name on it. I recognised it and I wanted to connect the words on the wall with the things I already knew. But the plaque held my attention with what it revealed at the last, the existence of Boyd's daughter and her dedication to his memory. For a man to have an adult daughter who not only had been shaped by him but also admired him, loved him, cherished what he'd accomplished in his brief time on this planet, was something that stirred me deeply and provoked in me the yearning for someone like that in my own life. But then what held me to the spot, to the towpath, was the fact that she, as an old woman, had decided to put the plaque right there, in the place where Boyd had spent the least of his professional years. As if trying to anchor him to London. As if to secure him to her in memory, in history, when she'd failed to secure him to her in life. It was in the location of the plaque and the brevity of the years it encompassed that I heard those words from her, in her frail voice. Don't go. Please. Don't go.

Don't go.

It's what Child's wife had begged of him, too, before he set sail for Bristol. Don't go. Stay with me, *please*. Don't leave me here alone in my grief.

Their daughter, Henrietta, no longer ill, had been only recently interred.

But he insisted he must go. He must. He was compelled to go, he said, for the sake of the girl. His work beckoned him abroad. He could imagine no other means of seeking restitution for their loss. He would collect the songs for his daughter, as a gesture to her memory, and he would find a way for her to live on through his labours.

Wait with me, she said. Don't go.

The diamond at the tip of my finger threw off a spark of light.

That ring was the first down payment I made on a life I planned to live with someone else. I thought of it then, and I think of it now, not only as a token of my love for my wife, but also as a dedication to the future I'd intended to build with her. I'd fallen for other people before. I'd lived with other women before. But before I gave her that ring I'd never felt so at one with someone whose future seemed so indefinitely entangled with mine. I gave that ring to the world to come. Now, though, I realise that indefinite isn't the same as everlasting. Indefinite doesn't mean that something doesn't have an end. It only means you can't see far enough ahead to know when the end might arrive.

Before I gave that ring, I lived a different life. Giving it was a way of burying that existence. I remember putting it to rest. I remember preparing to move in together. I packed up the clothes I'd always kept in a single wardrobe, then I sold off the wardrobe along with the single bed, the single sofa, the bar fridge and the half-size bookshelves that had always furnished the grotty flats I'd rented. I disburdened my life of these dated belongings, a bachelor's paraphernalia, and I got rid of them with a thrill. I was suddenly a fanatic, an ardent devotee of the conjoining of lives, and I went about building a bonfire from the stuff of my earlier heresies. I was eager to burn the detritus of my old ways so that something wholly new could assume its place. I disposed of it all, entwined my days with my wife's, and then as one, as a couple, we took things even further and made plans for a new life in Switzerland. New lines of desire struck out for distant places and found their terminus in the

Alps. At their end, implicitly, was a child yet to be conceived, and all the energies we committed to following those lines, to reshaping our life around them, poured into that vessel, pooled there, giving a perceptible future to the dreams we pursued.

Nobody said, Don't go.

Everybody said, Go on. Begin. This is where things really *begin.*

But now things had burned again. Burned the vessel, burned the future. Burned without my having set them alight, though I couldn't linger in the wreckage. Who would say, Don't go, this time? Who, in the life I was slipping out of, was prepared to ask me to stay?

Time is all it takes to transform something sacred into a relic from a bygone age. Time and its events. I saw this when I returned home at the end of spring. Red berries had broken out on the yew at the edge of the forest, and the front garden overflowed with lilacs in full bloom. Did I still know this place? Was the house still rightly *ours* after what we had become? I blasted through the door, against the new wedge of envelopes that had built up behind it, and I moved through the hallway in the daze of one who has stumbled into a sepulchre.

Things had happened in Sydney. Facts had come into force. My wife had no recourse but to stay. I'd had to cobble together other plans. I flew to Brisbane with my parents, as intended, and spent a couple of days in my boyhood bedroom before I couldn't take any more. I paid extra to bring forward my return ticket to Europe. My parents had watched me pack up, in haste, painfully concerned for me and just as painfully aware that they had no notion of how to help. I couldn't care. I'd boarded the plane to Singapore conspicuously alone, feeling looked at by other passengers as one of the men I might have become, and finally I returned to Zürich with not a thing of any value to my name except the ashes I'd brought with me in the vase. In hindsight, there was an ease to the transit. Once I'd taken the first step, it wasn't difficult to go. What seemed impossible for so long was the decision to leave. Making it. Admitting it. Sticking to it and bearing it out. Not reclaiming my hand from one who would hold it to detain me, to delay my departure, but forcing myself to take the first step that would sweep me away from who I'd become.

Boyd was not unfamiliar with the rhythms of extended transit and must have known, as I do now, the echoes of those rhythms in journeys that loop back on others. Low-lying hills, seen from afar, southbound along the Iberian coast. White haze against clear skies and the darker blue of the sea. Passing by, and passing again, the shadows of former selves, the family man who made the journey to the southern hemisphere and then the other man, bereaved, who sought consolation in the heart of empire. The first man had distracted his wife and dandled his infant child whenever the slave ships passed within earshot. All along the Côte d'Ivoire, all across the Gulf of Guinea, you could hear the wretched moaning even at a distance, and if the wind charged in from the right direction you could smell the stench as well. The second man had sailed without wife and child. He'd sailed, too, without any law of any land permitting further trade in human chattel. When this man passed the ships that carried the bodies that fuelled the engines of progress on distant soil, he envisioned within them the faces of the men he'd seen every day in the colonies. Terrified Irishmen gazing out of the hold, wild-eyed, as they passed by slave castles atop mountains gleaned from far offshore. Urchins plucked from the gutters of London, of Birmingham and Liverpool, thrown into captivity with common thieves, with deserters from conflicts they'd been conscripted to fight, with usurers and debtors and other scoundrels who deserved torment of their own, deserved to be locked below decks for a time, to have their skin salted, to watch it grow hard and saurian, to stew in their own juices, to sprout stubble into untamed beards and have their faces wracked with defeat, and finally to be disgorged onto bleak, malicious shores and there to labour away, tree by felled tree, stone by heaved stone, year by exhausted year, day by hungry day, hour by stolen hour, minute by gruelling minute, for the fragmentary, piecemeal glory of the mother country. Had he survived into another age, another time, he might have someday looked skyward, from the midst of the Indian Ocean, and seen, far above, through distant clouds, the speck of the aircraft that ferried me, too, back and forth between two lives.

Or maybe what I mean to say is three lives, not just two. There's the life you've lived, up to the point at which you slide into a new one. There's the life you're preparing to live, the raft of hopes you hold for the future. But then, in that eternity of indecision, while you teeter on the edge of doing something irreversible, you also live through, and think through, all the possible permutations of the life you're about to forfeit.

I picture Boyd on the eve of his departure to Van Diemen's Land. He prowls his lodgings on Regent's Canal and picks and chooses which of his possessions would best accompany him. He runs a finger along the spines of the volumes in his library. He inspects the silverware, item by item, scrubbing out blemishes and blowing away dust, and he appraises the art on the walls and the quality of the furniture he has procured in his years in London. His escritoire. His lounge set. These things aren't just things. They are receptacles for who he is, what he has done. His vocation. His decisions. His commitment to a future that has crumbled. With his daughter in the sitting room, making plans with her husband-to-be, he picks up an item here, packs away an item there, and thinks on the course of the life he will now never live. He browses the pages of the books, the philosophy and poetry, that he will never again read aloud to his daughter. He traces the contours of the vase he will never gift her. He admires the colours of the paintings that will never amuse her firstborn child. He thumbs the rims of the tumblers and sippers, glasses for whiskey and port, which he knows he will never clink with his son-in-law to toast the births of the children to follow. Surely, though, he must gift his daughter some keepsake. He studies his reflection in the ornate mirror, a gift from his own father-in-law, which will now catch the reflections of those children, his descendants, entirely in his absence, capturing faces that will share his features but will never be his to admire. He has chosen not to lead the life he can picture in his mind's eye. He watches its possibilities wilt as the night grows dark.

What was I prepared to relinquish? I looked across the breakfast bar at my wife. Not at the ring on her finger. Not at the hand I held. Her face. Her eyes. The person I saw was a woman who'd long ago begun to determine her own path. In the way her skin had weathered, in the way her creases had worked into wrinkles, I saw the past we'd shared together, those years of anxiousness and hope and distance and unnameable things we could not retrieve. In her expression, though, I saw more. I saw the kindness in her I'd been reluctant to recognise of late, the gentle remarks she'd made in the course of our days to remind me, indirectly, to act in my own best interests, to adhere to my code and not let myself lapse into releasing what I harboured inside. I saw the patience in her that had brought us to this place together, long past the point at which she'd had every right to make a decision on her own. I saw her propriety over her own deeds, her right to reserve her name from the grunge I'd thrown at her. And I saw in her the will, the assertion of her selfhood, that let her assume a standing in the world every bit the equal of mine but in no way dependent on me, to live a life that was in every sense shared, organised consensually, co-operative without being subordinate. I saw in her an independent person. The revelatory thing was not that she was this person. The revelatory thing was that at last I'd let myself see it.

There were, I knew, so many things the two of us could still endure if I were to take the path of least resistance. I looked into her eyes and I saw a future rife with possibilities. I saw promotions and career setbacks, a newfound passion for the classroom, the exhaustion of grading end-of-term assignments into the first few days of vacation. I saw financial advisers, car loans, a mortgage, a timeshare purchase in a house in the Black Forest, daytrips across the border into France. I saw Boston again, and New York, and the Alleghenies, this time in her company. I saw cancer scares, a lump, a biopsy, a doctor's analysis, and I saw rude health and exercise routines and half-marathons run on the slopes of the Alps. I saw visits from family, hers and mine, at Easter, at Christmas, in our house or in a hotel at some halfway meeting point. I saw us returning to Australia for funerals. I saw myself wrapping an arm around her as she heaved and sobbed at the graveside of one of her parents. I saw her by me, at my desk, late into the night, plying me with coffee as I searched for words to weave a eulogy for one of mine. I saw the discomfort of friends expecting children of their own, uncertain about how we'd take the news, uncertain about how to break it to us or whether to keep it from us a little longer. I saw, perhaps, a decision to try to conceive another child. To start again if we could, if we weren't too late.

I saw things that lightened my heart. I saw moments of bliss, ecstasy, joy, the vitalising energies lacking in this book. I saw, too, the hum and whir of our banal day-to-day. I saw her making me toast for breakfast. I saw myself attending to her, a thermometer and a cup of tea, when she'd come down with an illness and taken to bed. I saw us outside in winter, working together to shovel a path through the snow. I saw dirty dishes in the sink and a bathroom run out of toilet paper. I saw her remonstrating me for always overloading the washing machine. I saw myself ripping open an envelope and finding inside her credit card bill, and clearing it all at once because she had a habit of forgetting it and racking up the interest. I saw the bland material of a life shared by two people.

I pressed my hand to hers, harder, and searched her face for clues to her thoughts. I looked at her and I saw all these things and I saw that we could have them if we wanted to. I saw that they could be ours as much as they already belonged to so many other people if I just kept my mouth shut or, for the sake of performance, opened it to sputter out platitudes and excuses. But I also saw that all these things were possibilities for my life, *my* life, which I was prepared to sweep away. Possibilities sprouted from them, proliferated as from seeds, and there I was, sword in hand, ready to sever them all at the first sign of fresh shoots.

My wife drew breath and began to speak again.

Sydney in summertime. The sandstone hums. Fruit bats squabble over something fecund, something fizzing and foaming in the sun, and onto the golden sand rushes water the colour of sapphire. Convicts haul heavy loads, buckling beneath the heat overhead, and wherever they grunt and complain there are cracking whips, taunts and jeers, spit, sweat, blood. The harbour seethes with creaking ropes and flapping sails, hessian sacks spanking the soil, horses that shit and snort, flies that swarm the wooden goliaths listing and bobbing at dock. Boyd peers over the edge of his vessel. Who's to say that even one molecule of the water that catches his reflection wasn't still there, centuries later, circulating through the currents of Port Jackson, to catch my face from the ferry on the morning I set out for Maroubra? Who's to say it couldn't dissolve all the years that distinguish us, couldn't mingle us together without our having met?

My wife was still talking about the ashes. She thought she'd asked me about my wants. She thought she'd secured my honest consent to let them scatter. She hadn't thought my failure to speak of what I wanted was a sign that I didn't at all want what she'd planned. She couldn't understand why I wouldn't speak. She didn't understand that I couldn't speak. She wanted to know what I wanted to do next. She wanted to know if I'd seek help for what troubled my soul and if, in fact, the two of us should seek help together. Us. Together. Things that no longer existed for me. Things that I could no longer feel existing in the world, things no longer firmed up by forces outside myself. She assumed the two of us still moved along the same trajectory, if not always in lockstep. Did she believe it, too, or was this only what she wanted to see? She couldn't admit that I'd been decoupled from her already and cast adrift by the tilt and sway of the Earth on its axis, the rise and fall of tides, the wind that carved a course through the world for me to follow. Brisbane and Zürich, then home to the Alps. Syria, Turkey, the blowback, the boy on the beach, and then an urge to move. London, King's Cross, Pentonville, bound for Aberdeen and the Mearns, but yanked back first to Sydney en route to Van Diemen's Land.

What I found in the Alps was a house that looked like a reconstruction of a past I'd dimly known. Snowmelt scored the mountainsides with radiant brooks, streaks of white water gushing through the springtime green of fields and forests. Indoors, of course, everything was as we'd left it. Bedroom and bathroom and kitchen were all in their usual conditions. Even the card we'd kept on the kitchen table remained untroubled. The cover still confronted me with a vision of my daughter's face, and, inside, her footprint still testified to her having been a person I could touch. But then, in the atmosphere of the rooms, in the feeling of what it all now meant to me, it was clear that a change of season had come over the place as well. Our house looked like the dwelling of another couple who'd stepped outside for a walk and would be returning any moment. All known, all recognisable, but also now a shade unfamiliar, a few degrees removed from a life I could believe in.

At night, my first night back, alone, I sat cross-legged on the living-room floor and flipped through a sleeve of old CDs. I'd left the laptop with my wife in Sydney, but on a shelf in the corner beside the fireplace we kept a stereo system. Numbers scanned, discs cast aside. Twenty-four to forty-five. Forty-six to fifty-nine. Seventy-one to ninety. I might've given that one to the stereo, skipped ahead to seventy-eight and pressed PLAY and waited for those straining notes, that mournful voice. *Though pleasant is—this winter night—* But I couldn't. I needed a different energy. The house needed it even more. The truth was that I'd agreed to see what had to be done to make the place ready for incoming tenants. We wouldn't renew the lease on it. I'd stay there through the springtime, to see out the end of the school year, and I said I'd take it upon myself to cleanse it of whatever marks we'd made. By the end of the summer, new lives would already have arisen within its walls and my presence, my wife's presence, my daughter's presence, would have been swabbed from the surfaces of things. I didn't need to hear mourning. Just being back was its own mourning.

So, a new disc. A new song. Two hundred and thirty-eight. The whimsical strum of a guitar, the jaunty jangle of a cymbal. A rhythm as of prancing horses or children frolicking in sunshine. A woman's voice, clear, fresh, singing as though smiling. A merry tune at odds with my mood and the rupture that sent me back to the Alps. Young people in love. Young hearts set upon hope. Compromises made, duties of mutual care fulfilled, happiness gained and futures secured. *O, four-and-twenty nobles*, she sang,

rode to the king's hall,
and bonny Glenlogie
was the flow'r of them all ...

Still, there was no way to stop the visions that paraded through the house as I listened. *O, four-and-twenty nobles—rode through—Banchory Fair*, she sang, *and bonny Glenlogie—*

I'd placed the ashes on the kitchen table, beside the card, beside my daughter's face and footprint. I'd secretly stowed the vase in my luggage. I packed it with care in a padded box I'd bought before leaving Brisbane, and I kept it sealed, to prevent further spillage, with the wadding I'd made from the silken doily. As soon as I could retrieve it I did, as soon as I'd landed and yanked my suitcase off the luggage conveyor, to check on it to be sure the glass had held and survived the journey. Then I'd carried it home in my hand, if *home* is the right word to describe my destination, and straightaway I set it in the place I'd once kept the urn. I returned the ashes to where they'd last spoken to me. I didn't think they'd speak again, but I needed to see them there. My reclamation. I could see them from where I sat.

At the wharf at Port Arthur, I'd stood and watched a gentle tide lap at the stony shore of Mason Cove. Boyd had disembarked around there, back before there was a wharf, when the sloop was dragged onto the sand and a plank was laid out for the commandant to set foot on terra firma. The drone of servants chattering, chains of iron clinking with the movements of the convicts, and in the distance the rhythmic chock of solid timber splintered by men at the axe. The buildings of the penitentiary complex had surrounded him, the tremendous brick edifices of the mess halls, the officers' lodgings, the houses of the magistrates and surgeons, even the humble chaplains' quarters. Within those buildings, and in the open air between them, prisoners practised their trades, produced goods and wares, tended crops, kept the grounds in order. None were permitted idleness, barring those who had their own private torments in solitary confinement.

Let's say Boyd started off, at pace, towards the guard tower at the heart of the site. At his back a path of dirt and stone hardened into bitumen and a car pulled up beside a woman, distraught, with her child in her arms. As Boyd walked on he passed by the tree that hid the elder girl, then stepped over the patch of grass her blood seeped into. In the distance a forest sprang up around the café, the gift shop, the shell of the building, the reflecting pool, the plaque, the names, and me. He moved amid the solid structures of the penitentiary grounds, his route disturbed by the terror of a crime yet to occur. He walked right through the sightline of the roaming glare. It couldn't see him. It moved on to those who could look back in fear.

Bed and sofa and kitchen table. These were the ruins I wandered among. Books on the shelves, lying around like fallen leaves, and the stereo in the corner of the living room. The front room full of belongings I still couldn't behold. Everything desolate, beyond reanimating, though washed over with melodic words that invited into the house a spirit of innocence, a simple beauty, which should by right have been dwelling there already.

There were *four-and-twenty maidens*, I heard, *brought to—the king's hall*:

> bonny Jeannie o'   Bethelnie
> was the flow'r of   them all …

So, I knew, Jeannie and Glenlogie were foreordained to become a couple. But chance would intervene in their union. Chance and a twist in the tale, a new direction.

The ashes were visible through the glass of the vase. The ashes remained still, though I'm sure I trembled while I looked at them and listened hard:

Down comes Hetty Gordon,
she comes trippin'
down the stairs,
and she's spoke to
Glenlogie, among all that—

I pulled the book from its place on one of my shelves. LOCAL HISTORY. That's what it was, after all. Child, I learnt, had found the song in the vicinity of Aberdeen. The village of Oldmeldrum, fifteen miles northwest of the city, had been known as Bethelnie until the union with England. Banchory lies perhaps twenty miles south of there. Twice that distance, due southwest, is the edge of the Cairngorm massif, a desert of heather and deer grass, and the trickle of water known as the Burn of Glenlogie. When Child collected the words to that song, what was he really preserving the remnants of? The dalliances of the aristocrats who'd made those places their playgrounds centuries before he arrived. Glenlogie, the nobleman, rides with his men through the market fair at Banchory, bound for Bethelnie, to meet his betrothed. But. But he has hardly had time to stop there, to freshen the horses and procure supplies, before he is called to the house of Lord Gordon and met by the man's unwed daughter. Hetty, we're told, is a clumsy girl, uncouth and undesirable, but instantly she falls for Glenlogie. She doesn't demand his hand in marriage. She simply assumes it can be hers if she opens her heart to him without inhibition. *Glenlogie*, she says, *Glenlogie*,

O, if you'll prove kind,
I lay me love on ye,
and I've told ye me mind …

One man, a collector of songs. One man, a collector of silences. I see a convict in solitary confinement. He has fading memories of a boyhood on Loch Alsh. He and his family were expelled when a newly awarded baron cleared the land. All they took with them were their clothes and their songs. Now the songs are gone. Forgotten, extinguished, subsumed by the purity of the man himself. The cell has extracted them from him and cleansed his mind of any place for them to take refuge. And me? Headstones and relics. They were what furnished my mind. They were what I'd taken to collecting. NEVER FORGET. BELOVED SON.

From those last words I lifted my eyes and scrutinised the shoreline for any signs of Shane. Sea winds blew from the east. The breakers jostled a tiny body, a tiny boy, turning his red T-shirt maroon and his blue shorts black. Froth and bubbles speckled the sand around his shoes. Still he lay with his face in the water. As the waves came in they submerged him, soaked him, glistened through his hair and rocked him side to side as if to wake him. Then they pulled back and left him inert. The sight of him had sent me to Shane. The sight had sent me to Shane along with the ashes I'd taken. I felt the hardness of the vase in the inner pocket of my autumn coat. I'd nestled it in there securely, still stuffed with the doily, so that now it pressed against my chest with the tension of a tumour. I needed help. I knew I needed help. I needed more help than I'd been able to elicit from Demirović. I needed to see the man again, to meet him once more on the beach and speak to him this time, to ask him how he did it, how he continued, after everything, after all his losses. I'd expected to find more of a monument. I needed to know how he'd managed to survive on just two words, when I felt as if endless blather wouldn't be enough to sustain me. And yet, and yet. Those were the only two words I could feel at the bottom of my own experience. What happened, happened: loss, cremation, scattering, and yet those two words begged for elaboration into all this.

But Shane wasn't there. The sole sign of life was a solitary thrush, grey and brown, warbling through the sky overhead. I wanted Shane to return; I stayed there and waited for him and hoped. I sat in the sand and idled, biding my time between his house and the house in which I'd once taken refuge. I must have looked for all the world like a hermit withdrawn to himself. Footprints were all I saw to indicate a human presence. Even then I couldn't be sure they belonged to the man I sought. The only certain traces of Shane were the ones I imposed on the site. Beside me loomed the house the government had paid for. Dark inside. Sunlight glinted off the windows. I squinted to see what I could, but I couldn't make out anything more than the sharp angles of a table and chairs in the kitchen. Had Shane and Kerry sat there and spoken to one another, wondering aloud what they ought to do now? Had one of them said, Don't go, when the word *divorce* slipped out?

Hand to my brow, I shielded my eyes from the harsh light overhead and spun in the sand to take in my surroundings. Child had favoured high ground in search of thin places to explore. Standing stones on barren hilltops, seen from crests in uneven earth, or clumps of trees glimpsed from gentle slopes. Atop the dune I turned and scanned the terrain. The sea lay flat to the east, with the grey coast stretching out to the north and the south. But far to the west, southwest, beyond where the land eased into rolling pasture, I could see the summits of the mountains rising like puckers in the pinched skin of the planet. Something inside me reached for them, a line of desire extending towards them and pulling me through the veil.

Bethelnie and Banchory aren't much to speak of. Villages at the foothills of the Cairngorms. Old estates and market towns of little note. The sites of songs about men and women consorting, cavorting, and playing fast and loose with the heart. Soulful declarations, snide dismissals. Revelations of profound emotions, commitments made and then broken in a moment's petulance. Hetty Gordon baldly avows her love for Glenlogie, but he insists he is promised away. He intends to marry Jeannie o'Bethelnie and he rides on to meet her.

When he leaves without Hetty, then, the plain young woman faints, falls ill, and *takes to her bed*—

with ribbons
and napkins   to bind up
her head.

When her father wakes her, shakes her by the shoulders until she flutters her eyes, the old man is shocked to find his daughter deathly sick. A physician is sent for. He can't see anything wrong with her. A priest is sent for. He can diagnose the problem. It's the blithe treatment of her declaration of love. It's Glenlogie denigrating her sincerity with no qualms. The priest writes a letter to upbraid the noble sir. Why should he behave so, to a suitable young lady? He behaves as he does because he is who he is. He is a man of comfort, of privilege, who believes himself free to do whatever he pleases, however he pleases, to live the life that best suits him, and who feels that, in any event, the world itself will in time conform comfortably to his preferences.

I understand him well. He is who I used to be. His world, the accommodating world, was the one I used to inhabit. Everything that followed my time with my wife in her parents' kitchen was a symptom of how privileged we actually were, how much control we actually had over the way things would happen for us. We could continue sitting together at the breakfast bar and there, in perfect peace, we could rearrange every aspect of our lives. We were educated people. We had qualifications. We could quit our jobs from a distance, via email, simply announcing we wouldn't return, and there was nothing anyone could really do to challenge our decisions. We could find new positions with relative ease. Or we could do nothing for a time. We had some savings in the bank, only a little but enough to meet our needs. We could set up an automatic transfer to cover our rent for a few more months. We could exploit different lines of credit, plus loans from supportive families, to fork out for new plane tickets that night and be out of the country, bound for elsewhere, by lunchtime the following day. We didn't have to fear our meeting with guards at a border. We barely had to look at them. We spoke the global lingua franca. We had skin that didn't attract unwanted attention. We were free, strong, and capable. We had more power over ourselves and our wishes than even the aristocrats in that song.

But none of those privileges gave us a direction to move in. Nothing we had in the here and now could force the world to accommodate the future we hoped in vain to reclaim. None of it gave us anything to say to one another. None of it could pull down the barriers that kept us from imagining better things for ourselves. Every privilege that allowed us to ease the aches of daily life took us no further than that. We daubed balms and unguents on the surfaces of wounds that were more than skin deep. I wanted to go back to that lost world, I raged for it, to make my choices, to take control, to be accommodated, but I couldn't find my way in again. I tried to return to it there, on that beach, as I stood waiting for Shane to come to me, to speak with me, or rather, to be spoken to and to speak in reply, to give me the consolations I longed for. In the end, I stood there alone and silent in the sun. The gateway to the old world had been barred. I flailed about as if orienteering without a map and compass, whirling on the spot to see where I might go now. Nowhere. Anywhere. Where else was there, but the muck?

The Burn of Glenlogie burbles down from the Cairngorm massif and through a broad valley of spindled shrubs, purple flowers, prickles and thorns. It trickles over the foothills that decline, eastward, to the coast, but it deposits itself into the depths of the moors before it reaches the sea. When I came across it at last, found it where it was hiding, it had the sound of a soft wind moving through a thicket of rushes. Its quicksilver surface shot over stones like a comet across the night. Child had stalked this terrain. Local history confirmed it. The pages I'd found in the beachside retreat gave the proof. With scarcely more than a knapsack and bindle, a notebook, a hipflask, and his shillelagh, he'd ascended the massif from lowlands in this vicinity and struck out to conquer it. But the Cairngorms aren't really mountains that rise from flat terrain. They're an agglomeration of plateaux, a welter of earth and rock that attains a new elevation, higher than the rest of Britain, from which the mountains climb up. To set foot on the massif is to stand in the sky. To traverse it is to anchor yourself to the beating heart of the land, to put yourself in contact with the barest facts of your existence. It's a harsh place, absolutely indifferent to the survival of the life that takes to it, and it can be painfully, blissfully lonesome. I stomped through the mud alongside the burn. I felt a sharp cold lifting off the water in a breeze that skimmed over the heath. For a while as I walked, I saw Child trudging beside me. He'd resolved to reach Braemar by nightfall. Thoughts of his wife and children gnawed at him, pestered his conscience. Was it terrible of him, he wondered, to have wished for a bargain with the divine? He'd have his daughter ill again, even ill for the rest of her life, if only he could have her returned to him alive. Was there cruelty in that?

Find the burn and follow it all the way back to its source, and you'll stand before the hump of the Scorrie rising steeply from the base of the glen. You have to scramble along the trail over the shoulder of the mountain, then follow the ridges from Glen Clova to the great open amphitheatre of Corrie Fee. This conical pit, this winnowing of the mountains, was carved out over millennia by the ice sheets that had retreated from as far away as the Bosphorus. Take a planetary perspective on things and bring the ice into view again. You'll find an umbilical link, cold and white, stretching from the Middle East all the way to the Scottish Highlands, and in its withdrawal giving shape to the Carpathians, the Pannonian Plain and the Drina, the Berner Oberland and the Alps, the Schwarzwald, the Low Countries, and all of the British Isles. I climbed up into the corrie, following the thread of the burn, now little more than a wisp of water down the mountainside, and as I gained altitude I could feel the land beneath me lurch. The ice sheets had kept the crust of the planet under such formidable pressure that even now, today, thousands of years after they finally melted, the pressure is still being released. The entire island of Britain continues to tilt, imperceptible to the eye, as if on a tectonic fulcrum. Every day the land imbalances a little more. The sea swallows its southernmost edge while the mountains in the north creep further into the sky.

I held the vase close to me, close to my chest, as I climbed through Corrie Fee towards the source of the burn. Before I'd left the kitchen, my wife had told me she wanted to know, plainly, what the ashes meant to me. She was mystified by the devotion I'd shown them. She couldn't see what it was that had urged me to take them. Did I regret the cremation? Did I see it as a mangling of the body? Did I know how distressing that would be to her, how off-putting, to leave her thinking that what she'd wanted, what she'd suggested in good conscience, was something I saw as a violation? Worse than a violation. An evisceration or disembowelling, on a different order of revulsion. Was there no way I could see the cremation as a purifying process, a reduction of the body to its elementary particles? Did I have nothing to say to that notion? Was there nothing she could say that would open me up again, bring me into a temper where I could share what I kept inside?

What could I say? I'd gone into silence. That was purification. That was the purest expression of what I felt and what I wanted. My actions were my actions. I couldn't think of a way to speak of what I'd done, to speak of it more clearly than it spoke for itself, and I couldn't think of any reason I should. I didn't know why we couldn't just deal with the facts. I didn't know why we had to continue performing for one another. This had become what I hated most of all. Our loss, yes, but also what it had turned us into. What we'd lost, really, was the ease of being who we truly were, of being ourselves with one another, and each of us had avoided the fact by staging some approximation of who we supposed the other wanted us to be. We didn't expose ourselves. We didn't open our hearts. Hetty Gordon, on her sickbed, possibly on her deathbed, receives a visit from Glenlogie. The letter from the priest has swayed his sympathies. What is the matter with this strange young woman? What can he do to allay her infirmity? In vain he casts about to pinpoint the source of her woe. That's what helps him to help her. That's all it takes. His arrival and his probing questions, his simple concern for her wellbeing. She hides nothing. She tells him plainly. She says the words he needs to hear in order to know her troubles. It's not just that she isn't by nature a performer. It's that there's nothing between them to perform. There are only the honest facts of their situation and a willingness to face them no matter what they entail. We'd had the facts in front of us for a time. We'd only lacked the simplicity to see.

I'd taken a moment away from the penitentiary to wander along the edge of Mason Cove. The waters unfurled around me from the gutters of Caledonian Road. I'd lingered by the shore, I remembered, and as I'd looked at the waves I'd seen Boyd behind me, over my shoulder, spending an idle moment on the sand. Van Diemen's Land was where he'd grown old. It was where he'd decided to go to grow old. Now I could see the decrepitude in his face, his shabby sideburns and untrimmed whiskers. Now I could see the pendulous swell of his belly, the catch in his step as old age pinched the nerves in his spine. These are the ravages of twenty years as Commandant of the Port Arthur Penal Settlement. Twenty years of scrupulous, unswerving fidelity to the daily mechanics of the penitentiary, the order imposed on the inmates by the clock, the minute-by-minute regulation of time, and the incremental perfection of silence that was forever his horizon. What was the lasting value of these years? He died alone at home in Hobart Town, in 1888, almost half a lifetime since he'd last seen London, and yet, today, his decades abroad have no place on the plaque that honours him.

For his part, though, especially towards the end, he made an effort to bridge the two halves of his life. Although he never returned to Britain to reunite with his daughter, he took pains to ameliorate her absence by etching her presence into his passing days. That's why, when he appeared to me, I could hear him approaching. He hummed a tune to himself. The tune was one he'd learnt as a boy in Bridge of Allan, taught to him by a mother whose roots extended farther north. It was a tune he'd taught his own child, and it was the tune that returned to him when he saw she'd fixed her sights on a particular man. Annie Gordon, the swooning girl, and her blatant, unashamed declaration of love. *Glenlogie*, he sang, *Glenlogie*,

O, if you'll prove kind,
my love is laid on ye
and I've told ye me mind …

I heard the tune well up within him, pushed out in a patrician mumble with only the barest melody to it. It flowed away from him, rippled out from that moment in time and then curled back on itself to return to me as I sat by the stereo in Switzerland and listened and felt it draw me on to Britain. The house was empty of spirit. I couldn't find comfort in it. I needed a more sympathetic space, a place where I could replenish the elements of myself.

There's no point denying that at some stage, in some way, as I sat with my wife, everything I used to be spilled out of me. At some stage I must have said I couldn't go on anymore, I needed time to myself, and distance as well, distance from everything we'd known together; I didn't see how to preserve what remained of what we'd shared without crawling through life being stalked by the sense that each of us was still attached to a corpse. Even if we could resolve our tensions, like neighbouring nations signing a peace treaty, there would still be this exclave wedged between us where our sovereign borders met. I must have said the word *divorce*, or perhaps I'd been too cowardly and my wife had said it and I'd agreed, or perhaps all we'd managed to speak of was time out or a break or a trial separation or some other euphemism for exactly what both of us knew we were heading towards.

I must have apologised. I must have sworn. I must have insisted when my wife refused to concede immediately, I must have loosened my hold on the reins when it became clear that she understood how surely I meant to go on with my decision. I must have cried. I have a memory of tears. I must have gone hoarse, I might have raised my voice, or then again I might have dropped my words to a whisper. I must have purged myself of all the bitter things I wanted to do to my marriage, I must have expunged the will to ruination I'd kept inside. I must have done these things because I am where I am. Still, I bear no memory of doing them. I have only a memory of the sensation of having done.

I shouldn't be in here, he'd told the men who detained him. I really shouldn't be in here. I don't remember, he didn't remember, what it was that he'd done to deserve being left to himself. But they would put him away for months in a cell of his own, no contact with the outside world. Hands bound, a shove at the back, then darkness. No escape from the raucousness of your own thoughts. They'll hang you for what you've done, but they'll break you first. What do you hear? Echoes of field songs. Hot wind through the baobab branches. A woman's voice, a child's, reverberating down through the decades. A woman's voice, a child's, a police officer's, a social worker's, and the indistinct chatter of children in the playroom. A woman's voice, Come to bed, a woman's voice, Don't go, a sickly child's whimper and wheeze, and then, dwelling in the solitude of your own creation, the voices of the men you've put away in there, the men you've dragged with you into your idyll of silence. The words they speak are yours. I shouldn't be in here. This is a mistake.

You speak to a person, directing your words particularly at them, but you feel the words bend around them as if colliding with a barrier that escapes the eye. Is there a word for that feeling? As the years ache by, as the decades ache by, Boyd slips into a realm distinct from that of his daughter. They communicate with each other, regularly and faithfully, exchanging letters across the hemispheres throughout the oscillations of their fortunes. She tells him of births and deaths, new friends, new houses, sojourns abroad. He tells her of prisoners arriving, serving out sentences, trying to escape, submitting to recapture. He tells her of skirmishes with the last few straggling tribes on the outskirts of the prison. He tells her of refinements to the separate system of punishment. He sits at his escritoire and unburdens himself to her. He sits in silence but for the quill scratching the page, but for the tinkle of its tip at the inkwell, and he channels into words all the thoughts that would otherwise rage through him, detailing them for the one person who he knows will hear him out. In a way, I imagine, the two of them grow closer, more honest, more intimate, even as they remain far apart. He looks at a blank page as a receptacle into which he can be forthright about his deepest concerns. But between them there is a sort of partition he can't break through. It causes them to move at different speeds. The letters he exchanges with her are missives between ghosts on separate planes of existence. By the time he receives one of hers, or by the time she receives one of his, the world described on the page no longer exists. She becomes a mother to darling twins. He receives an honour from the governor of the colony. She takes part in suffrage demonstrations. His health deteriorates rapidly. She becomes a grandmother. He retires to Hobart Town. They always learn of events too late.

At some stage, I know, I rose from the breakfast bar. I must have risen because at some stage I left the kitchen and the house. The interim is opaque. I imagine my wife sat still, observing me from afar, her hands shackled to the breakfast bar by what I'd said to her when I finally managed to speak. I imagine she watched me totter to my feet, swaying as I rose, defeated and deflated. I imagine she saw me not looking at her, just as I'd observed Hassan Demirović. I imagine she saw, written into my face, the smallness that had devoured me. The shrinkage of self. The withdrawal. The veins and knuckles tense in my hand as I held steady to the backrest of my stool. Then the retreat of a man who looked to be navigating a path through mist, who couldn't see the space in front of him any more than he could see the shape of the years ahead.

The final letter Boyd received from London came with a gift. Newly printed, bound in vellum, a book of ballads from England and Scotland. It arrived in the summer of 1888. That was the summer he took to his deathbed. Stains on starched collars, tantrums, halitosis.

Shallow breaths, a slowing pulse. Lugubrious days, sullen nights. But he still had his wits about him, spending his waking hours with his favourite titles in a house stuffed full of antique tracts. His daughter feared for his health and sent him the new volume to lighten his heart. The contents, she said, had been collected by an eminent scholar of poetry and popular song. She pointed out the inclusion of one of his favourite tunes, the one he'd always sung her. But, she noted, the scholar hadn't collected the song in *all* its variant forms. The two of them had always known the swooning girl as Annie Gordon. On the page, however, the scholar had given her name as Hetty. In every version of the song, variant after variant, it's Hetty Gordon who lays her love on the valiant Glenlogie and then takes fatefully ill. Since Tam Lin and Long Lankin and others appeared in so many guises, wearing so many different names, it's strange, that consistency, isn't it? As if the song had snagged on that one name and now it was the only name the girl would carry into posterity.

Boyd never replied to the letter, never gave thanks for the gift. The next correspondence sent to London from Hobart Town was a document from a notary public. It certified the death of James Arthur Boyd, due to natural causes, and outlined his solicitor's plans for the execution of his will.

Too late. Too late. I stood in the kitchen and felt, above all, that I'd arrived too late in the present moment, that everything that was happening now was happening too late, that I'd let it run on so much longer than it ever should have lasted. It was too late for me to change things. Nothing to do now, no change to effect, but to amputate the disfigured limb and cauterise the wound. Put a seal on it. It wouldn't fix anything. There would still be the pain of the injury and the remedies applied. But maybe it would hold off further suffering.

Boyd's daughter invested her bitterness in the plaque. Nearly twenty years after her father died, she battled to have his memory honoured by the city she'd made her home. So what if the more appropriate place to commemorate him was the penal settlement at the end of the world? The place had been decommissioned. There was talk of allowing tourists in. Nevertheless, the organisation with authority over the plaques respectfully declined her request for one. That's why she took it upon herself. She would honour him in his old lodgings. She restored him to his proper place. The plaque could not erase the fact that he'd abandoned her, but it could drag his memory back to her and become the locus of his posthumous life. All it needed to do was fix his name to a point in space. There he'd be, recessed into history, but able to flicker back into the world like lightning drawn to a rod.

I couldn't be so callous as to discard my wife. But neither did I have the reserves to remain awhile with her. I didn't want to be bitter towards her, or to make her bitter, or to become mired in recriminations. I didn't want to spite her. I just wanted to be away. I believe I told her these things. I stood beside her at the breakfast bar. I told her I didn't hold anything against her. I told her I hadn't taken the ashes to offend her, I'd just sunk too deep into my own head. I told her I understood why her clifftop ceremony had been important to her, even if I hadn't been moved by it. I told her I was sorry for all I'd done to offend her, even if I didn't regret any of it. I told her all this before I left, but only after I told her, not in so many words, that I could finally see her, distinctly herself, if at a remove from me. I stood beside her at the breakfast bar and rested a hand on her back. I broke my silence and compelled her attention when, first of all, I spoke aloud her name.

I'm reluctant to resort to a word with connotations of bliss. What I'll say is that when I let go of the ashes, I felt, in my body, an unexpected levity. It wasn't a sensation of lightness, still less a sensation of flying. It was something more like throwing open the windows on a boarded house and letting in a breeze for the first time in too long. I realised it had been almost a year since I'd last done something good. I'd done many things I knew were wrong, and others I'd believed right, or at least necessary, though I knew they wouldn't be for the best. I'd done too many things that hadn't caused the slightest disturbance, things intended specifically to avoid disturbance, though I went about them knowing that I shouldn't have done them at all. Nothing of what I'd done since those snowy days in December felt unaccountably good to do, the way forgiveness feels, or generosity, or understanding. But this did. I could breathe again.

Above Corrie Fee, rising from the knapps, a plateau of moorland and heather overlooks the scree and rockfall of the glens. Much of the plateau is wet beneath scrub, boggy with trickles of water the colour of strained tea. But beyond the murkiness, at the edge of the filth, there is a sterling tarn. I learnt of it from a footnote in the book I carried with me. It's easy to miss. At a distance it looks like a puddle. It's not deep enough to grow dark. Get close to it, though, and you'll see a plunge pool of pristine clarity. Cup your hands and dip them in. Taste the water. It's pure. It's fed by an underground spring, a subterranean pocket containing the last vestiges of the glaciers that once stretched across this part of the planet. In turn, it feeds the groundwater that sustains the surrounding burns and, further on, the River Esk. Streamlets spill from it like flashing tendrils, tinkling down the mountainsides and trailing lines over the land.

I removed the tiny vase from my coat and cupped it in one palm. I unwrapped the silken doily and extracted the fabric from the flute of the glass. Then I knelt beside the tarn, knelt in the mud at its edge, and I reached into the earth to retrieve a stone the size of a coin. I nestled the stone in the mouth of the vase and pressed it carefully into the topmost ashes. Sunlight played over the water like flames. The stone gave a little heaviness to the glass. A mountain wind, calm and cool, cleansed the air and rumbled a wordless hymn. At last I offered the vase to the tarn. I watched it bob on the surface as the water took its weight, and then, once accepted, I let it go. Slowly it sank to the bottom of the pool. It settled on the mossy base like a weary head on a pillow. I stood up again.

I could still picture that body. I doubt I'll ever forget it. For a heathen like me, the body is holy and there's no accounting for all that is lost when the body is gone. I can see her even now, shockingly motionless, as inert as a lump of empty matter, and yet so placid, so simply at rest, that the dread I felt when I saw her has become entangled with envy. I craved, I still crave, tranquillity like hers.

I watched the water ripple upwards from its source and overflow the tarn. I watched its runoff burble away in a dozen directions, babbling on to the horizon without rest or relent. That water dragged the remnants of a vanished epoch across the land and renewed its presence in the here and now. It brought daylight to atoms from deep within the crust of the Earth, atoms that carried memories of mastodons and mammoths, and it offered them up to the wind, the sun, the soil, to be changed into other forms, to take on new ways of being. Down there, too, I knew, it would worry away at the stone in the vase and carry up flakes of ash, the billion parts of that beloved body, to bring them sparingly to the surface. It wouldn't scatter them all at once. It would disperse them over the years to come like waves of light dancing across the spectrum of time. It would carry traces of a girl's existence, otherwise so fleeting, to parts of the globe she'd never had a chance to hear of, places that had never known the slightest thing of her. I stood back and watched her leave me, not ascending to a higher domain but infusing the planet beneath my feet. Working on my behalf, I saw, the water flowed on as always and gossiped news of her life to the world.

b
BRIO

First published by Brio in 2020

Brio Books
PO Box Q324, QVB Post Office,
NSW 1230, Australia

www.briobooks.com.au

978-1-922267-00-9 (print)
978-1-922267-01-6 (digital)

Cataloguing-in-publication data is available from the National Library of Australia

Cover and internal design by Brio
Printed and bound by McPherson's Publishing Group